Miss Burnham and the Loose Thread

www.penguin.co.uk

Miss Burnham and the Loose Thread

Lynn Knight

bantam

TRANSWORLD PUBLISHERS

UK | USA | Canada | Ireland | Australia
India | New Zealand | South Africa

Transworld is part of the Penguin Random House group of companies
whose addresses can be found at global.penguinrandomhouse.com

Penguin Random House UK,
One Embassy Gardens, 8 Viaduct Gardens, London SW11 7BW

penguin.co.uk

Penguin
Random House
UK

First published 2025 by Bantam
1

Set in 12/15pt Adobe Garamond Pro
Typeset by Jouve (UK), Milton Keynes
Printed and bound in Great Britain by Clays Ltd, Elcograf S.p.A.

The authorized representative in the EEA is Penguin Random House Ireland,
Morrison Chambers, 32 Nassau Street, Dublin D02 YH68.

A CIP catalogue record for this book is available from the British Library

ISBNs
9780857506467 hb
9780857506474 tpb

For my mother
In memoriam

Contents

Prologue

A Gentleman Friend
October 1924 and February 1925

'Will you be mother?'

Phyllis reached for his teacup. This would be the first time she'd poured tea for a gentleman friend. She hoped her hand would not shake. 'Do you take sugar?'

'Yes please. Two lumps.'

'Milk?' The milk jug trembled; she must not spill milk in his lap. Don't get flustered, Phyllis told herself. He may be just as nervous as I am. 'This is a pretty cafe,' she said to cover her embarrassment. The cafe was on one of the roads some distance from the park, in a small parade of shops in what had looked like a purely residential district. Unless you knew the area well, you wouldn't know the cafe was there. She had thought they would have tea at the Crystal Palace tearooms but, really, this was nicer, more discreet. 'How did you find it?'

'Oh, on my travels,' he said, managing to make south-east London sound almost exotic. 'I'm glad you like it. It is a bit out of the way, but I wanted to bring you somewhere that would suit you, somewhere more . . . individual.'

Her first compliment. Phyllis had never thought of herself as individual in any way. She lifted her teacup and studied the pattern printed there. Its posies complemented the cafe's crimson and jade-green cushions, their colours sharp against the dark, Jacobean-style chairs.

'Pretty china, too,' Phyllis said. 'I usually take tea with my mother.'

'She will be missing you this afternoon then, Miss Holmes. It's just the two of you, I think?' They had touched on this earlier, during a short walk around the park in which she had been grateful for the chance to talk about the greedy ducks and watch other promenaders. But there were no more distractions; it was just the two of them now.

'Yes. My father died last year.'

'I'm sorry to hear that.' In the silence that followed, Phyllis's companion made short work of a scone and brushed the crumbs from his moustache. She took a small bite from a slice of Madeira cake.

'I expect your mother vets all your beaus?'

Beaus: imagine. Phyllis blushed. But it was a nice sensation, as much pleasure as embarrassment, for once. There had been no other beaus, but dare she whisper that word now? 'Mother is happy for me to have friends,' she said more stiffly than she'd intended. It was so hard to get this right. And, truth to tell, there had not been that many friends and certainly no gentlemen among them. Phyllis looked up and saw that Mr Wilson was smiling. It was the first time since they'd sat down that she had lifted her gaze from the knot of his college tie. He had warm, brown eyes and crinkled lines on a kind face. She stirred her tea, emboldened. 'It's very pleasant to come out for an afternoon.'

'You must be a great comfort to your mother.'

Phyllis demurred. She pictured herself posting Mother's

letters, collecting her library books and sitting still, palms facing, while Mother wound wool around her hands.

'It's hard for ladies to have to get used to having no man in the house.'

It had been hard. No ally, just Mother's emphatic sighs and querulous tones: 'There's no sugar in my tea – you know I take sweet tea in the afternoon. You might allow me one of my few indulgences.' Phyllis had given up her own sugar ration to her mother during the war, and gladly. And now that rationing was long over and done with, found she was perfectly happy to go without. Not that her sacrifice had sweetened Mother any, she noticed.

'I expect you help in all sorts of ways,' Mr Wilson said. 'I always think it's difficult for a lady to take up the reins, to have to bear a man's household responsibilities.'

'We are lucky in that regard. Father left things in good order.'

Mr Wilson nodded encouragingly. Phyllis wavered: should she say more? She had been taught it was ill-mannered to speak of money, but perhaps people did these days. So much had changed since the war. And Mr Wilson did seem to expect her to say something further.

'Father set up a trust,' she said quietly.

'A trust?' Mr Wilson's voice faded.

Phyllis noted the change of tone. Perhaps he thought trusts a bad thing. Could Father have been wrong in that?

'Yes,' she answered, bolstered by the memory of her father's irreproachable judgement. 'The money was released two years ago, on my twenty-fifth birthday.' This seemed to reassure her companion, who now leaned towards her. Goodness, was he going to pat her hand? But no. Mr Wilson smiled: a broad, warm smile; genuine, too. It animated his whole face. 'I am sure your father was most wise.'

He was nice, really. And it was kind of him to ask about Mother and a comfort to hear him speak of Father in that respectful manner. Really, the afternoon was turning out better than she could have hoped. And it was nice to do something for herself for once. And this was a pretty little cafe, truly. And private; they might have been taking tea in their own home. Imagine: sitting at your own tea-table with a snowy-white cloth with crocheted edges and freshly laundered napkins to match. It would be a pleasure to iron napkins for her own tea-table. She must ask Sarah how to go about that.

Her companion's voice brought Phyllis back to the present moment. 'You haven't finished your cake, Miss Holmes.' There was a selection of cakes: a tiered arrangement of Madeira cake, iced squares and small buns scattered with coconut.

'Oh, no more for me, thank you. I've had an elegant sufficiency.' It was a phrase Mother used, together with 'Always leave something on your plate for Miss Manners.' That was very Mother, too.

'I can't believe you're watching your figure. Not a slim young lady like you?'

Phyllis's courage faltered. This observation was too personal. Mother would say he was not top-drawer. But Phyllis already knew that. And what did that matter these days? Mr Wilson seemed genuine, and he was kind, and that's what counted.

'Mother will want to have tea when I get back,' she explained. 'And Mrs Watkins always makes a cake – or buns.'

'Keeping our meeting secret, are you?' Phyllis flushed. 'That's your prerogative, Miss Holmes. A young lady should have her secrets. And Mrs Watkins . . .?'

'Our cook. We have a cook and a maid, Sarah. 'We are lucky there, too. They've been with us a long time and were very helpful when Father was ill. Father was an invalid for some years before he died.' This was not so difficult after all, not once you settled into it, although her heart would not stop fluttering. He was kind and he had a nice smile, and if the conversation was stilted, that was because she was not adept at this kind of thing. It will come with practice, Phyllis told herself. Mr Wilson smiled again. Already it was becoming easier.

And to think all this started four months ago. Since then, there had been other walks and other corner tables in little cafes here and there. They had even tiptoed around the floor at a tea dance once or twice. They had sat out most of the dances, but it was fun, all the same, to see how those who knew the steps got on. Once the summer came, they'd go boating. 'Imagine,' Reginald had said, 'me taking the oars while you sit back, reclining like a queen against the cushions.' The picture he painted was of a different Phyllis entirely. There were so many things they might do. They met every few weeks, whenever Reginald's work schedule permitted. The gaps in between were no hardship. Truth to tell, they were a large part of the pleasure Phyllis hugged to herself. It was thrilling to have a secret admirer.

He was easy to talk to; happy to listen, too. She found herself telling him all sorts of things she had never told anyone else. He was interested to hear her thoughts and to share his own, most especially his plans for striking out in business. And it was such a joy to order new clothes, and an even greater one that Mother did not know how many, nor where she was going, or with whom: 'You are seeing a lot of Marjorie Harper these days. I do hope you're not making a nuisance of yourself.'

Reginald became her armour, her shield against scalding remarks. 'You do look smart,' he'd say. 'I like being seen out with you; my pals would envy me.' Really, she had to pinch herself.

Part I

An Enterprising Young Woman

April 1925

1

Rose moulded a length of midnight-blue silk, twisted one end and conjured a flower out of nowhere. Now for the dark-green leaves. Hours she'd spent, finding the right mix of sugar and water to stiffen them. There: the leaves curled in just the right way, with just the right amount of stiffening. She took the silk ornament across to the dress stand and stitched it into place on the gown draped there.

Done. Rose stretched both arms and stepped back. This was what it was all about: sculpting and making clothes. Every moment should be like this one, instead of having to find a way through the maze of bills that arrived with startling regularity and the accounts book that even now waited to chide her.

Six months ago it had all looked more straightforward. Well, not exactly straightforward. Setting up the business had terrors of its own, but it had all begun so well: she had a handful of clients commissioning new designs and there were bread-and-butter customers wanting the serviceable work of letting out, taking in or restyling, which, though far from making her pulse race, was a necessary contribution to the pot. It was the autumn season and, with Christmas coming, there'd been evening gowns to make, and several of them. The memory of all that richly coloured chiffon and velvet still sent a shiver through her.

The speed at which new clients entered 'the Book' in those first few months had been immensely gratifying, but those new names had all but slowed to a trickle. January and February were always slow, but it was now the start of April and things had yet to pick up. For the past few weeks, Rose had opened the Book at the same page. It was only a pause, of course it was, and something she should have foreseen. This was south-east London, for heaven's sake, not Mayfair. For all the talk of those who'd done well since the war and had money to spend (versus those whose fortunes had dwindled), their wives and daughters were still likely to order only the one gown or frock, not a whole season's new wardrobe. The gentry had yet to discover the delights of south-east London.

Rose hoped to entice the gentry in due course, though she could hardly hope to do so yet. But there had been no other new clients for a while, either – that was the thing. And meanwhile the bills kept coming. Why had she not seen how large a pool of clients she would need – a far greater number than she'd initially envisaged. It could be an age before the likes of Miss Prendergast and Miss Thorn returned with new commissions – if indeed they did. What if they were merely being polite when they'd said they would be back? (Though, if that were the case, they would hardly have written such effusive thank-you notes.) This was just a lull, Rose told herself; there was bound to be a lull once Christmas was over, and the first flurry of interest had passed. This was just a late start to the spring. She would take a deep breath and advertise in all the right places, *Vogue* included. *Vogue* would require a very deep breath but, nothing ventured . . .

And, in the meantime, thank heavens for Miss Holmes and her unexpectedly long list of requests. What next for her, Rose wondered, after the midnight-blue dress? She had hinted at a new tea-gown, something pastel and dainty. It was a glancing thought, barely a whisper but, in Rose's mind, the new gown was already taking shape. Yes, everything would come together. The first year was bound to be difficult and they were barely six months in.

Rose looked out at the workroom – *her* workroom: the three deal tables she and her sisters had scrubbed back to life; the north light coming through the two large windows; the sturdy ring of tacking threads, like an outsize string of beads; her trusty thimble and inch-tape, her sacred shears and scissors; her sisters' own thimbles and inch-tapes marking their respective places at their own, smaller tables, with their treadle-machines tucked alongside. It was a chancy venture, particularly with home and business under the one roof and her two sisters working for her, but yes, they really were here. Even now, she could scarcely believe it.

Rose watched Ginny slice through the fabric that would add a contrasting panel – and four comfy inches – to Mrs Bradbury's stockinette dress, her elder sister applying herself to the task with the same thoroughness she brought to far more intricate work. She was wasted on something like this, as was their younger sister, Alice, who should be making up sophisticated frocks and not relegated to oversewing, as she was this afternoon. From where she stood, Rose could see Alice's lips moving and guessed that her feet were keeping pace with a jazz-time rag that was playing inside her head. Rose had no idea how Alice managed to achieve neatly finished seams while perfecting the latest dance steps, but judged it best to say nothing.

It was a complicated business being your sisters' boss, especially when the three of you had to become sisters again each evening. She and Ginny had both trained at Webb & Maskrey, the prestigious West End store, and so were drilled in that department store's ways; they knew one another as dressmakers as well as sisters. Alice, on the other hand, had been apprenticed to a different store and was their junior by some years. She was now twenty-one to Rose's twenty-six and Ginny's twenty-eight ... Which is why she is shooting a syncopated toe sideways every now and again, Rose told herself, whereas I'm contemplating the accounts.

Accounts were such a finicky business. A recent magazine article informed Rose that 'Anyone who wishes to be successful in business should attend to their accounts each week', but faced with the choice between slashing into yards of silk or totting up figures, there was very little competition. Nonetheless, every other week, Rose sat down with the Book, as she was about to do now.

The Book held the details of each client visit, from their very first day in business, 20 October 1924: Miss Hadfield, measure for rust-red tea-gown with lace trimmings; 27 October, first fitting; 4 November, second; 10 November, third. And then a breakdown of materials and costs: four yards wool delaine @ 2s 11d per yard; 12-inch open-work lace, £1 3s 7d; six covered buttons, 9½d; 1 belt buckle, 1s 6d; two reels Rust Red Sylko, one Ginger, 4d each.

. . . Mrs Merryweather, blue velvet devoré; Miss Croxley-Smythe, butterscotch charmeuse lace; Miss Holmes, cream-and-pink wool crepe . . . and so on. And here was Mrs Pell's coffee-coloured shantung silk, with its slip accounted for separately to disguise the actual cost of the dress. Mrs Pell exuded wealth, but she had to ask for every penny. She'd made light of the fact – or tried to: 'Gerald is so stingy. I'd like to get back at him', and who was Rose to object? Instead, she had done what she could to help. Few husbands liked to enquire too closely about items of underwear.

Rose turned to the next page: . . . Miss Thorn, royal-blue day dress . . . Miss Jennings, restyle tailored suit . . . Thank goodness for the evening course in tailoring that enabled her to offer suits and coats. Miss Jennings was the one professional woman in the Book, but Rose hoped there would be others before long. She took great pride in having a client who had made her way through the ranks of the Civil Service. To date, Miss Jennings had requested only the one restyling, but she'd been pleased with the result and, fingers crossed, a request for something new would follow. But that would be further in the future, Rose reminded herself, not the coming weeks; the bulk of the list she'd been reading was of past glories, none of which would help right now . . . But here was Miss Holmes again. Thank goodness.

Truly, it was heartening to see how Miss Holmes had blossomed and discovered the confidence to step out in new clothes – and equally heartening that she was commissioning so many of them. The tea-gown Miss Holmes mentioned at her most recent fitting (and this, even before her latest new dress was complete) would be a pleasure to design and there was already talk of a summer coat – something ladylike but practical, for walks in the park and boating.

Her last account was still outstanding, as was, of course, the cost of the 'special' blue dress with its scalloped hem, exquisite silk and elaborately crafted flowers, not to mention the hours of labour involved. Late payers went with the territory – many Webb & Maskrey clients didn't settle their accounts from one year to the next; the more elevated the client, the greater the credit extended – but Miss Holmes was remarkably prompt. Rose was confident of a large cheque by the end of the month.

Which brought her back to the bills, each one an accusation. That's what she was beginning to feel. Why did bills land with such frequency, but payments take an age to arrive? Rose set the latest bill – for some intricate beading – against Miss Holmes's name. The beading was just the thing for her special dress, but the queasiness Rose now felt when each new bill appeared was becoming a permanent sensation, and the knot in her stomach every bit as tight as the intricate beading itself.

The initial cost of materials, the price of coal . . . She and her sisters could wrap up well and wear fingerless gloves, but coal would still be needed to heat the irons on the workroom stove and then there was the fitting-room fire. She could hardly have her clients shivering in their birthday suits or ask them to come to appointments wearing their thickest vests.

Rose turned back to the Book. Here was Mrs Carlton, an optimistic bride when Rose first saw her at Webb & Maskrey in the spring of 1914, but now a desperate wife seeking refuge in clothes. If she could fill her days with dress fittings and like distractions, she would be able to spend less time looking at her husband's disfigured face.

The thought of Mrs Carlton returned Rose to those early years, when 'perfection' was the keynote of the Webb & Maskrey workroom she'd joined at the age of fourteen, and in which she'd made her way from Apprentice to Improver, Assistant, Hand and, eventually, Fitter. The terrifying instruction 'Nothing less than perfection' had regularly issued from the Chief Fitter's lips. Rose could still recall the sensation of knuckles being pressed into her back as Miss Feldman walked the room, pausing at the shoulder of whichever unfortunate seamstress was her target that day, to repeat her well-worn mantra. Those long months of terror and anxiety when Rose first joined the store, her insides turning to water at instructions barked with insufficient explanation but which must be carried out. Precision alone was not enough; you needed to be swift: keep up or find a new post. Exact stitches of equal length were deftly executed, and all errors caught and made good, no matter how many hours of unpaid labour that involved. Good seamstresses were slow to train; dismissal could be instantaneous.

Rose had such bright ideas when she first started but, like all apprentices, she'd had to learn – literally – from the ground up. Some glorious creations had evolved in the Webb & Maskrey workrooms, but most apprentices had a greater acquaintance with the patterns on the fitting-room rugs as they moved back and forth on hands and knees, picking up quantities of pins with the enormous magnets supplied for that purpose. Experienced hands made alterations at an astonishing speed. Within a few years, Rose was doing the same herself. And now, here she was, fielding her own business.

Her own business. Rose could still see the raised eyebrows and questioning looks she'd encountered when she announced to the workroom that she was leaving Webb & Maskrey to take up the lease on 9 Chatsworth Road. Their faces expressed surprise on several fronts: that a landlord would be foolish enough to rent property to a young woman; that a woman would consider setting up in business in the first place; and, on the part of some, a willingness that she should fail. Working alone was all very well if that meant you and your Singer at your kitchen table, but leasing premises and employing staff, even if the staff were your own sisters: who does Rose Burnham think she is? Queenie Blake was the only one to sneer out loud: 'So you're going to be one of those "business girls" we read so much about?' Few of the other seamstresses said as much, but Rose could read the messages behind their disbelieving looks.

Rose shut the Book and straightened her back. She must not fail. Those doubting Thomases would not have the last word.

2

Rose was halfway through her breakfast toast at one end of the table; a pile of notebooks and spools of raffia and ribbon were splayed untidily on the other half, where Alice was sifting through her bag. The sitting-room table had a great many uses and breakfast was generally catch-as-catch-can.

Ginny sat down beside them, poured herself some tea and then propped a book against the teapot. 'Sorry,' she said, 'but I have to finish this. I'm only ten pages off discovering who did the dastardly deed.'

Rose read the title: '*Bitter Leaves*', she said. 'I wonder you think it safe to drink the tea.' But Ginny was already on to her next paragraph. Rose turned to Alice. 'So, what is it today?'

'I'm meeting Clara Bow for a spot of shopping in Bond Street before we lunch at Claridge's – I *wish* . . .' Alice paused. 'It's "Steaming and Shaping Felt" this morning,' she amended, 'and this afternoon we're showing our decorations for different styles of hat, hence my raffia extravaganzas. And you?'

'I'm going to Webb & Maskrey to see their latest model gowns and then I'm back here for Miss Holmes.' Rose noticed the time. 'Hadn't you better get a move on? The Trade School will take a dim view if you're late.'

'Oh, blimey, yes.' Alice gathered up notebooks, raffia, ribbons and wayward threads, and crammed the lot into a remarkably small bag; Rose affected not to notice the chaos. 'Right, that's me done – I'm off.'

Ginny finished her novel, stretched her arms and leaned back in her chair. 'Isn't it quiet?' she said some moments later. They could hear a tram rattling down the adjacent street and the tap dripping in the scullery, but Rose knew what she meant. 'And isn't it wonderful to be able to just walk upstairs and start work without having to navigate muddy streets with chilblained feet and splattered stockings, and to be able to work late – or start early – without ever leaving the house?'

'Bliss.' Rose still marvelled at that.

'I'd better get going,' Ginny said. 'Mrs Bradbury will be here at nine to collect her dress.'

'And the West End beckons for me.'

Rose hurried to catch her train into central London. Once there, she headed in a direction she knew so well she could practically have walked there with her eyes closed. The spring sunlight was glinting on Webb & Maskrey's plate-glass windows, showing off the store to good effect. Rose pushed open the nearest door. Ashes of Roses: how exquisite. The scent assailed her the moment she crossed the threshold. The blend of luxury, colour and perfume was immediately soothing. Rose felt her shoulders relax.

What a pleasure to return to her alma mater as a customer. Today, she could linger beside any and every counter; she could even sit on one of the chairs, should she wish to do so – something strictly forbidden to employees. Rose smiled and walked tall. She was wearing a hand-painted scarf, one of her own creative endeavours. A wisp of silk in blade green, with a flash of yellow, it was echoed in the broad band around her hat and provided a marked contrast to her coal-black suit. Rose had already caught an admiring glance of recognition from Miss Purfew on Gloves, who, in turn, exchanged glances with her young assistant, and was now crossing the aisle to tidy a counter that required no tidying, in order to get a better look.

There had always been an element of competition between the shop assistants and the dressmakers. Assistants were front-of-house – and didn't they know it; some were so haughty they could barely bring themselves to serve their own customers – whereas seamstresses were backroom girls and, as such, were designated to a lower rung. Rose had always resisted this demar-cation, which, in her estimation, was completely wrong-headed: dressmakers had the skills to transform you, shop assistants took the glamour they created and sold it. But these old rival-ries were no longer her concern. Rose gave a gracious smile and moved on.

How fortunate that a trip to look at Model Gowns was entirely justifiable. It was vital for Rose to stay abreast of the latest trends and see what her clients might find here. Although she defined herself as a designer-dressmaker, she had to acknow-ledge that some clients may simply want her to tweak and adapt a design they'd seen elsewhere or, indeed, copy a model gown stitch by stitch.

The Model Gown department was bathed, as ever, in a rev-erential hush. The carpeted floor-space was arranged to create a central runway, a silent aisle down which the latest gowns swished and glided, shown by mannequins far younger than the small group of customers who observed their every move from the velvet-covered chairs placed on either side. Rose found a vacant seat and sat down to watch the mannequins sashay in dresses belted on the hip, or else draped or gathered there, then pause and turn around to show off their own sharp features before sashaying further down the room. Some of this season's evening gowns dipped at the sides, Rose noted, but were shorter than last year's. Embroidery was conspicuous, as was beadwork: there were silken sunrays, spangled moons and cascades of bugle beads; wired silk flowers, too, similar to the ones she'd fashioned for Phyllis Holmes.

Now that skirts were shorter, the eye was inevitably drawn to shoes – and to calves, although there was little one could do with those, except perhaps resist the bolder new shades of stockings if one was not exactly svelte. For her own part, Rose loved them: heliotrope, gingerbread, marine blue . . . such a change from the flesh-coloured stockings many people now wore, but she wasn't here to shop for herself. Spring shoes were on display this morning – town shoes with buttons or buckles, and sturdy, lace-up brogues; wedding shoes, too – an inevitable herald of the season.

Whenever Rose looked at shoes, she remembered her father, who had worn out his own shoe leather as a commercial traveller. When asked what he sold, he'd say, 'Footwear', because footwear sounded manly, but his speciality was ladies' boots and shoes. Rose remembered the special care he took when handling bridal shoes: so pale, so exquisite, so expensive. 'You can look, but do not touch,' he'd say, holding a box aloft and opening a nest of tissue paper to reveal watered-silk shoes with diamanté buttons, or creamy satin pumps. Today's shoes were no less magical – dove-grey silk with a spangled trim and Louis heels – as was their name: Titania. Even the tissue paper in which they nestled seemed to have a special rustle.

There were numerous bags on show, too: slinky or metallic,

soft drawstring or hard clasp, velvet, straw or leather. There was also the perfect midnight-blue pochette to complement Miss Holmes's special dress. She must mention that to her this afternoon.

Rose made her way back downstairs, where she joined the mêlée of shoppers, some moving purposefully, others drifting with the tide, content to look at everything on offer. Several customers, a lone man among them, had formed a semicircle around a young woman who was evidently demonstrating some gadget or other. Her voice carried across the store, drawing more people towards her. Intrigued, Rose joined them. The white-coated speaker was gesticulating at a domestic appliance – if appliance was the right word for the gargantuan contraption which, at first sight, was an unattractive tin tub.

'Ladies,' she intoned, 'and gentleman,' she added quickly, 'I'm here to introduce Excalibur. Let this mechanical wonder solve the problems of modern life. You need have no more worries about finding domestic servants with a mechanical housemaid in your home.' She gestured with both hands at the metal beast, her white coat adding a veneer of science to the proceedings. 'Excalibur will wash your dinner plates as well as your laundry and, what is more, its clever attachment' – she pointed to an unwieldy-looking nozzle strapped to the tub's left side – 'will clean your floors. And . . .' – the young woman paused, wide-eyed, as if she could not believe her good fortune – 'you need only reapply its lid . . .' – there was a further pause while she struggled to manoeuvre the awkward lid into place: 'Easy-peasy,' she said, to cover her embarrassment. 'And,' she said more loudly, resuming her script, 'hey presto, you also have an ironing board. What housewife could wish for more? Your home will gleam and glisten; you will have no wages to pay and no need to even say "thank you" to your efficient mechanical maid. Sit back and put your feet up. Let Excalibur do the housework for you.'

It was a deft performance, complete with smiles and flutterings, bobs and tucks. 'You, Madam, let me show you . . .' Or 'You, Madam, are you tempted?' But when the young woman paused again in her delivery and turned her back on her audience for a moment, Rose saw her smile disappear. No wonder: fancy spending your day extolling the virtues of that lumbering beast. Who would want their clothes washed in the same tub as their dinner plates? And who was going to load and unload the mechanical monster, let alone drag that heavy-looking hose around the floor? For once, a simple mop and pail had its appeal.

These thoughts, and the demonstrator's continuing presentation, were interrupted by commanding tones: 'Well, if it isn't Miss Rose Burnham, the Queen of Chatsworth Road. Good morning, Miss Burnham. What brings you here?'

Rose recognized the voice straightaway. 'Miss Greene,' she said, turning to face the speaker and matching the greeting, tone for tone. It was her old friend and colleague Madeleine Greene. She hadn't seen Maddie for – how long was it? Three years? Several heads turned in their direction, frowning at the interruption and those responsible for it. Trust Maddie to make an entrance, no matter what she disrupted.

Rose smiled and lowered her voice. 'Good morning, Maddie. I'd heard you were back.'

'Indeed. Second Window Dresser at your service,' Maddie said, and gave a pantomime bow. She grabbed Rose by the elbow and steered her towards an anonymous door that opened on to the back stairs. 'I've brought you in here,' she said, once they were safely ensconced in the area designated for staff use, 'because I could see Miss Carter advancing towards us.'

Rose laughed – Miss Carter's seniority was as legendary as her temper. 'You haven't changed a bit.'

This wasn't entirely true; Maddie looked older than when Rose last saw her, but she still had the knack of twisting her hair on top of her head in a style that looked entirely individual, and of smiling in a way that Ginny always said reminded her of a purring cat.

'Nor you, though I thought you'd be wearing something *breathtaking*' – she emphasized the word – 'in homage to your swanky new enterprise.'

'Oh, you've heard?'

'Haven't I just. You know the Webb & Maskrey grape-vine . . .'

Maddie and Rose had risen through the ranks together. Hired as apprentices at the same time, they had found themselves seated at the same table, but when Maddie later exchanged dressmaking for window dressing, it became harder for the two of them to meet, and harder still when Maddie left the store to nurse her mother. Their meetings had become less frequent and soon dwindled to the occasional postcard.

'And as for taking your breath away,' Rose said, 'the terror of having your own business does that. But it's hardly swanky. It's just that it seemed the right time to take the plunge. I found a good spot and a landlord who was prepared to give a woman a look-in.' There was no reason to mention how nerve-wracking everything was, that it had all come together rather sooner than she'd envisaged and that the rent was only guaranteed for another six months . . . Maddie didn't have a business bone in her body.

'Good for you.'

'But it really isn't swanky,' Rose insisted. 'We work in the front rooms, upstairs and down, and live in the back. It's a squeeze for the three of us but it makes such a difference having a dedicated workroom and a fitting-room that is just that – no more barking your shins on parlour furniture or having dress stands draped in sheets loom at you during the night.'

Maddie laughed.

'But I'm doing all the talking,' Rose said. 'What about you?' Maddie always had been good at asking questions without revealing much herself. 'It's an absolute age since I last saw you. I was stunned when I heard you were back. And rooming at the ladies' hostel, you brave creature.' She rolled her eyes. 'You might have let me know.'

'Oh well, here I am,' Maddie said in her usual airy fashion. 'After Mum died, I realized that I couldn't bear working any-where else and, thankfully, they took me back.'

'That is good news.' Surprising, too; Webb & Maskrey rarely gave second chances. But then Maddie always landed on her feet. It was good to see her again, and here they were talking as if they'd seen one another only a few days earlier.

'And what's this I hear about your name?' Maddie asked. 'I thought the business would be called "Madame something-or-other", but I gather you're using your own name.'

'Well, I did consider "Madame Rose", but I thought that would make me sound old, or else like a fortune-teller. So, though I like to think I have an eye to where fashion is heading, that wasn't the label for me. Ginny suggested "Madame Eglantine".'

'Eglantine?'

'A joke,' Rose said. 'It's a wild rose – beautiful, but with sharp thorns.' Maddie laughed. How easy it was to slip back into their old friendship. 'You must come and see us,' Rose said. 'I'm sure Ginny and Alice would also be pleased to catch up.'

'How are your sisters – "the Burnham Girls"?'

'Oh, Ginny is the same old Ginny. Steady, reliable, putting a brave face on things . . .' Rose brightened. 'And Alice has discovered a hankering for millinery and is doing a course at the Trade School. It's only one day a week, although you wouldn't think that to hear Alice. I met her there the other evening; it's not changed a bit since our day.'

'It's Alice's birthday on Saturday,' Rose added. 'We're going dancing. It's the first time we've been out for months. Why don't you join us? You can tell us all your news then.'

'I'd love to, but not this weekend. I'm going to my sister's. I generally visit Bella at weekends. I need her roast dinners to sustain me for another week of hostel life. Thank you, though. Another time, I'd love to. But now I must fly, or Miss Carter really will catch me out.' Maddie pulled a face at the thought.

'I must go, too,' Rose said. 'I've a client coming at three. Drop me a line and we'll arrange something.'

Rose pushed open the staff door and was sucked back into the stream and its competing and beguiling scents. If only customers knew that this pot-pourri of sophistication was nothing like the passageway she'd just stepped out of or, indeed, the upstairs workrooms, which, although warm and entirely adequate, were the equivalent of the backstage of a theatre or a servants' hall.

The ground floor really was looking rather luxurious since its recent refurbishment. Perfume bottles with tasselled stoppers, and swansdown puffs sitting atop chubby pots of dusting powder, were now seen to best advantage, instead of being

25

concealed in drawers. And their displays, newly reflected in multiple mirrors, created a sense of abundance that was quite dazzling. A cardboard smile assured Rose that Pond's vanishing cream, with the subtle fragrance of rose geranium, would remove all traces of fatigue. It would take more than vanishing cream, she thought.

3

There was a knock on the door shortly before three o'clock, only it wasn't Miss Holmes but an unknown man whose suit was beginning to shine. He tipped his hat and, in what might have been a continuation of that greeting, opened the suitcase he was carrying. Tidy rows of brushes, cloths and dusters pleaded from within its jaws.

'Could you help an ex-serviceman, miss?'

Now that she looked at the man more closely, Rose thought they were probably similar in age, although he looked older, and the row of medals pinned to his chest made her feel even more self-conscious in her pristine dress. Reaching into the case, she chose one of the largest brushes.

'Where were you?' she asked.

'Ypres, the Somme, you name it. And now look at me: a two-a-penny hero selling brushes door-to-door.'

'My elder sister's fiancé died at Passchendaele,' Rose said, as if by saying the word she knew what she was talking about.

'I'm sorry.' But the soldier's tone suggested it was all the same to him.

He pocketed the coins she'd offered and turned to go. Immediately, Rose thought of Ginny's Tom and of something he'd said on his first leave. They were drinking tea at the kitchen table, his long legs getting in the way as usual. Ginny had just stepped out of the room and, taking advantage of her absence,

Tom had turned to Rose and said, 'It's nothing like they say it is, you know.' Useless, Rose thought now, to think I am conferring bounty by handing over a few coppers. 'Thank you,' she called out to the soldier's retreating back. He was already partway through the gate.

Rose lifted the special dress and carried it downstairs; such a careful cradling, the walk from workroom to fitting-room almost a processional, a ritual in which so much faith was invested. The dress had been almost ready at the previous fitting, but Miss Holmes had yet to see the effect created by the two stiffened flowers positioned at the hip, which were designed to draw the eye to her slender figure and away from her sloping shoulders. This would be the first occasion Miss Holmes – and Rose – would see the midnight-blue dress as a living, floating accomplishment. Even Rose had butterflies as she fingered this effervescence of silk.

Rose sometimes stepped into the fitting-room for the sheer pleasure of seeing it was there. In her estimation, this was the best room of all. She had worked hard to achieve the right blend of what she hoped was understated chic and practicality. She loved the pale-blue walls, was pleased with the furniture and even more delighted by the fact that it had come from a big-house sale. She had seen an advertisement in the local paper – how lucky that it had caught her eye just as they were starting out. Armed with directions, she and Ginny had caught a train to Kent one afternoon and walked the remaining mile to Burbage House. How fascinating to step inside someone else's life, especially when that life was in the process of being dismantled, the only son and heir killed at Mons. His parents, finally conceding defeat a decade later, had now put the house and its contents up for sale; many of those items were laid out on trestle tables or distributed across the lawns when Rose and Ginny arrived.

Rose had marvelled at the set of meat plates in descending sizes, but concentrated instead on furnishing the business. Their outing was such a success that she and Ginny had needed to hire a man with a large cart to carry away their booty – the three deal tables that were now upstairs; the two handsome cane chairs that sat in the fitting-room on either side of a small table with its discreet piles of *Vogue*, *The Lady* and *Fashions for All*; the folding screen that shielded their clients' modesty while they undressed; and two good-sized patterned rugs. Best of all, though, was the commodious sideboard from the servants' hall – 'as befits our station' – which, when scrubbed and repainted in the palest blue and embellished with arty florals, might have originated in the Omega Workshops. A spray of Chinese Lantern stems provided the fitting-room's final touch, their bright orange globes adding a distinctive note of colour that was reflected in the enormous mirror that ran from floor to ceiling on the opposite wall.

Rose paused before the glass and studied her reflection there. She was used to assessing other women, to gauging their height and size, and to knowing at a glance which colours and styles would flatter, and which do nothing for them. What would those same women make of her? She was tall and slim, with thick, brown hair cut into a dense, tight bob, but Rose knew that a description of how she looked did not do justice to the way she carried herself, or to that indescribable something which became a discernible flair when she tweaked and tucked and pulled and draped, sculpting something dashing and unexpected out of four yards of silk. Rose smoothed the black dress she wore to greet clients and allowed herself a final assessment of the room. Yes, she and it were ready to greet Miss Holmes.

Dear Miss Holmes. Rose regularly added this epithet when she thought of Phyllis Holmes. No other client's name was prefaced with 'dear', but it would otherwise have been 'poor Miss Holmes' and that would be self-defeating. Though, in truth, that is how Rose had defined her during those interminable Webb & Maskrey appointments in which Miss Holmes, accompanied by her mother, was pressed into styles she should have left behind years before. And yet, somehow, Miss Holmes had found the courage to forgo Mother and the department store and follow Rose to her new venture.

At first, it was a delicate business. 'If you are going to wear this year's styles,' Rose told her, 'you will need new underwear. Today's printed chiffons are unforgiving.' That was her chance to relieve Miss Holmes of sackcloth-and-ashes bloomers and vests cobbled together with tape. Miss Holmes was willing to be guided – up to a point, that is. Even Rose's powers of persuasion could not make her relinquish her corset, but she had at least been steered towards something more pliable.

'Father's money,' Miss Holmes had said faintly when Rose, who had issued clear instructions on what she should purchase, complimented her on the result; Miss Holmes blushed. 'Father's money,' she repeated, even more faintly. The words 'father' and 'corset' did not belong in the same sentence.

Thereafter, the speed at which Miss Holmes ordered new clothes had been startling. In the last five months, Rose had made her a shell-pink-and-cream wool crepe skirt with a matching jacket, a day dress in silk georgette and two in printed crepe, an afternoon frock in damson velvet devoré . . . And now 'something understated, but special', Miss Holmes had insisted, leaving Rose to conjecture exactly what 'special' meant. A beguiling dress, Rose thought, for surely Romance lay behind all this spending. This was more than a new thirst for clothes.

She could feel Miss Holmes's heart beating as she helped her into the dress, her quivering breaths keeping pace with each hook and eye. Rose's own heart beat almost as fast; it was like holding a bird in her hand. She wanted to prolong the moment before she asked Miss Holmes to turn around and face the glass. Rose slipped the final hook into place and stepped back. And with one bound she was free, she thought, wondering where this dress would take Miss Holmes. 'Now you can turn and look.'

For one long moment, Rose waited.

'It's perfect,' Miss Holmes said. 'It's everything I wanted and more.' Tears sprang to her eyes, her lower lip trembled. This was not the first time Rose had seen a client moved to tears by the transformation achieved by a special dress; to stand before a mirror and see another woman look back at her. Rose felt giddy with success.

But Miss Holmes's tears continued falling and her face began to collapse. 'Yes, this is exactly what I'd hoped for, and more.' She started sobbing. 'But I can't have this dress.' She was weeping freely now and weeping in a way that suggested she had needed to weep for a long time. Rose moved towards her – formality be damned, she needed to comfort her – but Miss Holmes was encased in her private grief and made no attempt to stem her tears. Reluctantly, Rose stepped aside. She had no place in this.

Rose had found herself at the heart of other dramas with clients in the past and knew she would have to wait until Miss Holmes felt able to compose herself and explain. And, in explaining, surely all would be well?

'I'll get you a glass of water,' she said. What else could she suggest? Miss Holmes needed some time alone. And so did Rose. This was nothing like the scene she'd envisaged, had been imagining for several days – that glorious moment when Miss Holmes turned to her and smiled. That picture had dissolved and all her certainties with it.

Rose took her time to walk down the hall to the scullery, turn on the tap and run cold water into a glass. She looked through the window at the tree in her neighbour's garden and counted its scratchy branches and the leaves coming into bud. By the time she returned to the fitting-room, Miss Holmes looked blotchy and chaotic, but at least her tears were subsiding.

Miss Holmes sniffed. 'I shouldn't have let myself try on the dress when I knew I couldn't have it.'

Oh, please don't say that, Rose thought. Not like this, not out of the blue. She dared not even allow herself to think what it would mean for the business if Miss Holmes did not take this dress. And Miss Holmes herself, her unspecified adventure, her blossoming these last months . . .

'I'm sorry you are so distressed,' Rose said. 'I don't know what has happened, Miss Holmes, but I don't want to add to your woes. Why don't you come and see me when you're feeling better, and we can talk then.'

'Thank you.' Miss Holmes managed a watery smile.

'Let me help you get changed.' Poor Miss Holmes, it was like undressing a child exhausted by her own tears. But it couldn't be as bad as it seemed. There must have been a lover's tiff – if a man *was* involved; a misunderstanding of some sort. Surely it was nothing more serious? 'I have to go upstairs now,' Rose said, 'but there's no need to rush. Please sit here as long as you wish.'

She could not possibly send Miss Holmes out into the street looking as bedraggled as she did at this moment. She knew Miss Holmes wouldn't want her to witness the effort required to restore herself, and Rose did not want to see it, either. She needed to leave the room before her own composure slipped. She returned the blue dress to its padded hanger and there it hung, perfect but lifeless, its moment of glory passed. Rose had the sense of a thread being pulled. One tug and everything could unravel.

4

For one night, though, Rose must push these thoughts aside and focus instead on her sisters. It was Alice's birthday, and they had come to the Amalfi to celebrate. Halfway through the evening there was an interlude, with a demonstration by a professional dancer. 'Fiffinella' was in her element, twisting her feet and smooching in a series of slinky movements that were all elbows, knees and toes. She turned on the balls of her feet in a wiggle that was also a strut and, holding her right arm aloft, flickered her fingers like flames. 'Jazz, baby . . .' the band-leader crooned.

Rose had forgotten how popular these demonstration evenings were. The music changed and 'Fiffinella' switched to a series of steps designed to give your foxtrot that extra-special touch. Rose knew this one; Alice had been practising all week – taking six steps backwards, beginning on her right foot (and counting one to six), stepping forward on her right foot, *lightly* (counting seven), then forward with her left and back again, *swiftly*, on her right (*and* eight). She scoured magazines and newspapers for tips and knew the names, if not necessarily all the steps, for the latest crazes: the jog-trot, the ragtime jazz and now the foxtrot fancy.

Rose leant across the table to make herself heard. 'It's an absolute age since I've been here.'

'Me too,' Ginny said. 'Although it hasn't changed. What do

you think of it, Alice?' But Alice and her friend Maud were too engrossed in Fiffinella's footwork to comment.

The Amalfi had become popular during the war – frenetic evenings suiting the frenetic lives of the young men home on leave. Rose had only ever been an occasional visitor but some of her colleagues had come here week after week to lose themselves in the darkness and the rhythm. How on earth they had managed to stay upright was beyond her. After only a few turns around the floor, Rose had longed to soak her work-and-dance-weary feet.

A row of potted palms near the entrance created a walkway shielding the dance floor, which, once revealed, was seen to be illuminated by a series of lamps on small tables dotted about the room. Their spectral light and the five-piece orchestra in black tie and tails provided instant glamour. This haunt was somewhat tame compared with the more prosperous West End clubs, but it nevertheless had a certain something.

Now Fiffinella was performing a series of shimmies. Each time she moved, the brilliants on her dance shoes glittered. Alice nodded approvingly and turned to speak to Maud, but the beat was too insistent; her words disappeared.

The music came to a halt, its squalls replaced by applause. Fiffinella took a bow, and her audience came to life. Now it was their chance to perform. 'Our turn now. Shall we?' Rose held out her hand to Ginny. Alice took up with Maud and disappeared on to the dance floor while her sisters were still finding their feet. It was a mixed crowd this evening: tentative couples taking halting steps beside proficient dancers who circled the floor without pausing. Some young women were accompanied by young men. A larger number, however, had paired off together, perfecting the latest steps and having a lark, apparently oblivious to the shortage of male partners. Among the men present, there was a clear demarcation: there were quite a number of younger and older men, but fewer of the same age as Ginny and Rose.

'I'm glad we decided to come,' Ginny said, as she and Rose moved off to a simple foxtrot. 'It's lovely to be out for an evening – and to work off that birthday cake. And besides, we have another reason to celebrate: everything seems to be coming together.'

Rose concentrated on her footwork.

'I know it's still early days,' Ginny continued, 'and things are slow at the moment, but we're not doing too badly, are we, thanks in large part to Miss Holmes?'

'No,' Rose said, glad that she wasn't looking directly at her sister. She had yet to tell Ginny what had happened with Miss Holmes. All would be well when whatever misunderstanding was put right, Rose told herself, repeating the words she'd been reciting for the past two days. She must not let the other afternoon unnerve her; she would not give Miss Holmes another thought this evening.

'That was my toe,' Ginny said.

'I'm sorry.' Rose gripped Ginny's hand and looked past her left shoulder at their fellow dancers. 'I wonder where all these couples met?' Then, too late, she remembered how often Ginny and Tom had gone dancing before he was conscripted and everything changed. They circled the floor in silence.

'There'd be nothing to stop you marrying, you know,' Ginny said eventually. 'Not if you met someone.'

Rose paused mid-step. 'Whatever put that into your head?'

'I don't know, thoughts of the future and so forth.' And the past, Rose knew. 'I know you want to take care of us, Rose.'

'I promised Mum.' During those long, hard weeks, coming home from the store to sit at her bedside. Five years ago now, and coming so soon after Dad. Rose could still feel herself holding her breath each time he coughed. And then for Mum to get sick, too . . . Grief caught at her throat; she squeezed Ginny's hand.

Ginny spoke into her silence. 'I know you promised Mum, and I understand why, what with you making such strides at work, and the war and everything.' 'Everything' included Tom's death, although Ginny didn't say so. 'But that doesn't mean you need to sacrifice your own happiness for us.'

Rose looked at her in astonishment. 'But I couldn't be happier: my own business, even my own label stitched into the back of the clothes.' *Rose Burnham* flashed before her eyes in a flourish of black on white. 'You know how long I've wanted this. And anyway,' Rose laughed, 'what man would be happy with me up at five to finish something, or working past midnight?'

'Someone who believed in you.' Ginny looked into the middle distance.

But that's *your* dream, Rose thought. She wanted to lighten the mood. 'How many men have you met who are willing to play second fiddle? I don't see any likely candidates here, do you?' Laughing, Rose gestured towards a group who, convinced their single state would not last long, were claiming the margins of the dance floor.

Ginny smiled. 'Not this evening.' 'Tea for Two' was replaced by 'Kiss in the Dark'. They picked up the rhythm again.

'You're leading, Rose. *I'm* supposed to be leading.'

'I'm sorry, I wasn't thinking. Why don't we sit this one out?'

Back at their seats, the sisters surveyed the room. 'Look over there,' Rose said. 'More wolves in sheep's clothing.' She pointed to the far corner, where two young swells were chatting to Alice and Maud. The one who'd attached himself to Alice was standing with his hands in his pockets and a confident smirk on his face. She seemed unimpressed. This ritual went on for some minutes before they moved on to the dance floor. Alice's expression was as poised as her footsteps but the young swell evidently did not pass muster. Alice covered the floor without undue exertion and deposited him the moment 'Kiss in the Dark' came to an end.

'Nice time?' Rose asked when Alice rejoined them. Maud was not far behind, having jettisoned her own partner almost as quickly.

Alice grimaced. 'Mine thought he was God's gift.' She reached into her bag, extracted a small bottle and splashed herself liberally with scent. Fortified, she turned to Maud. 'Again? But let's dance together this time.'

The band struck up a breezy foxtrot. Rose turned to Ginny. 'Do you think she's happy working with us? You don't think she felt obliged to say yes because she knew I needed another seamstress?'

'When has Alice ever felt obliged to do anything?'

'She does seem happier, especially these last few months.'

'Since she started millinery classes, you mean? She's like you, Rose, far happier if she has something of her own on the go – and millinery is something you and I can't do. And I don't think she enjoyed the pecking order of department-store life. She's more like you than you think.' Ginny peered into the darkness. 'Isn't that Maddie Greene? I'd heard she was back at Webb & Maskrey.'

'Yes, I meant to tell you. I bumped into her the other day.

But it can't be Maddie.' Rose craned her head to look. 'I invited her to join us but she said she'd be at her sister's this weekend.'

'Are you sure? It looks like her. Over there, near the far pillar. Look – that couple to the left of the orchestra, disappearing behind the palms.'

'That *was* her,' Rose said. 'How strange, although I couldn't see who she was with. Well, that's a bit much, when I'd asked her to come out with us.'

'Perhaps she received an irresistible invitation,' Ginny said. 'He certainly was a looker *and* was nifty on his feet. Perhaps he is her secret beau.'

'How extraordinary. I shall have to quiz her when I see her next . . .' But why had Maddie not simply said that she was spoken for this evening?

Alice reappeared. The orchestra progressed to a tango; the trombone flung its highest notes towards the ceiling. 'What now, birthday girl?' Rose asked. Secretly, she hoped they were heading home.

'Just one more turn.' Alice pulled Rose to her feet.

5

Rose reached for a fresh sheet of paper. She loved mornings like these, when she had a few clear hours and could dive into work without fear of interruption. What a perfect start to the week. She began making loose, sweeping sketches, limbering up for the morning ahead. She was just fleshing out her ideas when her concentration was broken by a knock on the door.

Ginny looked up from her sewing. 'Are we expecting anyone?'

'No.' Rose turned to Alice, who was pinning a dress on to Bertha, the stoutest of their dress stands, and was now doing so with studied absorption. Roll on the day when they could afford an apprentice. 'I'm sorry, Alice, but can you go?'

Their visitor was Miss Holmes; there would be no more drawing this morning. Rose could hear their voices in the hallway, Alice speaking more loudly than necessary in order to alert her sister; Miss Holmes quiet and polite, as always. Rose put down her pencil and went downstairs.

'I'm sorry to come unannounced, Miss Burnham, but if I didn't come today, I'd lose my nerve.'

'Of course, Miss Holmes,' Rose said, 'you're very welcome – do come in.' But her mood immediately changed. This couldn't be a good sign; she'd not expected to see Miss Holmes again quite so soon, and had hoped not to see her like this.

'Thank you, Alice,' Rose said, as Alice turned to go back

upstairs. 'Why don't we step into the fitting-room, Miss Holmes. We'll be quiet there.'

Miss Holmes didn't wait to sit down before she started speaking. The words came out in a rush. 'The thing is, Miss Burnham, I've made a dreadful mistake. Someone has taken advantage of my good nature.'

'Oh, surely not? I'm so sorry to hear this.' Rose stepped towards her and put out her hand, but Phyllis Holmes retreated into a small, tight ball and perched on the edge of a chair. 'Whatever has happened, Miss Holmes?'

Miss Holmes said nothing but sat shielding herself with her bag, a flat leather bag shaped like a document case. She was clutching the bag so tightly, it might have held vital papers. The veins stood out on her hands. She was wearing green this morning, a dark shade of green that did her no favours and was more suited to 'then' than now. But 'then' had evidently reasserted itself; the Miss Holmes of recent months had vanished. Rose stood by helplessly while Miss Holmes worked herself up to whatever it was she needed to say.

Eventually, she spoke. 'I met a gentleman, Miss Burnham. Or at least, I thought he was – a gentleman by temperament, that is. I thought my life had changed – and so it has, but not in the way I expected.' She took a deep breath. 'The man I met has disappeared and I don't know how to find him.' She gripped her bag even more tightly.

'I'm not quite sure I follow . . .' Rose said, groping to digest what she'd just heard. 'Perhaps there has been some misunderstanding?'

Miss Holmes looked at Rose but said nothing. The coals shifted in the grate, the hall clock ticked more loudly than usual. They could not sit like this all morning; she would have to encourage her to speak. 'This gentleman, Miss Holmes,' Rose said tentatively, 'when did you last see him?'

'Five weeks ago. February the twenty-sixth.'

'And you have heard nothing from him since?'

'No.' Her reply was scarcely a whisper.

'Did anything particular happen on that occasion? Something that could account for . . .'

'Oh, yes – everything,' Miss Holmes said. The stress she placed on 'everything' was painful to hear. 'The whole afternoon was about making plans. You see, that's when I gave Reginald – Mr Wilson' – Miss Holmes looked up – 'the capital to help those plans along. He's setting up in business, you see.'

'I see,' although Rose hoped she did not. 'But what . . . how?' She clasped her hands to steady herself; she must maintain her own poise. She hardly liked to frame her next question. 'This . . . investment, Miss Holmes . . .' Rose could not complete the sentence. She sat down before her knees gave way.

Miss Holmes squeezed her eyes tight shut. 'Eight hundred pounds,' she whispered.

'Eight hundred pounds,' Rose repeated. Her level tone amazed her. She'd be lucky if she saw a quarter of that amount this year. She forced that thought aside and wondered what on earth she could safely say next. She seemed to be having two different conversations, the one shrieking inside her head, her hopes and fears colliding, and this other, public one in which she sounded perfectly calm.

Miss Holmes looked across at her. 'You think I've been very foolish, don't you? I have been very foolish, haven't I?'

'I think you must have been cruelly deceived. What do the police say?'

Miss Holmes retreated into an even tighter ball. 'Oh, I couldn't go to the police. I'd be so ashamed.'

'And,' Rose hardly dared ask, 'what about your mother? What does your mother say?'

Miss Holmes's answering look was pitiful. 'What will I say to Mother? I can't tell Mother I've lost Father's money. This sort of thing doesn't happen to people like us.'

'Well, it may not come to that. There may be a perfectly straightforward explanation.' (Though not necessarily one she'd want to hear.)

'Yes,' Miss Holmes said. She leapt at that possibility. 'Perhaps Reginald has had an accident and lost his memory.'

'Perhaps.' Inspiration struck: 'What about the friend who introduced you? Surely you can ask your friend to enquire on your behalf?' Miss Holmes squirmed. 'I know that would be embarrassing,' Rose continued, 'but you'd at least be able to reach your . . . gentleman . . . and demand an explanation.'

Miss Holmes stayed silent. If anything, she looked even more shrivelled.

'You did meet him through a friend?'

Miss Holmes looked down at her lap.

'Or at a dance, perhaps?'

Miss Holmes shook her head. Her whole body crumpled. 'I'm not sure I can tell you.'

Rose smiled encouragingly, though it required all her effort to do so. Now what was Miss Holmes going to say?

'I met him through a matrimonial agency,' she mumbled.

'Oh!' Rose exclaimed. 'Oh,' she repeated, in what she hoped was a more measured tone. 'I read something about matrimonial agencies only the other day.' Did that fib sound convincing? She'd no idea such places existed. But that was beside the point;

Miss Holmes needed all the reassurance she could muster. 'It's so hard to meet gentlemen, isn't it? If I weren't so busy with my clients, I'm sure I'd approach an agency myself.' Rose heard her voice run on. 'And anyway, that's good news: the agency can trace him for you.'

Miss Holmes looked appalled at the very idea. 'Oh, I couldn't possibly contact the agency again, Miss Burnham. They will have taken Mr Wilson on trust, just as I did. And . . .' she hesitated. 'I couldn't bear to have to explain.'

No, of course not, Rose thought, looking at her pleading, strained face. It has taken all your resolve to tell me. 'I'm so sorry, Miss Holmes. And, this . . . agency,' she said, floundering. 'How exactly did you find them?'

'Oh, it was all above board. I saw their advertisement in the local paper.'

'I see. And may I ask their name?'

Miss Holmes blushed. 'Cupid's Arrow,' she said.

6

Cupid's Arrow. Rose repeated the name as she headed back upstairs after saying goodbye to Miss Holmes. What an outrageous story – if only that was all it was, a story. Rose gripped the banister to steady herself. When she reached the landing she put her hand on the workroom door, then changed her mind and opened the bedroom door instead. She could not face her sisters until she'd digested what she'd just been told.

The bedroom was a cold room, with twists of newspaper in place of a fire in the grate, but that did not matter this morning. Rose sat down on the bed. She was struggling to understand how someone so reticent, so sheltered, so *respectable* could find herself in this situation. And yet it was probably those very same qualities that had led Miss Holmes to this. Unless there really had been a misunderstanding and . . . and what? From whichever angle Rose examined it, Miss Holmes's predicament was all too convincing.

But what of their own predicament? If, at the end of the month, there was no large cheque from Miss Holmes to pay for the silk and the bill for the beading and all the rest, where would that leave them? What would it mean for the business? That question confronted Rose, but what could she actually do? She couldn't face the bank manager again. The memory of her visit last year was all too galling: 'My dear Miss Burnham . . .' He'd leaned back in his chair, exposing his spreading girth and gleaming watch-chain. 'If the bank were to extend further credit to every young lady who can sew a fine seam, where would we be then? You are just starting out and must prove your worth to me. Just because one or two well-heeled ladies like your frocks, does not mean you will succeed in business. Trust, like money, must be earned. Business is full of harsh lessons; let this be the first one for you. And' – he'd glanced out of the window – 'a word to the wise: success in business requires sacrifices. Don't go thinking that because the sun is shining you can take a day off.' The cheek of his parting shot; she'd spent most summer days of the past twelve years in an airless workroom. What experience did he have of that?

A litany of her failings paraded before Rose. She had been too reliant on Miss Holmes, had underestimated some setting-up costs and overlooked others. If she knew about late payers, why had she not considered how much money she would need in hand at the start, and how very many clients would be needed to establish the business? Rose pictured the fitting-room downstairs and its perfect, pale-blue walls. That quiet blue room was the culmination of everything she'd ever wanted. How could something so present, so substantial and so real, be yet so insecure? And all because some devious swindler had sweet-talked Miss Holmes into giving him her money.

But what a leap for Miss Holmes to have approached a matrimonial agency in the first place. How ever did she screw up her courage? Rose thought back to her Webb & Maskrey days and to Miss Holmes standing goose-pimpled and shivering, yet perspiring, her mother presiding over every appointment, domineering even when silent, their fitting-room behaviour a microcosm of home. Rose recalled an occasion when tears had coursed down Miss Holmes's cheeks and, silently and discreetly, she'd caught them on her tongue. 'Why don't you take Mrs Holmes to see the new season's coats,' Rose had asked one of the store's senior hands. 'Miss Holmes and I can finish here.' She'd led Phyllis back into the cubicle and, after watching her dab at her tears ineffectively with a tiny lace-edged square, offered her own large handkerchief instead.

'Thank you, Miss Burnham,' Miss Holmes sniffed. 'I will bring it back, freshly laundered.'

'Oh, don't worry, miss,' Rose said. 'Leave it with me when you go.' Imagine Miss Holmes having to admit to Mother and whoever did their laundry that she had in her possession, and would need to return, the fitter's handkerchief.

Rose had helped her to dress on that occasion, too – then, as now, years later – and had suggested Miss Holmes sit near the scalding pipes to put some colour back in her cheeks. By the time her mother reappeared, suitably subdued and stroked, Miss Holmes was at least presentable and better able to face the world. Dear Miss Holmes, who had always done as she was bid. Until now, when, somehow, she had finally summoned the nerve to burst out of her shell and grasp her own life. And look where that had got her.

Rose looked around the room she shared with Ginny. It was a plain room with a homemade quilt, a simple bedroom suite and the rag rugs they'd made for either side of the bed. Alice had the room down the hall, a small room that was becoming smaller by the day as her milliner's accoutrements encroached on it from all sides. So much so that Alice's hatter's block had found its way here and was now screwed on to the dressing table. When Rose woke in the night, 'Yolande' looked back at her. 'Why Yolande?' Ginny had asked. 'And why must every object have a name?' Yolande not only had a name, she had a personality, especially now that Alice had added long-lashed eyes and a pouting smile to her canvas face. 'You wouldn't get caught out like this, would you, Yolande?' Rose asked now.

She and her sisters were lucky. They had each other and would surely protect one another from stumbling into something like this. Not that they had any money to give away in the first place ... But was Phyllis Holmes so easily duped? Of course she was, Rose thought. She pictured the countless giddy young women whose evening gowns she'd stitched. How many of them had danced with the same man twice in a row and so thought their future was fixed?

Rose had to steel herself to go through the accounts again. The Book seemed heavier this afternoon when she lifted it down from the shelf. She already knew what she would find there: the flurry of appointments against the name 'Miss Holmes' and the details of all her payments from November onwards. And, yes, it was just as Rose had feared: the words 'paid' appeared in the final column against the first five garments, but the account for the velvet devoré was still outstanding, as was, of course, the cost of the special dress whose account she had yet to present.

It was not just the fact of the unpaid bill and the rejected dress Miss Holmes could not now pay for, but the orders, month after month, she would now no longer make. Rose blanched at the evidence before her: why had she not questioned why Miss Holmes was commissioning so much? She was one of their very first clients, her confidence increasing alongside theirs; it had been hard to tell who was the more excited. The regularity of Miss Holmes's requests and her pleasure in each one had stopped Rose asking herself a fundamental question: what will happen if – when – these commissions stop?

'The Burnham Girls' and Miss Holmes. Such different lives they'd led – she and Ginny hoisting up their skirts to hop on to trams and buses, making their independent dash to work while Miss Holmes was still in the schoolroom – and yet now their fates were inextricably linked. If she did not settle her account and ordered nothing further, things would be decidedly bleak. Alterations here and there would not solve it and, although new clients would come, they couldn't magic clients out of nowhere. Rose stared at the red-lined columns and willed their figures to change, but no matter how hard she willed it, the sums stayed exactly the same. Rose felt adrift; that all too familiar knot of anxiety twisted and tightened.

If the very worst happened and it all fell apart, they would still get jobs . . . Wouldn't they? Of course they would, but not necessarily jobs as good as the ones they'd left. They'd have to take anything on offer. But not at Easton's; spare us Easton's, with its windows stuffed with eiderdowns and cut-price frocks. Now you're being melodramatic, Rose admonished herself. But was it melodramatic, with things as fragile as they were? She glanced across at Ginny, who was sewing with the studious contentment of someone who has faith in the future. Now she would have to trample on that.

Alice was quietly working to her own private accompaniment, as usual. Alice would land on her feet and had youth on her side, too. In a few months' time, when she finished at the Trade School, Alice could opt for millinery, though she'd still end up in a workroom somewhere, unless a bijou shop took her on. But bijou shops paid even less than department stores and were far less stable. If nothing significant turned up in the next few weeks, what were they all going to do?

Why, oh why, had she encouraged her sisters to join her at

the beginning, instead of waiting until things were more certain? But that question wasn't even worth asking. Who else would listen to your plans and work alongside you willingly, for long hours and little pay, if not your own sisters, and extremely skilled sisters at that? She could never have hired experienced outside hands. But how would they all get by? The knot gave a further twist.

Rose pictured yet more bowls of Ginny's pearl-barley stew with dumplings. (Sorry, Ginny.) Paring and scraping was fine – even fun – at the start of an adventure and a brand-new life, but not day after day, with the knowledge of abject failure, and with years of paring and scraping ahead. And where will we all live, if I have to give up the lease on this place? Oh, please, not the ladies' hostel . . . Rose saw her ambitions in tatters, her proud dreams reduced to rags.

No – that must not happen. She must come up with a plan.

7

Later that afternoon, Rose slipped out to buy the *Sydenham Gazette* and brought it up to the workroom. She thumbed through page after page of local news until, there, towards the back, sandwiched between advertisements for Twink dyes and Sunlight Soap, was a discreet panel with the name 'Cupid's Arrow' centred within it. In smaller print – whispering, almost – on the line below, Rose read the words: 'Matrimonial Agency'.

'Do you seek companionship and fellow feeling?' the advertisement enquired. 'Let Cupid's Arrow secure your heart's desire.' Rose winced. She didn't like to picture Miss Holmes eagerly reading these words. She saw her cutting out the advertisement at home, in secret, as the nights were drawing in. What would Mother have said, had she found the blank space that stood for the gap in her daughter's life? Poor Miss Holmes – and these same saccharine words had introduced a trickster to her, and now threatened to undo the business. Rose pursed her lips. Cupid's Arrow had a lot of questions to answer. Fancy allowing a deceiver on to their books, a deceiver who, unless he was stopped, could be deceiving some other woman right now. Someone should find and uncover him. An idea began to take shape . . .

The even-smaller print at the base of the advertisement made Rose pause. 'Introduction fee: 2 guineas.' Two guineas. However could she justify spending that amount, with money as tight as it was? But what other way was there of championing Miss Holmes and perhaps even retrieving some of the money she owed them? Rose paused again. Put like that, it sounded quite convincing, but *two whole guineas*? How many bolts of silk could she buy with those? Perhaps best not mention the fee.

'There's something I need to tell you.' Rose caught Ginny's quizzical look, saw her ready herself for whatever was coming. Alice looked up briefly but continued sewing. 'Everything has been going beautifully,' Rose said. That was an exaggeration. She tried again, 'Well, everything began as well as we could have hoped. Better, really. We've had new clients commissioning new clothes, numerous restylings, and three Webb & Maskrey faithfuls have followed us here, including Miss Holmes, who has amazed us all by commissioning one thing after another.'

'Oh, yes,' Alice said, 'I forgot to ask: was Miss Holmes thrilled with her special dress?'

'That's what I need to talk to you about.' Rose took a deep breath. 'Up to now, we've relied rather heavily on Miss Holmes. In fact, going through the Book, even I'm surprised to see quite how many outfits she's had, and the fact that she came to us so soon after we started has rather disguised the overall picture. Unfortunately,' – unfortunately: that word was not nearly big enough – 'unfortunately,' Rose repeated, 'right now, we don't have enough new clients and we've no new commissions lined up. I'm afraid that things are rather more precarious than I'd expected.' Rose paused before delivering the final blow. 'The thing is, Miss Holmes can't pay her outstanding bills and won't be ordering anything else.'

'What?' Now she had Alice's full attention.

'Miss Holmes has been taken in by someone – a swindler, a

bounder, a confidence trickster – a man who promised her the earth, or made her think he had, and then took her money.'

Alice looked incredulous.

'That's dreadful,' Ginny said when she finally found her voice. 'What do the police say?'

'Miss Holmes hasn't told them. She's too ashamed.'

'Ashamed that someone stole her money?' Alice asked. 'How can that be?'

'It's more complicated than that. I say that the man took her money, but she actually gave it to him. He deceived her into thinking they had a future together and so she gave him her money.'

Alice put her head in her hands.

Ginny sat back as if winded. 'Oh dear, no. Poor Miss Holmes. How on earth did this come about?'

Rose explained how Miss Holmes met her fake charmer. 'So,' she concluded, 'you will understand why Miss Holmes can't have her special dress or settle her outstanding account.' Rose looked at her sisters, each sitting with her hands in her lap and a disbelieving look on her face. She had never sat in such a quiet and inactive workroom, and it was her fault they were sitting like this.

'All that work . . .' Ginny said, 'and the costs . . .' Her voice trailed away. It seemed she could barely summon the words she wanted.

And nor could Rose. 'I know. That's what I've been struggling with. We will have to tighten our belts even further.' Alice's eyebrows practically reached her hairline. 'Yes, I know things are already tight, but we'll have to be even more frugal.'

Alice looked despairingly at Rose. 'Will I have to give up the Trade School? I've paid this term's fees, but I have to produce three presentation hats before I finish, and they'll need felt and so forth.'

'No, Alice, you won't, and your final presentation is still some months off. Don't worry. A lot can happen by then.' It had better, Rose thought. 'New clients will come,' she insisted, 'and we will do what we can to find them and to secure more basic work, and, in the meantime' – Rose paused again, for emphasis – 'there is the question of Miss Holmes.'

Dear Miss Holmes. Her parting words yesterday had been almost too much to bear. 'Thank you for your kindness,' she'd said. 'Do you know, Miss Burnham, you were the very first person to ask my opinion? No one had ever done that before. It was years ago – my sage-green dress: do you remember?' Rose did not, but the expectation on Miss Holmes's face made it impossible for her to say so. Instead, she gave what she hoped was the right kind of smile, and so Miss Holmes continued. 'You asked which colour velvet ribbon I would like for the detailing on the bodice. I chose brown – a lovely acorn brown – and before Mother could speak you said, "That's exactly what I would have chosen, Miss Holmes. That shade will enhance the dress and suit your colouring." And so Mother accepted your view. No one had ever asked me to choose anything before. I had always taken what I was given.'

What a dreadful mess this is, Rose thought. 'The whole thing is unspeakable,' she said, looking from Ginny to Alice. 'And to think I helped this wretched deception along. Unwittingly, of course, but I designed the clothes she wore to meet this man and didn't stop to ask why she was commissioning so many. I could have found out something, if I'd tried. I do feel partly responsible.'

Rose headed off Ginny's objections. 'Yes, I know I'm not,

but all the same, Miss Holmes is immensely distressed – as of course she would be – and I must do what I can to help. She's seen us through our first few months. I can't step away from her now. And the harsh fact is that without any new commissions from Miss Holmes – no new tea-gown, no light summer coat in which to go boating – and with no other new clients in immediate view, we're not exactly overstretched. We do have the time to help her, and I think we owe her that. We owe it to ourselves, as well. In deceiving Miss Holmes, that blackguard has also taken *our* money.'

Ginny looked wary. 'What are you thinking?'

'I think I should track him down and expose him, and maybe even get some of that money back.'

'And how on earth do you intend to do that?'

Alice interrupted them. 'I know: why don't I sign up with Cupid's Arrow and play that scoundrel at his own game?' She tossed her head; her bobbed hair swung with her. There was no mistaking Alice's outrage, nor her determination. And how funny, Rose thought, that they had both come up with the same solution. Rose pictured Alice gaining on a sinister figure lurking in the lamplight, heard the strong bass notes of a drama reaching its climax . . .

Ginny looked despairingly from one to the other. 'What *are* you thinking?' she repeated, with a new note of dismay. 'Much as I enjoy reading detective stories, I've no desire to be in one.'

Rose came back down to earth. 'That's good of you to offer, Alice,' she said, choosing to ignore Ginny's comment, 'and I'd be grateful for any help, but I got us into this mess so I should be the one to get us out of it. I'll go to Cupid's Arrow. And besides,' Rose added, seeing how reluctant Alice was to relinquish her plan, 'if we are to lure the same man, we need someone who more resembles Miss Holmes.'

'But neither of us are anything like her.'

'No, but that transformation will be easier for me. Try as you might, I think you would find that difficult.' Rose adopted a demure expression and folded her hands in her lap.

'I see what you mean,' Alice said. 'And you could wear the blue dress; you're taller than me, so it would fit you. And at least it would then get an airing.'

'It is a beautiful piece of work, Rose,' Ginny said, rather more diplomatically.

'And then you could truly be a Miss Holmes type.'

'That's a brilliant thought, Alice, but I rather hope we'll be able to sell that dress at some point, so it would be a shame to risk it for this. On the other hand, it does say "money" and "Miss Holmes" straight away, and that would be a distinct advantage. But perhaps I should save the blue dress for an outing with the man himself.'

'Yes, that would be something,' Alice said. 'I'd book a ring-side seat for that.'

'There must be a safer option,' Ginny insisted. 'Can't you discuss this with Mrs Lingard? I'm sure she would be able to help.'

'I've thought about that, Ginny, but she's already sent Miss Prendergast and Miss Croxley-Smythe our way, and only the other week I told her how well things were going. I can't ask for more help now.'

Ginny sometimes joked that Rose was Edith Lingard's good deed. When they'd first met, Rose was a junior hand too lowly to venture an opinion, but she'd boldly suggested an alteration that, in Mrs Lingard's estimation, thereby rescued an otherwise unacceptable dress. Mrs Lingard asked for Rose to be present at future fittings, and her standing was such that the Chief Fitter dare not object. Thereafter, Mrs Lingard had maintained her interest in Rose. Even so, Rose had been surprised to be summoned to her home last year, and even more surprised by what she was told when she got there.

'My dear Miss Burnham,' Mrs Lingard began, 'I've spent a lifetime having decisions made for me. My parents steered my youth and, after I married, my husband took care of everything. Since his death, I've had to learn to think for myself and I find that I rather like it. I take advice, of course, but I'm entitled to indulge myself – within reason, so my accountant tells me. So, allow me to do so now. I gather you are starting up in business. A risky venture, but you seem to be an enterprising young woman; I've seen the evidence of that over the years. I know you have flair, but I'm well aware that a flair for design by no means guarantees a head for business. I think, however, that you have the steeliness required. So let me help you by guaranteeing the rent for the first year.'

Rose had opened her mouth to protest, but Mrs Lingard raised her right hand to silence her. 'These are difficult times, Miss Burnham, and if you are going to strike out alone it would help to have some support, especially from someone who can introduce new clients. There is one condition, however: I want you to come and see me twice a year. Call it a board meeting, if you will. In other ways, I will be silent, but I will be here if you wish to consult me. And before you ask how you can possibly repay me, I will tell you: your success will be the return on my investment. My newspaper tells me this is a new world for women. I'd like to contribute to that.'

Rose blinked, but Mrs Lingard had not finished. 'There will

be setting-up costs too, I realize. A loan should help with those. My accountant will arrange the details.' Rose blinked even harder. 'To cover your initial outlay, for fabrics and also furnishings,' Mrs Lingard said, naming the very items Rose was already mentally purchasing. 'I'm sure you have ideas.'

For such a recent convert to business, Mrs Lingard seemed to have a firm grasp of its requirements, but then, Rose thought, she had probably spent years on committees, distributing funds. It was strange how often women were assumed – or assumed themselves – to know nothing about money, when they were adept at that very thing. Rose felt light-headed. This conversation was too dizzying for words – and yet, somehow, she must find them. 'I don't know what to say, Mrs Lingard . . .'

'I think "thank you" is customary.'

Rose often replayed this encounter, delighting in and taking courage from it. She and Mrs Lingard had had their spring meeting only a few weeks earlier, which was why she couldn't possibly go back to her now. The whole thing would be too shaming. 'I have thought about it, Ginny, truly,' Rose repeated, 'but to have to explain this to Mrs Lingard would mean falling at the first hurdle. She would be kind, of course: how was I to know a valued client would be duped by an out-and-out scoundrel? But she'd conclude that I'm not ready to run my own business. I'd really rather try and sort things out ourselves. At least then there's a chance we can resolve this with no one else being any the wiser. So,' Rose paused, 'that's decided: I'll sign up with Cupid's Arrow, lure the deceiver and see where his sweet nothings lead . . .'

'I'm really not sure about this,' Ginny murmured.

'Don't worry, I may only need to meet him the once.' If she could convince Ginny of that, she might even convince herself.

'Think of it as dressing up,' Rose insisted. 'Miss Holmes dressed up for what she thought was her future, poor woman; I'll be dressing up for ours. I'll go through our wardrobes and see what I can put together.' Thank goodness they each held on to clothes for restyling and were able to magic something special out of nothing much. Alice looked appalled at the idea that anything of hers could in any way resemble something worn by Miss Holmes. 'I expect I'll be able to find something among Ginny's and my things,' Rose reassured her. 'Perhaps one of Ginny's blouses with soft lapels . . .' Now it was Ginny's turn to look affronted.

Rose continued: 'And I can put my hair in earphones. I've still got the hair I kept when mine was bobbed. If I use plenty of pins, I should be able to keep the coils in place. Yes,' she said excitedly; her plan was coming together. 'I'm sure I can transform myself. But if I *am* going to do this, I must do it quickly, and do it before I lose my nerve.'

PART 2

Cupid's Arrow

8

The next morning Rose found 5 Bolton Street on a busy thoroughfare, tucked in between a baby-linen shop and a baker. Its anonymous black door was slightly recessed and its sign so discreet that the casual passer-by would scarcely notice its existence. The door opened into a dark, narrow corridor with stairs at the far end. Cupid's eyesight had better be good, Rose thought, as she groped her way towards them. Upstairs, however, things were brighter. Rose knocked on a buff-coloured door and, after a moment or two, a thin voice said, 'Come in.'

The thin voice belonged to a young woman in a crocheted dress who greeted Rose, whispered 'Excuse me', and then retreated to an adjacent room. Rose caught a glimpse of a desk and a telephone before the young woman shut the door and started speaking. Try as she might, Rose could not hear what was said.

The waiting room was small but sunny and appeared to be cut from a larger space. It was furnished with four hard chairs and a table that held a selection of magazines. All out of date, Rose noticed. A pot of late narcissi provided an unexpectedly homely touch and was filling the room with scent. Rose walked to the window and looked out at the buildings on the other side of the road. A large enamel sign on the wall opposite advertised Lipton's Teas ('so refreshing'); a second, smaller sign proclaimed the virtues of Robin Starch.

'I'm sorry about that,' a voice spoke behind her. 'Telephones so often ring at the wrong moment.' Rose turned and saw that the young woman, now framed in the inner doorway, was a mere slip of thing; too young, surely, to be Romance's ministering angel? 'Miss . . .?' the young woman asked.

'Miss . . . Lipton,' Rose replied.

'Do come through, Miss Lipton. I'm sorry to have kept you waiting. I'm Miss Lane, the manager of Cupid's Arrow.'

Rose was shown into the other room and offered a chair. A small pot on the desk held narcissi, like the pot in the waiting room. 'What a lovely fragrance,' she said.

'Isn't it? I brought them in this morning.'

How reassuring. None of this was what Rose had expected, though she had not known what to expect. Miss Lane's smile was equally reassuring as she opened the drawer in the box file on her exceedingly tidy desk and retrieved a blank card from within. The box itself was crammed with cards; it was impressively full, in fact. Were there really so many clients on Cupid's Arrow's books? Miss Lane placed the blank card in front of her and unscrewed her fountain pen. She had obviously spent some time buffing her nails.

'You have a nice office,' Rose said. Their conversation had to start somewhere. 'Have you been here long?'

'Since the autumn,' and again came that soothing smile. The autumn: Rose calculated the timing of Miss Holmes's broken 'romance' and recalled how happy she had seemed back then. She was about to ask another question but stopped herself. Patience, she cautioned. You are now Miss Lipton, not Rose. You are the interviewee. She gave what she hoped was a genteel smile and clasped her hands in her lap.

Miss Lane evidently took this as her prompt. 'Thank you for

coming to see us, Miss Lipton. We at Cupid's Arrow are here to help Romance find its wings and fly.' Rose concentrated on the narcissi. 'Our role is to match suitable ladies with suitable gentlemen. We ask only the most discreet of questions to set you on your way, and we use your answers to match you with a prospective suitor. The gentleman in question then contacts you – the gentleman *always* writes the first letter – and, if romance blossoms, all to the good. If, however, you find that you would like to meet a different candidate – after all, we each have our preferences, and however closely we monitor our ladies and gentlemen we cannot promise that Cupid's arrow will strike the right heart straight away; if you wish to meet a different gentleman, please let me know and I will arrange for someone else to get in touch. I should emphasize that confidentiality is our watchword. Discernment, too. It is our proud boast that we at Cupid's Arrow almost always introduce the right gentleman to the right lady.'

Except in the case of Miss Holmes, Rose thought, but – golly – that was an impressive pitch. Miss Lane must have learned it off by heart. She didn't even falter when reciting that romantic guff. Miss Lipton responded with what she hoped was a nervous but encouraging smile.

'Now, do you have any questions, or shall I take down one or two details?'

'Questions, oh gosh, questions . . .' Rose had already decided that Miss Lipton should be a bit fluttery. 'No, not really, not at the moment.' She hoped she wouldn't have to answer too many questions, either, otherwise her carefully judged accent might slip.

'A few details first, then. Your full name, please.'

'Miss Allegra Lipton.' Allegra? Was that really a good idea?

'My parents had ideas above their station,' Rose added, to soften her fanciful choice. There was no point in pretending she was in the same social bracket as Miss Holmes, but she had her cover story ready for the right moment.

Miss Lane didn't react. 'Address?' she asked, pen poised.

'My address? Well, that's a little bit complicated. I'd like to give you a different address, if you don't mind? My mother is a little . . . How can I best define Mother? Mother is a little . . . old-fashioned, and would not like me receiving correspondence from gentlemen.'

'Of course, Miss Lipton. That's a mother's prerogative. I quite understand. We can't all be up-to-the-minute.'

How clever, Rose thought, to thereby flatter me that I am. 'Yes, it's silly really,' Rose said, 'but I think Mother is nervous of – how can I put it – gentlemen callers whose intentions may not be entirely honourable. She has become concerned about . . .' Rose hesitated and then volunteered: 'Fortune hunters . . . Silly, I know.'

'Fortune hunters?' Miss Lane gave a different smile. She seemed to find that prospect amusing. 'Well, we must all be on our guard against those.'

'Yes . . . Anyway, my address. I have a little job – well, it's more of a pastime really. On two or three mornings a week I am employed by a dress designer. I show ladies into the fitting-room and assist them there. To ensure they are comfortable – you know. The designer's clients appreciate a little extra help.' Steady, Rose, she thought. Will Miss Lane swallow this fiction? She was hardly a West End couturier. 'I work just a few hours a day. It's not as though I *need* to work any more; I just like to get out of the house. Otherwise, I'm at home with Mother.'

Miss Lane seemed to accept this explanation. 'How

interesting,' she said, and made a note of the address Rose gave her. 'I will add your employer's details: *Contact Miss Lipton care of Rose Burnham, designer.*'

'Thank you.'

'Now to some particulars: how tall are you, Miss Lipton?'

'How tall?'

'Yes, we like to make a note. Few gentlemen are comfortable with ladies taller than themselves.'

Oh, I see. Five foot six, I think.'

'Thank you. And,' she squinted across the table, 'blue eyes, if I'm not mistaken. Blue eyes and dark-brown hair, and a slender figure. That's always welcome.' Marriage market or cattle market, Rose thought. 'Twas ever thus . . . Miss Lane made a further note and then looked again at Rose. She was even more eagle-eyed than Rose herself, when she assessed new clients. But surely Miss Lipton would squirm before all this unwanted scrutiny? Rose frowned and looked down at her lap once more.

'And your education, schooling . . .?'

'My schooling?' She must not keep parroting Miss Lane's questions, but she had not anticipated this one and needed time to think. Park Street Elementary clearly would not do. Rose saw herself arriving at Webb & Maskrey for her apprenticeship interview, carrying the sample run-and-fell seams she'd practised at home and the buttonholing her mother had taught her. 'At home,' Rose said, waking up at last. 'Yes. Mother wanted me at home,' she fudged.

'A governess?' Miss Lane smiled again. She might have been savouring a delicious sweet.

'Yes, sort of.' Why not, thought Rose. A host of novelistic schoolmarms rose up before her. But Miss Lipton must not be too clever. 'I can't say I learned very much.' She looked down again at her lap.

'Oh, I wouldn't worry about that, Miss Lipton. Most gentlemen like wives who will listen, not young women who want to voice what they know. And what of hobbies, pastimes?'

'Sewing,' Rose said, on safe ground at last. 'And reading.'

'Needlework? Embroidery?'

Rose nodded, but not too vigorously. She must be careful not to dislodge her false hair.

Miss Lane noted the ladylike accomplishments but did not ask Rose to elaborate on her reading habits.

'Now, tell me a little more about yourself.'

Rose hesitated and then began what she'd rehearsed. 'Well, there's not all that much to say. I live at home with Mother. I suppose you would say that Father left us comfortably off. Fancy – we'd no idea. I'm not the sort of girl who thought she would ever have money, so it's all very exciting, really, though I am of course sad that Father didn't have the chance to enjoy it.' Was this too much? 'You see, he did rather well during the war. Father was in business. I'm not sure exactly what – he always said he liked to have plenty of irons in the fire.'

Rose gave a nervous giggle. 'Oh, I probably shouldn't have said that.' She saw Miss Lane take it all in. 'He died two years ago. It's just me and Mother now. I'm comfortable at home, but I would so love a place of my own and someone to talk to of an evening. Mother goes to bed early, and the evenings can be long.' Rose looked out of the window and gave a wistful sigh. 'The days are quite long, too. I am happy at home with Mother, but I would so love my own home.' Rose came to a halt. She hoped she hadn't overdone it.

'Of course, Miss Lipton,' Miss Lane said. 'And we are here to help you find one. The days have passed when young women wished to be companions to their mothers, although of course many are. But it is difficult for young ladies to meet suitable gentlemen without assistance, especially when the war took so many fine young men.' She paused, before adding, 'Hence the usefulness of Cupid's Arrow.'

Rose gave half a smile and lowered her eyes. If she looked straight at her disarming inquisitor, she might slip up.

'I assure you, Miss Lipton,' Miss Lane said, 'there is no shame in this arrangement. I admire your perspicacity in taking matters into your own hands. These are hard times; one must do what one can to furnish one's future happiness.' She might have been quoting *Home Chat*. 'Now, can you describe your ideal man?'

Goodness. Douglas Fairbanks, Ramón Novarro, Rudolph Valentino? But Miss Lane was unlikely to want a list of the nation's heartthrobs. And, after all, Miss Lipton needed to be demure as well as susceptible. 'Tall . . . handsome . . . but isn't that what all your clients request?' Rose gestured towards the card index. 'I see you have a great many.' She was itching to reach into that box and uncover its secret hoard of . . . hoaxers or mere hopefuls? She wondered how to elicit information without breaking cover. 'Aren't we all seeking the same thing? Indeed, I wonder if I have been foolish to come here. Speaking so personally, confiding in you – it's not something I'm used to.' Rose fumbled with her bag.

'Miss Lipton, let me reassure you . . .' Miss Lane wasn't really cut out for this role, Rose thought. She was too young to play motherly adviser and too young, surely, to understand the desperate fear of loneliness that stretched before the Miss Holmeses of this world. But Miss Lane compensated with another of her bright smiles. Rose noticed the uneven stitches around the neckline of Miss Lane's crocheted dress. She pictured her crouching over an insignificant fire on a Sunday evening, having to be miserly with the coal, peering at her crochet work, a cup of cocoa standing in for supper. She probably needed all the narcissi she could scent her rooms with. But she must not start to feel any sympathy for this young woman who had been careless enough to send Miss Holmes a wrong'un and who was now saying, '. . . we have endorsements from far and wide. Of course, I can't give you the names of the many young women whose lives have been changed by Cupid's Arrow – that would breach confidentiality, and you will appreciate how vital confidentiality is in matters of the heart – but many ladies, titled ladies among them, have left these offices floating on air.'

'Gosh,' Rose said. That did not sound wise, given the gloomy staircase and passageway they would have to navigate on their way out.

'Yes, many of our clients anticipate the sound of wedding bells.'

'Really?' Poor Miss Holmes among them.

'Now,' Miss Lane flourished her pen once more and adopted an intimate tone, 'how would you describe *your* Mr Right? What qualities does he have? Is he a war hero, or someone a little older? Does he play cricket, for example? Is he a fan of motoring? Some of our ladies ask to meet a gentleman with a car; others like someone bookish, or a gentleman who likes dancing.' She looked again at Rose, as if to assess her foxtrot. 'Well, perhaps not dancing,' she said. 'We aim to match the qualities of our respective clients. Mind you, one lady who said she was not at all outdoorsy went on to marry a keen cyclist. There's no knowing where Cupid's arrow will strike.'

Indeed. Rose cleared her throat. 'Actually, I do like to dance, occasionally. And I love reading,' she repeated. How had Miss Holmes answered? 'And walking in the park.' Hadn't Miss Holmes said something about walking in the park? Miss Lane made a note.

'And, finally, how would you characterize yourself, Miss Lipton? Are you Miss Femininity or Miss Effervescence? Miss Town Mouse or Miss Country-House-Dweller?'

Golly. Her interviewer was obviously following a crib sheet, but whoever had dreamed up this? Rose thought it best to stay silent.

'Miss Femininity, I think.' In Miss Lane's eyes, silence was obviously a good thing. She made a further note and fastened her pen. 'Well, Miss Lipton, I am sure we'll be able to find the right gentleman for you. But just one or two formalities before we close. We will of course need a photograph. Mr Jones, the photographer further down Bolton Street, has supplied some rather splendid studio shots.

'Mr Jones,' Rose repeated.

'Yes – number seventeen. Alfredo's Snaps. Now comes the delicate moment when I must ask for your fee.' Rose slid an envelope across the table. Two whole guineas: she could still barely countenance the thought.

'Thank you.' Miss Lane looked at but did not touch the envelope; she would not tarnish their conversation by opening it in front of Rose. Slowly, reluctantly, Rose returned her hand to her lap. She could almost hear the guineas screech at the affront of being spent like this. If only the envelope were on a piece of string and she could yank it back again. But it was all in a good cause, she reminded herself. In a matter of days, she could be face-to-face with the man who had deceived Miss Holmes and taken the money.

Miss Lane pulled the box file towards her. 'Well, Miss Lipton, as you see, I have made a note of your details. I will now go through our records so that, when you send your photograph, I'll be able to forward it to a possible match. He will then write to you, so that you have the opportunity to assess him on paper before you decide to meet. But I assure you that . . .'

'Do you interview the gentlemen?'

'I don't – that wouldn't be right. The gentlemen are vetted by a male colleague.'

'I see. Well, thank you,' Rose said. 'I'll get my photograph taken for you.'

'Yes, please do.' Miss Lane stood up and steered Rose towards the door. 'Good luck, Miss Lipton. I do hope Cupid's arrow strikes soon.'

9

'And which backdrop would you like?'

Mr Jones of Alfredo's Snaps stood before her. His chalk-stripe suit and generous moustache completed the caricature of the dapper Edwardian he must have been once upon a time: the young photographer, setting up his tripod, bustling from one wedding to the next. And now here he was in a frowsty little shop on the high street. 'I can do plain,' Mr Jones continued, 'with you seated beside a little table, or else a country lane. A country lane is always popular.' He invited Rose to step around the corner of the studio where, sure enough, just out of sight, a pastoral scene painted on a canvas backdrop awaited. If Rose closed her eyes, she might even feel the breeze ruffling her hair.

'And I've furniture to set the scene.' Mr Jones gestured at a stiffly upholstered chair rather like a throne and the aforementioned little table, a spindly affair in bamboo. 'I've a nice plant, too' – he pointed to a glossy aspidistra gleaming within a jardinière, the prop in family albums down the years. And so it proved: 'My wife's nurtured that plant for over twenty years. Milk is the trick, she tells me. She dabs milk on the leaves.' It did look remarkably resilient.

'I don't think the plant,' Rose said, 'although it is a beauty,' she added quickly. 'A country lane might be nice, but I'll be guided by you.' She looked up at him from under the brim of her hat and beamed. But Miss Lipton would not beam. Rose tried to turn her smile into something more tentative and succeeded in looking extremely uncomfortable.

'Well, it depends on the occasion,' Mr Jones said. 'Is the photograph for your mother or for a pal, or . . . is it for your sweetheart, perhaps?' Rose wavered. 'Now, I've been doing this for many years,' Mr Jones smiled, 'and your shyness suggests to me that this picture is for a gentleman friend. Am I correct?'

Rose was ready for him this time and offered an anxious smile of her own.

'Don't worry, miss. Your secret is safe with me. I'm always being called upon to take pictures of young ladies. Transform them I do – well, not that you need transforming, but a photograph can lend a softer light – and a pastoral scene provides the ideal backdrop. You've made a good choice. The country lane is very popular with young ladies and lends a nice romantic touch.'

The country lane was on rollers; Mr Jones now wheeled the backcloth further into the room and positioned the chair in front of it. 'Now, if you would just seat yourself here,' he gestured towards the throne-like chair, 'I'll set up the camera.' There weren't many chairs like this in country lanes, but Rose did as she was instructed.

'Back nice and straight – that's right. Both hands in your lap. If you could turn your head a little to your left, and perhaps look over your left shoulder? No, in your case, I think to the right. It doesn't always do for ladies to look straight at the camera. I always think a slightly sideways look conveys a more ladylike impression. Or you could glance down towards your lap? Some ladies prefer that pose. No? Fair enough. Now, don't move.' The bulb flashed.

'That's right. Keep still. I'll take one more to be on the safe side. Would you like one facing front or will you stick with sideways?'

The bulb flashed again. 'That's lovely. Now, would you like them sized for a particular frame or in postcard format?'

'Postcard, please,' Rose said. 'Two copies.'

'Right. They're sixpence a card, so that will be one shilling.'

While Mr Jones went to make a note in his book, Rose studied the panoply of best-dressed days and special poses ranged across his studio walls – everything from stiff-backed Edwardians told to watch the birdie, to a young girl doing the splits while holding pompoms aloft. There were dapper gents – and ladies – in their weekend finery, plus the odd unintentional comedy turn, including the woman whose hat was so crammed with overblown roses it resembled a squashed sponge cake. Bit by bit, the tone of the photographs changed. It was not just a case of different eras; there looked to be a different hand at work and a larger number of casual, outdoor snaps.

'I'm just admiring your photographs, Mr Jones,' Rose said. 'Quite a gallery. These two make a handsome couple.' She pointed at a man in a jaunty titfer who, right arm linked with his best girl, looked extremely pleased with himself.

'Oh, my lad took that one. You can't just rely on studio work to keep yourself busy, you need to go out and about. But that's a young man's game. Will Monday do for you?'

'Monday? Oh yes, thank you.'

'What name?'

'Miss Lipton.'

'Monday it is, then, Miss Lipton.'

Five days. All she could do now was wait.

10

Waiting was easier said than done. How on earth had Miss Holmes contained herself while waiting? Rose pictured her walking Mother's Pekinese or distracting herself with bits of embroidery, all the while listening for the postman's feet on the path. Rose had a different plan in mind: the next day was Maddie's half day; this would be a good moment to catch her before she left the store and find out what she could about her mystery dance partner.

'I'm looking for Miss Greene,' Rose told the shop assistant who appeared the instant she paused inside Webb & Maskrey's front entrance. 'I want to speak to her about the foulard silk gown in the window.' It was a lame excuse, but the young woman seemed to swallow it and, if questioned, Maddie would back her up. She had to concoct a reason or else Maddie would catch it; assistants were not allowed to speak to customers other than on shop business.

Maddie came towards her clutching an enormous lampshade and two violently clashing bolts of fabric. 'It would be so much easier if I could put this on my head,' Maddie said, gesturing at the shade, as soon as she drew near Rose. 'Can you follow me? If I don't put this dashed thing down, I'll drop it.' She raised her voice: 'Good morning, Miss Burnham. Miss Bancroft tells me you wanted to ask about a model gown you saw in the window. Please come this way.'

'Yes, that's right, Miss Greene. Thank you.' Rose fell into step beside her, but the minute they were out of earshot she came to a halt and said, 'We saw you at the Amalfi last week . . .' the cautious introduction she'd prepared, slowly working her way towards the subject, disappearing in the face of Maddie's confident manner.

Maddie looked embarrassed. 'I can't explain now. Will you still be in town in an hour? I should have finished by then. Can you come to the ladies' hostel at two thirty?'

Rose asked for Miss Greene for the second time that day and was directed to wait in the hostel sitting room. She had been here a few times over the years and could think of few rooms more unprepossessing. It had Windsor-soup chairs and Windsor-soup walls – everything was the same drab brown. It was more like a railway station waiting-room than somewhere to relax at the end of a working day. It was all very practical, no doubt, but there was nothing here to lift your spirits. There should be colour, Rose thought, colour and . . . privacy. There was no privacy here, nor any attempt to create it. Most of the chairs had their backs to the walls and, although one or two had been placed before low tables, there was insufficient space between the different groups. This was a room where you made polite conversation with parents depositing you here for the first time or talked to the aunt who had come to check up on you. You wouldn't choose to meet a friend here when you could go to an ABC tearoom or a Lyons' Corner House.

Rose was grateful she'd never had to room here. Although 'room' was hardly the word, when what the hostel offered was a curtained cubicle with a single bed, a mirror and a tiny set of drawers in which you were expected to cram everything except for your dress and coat, which hung from hooks on the wall. It was just as well that shop girls – and many of them were indeed still girls, or else young women – owned few clothes: a shabby coat, a work dress and a best frock, such as it was. It was a parsimonious scheme, herding exhausted workers into dreary rows and expecting them to thrive for the few years they lived there. And as for the rules, but she must not get started on those. Rose only knew what the cubicles were like because once, years ago, ignoring the coir mat stamped with 'No Guests Beyond this Point', Maddie had sneaked her upstairs.

'Rose,' Maddie said, interrupting her thoughts and coming to stand beside her. She was still wearing her Webb & Maskrey uniform – a navy-blue dress with a detachable collar – and yet managed to look stylish. 'I'm sorry to ask you to this dingy place, but I'm dead on my feet this afternoon.'

'Too much dancing, perhaps?' Rose asked wryly, as Maddie sat down in the chair opposite.

'I'm sorry I lied. I shouldn't have lied. But I felt such a fool. I feel an even bigger fool now.' Maddie's excessive apology told Rose how embarrassed she was.

'But why didn't you say you had a partner for the evening? Quite a nimble one, too, I gather,' Rose added, attempting to lighten the tone.

'Because of how I met him.'

'Heavens – have you joined a secret society?'

But Maddie wasn't in the mood to joke. 'The thing is, I do so miss going dancing.' Rose opened her mouth to protest, but Maddie continued: 'Yes, I know you invited me to join you and I hope you will another day, although you may not, after last weekend . . .' This was false humility on Maddie's part; she knew Rose would forgive her. 'But you have your sisters and are busy with your business. It's so hard to find partners these days and, when you do, you can't guarantee they can put one foot in front of the other. I'm tired of older men steering me around the floor and sweaty-palmed young ones squashing my toes; I just wanted someone I could dance with. The truth is that I wrote to an agency and that's where I found him. I wrote and said I wanted a dance partner.'

'Gosh. I didn't know you could do that kind of thing. Good for you.'

'I don't know if the agency believed me. I'm sure they thought I meant dancing as a prelude to something more, but I really am not looking for a husband. It was simply a dance part-ner I wanted.'

Rose wasn't sure which strand to follow. 'A husband?'

'Yes, it's actually a matrimonial agency. I came across an advertisement in a newspaper someone left lying about. The agency itself is in south-east London, only a few miles from you.'

'Oh, what's their name?' Rose asked, although she feared she already knew.

'Cupid's Arrow,' Maddie said, and gave an embarrassed laugh. She patted her hair, surreptitiously restoring the hairpins that were threatening to slide out of place.

'Your Valentino was shot from Cupid's arrow, was he?' Rose asked as lightly as she could. 'Well, you've found your match there, if he's a lovely dancer.'

'Yes, but I won't be seeing him again. Which makes me even more sorry I lied. We had an enjoyable evening; at least, I did. His waltzes and foxtrots are a dream. He can even shimmy. I couldn't believe my luck.' Maddie pulled a face.

'So, why won't you see him again?'

'Well, that's what's *odd*,' she said, leaning forward to emphasize her meaning. 'He mentioned going dancing again on Wednesday, but – and this is going to sound strange – it all went wrong when he saw that I live here. He said he'd walk me home, but when he saw the hostel, he looked quite queer and mumbled something about Wednesday being difficult. I'm sure the hostel is the reason he cried off.'

'But why would he do that?' Rose asked, a little too quickly.

'I think he was hoping for someone with money.'

'Really?' Rose tried not to sound as interested as she was. 'But why ever did he think you had money in the first place?'

'I borrowed someone else's notepaper to write to Cupid's Arrow. I felt a bit silly, Rose,' Maddie explained, in justification, 'and I didn't want to give my own address. Daisy Johnson, who has the cubicle along from mine, has a stash of paper printed with hers. Her parents live in Surrey, and she writes to them on the family notepaper. She's got a whole boxful of the stuff; I felt sure Daisy wouldn't mind.' Maddie gave one of her most beguiling smiles and looked at Rose.

But Rose's thoughts were elsewhere. 'Do you really think he dropped you because you don't have money? Are you sure there wasn't another reason?'

'I'm certain. He was full of compliments all evening and everything was going swimmingly until we landed here.' Her glance took in the walls and sturdy brown furnishings. 'I'd asked the agency to contact me care of the post office; I thought that would be exciting – safer, too. One never knows who one might meet. I think that when I first said I lived nearby, he thought my family had a London flat as well as a house in Surrey. Honestly, Rose,' – she tossed her head in a typical

Maddie gesture – 'I was so miffed when he dropped me like that that I tore his letter into tiny pieces.'

'Well, he's not worth it, Maddie, even if he is a good dancer,' Rose replied, all the while thinking, How extraordinary – this must be the same man.

11

Rose found Ginny in the workroom when she arrived home. 'You won't believe what Maddie just told me,' she said, and went on to explain about Maddie's fortune-hunting young dancer. 'So, I've been thinking . . .' Ginny looked doubtful. 'He must be the same man who courted Miss Holmes. Why don't you and I go back to the Amalfi and see if he reappears?'

'Go dancing? With things as they are right now?' Ginny threw open both hands in exasperation. 'Have you taken leave of your senses?'

'Not to dance, to observe. I keep going over what Maddie said about her dance partner and Cupid's Arrow. What if the Amalfi is the fraudster's usual haunt – the place he takes susceptible young ladies? It might be a West End club, but it's hardly chichi: we know it from our days at the store. What if the dancer escorts his victims there precisely because it's not the sort of place they'd normally go? There'd be an element of adventure in that, wouldn't there, and his ladies would be unlikely to run into any of their pals, and then have to account for themselves and how they'd met their dance partner. He took Maddie there, didn't he? What if we could catch him there with someone else? You could pick him out and then we'd know.'

'I suppose you do have a point,' Ginny conceded, 'although it hardly seems the kind of place he'd take Miss Holmes.'

'That's true. But he may choose his haunts to suit his victims, although it wasn't really Miss Holmes he was wooing, it was her money that interested him, and I rather suspect she would have gone anywhere he'd led her. Look at it this way: it could be several more days, even weeks,' Rose stressed, although she thought that unlikely, 'before I hear from Cupid's Arrow. I'll get my photograph on Monday and post it then, but who knows when I'll hear back. And meanwhile the bills keep mounting and this fraudster might slip away. I can't just sit on my hands and do nothing.' Ginny looked pointedly at the partially clad dress stands patiently awaiting their attention for various small alterations and restylings.

'Yes, yes, I know, but what if we were to see him sweet-talking someone else? We would know then, wouldn't we? A third victim would clinch it and I may not even need to pursue him via Cupid's Arrow.'

'There is that.'

Rose seized her slim advantage. 'Right, we'll go this evening. I don't think we should take Alice this time. She'd want to dance and wouldn't be short of partners, either, whereas you and I can sit and watch.'

'He's not coming.' Ginny scoured the dance floor. They'd been at the Amalfi nearly two hours and were sitting at the table they'd occupied the week before, in seats well placed to see the exit as well as the dance floor, and with the unexpressed hope that revisiting the same table might somehow help to conjure up the same man.

'He must be waltzing at the Waldorf,' Rose said bitterly, 'or serenading some poor creature at the Savoy. There are countless hotels and dance halls where he might show off his fancy footwork. Not to mention all the other West End clubs. I was naive to think he'd come back.'

'That poor man,' Ginny said.

'What?' Rose screwed up her face in disbelief.

'No, not him; not Maddie's dancer. That man over there: his partner has just abandoned him mid-stride. He must have squashed her toes once too often.' Rose glanced in the direction Ginny was pointing and saw a man with a limp marooned in the middle of the dance floor. He was about their age and looked uncertain whether to shuffle left or right, and how to make his escape.

'How times change,' Ginny said. 'Do you remember the eagerness with which some women claimed wounded soldiers to show they were doing their bit?'

'Yes, the more visible the wounds, the better. But that was then.'

'Indeed. But look at him floundering. You have to feel sorry for the poor chap. I'll just go and rescue him.' And Ginny was up across the floor before Rose could say anything further. The band launched into 'Whispering'; Rose sat on and watched the crowd jiggle and trot.

'Shrapnel,' Ginny said, when she returned from her rescue mission. 'It got his right knee. He never was much of a dancer, he says; now he's even worse, but was persuaded to make up a foursome. He's a policeman – a sergeant – apparently. I told him I read detective stories – I was just making conversation,' Ginny explained in response to the look Rose gave her, 'to put the poor man at ease. I was trying to take his mind off his feet. He says most plots are too far-fetched, that real crimes are more mundane than the ones you read in books. I was tempted to explain our problem and put him right on that score – but I didn't, of course.'

'You managed to learn a lot in a short time.'

'I had to think of something to say to help us navigate the dance floor and get him back to his seat. He really is an atrocious dancer. The friends he'd arrived with were all dancing; he was the odd one out. He plays golf, apparently – not that golf requires the same finesse. He seemed a nice enough chap, though. It's a shame I couldn't ask his professional advice. I expect he's come across numerous swindlers.'

'Well, it doesn't look like our swindler is going to turn up.' Oh lord, Rose thought, and we've squandered the price of two tickets – and a whole evening. But at least Ginny had referred to 'our' problem; that was a major advance in itself. Together, they would be able to find their way through this. First, though, she would need to be assigned her own Lothario . . .

12

The trap was laid far sooner than Rose expected. Within a few days of depositing her photograph with Cupid's Arrow, a mystery *billet-doux* addressed to 'Miss Allegra Lipton' landed on the doormat at Chatsworth Road. The letter, 'c/o Rose Burnham, Designer', was from a Mr Martin, who invited her to meet him at 3 p.m. the following Sunday. Were Mr Martin and Miss Holmes's Mr Wilson one and the same, or was her own romancer a lonesome innocent? There was only one way to find out.

Rose reached the lower entrance of the Crystal Palace park a good twenty minutes before the suggested time. She wanted to spot him – her Romeo, her quarry – before he spotted her. She selected a bench beside one of the plane trees in the central avenue and sat down. *Don't stand gazing about distractedly but walk quietly to a seat . . . Seat yourself, if you can, where you can conveniently watch the entrance. But watch unobtrusively, not with a fixed and desperate gaze.* Thank heavens for the etiquette section she'd found at the back of Mum's book on household management. To think that it had stood on the shelf for all those years without her benefitting from these pearls of wisdom, which, although directed at those fulfilling social engagements, could just as easily serve the trainee detective.

From her vantage point, she should be able to see Mr Martin from whichever direction he approached. And all too soon, there he was: a man wearing a dark-brown overcoat and hat entered the park via the lower gate and strode purposefully towards her . . . and oh, thank goodness, walked past. Rose felt her heart lurch in a decidedly unladylike fashion. Miss Lipton must compose herself.

Some ten minutes later another lone man in a dark-brown suit entered by the same gate. This was him; Rose was certain. He was evidently looking out for someone and altered his pace as soon he saw the green hat she'd said she would be wearing. This was just like one of Ginny's books. Should she appear reticent or smile in a welcoming manner? By the time Rose decided, he was only a yard away.

She nodded in acknowledgement, and, like clockwork, the lone man raised his hat. *If you do not know the lady very well, you should wait until she acknowledges your presence before raising your hat. While there is no need for the sweeping movement like that of the cavalier of other days, do not go to the other extreme and simply touch the brim with your forefinger, as many men have a habit of doing in these days. Raise the hat just clear of the head for a moment.* Mr Martin passed that test with flying colours. Gloves, too: he'd removed his right-hand glove in readiness to shake her hand. Golly, he must have read the same chapter.

'Miss Lipton,' he said. 'Mr Martin. Mr Edward Martin.' True or false, that name was at least an improvement on Miss Holmes's 'Reginald'. He was wearing an undistinguished coat and suit that, like so many other serviceable suits, said little beyond the fact that it was safe, functional and inexpensive. Brown was not a colour Rose especially favoured, but she could hardly hold that against him. At first glance, Mr Martin looked like a perfectly decent chap. But then, he was hardly likely to announce himself as a serial fraudster.

Rose grabbed her bag. 'Shall we walk?' she asked, rising from the bench before he had a chance to sit down. She was not ready for Mr Martin to sit beside her.

'I was about to suggest the same.' Her mistake; he should lead and she follow. All those years at the edge of other women's courtships, the journey from georgette to tulle, had introduced Rose to the pattern of romance, but not its details, and she could hardly have asked Ginny to recall her early encounters with Tom – that would have been too cruel. But she must be careful; Miss Lipton would not be so forward.

'I'm not very accomplished at this.' Rose did not know if she was speaking for herself or her fictional character.

'It would be strange if you were,' Mr Martin said gallantly.

They walked in silence to where the avenue and plane trees gave on to a series of paths. Walking beside him, observing how Mr Martin matched his pace to hers, Rose realized how ludicrously inexperienced she was – and not just at romancing. She didn't even know what Miss Holmes's deceiver looked like. 'Shall we take a turn about the lake?' Mr Martin asked. 'There might even be some boats out.'

Fit in cheerfully with plans made for your entertainment . . .
'Yes, that would be lovely,' Rose said.

Several mallards and moorhens were squabbling near the railings, but it was too early in the season for boating. Rose and Mr Martin stood and watched the ducks snatch at anything thrown in their direction by two young children whose nanny kept passing them pieces of bread. An older boy skimmed a stone, which bounced across the surface of the lake. Mr Martin followed its perfect trajectory with boyish admiration. He nodded in approval and applauded. 'Good show. Well done.'

'I always wanted to do that,' Rose said eagerly.

'Really?' Mr Martin looked surprised.

Rose stepped back into character. 'Of course, I would never have dared.' She was trying to picture the man she'd barely glimpsed at the dance hall and the little she had gleaned through Miss Holmes's tears. If only there were a handy crib for 'How to Catch an Arch Deceiver'. But Allegra Lipton wouldn't be worrying about this. She must hold her nerve. 'Your letter said you're a draughtsman. What does that involve?'

'Drawings, mostly.'

'Drawings?' Rose said a mite too enthusiastically.

'Technical drawings. And calculations.' Was this meant to shut her up, or did Mr Martin simply not want to talk about his work? It was a Sunday afternoon, after all. Rose looked down at his hands, but his gloved hands told her nothing; he might have been a labourer or a banker (though a banker would have worn better gloves). She must proceed via a process of elimination: his accent, his voice, his clothes suggested that Mr Martin could be the office worker he claimed to be. Perhaps he was what a few years ago was called a 'temporary gentleman'. Were those temporary gentlemen permanent now, or had some of them fallen by the wayside? It wasn't always easy to assess someone's place in the pecking order, let alone answer the simple question of whether they were being truthful or not. Mr Martin said he was an office worker and, for now, she had no reason to disbelieve him. This was harder than she'd anticipated.

'And I think you work for a dressmaker?'

'A dress designer,' Rose insisted. 'It's just a little job, more of a pastime, really. I help ladies in the fitting-room.' His questions could hardly follow her there, so how was she to move their conversation forward? The section on 'The Art of Conversation' in Mum's book could not have been clearer: *Remember not to speak about yourself to any extent, or to discuss your personal affairs*

in general conversation, or talk on things that must be avoided.
Strangely, this advice only appeared in the section advising
men; there was no equivalent guidance on 'The Art of Conversation' for women. Perhaps women should not converse. And
yet how did romances start – real romances, that is – if not with
real conversations?

Rose took a deep breath and said, 'I don't really need to work
these days.' Here goes, she thought, and reprised her story. 'My
father was in business, you see. I don't know what he did exactly,
but whatever it was did well during the war and so, thankfully,
Mother and I needn't worry too much. He died two years ago, so
now it's just Mother and me.' An unnamed wartime occupation
sounded about right, mixing embarrassment at her family profit-
eering, while other men died, with her own ignorance of the
actual facts and a smattering of Miss Holmes's details. Mr Martin
nodded but gave nothing away; perhaps he was affronted. Rose
was all too aware that, by referring to money, she had committed
the ultimate faux pas about which no advice should be needed.
She herself was still smarting from an unexpected encounter with
Miss Holmes that had taken place three days earlier.

Rose had been tidying the fitting-room when Alice brought
Miss Holmes in to see her. It was another unscheduled appointment and yet another occasion she would prefer to forget.

'Good afternoon, Miss Burnham,' Miss Holmes had said,
standing near the door and not quite meeting her eye. 'I hope
you don't mind my calling unannounced once again, but I've
brought you a little something on account.' She lowered her
voice, although there was no one to overhear them; Alice had
disappeared the minute she'd introduced Miss Holmes. 'I'll pay
a little more later, as soon as I can manage to do so.' Miss Holmes
blushed and, looking down, aimed an envelope at Rose.

'Dear Miss Holmes,' Rose said, taking it from her; the envelope felt light and slight in her hand – 'a little something' was indeed the appropriate term. 'This is extremely thoughtful of you. I appreciate the gesture, but I can't take this. It wouldn't be right.' Rose offered the envelope back.

Miss Holmes winced. 'Miss Burnham,' she said, her outstretched hand hovering at Rose's fingertips, uncertain whether to accept the proffered envelope or re-present it. Rose saw how much this transaction pained her; read the extreme embarrassment on Miss Holmes's face. They were discussing money, that essential but grubby topic about which a lady should not speak. What would Miss Manners say? Miss Holmes hung her head in discomfort and shame; she might just as well have been heading for the debtors' court fastened to a ball and chain.

This exchange was a ghastly parody of the moment a few weeks earlier when Rose had handed a very different envelope to Miss Lane. And now here she was on a Sunday afternoon enjoying – enjoying? – the fruits of that particular transaction. And once again money had reared its head. The etiquette adviser would be thoroughly ashamed of her.

'Miss Lipton . . .?' prompted Mr Martin.

'Sorry . . .?' She must concentrate and think what she could easily ask. She couldn't ask Mr Martin about his wartime experience – that really would be infra dig. She most certainly could not ask the one question to which she wanted an answer: had he met and swindled Miss Holmes? It was dawning on Rose that there were numerous questions she could not ask outright, and many that may take several conversations to uncover. What had she begun? And what if the poor man were in earnest? Poor man indeed, if he was. She did not want to mislead him. Rose glanced at her companion from under the brim of her hat. He didn't look to be in earnest, but then, how would she know?

'Would you like a cup of tea, or shall we carry on strolling?'

'Let's carry on strolling,' Rose said. 'It's so lovely out this afternoon.' *When asked to make a choice, make it. A guest who perpetually 'doesn't mind' what she does is irritating in the extreme.*

Mr Martin seemed relieved, perhaps at not having to spend 2s 6d on two cream teas. 'Let's walk along the terraces. From the topmost terrace, there is a marvellous view across London and on to the North Downs . . . And you like needlework, Miss Lipton? That's a useful accomplishment. Ladylike, too. I like to see a woman sewing.'

'Yes, men do.' Rose pictured herself scrabbling on hands and knees for pins, although that was hardly a scene Mr Martin would recognize. A woman bathed in a beatific light while sitting quietly, darning, was probably what he'd had in mind. But her remark was unkind. Mr Martin may have been thinking of his mother. She must do better at this.

'Shall we walk on?' Mr Martin asked. The Crystal Palace itself was putting on its own display, its hundreds of glass panels twinkling and glistening in the afternoon sunlight. 'What a picture,' he said. 'We've got the right day for it.'

'The Crystal Palace,' Rose said. 'It sounds like something out of a fairy tale. I've always thought that a lovely name – something fit for a princess.'

Mr Martin smiled. 'It is like a fairy tale, you're right. And there are monsters here, too – stone creatures – to add to the story. We could come here again, if you like, and look at the dinosaurs. They're something worth seeing.'

'I'm sure they are. Yes, why not?' She seemed to have agreed to a further assignation.

13

'What did you make of him?' Rose had barely stepped into the sitting room before Ginny asked this question. The same enquiry was written on Alice's face. The table was laid for supper, but there were larger appetites to satisfy first.

In reply, Rose took off her hat, threw it in the air and caught it. 'What a joy to be free of Miss Lipton. It's just like removing a corset.' She put down the hat and began to dismantle her hair. 'Thank goodness,' she said, when both earphones were uncoiled. 'Those pins really do pinch. I should have thought of that before settling on my disguise.' Rose shook her head in relief and dropped into the nearest chair. 'What's for tea?' she asked, adopting a further diversionary tactic.

'Bread and scratch-it,' Ginny said, sitting down at the table. She indicated the pot of dripping and the remains of a jar of jam. Rose sighed. At least there was still some jam, and it was blackberry, her favourite. 'Alice will do the honours with the toasting-fork while you Tell All.'

Alice, who had taken up a position by the fire with a plate of bread, now extended the fork to its longest reach, skewered the top slice and held it before the flames. In no time at all it was toasting nicely. 'Come on, Rose,' she said. 'We're all ears. What did you make of him?'

She had kept them waiting long enough. 'It was more diffi-cult than I'd expected. I kept wondering all the while what he or I were supposed to say next to advance our romantic encounter. I'm sure it wouldn't normally be like that. I do wonder how on earth Miss Holmes coped.'

'When I met Tom,' Ginny said – Rose held her breath, and she and Alice exchanged glances; it was the first time in a long while that Ginny had mentioned Tom – 'I had no idea where things would lead. I'd seen him once or twice at a distance, but it was at that picnic in the woods – do you remember, Rose? – when things changed. We fell into step on the way home, and he asked if he could see me again. The next week we went back to the wood by ourselves. I'll never forget that evening – the scent of wild garlic and the whole wood a haze of bluebells. It was the first time he and I were alone. We walked and talked until darkness fell. Whenever I see bluebells, I'm back there. After that, Tom used to wait for me outside the staff door, do you remember?'

'I do, and with a different posy each week. I don't know how he'd have managed if yours had been a winter courtship . . .'

'He'd have thought of something.' Ginny's smile transformed her face. 'But my point is that we had time to get to know one another. For Miss Holmes it would have been different. She knew – or thought she knew – that the man she was meeting was every bit as set on building a future together as she was. Of course, that didn't mean they were bound to hit it off, but she went to their first meeting with many more ideas and expectations running through her head than I had when Tom and I started walking out. Her Mr Wilson was a prospective husband from the very first moment. That must have coloured how she saw him and how she interpreted everything after that. If he wasn't serious, why approach an agency? Especially when so many eligible women want husbands. The fact that he'd been vetted and lined up as someone just for her would have made him even more plausible. Here was someone who was presented as the perfect match or, if not perfect, a suitable candidate, at least.'

'Although that's what's odd,' Rose said, taking the piece of toast Alice proffered and adding it to the growing pile. 'Miss Holmes and Mr Wilson are so obviously not cut from the same cloth. He presented himself as someone starting out in business, whereas she is the daughter of a well-established manufacturer. In that regard, they were hardly well matched. Wasn't that quite a risk – on the agency's part, I mean? Though I suppose,' Rose said, answering her own question, 'Cupid's Arrow was relying on his charm and Miss Holmes's desperation – unless, of course, she made it clear that she would happily meet anyone they suggested, regardless of his background, although that would make her pretty unusual, and you certainly wouldn't think that to look at her or hear her speak.'

'But, from what you say, this man made her believe they had a future together. And if you want to believe something, you will.' Ginny smoothed the tablecloth with both hands, as if to underline her meaning.

Alice looked up from the fire. 'Cupid's Arrow: it sounds more like "Cupid's Dart" to me. Miss Holmes was well and truly taken in.' She reached for another slice of bread and stabbed it with the toasting fork. 'But I still can't think why she would be so gullible as to give this faker her money.'

'*We* know he's a faker, Alice,' Rose said. '*She* didn't. And he wooed Miss Holmes over some four months, so he appeared to be courting her in the usual fashion.' Lord, she thought, I can't spend four months establishing if Mr Martin is genuine. I'll have to speed things up.

'Well, then, why would she suspect anything?' Ginny asked. 'And your Mr Martin, for example, does he seem sincere? If you were Miss Holmes, would you believe in him?'

'I hardly know the man.'

'Exactly, but you want to find out more.'

'Yes, but only because I want to know if he is the deceiver . . .'

'But if you were Miss Holmes, you too would also want to see him again, albeit for different reasons.'

'True.' The toast was ready. Rose picked up the now-full plate, followed Alice to the table and sat down.

'And before you know it,' Ginny said, helping herself to toast and smearing it with dripping, 'you like the man, and so you think that all is fine and dandy. You don't imagine you'll be caught out. That's something that happens to other people.'

'Well, *I* wouldn't be taken in,' Alice said. 'Oh,' she scowled at her plate. 'This marge is sour. Can't we at least have butter on our toast?'

Rose ignored her complaint. 'You might not have been taken in, Alice, but don't forget that Miss Holmes had no one to confide in. If it were you who had met this charmer, I would be asking, is he handsome? What does he look like? Tell me all about him – and not just because we're sisters, but because you and I speak the same language. I also think I know the kind of man who would attract you . . .'

'Oh, do you, indeed?' Alice laughed.

'But I can't ask Miss Holmes, because she's not my sister and, what's more, she is a client. She can confide in me, but I can't presume on our relationship to that extent. It's fine for us to talk pin-tucks and ruching, and I spent years perfecting a silent sympathy when her mother was being unkind, but all of that's a million miles away from talking heartthrobs, let alone heart-ache.' Rose looked down at her uneaten toast.

'But you *did* talk to her,' Alice said in a completely different tone. 'And, more importantly, she talked to you. She also felt safe enough to weep. You are the one person she's confided in; you seem to be the only one she trusts.'

Rose dipped her head, acknowledging the weight of that responsibility.

14

'Sydenham 3491 . . .?' The voice that answered the telephone was the one Rose wanted to hear. It didn't take long to explain. 'Next Wednesday at two: that would be perfect,' Miss Holmes said, before Rose even had the chance to suggest a time. 'And then we won't disturb Mother,' Miss Holmes continued, in the tone of one used to being overheard. 'Mother plays bridge on Wednesday afternoons.'

The Laurels was a broad, three-storey house with a substantial tree in its front garden and two distinct entrances. The ornate double gate that led straight to the front door was clearly intended for visitors; a smaller gate to the right of the property was marked 'Service'. Here was a conundrum. A dress designer was no servant or casual caller, but what would Mother deem appropriate? But Mother was not at home, Rose reminded herself, and Miss Holmes had evidently been looking out for her; Sarah, the maid, crisply dressed in afternoon cap and apron, opened the front door before Rose reached it and showed her straight into the sitting room.

A sampler on the wall announced 'May Truth in its Beauty Flourish Triumphant'. But does the truth always flourish, Rose wondered, and would she get any closer to it this afternoon? Although it had only just passed two o'clock, the sitting room was in semi-darkness; the heavy brocade curtains at the windows impeded what light there was in this cold and unwelcoming room. Everything looked to be just so, including the small circular table that held a series of photographs in ornate silver frames: a baby in a christening robe propped up against tasselled cushions; a small boy in one of the lacy frocks well-to-do Victorians had favoured; the same child, a few years later, posing with a ball. There were several pictures of the boy at different ages and oh – good heavens – that child grown into a young man who, now wearing uniform, was facing his duty as well as the photographer's lens. A black-edged 'In Memoriam' card told the rest of his story. How had she not known that Phyllis Holmes had had a brother? A light cough told Rose that Miss Holmes had entered the room. 'Gilbert,' Miss Holmes said quietly. 'Killed on the Dardanelles. We had a service here, at St John's.'

'I'm sorry,' Rose said inadequately. 'I didn't know.'

Phyllis sighed. 'Won't you sit down, Miss Burnham?' She gestured to one of the two comfortable chairs near the hearth. 'Mother sends a notice to *The Times* on every anniversary.' And, Rose thought, the two of you sit before this shrine each evening. Not that you need a public notice or a shrine to remind you. Did her son's death account for the sense of muted but outraged displeasure Mrs Holmes almost always managed to convey? The sense that her daughter was not quite up to snuff. Was this a grieving mother wondering what to do with a daughter so unlike herself? But the comparison between son and daughter must have started years ago; a quick glance told Rose there were no equivalent photographs of Phyllis in this room.

'I asked to see you, Miss Holmes,' Rose began, 'because I really would like to help you, if I can. It must have taken great courage for you to confide in me and I thought that if the two of us put our heads together, we might uncover something that would help to track down the man who deceived you.' She could not possibly admit that she had signed up with Cupid's Arrow in order to achieve that very thing. And, at this moment, sitting in this room – and possibly in Mother's chair, although she sincerely hoped not – Rose felt she had dashed headlong, like some clumsy schoolgirl, without fully comprehending the reality of Miss Holmes's situation. But there was no getting away from it: she had gone to Cupid's Arrow, she had started something, and she did want to see where it led. 'Would you mind if I asked you one or two questions?'

Miss Holmes looked dazed but compliant. 'Of course, go ahead, although Mother will be back at four.'

'Don't worry, Miss Holmes, we'll be finished long before then.' Rose had no desire to bump into Mother. But how were they going to proceed? And how was she going to coax Miss Holmes to confide in her again? Miss Holmes looked as tightly buttoned as the dress she was wearing this afternoon. Its muted tones matched their surroundings; even Rose's fitting-room black, chosen for its sobriety, seemed too strident for the room.

Miss Holmes picked up the handbell to ring for tea, but was that a slight hesitation? Surely not. Courtesy alone demanded tea, and Miss Holmes was never anything less than courteous. This was all so strange, Rose thought. She felt every bit as awkward and undecided as her host about the etiquette of this occasion. She was used to seeing clients on her own territory, but then this wasn't exactly her usual work. In fact, the more she thought of it, the odder the whole thing seemed. What on earth had she embarked on and what did she expect to achieve? Miss Holmes rang the bell and, when Sarah appeared, requested a pot of tea – 'and biscuits, please,' she added a moment later.

'How are you, Miss Holmes?' Rose asked as soon as they were

alone again. 'How have you been since I last saw you?' She dared not ask how Miss Holmes had occupied her time: changing the water in the dog's bowl, doing little bits of embroidery . . .

'I'm well, thank you, Miss Burnham.' Miss Holmes was well versed in the conventions.

This was no good. She would simply have to plunge in. 'The gentleman . . .'

'Reginald . . . Mr Wilson . . .' It clearly pained Miss Holmes to say the name out loud.

How ever was she going to ask what Mr Wilson looked like? She would have to work round to that. 'Can you remember exactly what Mr Wilson told you? Anything at all that might help?'

'Well, he said so many things. He took such an interest in me and asked such thoughtful questions. At our very first meeting he asked, did I have family or was I alone in the world? When I told him there was only Mother, he said he was glad I had someone; that a charming young lady like me should not be alone. I thought that was sweet of him . . .' Miss Holmes faltered. '. . . at the time.'

The tea came (presented in nicely patterned china, Rose noted, although it was unlikely to be the best tea-set). Tea was a welcome interruption, and yet their conversation had barely begun. Miss Holmes placed the strainer on to each teacup with great deliberation. Pouring the tea seemed to require considerable concentration, and they were evidently both grateful for the further distraction of sugar tongs, teaspoons and milk. Once the tea was poured, Miss Holmes indicated the plate of digestive biscuits. Rose took a soft bite from the biscuit nearest to her. The maid was evidently well trained; Miss Holmes had not had to say, 'I think not the best biscuits, Sarah.'

'In November,' Rose said, putting down what remained of the digestive, 'I made a cream-and-pink wool crepe suit for you. Was that for a meeting with Mr Wilson?' If she could date their first meeting, she could perhaps more easily establish how he had gone about things.

'Yes.'

'Your first meeting?'

Miss Holmes took a sip of tea before answering. 'No, our second. By then, I felt I knew him a little. I remember we went to a little café called Pamela's Parlour.' The very name seemed to inspire a private reverie.

Rose took her own sip of tea; the need to keep cup and saucer steady forced her to speak more calmly than she felt. 'And could you remind me how often you saw him?'

Miss Holmes looked stricken. 'Every fortnight or so. Sometimes three weeks, or longer, even. He was – is – a commercial traveller, you see.'

'And did Mr Wilson speak about his work?'

'Not really, except to say how much he regretted having to work away from home, but that things would be different once he had his own little business . . .' Miss Holmes tailed off. 'He admired my clothes – your clothes, of course; said how much he enjoyed being seen out with me, that other chaps would envy him. That's why I wanted new outfits.'

'Of course,' Rose said, although this admission stung. She already felt complicit in this awful business. She looked down at her teacup. 'And where else did the two of you go?'

'Oh, one or two parks, if it wasn't too cold and the weather was fine, and to other tearooms here and there. He liked to visit different places, not always go to the same spot. He said he liked to explore different streets and discover what was around the corner. We had tea in Streatham one afternoon. We had to catch two trains to do that.' The recollection appeared to distract her. Miss Holmes picked up her teaspoon and put it down. 'There was a small town somewhere in Kent . . . He spoke fondly of a cottage there.'

With roses around the door, no doubt. Rose leaned forward. 'But you didn't go to see the cottage?'

'No.' Miss Holmes shook her head. 'But he told me all about it and he showed me a charming photograph, just like a picture postcard. He showed me a photograph of his mother, too. It was so reassuring to know he cared for his mother; I do so much for mine, you see.' Rose sipped her tea; she thought it best to say nothing. 'He was a quiet man – not taciturn, but thoughtful,' Miss Holmes continued. 'He always thought before he spoke. He wasn't in a rush like the young men you read about today.'

'And did you meet his family?'

'Oh, no. He lives in lodgings and his landlady does not welcome visitors.'

'And you didn't introduce him to your mother?' Rose knew the answer to this question, but felt she should ask.

Miss Holmes looked even more pained; Mother's presence invaded the room. She fiddled with the buttons at her throat. 'There never seemed to be the right time.'

Rose glanced through the window. It was easier to look at the garden than to keep her eyes on Miss Holmes. 'Did you think your mother might not like him?' That was a certainty, but she must not convey her own feelings on that subject.

'Well,' Miss Holmes wavered, 'Mother is quite . . . particular,' she said eventually. And then the words tumbled out. 'Mother thought I was meeting an old school friend. I just wanted to keep things to myself for a little while longer, Miss Burnham. I've never had a secret, you see.'

'I'm so sorry, Miss Holmes. I know how difficult this must be.' How to get back on to safer ground? She couldn't have Miss Holmes in tears all over again. 'And you say Mr Wilson is a commercial traveller?'

'Yes. He was an electrician before the war but is now having to work in sales. But he said he was saving hard and,' Miss Holmes paused, 'that all he needed was a bit more capital to set himself up in business.'

Rose winced. Talk of the lost money was no less distressing second time round. And, sitting in this mausoleum of a sitting room, it was all too easy to understand why Miss Holmes was so keen to escape. 'Did Mr Wilson . . .' How best to phrase the next unavoidable question? '. . . make any promises to you?'

But Miss Holmes knew exactly what Rose meant. How could she not, when she must go over and over this ghastly scenario, retracing every single step. 'Not in so many words. But he squeezed my hand – my left hand – and said that when we next met, after he was done with a special order that was taking up a lot of his time, he was going to make me very happy – both of us very happy, in fact. As he said that, he lifted my left hand and gave my fingers a shake. I did not mistake his meaning, Miss Burnham; I did not. And later that afternoon, we happened to pass a shop with two handsome chairs in the window and Reginald – Mr Wilson – said wouldn't we make a grand pair sitting in chairs like those on either side of our own roaring fire? He'd already mentioned that the cottage in Kent has a fireplace so big you can step inside it.'

Rose looked down. If she gripped her cup any harder, it would break. She put the cup down on its saucer and leaned towards Miss Holmes. 'When was this, Miss Holmes? Was this the last time you saw him?'

Miss Holmes nodded. 'Yes. February the twenty-sixth. I can picture every moment of that last afternoon. We were walking down the street; it was just after I had given him . . . the . . . the assistance.' The word 'money' was obviously beyond her. 'Our fingers touched. Surely, I did not imagine that?'

Rose sat back in her chair; she sat as far back as the stiff cushion would permit. This conversation was excruciating. She should not be here, asking these intrusive questions, putting Miss Holmes on the spot. 'And you have heard nothing from Mr Wilson since?'

'No. I wasn't worried at first, not with Reginald working away. And because of that special order, he'd said not to worry if I didn't hear from him for ten days or more.' How clever, Rose thought. 'But it's now been almost two months . . .'

'But, until this point, the two of you regularly exchanged letters?'

'Oh, yes. I've some half a dozen letters or more, but Reginald – Mr Wilson – always wrote from hotels, on their lovely headed notepaper – with him being a commercial traveller, you see. I replied care of Cupid's Arrow.'

'Yes, of course. And have you tried to contact Mr Wilson yourself, by any chance? I know you were reluctant to approach Cupid's Arrow again.'

Miss Holmes stalled. She appeared to study the dregs in her teacup. 'Yes,' she said quietly, 'I wrote to one of the hotels where Reginald stayed.' Her voice reached a desperate crescendo. 'The letter was returned, marked, "Gone Away".'

What a brutal phrase, Rose thought. Miss Holmes returned her gaze to her cup, for which Rose was extremely grateful; she didn't want to catch her eye. Poor Miss Holmes – and what shame upon shame: someone would have had to open her letter to obtain the return address.

Rose needed to find a different question, and quickly. 'Do you know the name of Mr Wilson's employer?'

'I'm afraid not. I had thought he'd told me a great deal, but I now realize how little he actually said. Reginald talked without really giving me details.'

'I see,' Rose said. Finally, she felt entitled to pose the one question she'd been longing to ask all afternoon: 'Do you have a photograph of Mr Wilson?'

'No.' Miss Holmes's voice broke. 'Not even that. We were going to have our picture taken together but, on the day we'd planned, Reginald had to work late unexpectedly, so he was still wearing his work suit. He said he didn't want to show that off; nothing but the best would do for me. We were going to have our photograph taken another day.'

'I'm sorry.' He seemed to have thought of everything, Rose noticed: hotel notepaper, no photograph taken with Miss Holmes, a picturesque cottage that may have been an actual postcard – perfect smokescreens, and ten days (and counting) in which to cover his tracks. Ginny was right: how easy it must be to deceive those who wish to believe what they are told. The whole time that Miss Holmes thought he was preparing for their future, she was building castles in the air.

Miss Holmes broke into Rose's thoughts. In a quavering voice, she asked, 'What will I say to Mother? I can't tell her I've lost Father's money, but how will I pretend otherwise? I've never worked and I'm not trained for anything. I don't know what I can do.' Rose recalled those discreet advertisements printed at the back of ladies' magazines: 'Crewel work, tapestry pochettes, writing-case covers. Reasonable rates. Apply to Miss So-and-So, Worthing.' They reeked of genteel poverty.

'I'm so sorry, Miss Holmes. This must be a bitter blow and so very distressing.' An inadequate response, but Rose wasn't sure what real comfort she could give. Miss Holmes glanced at the clock. Rose followed her lead and stood up. Whatever else happened, she did not want to have to explain her presence to Mother. 'I've taken up enough of your time, Miss Holmes. Thank you so much for seeing me this afternoon. As I say, I would like to help, if I can.'

Rose turned to pick up her bag. There were some letters on the bureau. 'Would you like me to post these, Miss Holmes? I have to pass a postbox on my way.'

'Thank you, but no,' Miss Holmes said firmly. 'They're Mother's letters, and she would want me to post them for her. And it will give me a walk. I could do with a walk. I haven't been out today.'

'That *is* a good idea,' Rose said, grateful that she could at least sound cheerful about something. She looked again at the gloomy interior, getting gloomier by the minute. 'Good afternoon, Miss Holmes,' she said.

'Good afternoon, Miss Burnham – and . . . thank you. Sarah will show you out.' Miss Holmes smiled, but there was a note of strain between them. Had she pried too deeply, forced Miss Holmes to reveal too much? And what had she learned that could identify the fraudster? Miss Holmes's Mr Wilson may be a commercial traveller; he may have connections in Kent; his mother may still be alive – all of which could be complete fabrications. Whoever he was, 'Mr Wilson' had worked hard to cover his tracks. If she was going to catch him out, she would need to be equally inventive.

15

The following morning the rhythm of the workroom was disturbed by a telephone call. The telephone rang so rarely that Rose and her sisters leapt each time they heard it, especially as it was on the landing just outside the door. It still seemed extraordinary to have one in the house at all. Rose had considered delaying the installation, but she had to be able to attract the right kind of client; that was the nature of business. Rose stepped out of the workroom, picked up the receiver and put it to her ear.

'I don't believe it,' she said, coming back into the room looking dazed, some ten minutes later. 'That was Mrs Townsend, Webb & Maskrey's Mrs Townsend. Mr Townsend's wife, that is.' Alice looked up. 'The Chief Cashier,' Rose explained, Alice being less well versed in the intricacies of the store's pecking order. 'She's coming here on Monday morning.'

Ginny looked up expectantly: 'And . . .?'

'Their younger daughter, Mary, is getting married,' Rose explained, speaking as if she was having to decipher her own words, 'and Mrs Townsend wants to discuss the wedding clothes and her own outfit.' She sat back down. 'I'm staggered – well, not staggered exactly, but I hadn't expected this. Nothing is fixed, of course. She may not like what I suggest – and heavens, what *will* I suggest?' Rose made a grab for her notebook. 'I've only got a few days.'

'But why aren't the Townsends going to Webb & Maskrey?' Alice asked. 'Surely they would go there?'

'Mrs Townsend didn't say, and I could hardly enquire, though I suspect that Webb & Maskrey would be a mite too close to home – the intimacies of the fitting-room, and all of that.'

'Yes, of course.'

'But this is marvellous news, Rose – or could be,' Ginny said, her face breaking into a smile. 'I know nothing's certain, but she wouldn't come here at all if she wasn't confident about your work. Someone must have spoken very highly of you. And it's the first of May, too – that must be a good omen. Well done you.'

'Well done all of us,' Rose said, finally coming up for air. 'If this comes off, we'll all be hard at work.' She saw the workroom busy with clothes, heard the oohs and aahs of the congregation and their pleasure in observing not only the bride, but the exquisite detailing of her mother's outfit and the marvel in silk in which the bride departed for her new life . . . And with those thoughts Rose picked up Nancy, the slimmest of their dress stands, and waltzed her around the room.

The Townsends were due at ten o'clock. Everything was ready for their arrival, but Rose wanted to check the fitting-room one more time. She always checked the room before receiving clients, but today she needed to do so with a particularly critical eye: front-of-house mattered when you were planning to put on a show.

Rose had known Mr Townsend for years, albeit at a respectful distance. She had also heard something of his wife's reputation, but this would be the first time they'd met. Eleanor Townsend was known to have a well-developed sense of her due and an equally strong faith in her own impeccable taste. As such, she was bound to broadcast her approval – or otherwise – of Miss Burnham's enterprise. And her approval mattered even more now. This wasn't simply a case of pride and past associations (though there was nothing simple about either of those), it was a chance for Rose to prove herself and, she hoped, secure the business at the same time. Yes, a successful wedding would be a passport to future clients and other formal occasions, the backdrop to flashier, more adventurous commissions and the ballast that would help 'Rose Burnham' thrive.

But this is not yet secure, Rose reminded herself: Mrs Townsend can easily go elsewhere if she doesn't like my ideas – or takes against the fitting-room, or even the slightest thing. Rose straightened the cushions once more for good measure and ran her index finger along the mantelpiece to check for invisible dust. She stooped to make a tasteful fan of the various magazines on the low table and then, rejecting that arrangement, put them back into their separate piles.

Mrs Townsend and Mary arrived promptly. Rose saw Mrs Townsend survey the fitting-room and take in every detail, as she herself had done only ten minutes earlier. Mrs Townsend then put down her bag, removed her gloves and said by way of introduction: 'Of course, as I am sure you are aware, Miss Burnham, Webb & Maskrey are currently preoccupied with the arrangements for the Drayton daughter's wedding' – Rose recognized the name of a respected bigwig – 'and so we couldn't think of going there; Mr Townsend tells me the dressmakers are working their fingers to the bone. As indeed is every department: there is a great deal to consider – the wedding gifts to organize and deliver, as well as new outfits for the whole family and several of the guests. Apparently, the wedding veil alone will have fifteen yards of lace.'

If this was to be Mrs Townsend's explanation for the commission, Rose was happy to accept it. And, in truth, it would have been nigh-on impossible for the Chief Cashier's wife to stand almost in the altogether in front of girls who were practically required to bob and curtsey to her husband. But please, Rose thought, not fifteen yards of lace.

Eleanor Townsend was handsome and tall, yet well proportioned, with dark, greying hair nicely framed by her hat. She was dressed to good effect in a dropped-waist day dress whose fashionably long line of glass buttons ran from neckline to hip. Her daughter Mary had yet to acquire her mother's sense of style – or any style at all, come to that; she still looked and dressed like a schoolgirl. She was wearing a hand-knitted jumper of a pattern similar to those sold for sixpence by *Fashions for All,* but her choice of beige wool was unfortunate.

'I'm thinking of cerise for myself,' Mrs Townsend said, naming a colour currently in vogue, 'and I have some tip-top ideas for Mary.' Mary nodded and smiled but said nothing. Mrs Townsend produced a list of her requirements: her own wedding clothes, the bridal gown and underclothes, plus two bridesmaid's dresses, one for a young niece and the other for her elder daughter, Grace, who wasn't at all keen on being dressed in the same style as her young cousin and would be attending separately for her fittings. For the next hour or so, Mrs Townsend and Rose debated tulle, taffeta, chiffon, lace and organza, discussed the merits of embroidery versus beadwork and pondered the question of ivory versus champagne silk. Mary, the bride to be, had little chance of influencing or interrupting her mother, but as there would be several bridal fittings, Rose thought it wise to satisfy her mother's demands first; once these were resolved (and contained), it would be far easier to focus on the actual bride. With the preliminary discussions finally complete, Rose rang the handbell, the signal for Alice to come and note the Townsends' measurements in the record book.

'A Regency lady. How quaint,' Mrs Townsend said, referring to the small bell.

'Yes, it belonged to my grandmother.'

'How fitting.'

Mrs Townsend's frame made her easy to measure; there was no unsightly stoop or uneven hips to correct. Seeing her deprived of dress, petticoat and modesty vest, and reduced to stockings and corset, Rose was reminded how vulnerable older women looked when stripped of their outer layers and how trusting they were required to be. Mrs Townsend's bombast quickly gave way to a more accommodating manner.

Rose moved around her, measuring nape to waist, nape to full length, width of back, on to elbow and cuffs. She asked Mrs Townsend to raise her arms, then brought her tape across her breasts. 'Forty-two,' she said, so that Alice could make a note. Oh, the glamour, she thought, as her fingers brushed against damp tufts of underarm hair protruding from either side of a corset whose elastic was not quite as taut as it had once been. At least Rose didn't have to hold her breath, as so often happened with less fastidious clients. 'Thank you, Mrs Townsend. If you would now turn around, please.'

Waist, hips, front length, side . . . Again, Rose thought how the relationship between a dressmaker and her client was one of a peculiar intimacy; it was hardly surprising that the fitting-room readily took on the air – and occasionally the role – of the confessional. Today, however, the talk was of wedding plans and nothing else. Mrs Townsend regained her composure along with her clothes and did not stop talking the whole time her younger daughter's measurements were taken. Fortunately, Mary was a biddable bride, turning round when commanded and raising her arms when invited to do so. She scarcely contributed a word to the conversation; she was obviously used to her mother's talk. They had wondered about May, rejected June and finally chosen September (August was such a trying month, the weather either too hot or else a great disappointment). What did July do to offend her, Rose wondered, but thought it best not to ask. Mrs Townsend hoped for good weather without showers or cool breezes. Of course, and as always with a wedding, she instructed Rose, there was the right balance to strike between elegance and warmth. One also had to consider the weather when planning the bridal train. Were the Draytons having a train, she wondered.

'I wouldn't know, Mrs Townsend,' Rose said.

With all measurements taken and noted, talk of the weather and clothing gave way to Mrs Townsend's ideas for the bridal bouquet, the bridesmaids' posies and even the wedding breakfast – galantine of chicken or ham? – but at last the appointment ended. It had been agreed that Mrs Townsend would not wear cerise, but a dove-grey dress and a matching coat with a dusky-rose silk lining, dusky-rose buttons and a soft, funnel collar – perfect for unreliable weather as well as being absolutely *now*. She had also been dissuaded from elaborate gusts of champagne silk into something simpler for Mary: 'Simplicity is today's keynote,' Rose insisted. Suggestions had been made for the bridesmaids' dresses, an appointment booked for Mary's first fitting in ten days' time, and for her sister Grace's first visit. With this much accomplished, Rose returned to the workroom. Her head was throbbing – she longed to sit down – but it would be worth every vexing minute.

Ginny looked up. 'So, that was Madame à la Mode . . .'

'Let's hope her elder daughter isn't anything like her mother.'

Grace Townsend was a breath of fresh air. She arrived for her first appointment in a brand-new hat, announced that she had come straight from Miss Mabel Porter's elocution and deportment class, and wriggled out of her clothes without needing any encouragement.

Nor did she need an invitation to talk. She had shingled hair and was wearing exuberant bangles, which jangled and raced towards her elbow each time she raised her left arm. Grace reminded Rose of Alice and, like her younger sister, she evidently knew her own mind. 'All those years of Mother telling me what to wear; I can't think how I stood it. I can't tell you how relieved I was to leave all that behind. No more woollen underwear, for starters. Mind you, on days like today, I can see she may have a point.'

The moment she'd entered the room, she'd informed Rose of her wishes: 'I don't want anything mimsy, and nothing floral, either. Mother says . . . but I know how to get round Mother. Most of the time, that is.'

I bet you do, Rose thought. She saw Grace Townsend assess herself in the fitting-room mirror and not quite suppress a smile. When Grace turned to the left and the right while being measured, she gave the impression she was practising movements learned in class.

'It was elocution this week,' she said. ' "Do not pass behind the automobile until you know the road is clear." What do you think? Am I enunciating properly? We have to draw mouths shaped like vowel sounds in the back of our exercise books. Good heavens,' she said excitedly. 'That sentence could almost be an elocution exercise itself. I'm rather pleased with that. And last week I walked five yards while balancing a book on my head. It's all tosh, of course, but Mother likes the idea, and it gives me an hour to myself.'

'I'd actually like to learn typewriting,' she continued, 'but Mother did put her foot down at that. She says it's pointless training girls for the Civil Service or other office work, when it will all come to nought the minute they wed and have to leave.' She had her mother's inflection off to a tee. Ah, Rose thought, Mrs Townsend is not quite as modern as she would like me to think. 'Which is a great shame,' Grace continued, 'because I will have to earn my keep. Just because Mary has found a young man does not mean there will be one for me. Anyway, I'm quite happy to be "surplus" and intend to make the most of it.'

Grace twisted round to look at Rose, who was now measuring the length of her new client's back. 'How did you set out in business, Miss Burnham?'

'Oh, that's a long story, Miss Townsend. I'd be happy to tell you, but shall we save that for another day? If you could just stand still . . .'

16

She had pulled it off, Rose reminded herself the next morning. She had secured the Townsend wedding and, hopefully, the business. To guarantee the spell, and her own good luck, Rose crossed her fingers on both hands.

She couldn't have worked harder. There she'd stood, ideas spilling forth, agreeing or disarming at the appropriate moments, elaborating on – gushing, more like – her many ideas and the opportunity this would be to put them into practice (all the while ignoring the small inner voice that whispered, Rose, this is only a suburban wedding). It may only be a suburban wedding, but it would be a smart one at that, and was just what they needed right now. We are saved, she thought, delivered from evil. That was a bit strong . . . We are saved from the workhouse to sew another day. Rose wanted to pirouette and sing. Instead, she allowed herself a series of celebratory twirls in front of the workroom's cheval mirror.

Towards the end of their appointment, Mrs Townsend had announced how perfect it would be if Miss Burnham designed not just the bridal gown, but Mary's going-away outfit, too: 'There would be a certain symmetry in that, don't you think?' And, of course, Rose agreed. That was exactly what she'd been hoping for.

Yes, she had pulled it off – they all had. Part-way through the morning, Mrs Townsend had said that she would like to meet

Ginny as well as Alice – and had spoken in such a way that Rose felt obliged to invite Ginny downstairs there and then. But what she'd feared would be an eagle-eyed appraisal of the three Miss Burnhams had turned instead into a lovely moment, with a real sense of pride and a realization that yes, she and her sisters genuinely were an impressive team and that, individually and together, they were a go-getting business. Now they had better get on with it.

Hence the lists Rose was now making – of lace and silk and braid, and the trimmings for the petticoats as well as for the dresses, and the buttons, ribbons, hooks and eyes, and other paraphernalia, and the numerous matching shades of Sylko that would be needed, all of which must be included when it came to calculating costs. The list already ran over two foolscap pages; Rose hardly dared to translate that into pounds, shillings and pence, although of course she must. And later there would be the pleas for small (and even large) adjustments – 'Oh, I know I'd set my heart on cream, but I really think peach trimmings will work best.' (And this after said cream trimmings had been seen and approved and were almost ready.) All of which would mean more work – which was wonderful, of course, if somewhat frustrating – and would be paid for in due course, but due course would be some way off. Oh, the necessary juggling and the robbing of Peter to pay Paul – or Pauline, in this instance – that would be needed to balance the books.

Balance the books: that gave Rose pause. How on earth was she supposed to do that? There would, of course, be a lag between ordering and paying for all these folderols and fabrics, just as there was always a lag between completing a garment and a client settling her bill. But how to reconcile the two with no Miss Holmes in the background, ordering like clockwork and paying on the dot, and with no other new commissions providing back-up? And there was one other major factor to consider: how was she to manage 'the Miss Holmes affair' now that her time would be needed for the Townsend wedding? Never mind juggling, this would be a high-wire act. Could she pull this off, too? Yes, she could. Time must become elastic, Rose told herself. She must not desert Miss Holmes.

And so, the high-wire act began. 'Mary will be our sole focus today,' Rose said, ten days after their first meeting, stepping aside to allow Mrs Townsend and her daughter into the fitting-room. 'Today we will pay close attention to the bride.' Mary blushed on cue. Her mother sank into the nearest chair and picked up a copy of *Vogue*. If she was not going to be the centre of attention, she could at least catch up with the latest proclamations on style.

'The dress will be in two tiers,' Rose reminded them. 'A silk underdress, worn beneath a shorter lace slip. The underdress will provide length; the overdress will carry the detail, with beads scattered across the lace and silk rosebuds grouped at the throat.' Rose sketched in the air, both hands darting and flashing. For a few bright seconds roses bloomed, beads sparkled. 'The overall design will be replicated in the dresses your sister and cousin will wear, but theirs won't have such intricate embellishments. I'll show you my sketches again in a moment.'

With Alice's assistance, Rose guided Mary into the first of the sleeveless toiles that would serve as a model, making sure to safeguard the tacking threads and keep an eye out for pins. 'This is to allow us to judge length and line. The beautiful fabrics – and the intricate work – come later.' She smiled encouragingly. The result would be simple but exquisite, she hoped, with nods to modernity, without being *too* modern; she doubted that Mary Townsend would be able to carry that off.

Rose issued her usual warning: 'First fittings can be anxious occasions, especially for something momentous. You have come with a head full of silk and lace, and here am I offering you muslin, and only a partial garment at that. You will need to have a leap of faith, Mary; Mrs Townsend,' Rose appealed to Mrs Townsend, knowing hers would be the leap of faith required and that, for all her apparent immersion in *Vogue*, she was watching their every move.

Alice now helped Mary into a second toile several inches shorter than the first. 'Remember,' Rose said, 'the switch to silk and lace comes later, as will the sleeves.' She wanted to confirm Mary's measurements before taking her shears to yards of expensive cloth, and sleeves were later additions.

Rose steered her towards the mirror. 'I hope you'll be excited by the thought of what's beginning to emerge, Miss Townsend, but do please remember: this is very much a work in progress.' There was always so much at stake with weddings, and considerable reassurance required. Brides-to-be were just as likely to dissolve in tears, or explode into tantrums, as they were to smile. All too often, young women approached the mirror in a fizz of anticipation, only to discover they were not Cinderella after all.

Mary Townsend seemed uncertain how to assess the young woman who stood before her. Rose left her examining her reflection while she crossed the room to pick up her sketches. Before she had chance to present them, however, Mrs Townsend sprang to her feet and took them from her, scrutinizing every detail. Then, in silence, Mrs Townsend passed the sketches to her daughter.

Mary's eyes now moved from mirror to drawings and back again. 'Mother?'

'Yes, my dear. Yes.' Mrs Townsend came to stand to beside her. 'I think we are making progress. A long way to go yet, of course, but yes . . .' Nothing too enthusiastic, then, Rose thought. She was going to be one of those clients who reserve judgement, although, to be fair, not everyone could grasp the finished effect from a toile and a series of basted panels. Thank heavens for the detailed sketches.

'Yes,' Mrs Townsend spoke for her daughter. 'The two-tiered look will have poise. And floral decorations seem to be every-where.' She indicated her copy of *Vogue*.

Given permission to smile, Mary beamed: 'Thank you, Miss Burnham. I particularly like the thought of the beading and the roses. It's going to be lovely, I think.'

'I'm glad.' Rose smiled. 'The tiers elongate the line and have presence; the beaded lace adds elegance and will soften the look.' Thank heavens, she thought: mother and daughter in accord. We're in business. 'I'm delighted to hear that you're happy, Miss Townsend. You can get changed now.'

How many wedding dresses had she made over the years? Rose couldn't begin to count the number. It had been a Webb & Maskrey custom for each hand to stitch one seam of a wed-ding gown with a strand of her own hair – a superstition guaranteed to ensure her own future wedded happiness. When Rose took her turn, her smile was every bit as private as that of the girls before her, but she knew from their talk, as they put on their coats to go home, that the hopes she'd expressed were dif-ferent. This is for the future, she had told herself, but her dream was for her own clients and workroom, and for a fitting-room not unlike the one she was standing in now, with art-border rugs, cushioned chairs and a pile of fashion magazines tastefully heaped on a low table. Hers was a dream of independence. With each thread Rose had stitched, that dream had come closer. Now it was finally here.

'Let me help you,' she heard Mrs Townsend say to Mary. She was a somewhat subdued Mrs Townsend this morning. Perhaps the sight of her youngest daughter in a wedding gown, albeit merely a preliminary glimpse, had caused her to reflect on the passage of time; it must be strange to see your child transformed into a bride before your eyes. Rose knew nothing of Mary's fiancé but could not imagine her marrying someone Mrs Townsend did not like. Neither daughter seemed to do any-thing without their mother's permission, even if Grace's leash appeared to be longer than her sister's. Seeing Mary Townsend's tentative smile, Phyllis Holmes unavoidably came to Rose's mind. Had she pictured similar preparations for her wedding to Reginald Wilson, imagined herself standing with her own mother, assessing her wedding gown?

Mrs Townsend's voice cut across Rose's thoughts. 'I've been thinking about shoes, Miss Burnham.'

'Ah, Webb & Maskrey have some lovely shoes this season, Mrs Townsend,' Rose said diplomatically. 'I'm sure you will find just the thing there: ivory silk shoes for Miss Townsend, and I saw a pair of dove-grey shoes that would be perfect for you.'

'The shoes I've seen have a small metallic sphinx on the toe.' Mrs Townsend's tone brooked no disagreement.

'A sphinx? How novel.'

'Yes, I thought so, too. It's nice to add an individual note to even formal occasions, don't you think?'

'I . . . yes, indeed,' Rose capitulated. Was Mrs Townsend

going to score points until the very last fitting? There would be some trying sessions ahead, if that were the case. But at least she had not suggested exchanging her dove-grey silk coat – which currently lay in several complicated pieces upstairs – for something in Nile Green or Luxor Red.

17

' "Black marocain afternoon dress, exclusive model, touches of sealing-wax red . . ." How snazzy.' Alice was reading aloud from the fitting-room copy of *The Lady*. ' ". . . Worn only once, 6½ guineas, original cost 12 . . ." I wonder what the story is there? Some of these private sales are intriguing. There's someone here who seems to be selling her whole wardrobe: "Evening dress, white net with embroidered blue beads, £4. Apricot silk, 30 shillings. Flame satin, 25 shillings. Brown wool coat and skirt . . ." She must be going down in the world.'

'There's a lot of that about,' Rose said. And us here, crossing our fingers, she managed not to add. The sisters were in the sitting room. Ginny had banked up the fire against the cool evening and was curled up with a novel. Rose was sitting in the opposite fireside chair with a notebook in her lap; Alice was at the table. 'How about this one? "Black silk stockinette semi-evening frock, trimmed with beads, £2; brown knitted coat and skirt, 30 shillings." '

'They're sober choices,' Ginny said, without raising her eyes. 'She sounds like a sensible woman. Must be tightening her belt.'

'But I bet the stockinette dress has seen better days and the knitted suit will be going – if not already gone – at the knees and elbows.' Alice continued reading: 'And how about "a pinkish-mauve charmeuse evening gown with a trimmed ostrich-feather mount and beads"?'

Rose looked up. 'That's quite something. There's a little bit of everything there.'

'It sounds positively pre-war,' Alice said. 'What's that you're reading, Ginny?'

'It's a novel Sergeant Metcalfe recommended. One of the ones he mentioned when I rescued him on the dance floor that night Rose and I went back to the Amalfi. I must say, for a man who maintains that detective novels don't mirror real life, he seems to devour plenty of them. In this one a couple of amateurs solve the crime alongside the police.'

'Well, there you are, Rose; that's encouraging.'

Rose was about to say that things had come to a pretty pass if they had to bolster themselves with the plots of detective stories, but Alice had already moved on. 'And here's another "worn only once": "Tailored costume, pink-and-cream-speckled wool crepe, bound silk braid, silk lined, pretty . . . distinctive . . ."' Her recitation slowed. '". . . pearl . . . buttons . . . designer-made . . . worn only once . . . 35 shillings."' Alice looked cautiously at Rose. 'Doesn't that sound remarkably like . . . '

Ginny answered for her. 'She wouldn't.' She looked at Rose. 'Surely Miss Holmes wouldn't sell her lovely suit?' Ginny put down her book. 'Would she?'

'She might,' Rose said. 'If she felt she had to.' Another chasm opened up before her. 'What date is that magazine?'

Alice checked the front page. 'Fourteenth of May – it's the latest issue. But there must be other pink-and-cream suits out there . . . '

'I'm sure there are,' Rose said, although not necessarily suits with distinctive pearl buttons. Oh, and good heavens, she thought, if that is Miss Holmes's suit, my label – my name – is stitched into the jacket and skirt. This was not the kind of publicity she wanted; she'd no desire to court the second-hand market. She must find some answers soon.

As if on cue, another envelope arrived from Mr Martin: an invitation to visit the dinosaurs the next weekend. Rose groaned at the prospect but knew she would have to go.

Even the weather was on Mr Martin's side. May was presenting itself in all its glory – ideal circumstances in which a young couple might bill and coo. Miss Lipton and Mr Martin reached a grassy bank in the region of the park designated for its prehistoric monsters, the life-sized stone models built in the nineteenth century to educate the public and complement the Crystal Palace. They selected a bench from which they could look down on a group of ghoulish creatures positioned around a man-made lake. Some had long tails; others, elongated jaws preparing to snap, or else broad wings ready for flight.

'That's a plesiosaurus,' Mr Martin was saying, 'and that big beast is a megalosaurus.' He had evidently done his homework.

'That sea creature has a beady eye.' Rose pointed to a dolphin-like monster poised as if to launch itself into the water. 'Although his eye resembles a boiled sweet more than anything and gives him a deceptively friendly look. All the better to see you with,' she added in ominous tones. Mr Martin looked puzzled. ' "Red Riding Hood",' Rose said. 'The fairy tale, you remember?'

'Oh yes,' Mr Martin said, although he obviously did not. 'Have you seen that beast over there, the one with the extremely sharp teeth?'

'Yes, quite a character.' Rose had no idea to which creature he was referring. He could have been describing several of the monsters there, the slick-tailed mammals or the scaly giants with terrifying jaws and wide eyes, none of which you would

125

wish to encounter. Come to think of it, stone replicas or not, this corner of the park must be pretty spooky by moonlight.

'They say you can tell a lot from people's eyes, don't they?' Rose said, congratulating herself on the thought. 'Yet it can be so hard to remember their colour and even harder to describe someone's face. For instance, I'm not sure I could give you an accurate description of Miss Lane.' She paused. Mr Martin looked askance. 'The manager of Cupid's Arrow,' Rose said. He nodded. 'Funny, isn't it?' she continued. 'She asked me such a lot of questions, and although I would of course know her if I saw her again, I can't guarantee that I could describe her accurately now. I suppose that's because I was so nervous. It's an ordeal, isn't it, answering personal questions?'

Mr Martin nodded again and said, 'I think she had blue eyes.'

'Really? Oh. I'm sure gentlemen are better at these things. Did she interview you, too? I thought a gentleman always interviewed the gentlemen.'

'There was no one else available that day. She took pity on me because I so wanted to sign up. And just think: if she hadn't done that, I may not have met you.' Mr Martin now presented Rose with the brown paper bag he'd been clutching which, it turned out, held a trim box of violet creams. 'I hope you won't think I'm taking liberties, Miss Lipton, but I thought you might like these.'

'Why, thank you, Mr Martin. How kind.' Violet creams and dinosaurs: what a combination. This was surely a first. And was this not advancing things a little too swiftly? Would Miss Lipton accept chocolates – however delicious – from a man she barely knew?

'Oh, call me Edward, please.' Oh dear: even swifter.

'Edward,' Rose said, as if tasting the name on her tongue. She wanted to say, 'No, thank you,' and hand it back again.

'And may I call you Allegra? It is a little unconventional, I know, but you strike me as the kind of woman who is not confined by conventions.'

'Oh, gosh.' And couched in such flattering terms. What would Miss Etiquette say? '*My dear, do not . . .*' It was far too soon – of that, Rose was certain. She had no wish to say yes, but she must encourage Mr Martin to reveal himself and, for that to happen, a closer acquaintance was essential. And, of course, he could hardly be 'Edward' and she remain 'Miss Lipton'.

But what an enormous leap. Her own name, 'Rose', was only used by family and close friends. Even at Webb & Maskrey she had always been 'Miss Burnham', a title so hard-won it still gave her pleasure to hear it. Her mother, who had been a lady's maid before marriage, had said how fortunate Rose was to have a job in which she would be known as 'Miss'; she'd always been plain 'Annie' or, worse still, known by her surname: 'Marsh'. What was in a name? Quite a lot. But Rose was not herself today; she was Miss Allegra Lipton. And Miss Lipton must say yes. Rose nodded and gave what she hoped was a tentative smile. The deed was done. Their romance had progressed to first names.

Which questions had Cupid's Arrow asked Mr Martin to lead them to this point, Rose wondered. Are you Mr Explorer or Mr Suburban Gardener? Do you play cricket or bowls? Which of Miss Lipton's avowed qualities had tugged at Mr Martin's heartstrings? He was studying her face with a sidelong look he evidently thought the brim of his hat concealed. Rose blushed – a genuine blush, but convenient, too. It was time Allegra Lipton blushed. She proffered the box. 'Would you like a violet cream?'

They munched in silence or, rather, Mr Martin munched; Rose nibbled; she thought Miss Lipton would most likely be a nibbler. 'My father used to buy violet creams,' Rose ventured, after what she judged to be a decent interval. Presumably Miss Lipton's father could have had a liking for violet creams. 'He bought a box each week, never missed. Once his business started to prosper, that is. He maintained he brought them home for Mother, but he had quite a sweet tooth on the sly. "And now we can treat ourselves to as many sweets as we like," he'd say. I think that gave him as much pleasure as anything,' Rose emphasized, 'once he came into money.' She couldn't put it more clearly than that. It was her turn to risk a cautious glance at Mr Martin. His face gave nothing away. He didn't betray even the slightest interest in where this conversation was heading.

'My mother still buys his favourites. Of course, we are lucky to still be able to treat ourselves,' Rose added, in case the message remained unclear.

'It's nice that your father left you well provided for,' Mr Martin – Edward – said. 'Shall we take this path? There's a cherry tree in blossom up ahead. Do you know how many trees there are in this park and how many different kinds? Oak, ash, beech, blackthorn, hornbeam, chestnut . . .'

'Golly,' Rose interrupted, before Edward Martin could extend his list. Oh dear. It was dinosaurs and trees that tickled Mr Martin's fancy, not pounds sterling. She'd wanted to nab a chancer, but had been paired with an unworldly man.

18

'It was introductions this afternoon, Miss Burnham,' Grace Townsend explained. 'You must always introduce the gentleman to the lady and, if you are introducing two ladies or two gentlemen, you must introduce the more junior person to the senior. You should also offer them a topic of conversation. We were asked to come up with examples, so I suggested, "Miss Pickford, may I introduce Mr Fairbanks? I'm sure there are many ways in which the two of you could collaborate." Or "Miss Glyn, may I introduce you to Mr Jack Hylton, the band-leader? I'm sure the two of you will be able to make sweet music." Miss Porter clearly thought that one too saucy, so I toned things down: "Miss Tinkerbell, may I introduce Mr Peter Pan? He is learning to fly, so I am sure you will have a great deal in common."

Rose took Miss Townsend by the shoulders and adjusted her position. She needed to check the line of her bridesmaid's dress. 'It's quite simple, really,' Grace said, 'once you know how to go about it. But you do have to be careful. For example, if I were to introduce my father to my mother – which of course I would never do – I might say, "Mrs Townsend, may I introduce Mr Townsend? He is Chief Cashier at Webb & Maskrey, but his secret passion is bowls. On summer evenings he is more often to be found on the bowling green than at home." And I'd then turn to him and say, "Mrs Townsend enjoys wool-work and

other forms of embroidery, which may make small talk difficult." But that wouldn't do, far too truthful; an introduction
should be light and easy, and enable conversation to flow.'

Rose felt an unexpected pang of sympathy for Mrs Townsend,
a bowls widow left alone with her sewing, but Grace was not
expecting a response. She swept on. 'Did you know that a lady
must . . . but a gentleman need not . . .' But Rose had stopped
listening; that was the only way to manage when Grace
Townsend was in full flight.

'This is all fascinating, Miss Townsend,' Rose said some
moments later, 'but I now need you to stand perfectly still. If
you want your dress to look more sophisticated than your
cousin Emily's, I need to do something with this neckline.' That
did the trick: there was not a peep from Grace while Rose took
up the length of silk she'd brought for this purpose and coiled
and cajoled it to create a fuller shape. 'There, that's better. What
do you think?'

'Gosh, thank you,' she said, when Rose had finished pinning
the silk into place. 'Mother was right. You really are something,
Miss Burnham.'

'We aim to please,' Rose said, and smiled. Crikey, a compliment from Mrs Townsend.

Grace Townsend was back in her own clothes as quickly as
she'd shed them. She looked the part this afternoon, in a copper-
coloured dress and becoming hat. Her bangles were also
copper-coloured. As she turned to leave, she smiled and said, 'I
do hope you don't mind, Miss Burnham, but I mentioned your
name to my deportment teacher. I told Miss Porter you are
making me a smashing dress and how elegant your own clothes
are,' – You really are a charmer, Rose thought – 'and she said,
"How interesting", because she's looking for someone to talk to

the class about how to dress well – "Appearance is a Girl's Best Friend" and that sort of thing. I think you may receive a letter in the next day or so, inviting you to speak on the subject. I do hope you'll say yes.'

'It was kind of you to mention me, Miss Townsend. I don't usually speak in public, although I suppose I could . . .' Though how on earth would she fit that in, on top of everything else? And yet, she could not afford to say no. The talk could prove useful: all those young women, some of whom would tell their mothers . . . Mothers *and* daughters covered in one go.

'Oh, good. And by the way, Miss Burnham, do please call me Grace. I can't be doing with "Miss Townsend" all the time. And, after all, you have seen me in my scanties.'

Miss Porter's invitation arrived the very next day. How prompt; how terrifying. The note was courteous and to the point: would Rose please advise her young ladies 'How to Dress for Success'.

'But what will you say?' Ginny asked, looking up from stitching the panels destined for Mrs Townsend's coat; Alice was tackling the inside seams for the lining of Mary Townsend's bridal gown, eyes fixed on the long straight line she and her treadle machine were creating.

Rose studied Miss Porter's letter. 'I don't know. I haven't had a moment to think. And there's not much time. She wants me to talk next week! I could do a "Miss Mabs", I suppose – don't wear blue with purple and be sure your bag matches your gloves – but that would be dull, and her students can read all that in a magazine.'

Alice perked up. 'Well, I think it's a terrific idea; and you'll be able to hand out your card, and that's bound to bring in new business.'

'That's what I thought,' Rose said, gaining confidence.

'See: this is the way forward,' Alice said. 'It's not like the days of yore. You need to go out into the world and advertise what you can do.'

'Except, most of the people at the class will make their own clothes, or else buy ready-to-wear. The daughters of the well-heeled ladies who can pay higher prices learn deportment and etiquette at their mother's knee.'

'I'm not so sure,' Ginny said, pausing in her work to look at Rose. 'More of those daughters now need to earn a living; their mothers won't know anything about that.'

'True. And, anyway,' Rose consulted the letter again. 'I'll only have to speak for twenty minutes. Miss Porter seems to think there will be lots of questions. I'll be able to answer those off the cuff.'

'And what's that other envelope?' Ginny asked.

'Oh, good heavens,' Rose said, as she retrieved a thick sheet of cream paper, 'it's from Mrs Lingard. I'd completely forgotten. The business with Miss Holmes and the Townsend wedding quite put it out of my head. Mrs Lingard is organizing a charity fête to raise money for babies' cots at the orphanage, and wonders if we'd give a mannequin parade. The fête is at the end of June.'

'Surely not,' Ginny said. 'That's only four weeks away.'

Alice laughed in disbelief.

'I expect she thinks we've some spare model gowns we can show.' Rose sat with the letter in her hand. The high wire had just been raised even higher; its height was now vertiginous. And yet they could not refuse their guarantor. 'We must say yes – we can't not. We can't let Mrs Lingard down and we do need the publicity. It's wonderful, of course, but how maddening.' Terrifying, too. Was it always going to be like this? 'Fancy being asked to do everything at once,' Rose said. 'It's impossible, and yet, somehow, we must make it work.'

'But what will we show?' Ginny asked, reverting to practicalities. 'You can't risk the model gowns and you can hardly parade Miss Simpson's restyling . . . and yet there's no money to buy new fabrics.'

'Well,' Rose said, thinking fast. 'We can take Miss Holmes's special dress, and if we present the show as a homage to summer, we can easily run up four simple drop-waist frocks; cotton doesn't cost all that much. Two could have petal skirts and sleeves, the others capped or even sleeveless . . .' She reached for that morning's newspaper, the nearest thing to hand, and started sketching in the margins and along the masthead. 'They can have hip-level belts or sashes. I saw two heavenly buckles at The Fancy Drapery the other day. They'll do, for starters. Jade green, bronze and rose-pink, sky-blue and . . . dare we run to tango? Are the ladies of Sydenham ready for tango? Well, perhaps not tango – although I like a flash of tangerine myself. I know: chrome yellow. The petal skirts would swish beautifully each time the mannequin turns.'

'These flights of fancy are all very well,' Ginny objected, 'but petal skirts need lining and overstitching; there's a lot of work in a handkerchief skirt, as you well know. The fête is only four weeks away and we'll be making these alongside all the Townsend regalia, not to mention you continuing to play detective now and again. We're already working late into the evening – at least those of us who are not about to go out and give talks . . . And,' Ginny continued, 'where are we going to find the mannequins? And how are we going to pay for these frocks?'

'All of this is true,' Rose said, choosing, as usual, to ignore the most difficult questions, but knowing she must concede something. 'Well, perhaps not petal skirts; we'll keep any complex work to a minimum. But don't forget, these frocks are all about show – they'll be seen from a distance, so won't require anything like the usual amount of finishing. No one is going to examine their hems or linings. The point is the effect they'll create. We'll be fine, as long as they look right on-stage, or whatever passes for a stage at a charity fête. If we choose bright colours, the audience will watch the parade of colours as much as the clothes. Yes, and with patterned paper parasols . . .' Rose was already picturing the final tableau. 'And we could do with a couple of lightweight coats; or one coat, at least. What about the embroidered coat you were making, Alice? That green-on-cream will look striking on a catwalk and will easily be seen from a distance.'

'But I put that coat aside when things got difficult. And I was making it for myself.'

'Well, if you finish the coat but don't wear it, it will still be pristine.'

'But the fête is in no time at all . . .'

'Yes, but you won't mind, will you? It's in a good cause. And we'll be able to show one or two of your hats in the final tableau . . . And I'm very much hoping you will agree to be one of the mannequins?'

Pacified, Alice accepted.

'And, as to the other mannequins,' Rose said, producing her trump card now that she'd had time to find it, 'I'm sure Grace Townsend won't be able to resist, and I'll ask her to invite the two likeliest candidates from her deportment class to make up the numbers. From what I've seen, Grace has a good eye; I'm sure she'll know what's required. And I'll speak to Maddie, too. She might be able to help out in some way on the day. We can measure and instruct – and vet – Grace and her mannequins, and then we can all get cracking.'

Ginny looked at Alice but said nothing. What else could they do?

19

It was almost overwhelming. The slub silk for Mrs Townsend's wedding coat was refusing to drape in the right way and, as if the slub silk (and the sphinx-head shoes) were not enough, Mrs Townsend was now making exclamatory noises about her whole outfit. Mary's going-away dress was still undecided, and Ginny had of course been proved right about the dresses for the charity fête. No matter how simple, they still needed making and would somehow have to be squeezed into an already impossible schedule. And now there was this talk Rose had said she would give.

'We dress for ourselves, as well as for work and social occasions . . .' Don't go on about work, Rose reminded herself, turning the corner into Markham Lane. Not all these young women will have jobs. The magazines might say the world is full of business girls, but there are still plenty of young women at home. An advertisement for cold cream came to mind – 'For the home girl whose duties are usually arduous, exacting and monotonous . . .' Oh dear – that thought brought Rose back to Miss Holmes, and that wouldn't do this evening.

She started again. 'We dress for ourselves . . .' She had now reached the end of Markham Lane and turned right into Arden Street. 'We want to feel that the clothes we wear represent who we really are . . .' But there was no more time to rehearse; she was almost there and, anyway, she knew what she wanted to say. Rose took a deep breath and entered the building.

She heard the deportment class before she reached the first landing – the tail-end of a class, at least. As soon as Rose entered the hallway, she heard commanding tones and could see dark shapes through a frosted-glass window. 'A little more poise please, Miss West; that's right, Miss Simmonds. Picture a long piece of ribbon being pulled from the tips of your toes, up through your body to the very top of your head. Lovely, ladies. Diaphragms in . . . and . . . hold.'

Rose knocked and entered, straightening her own back and tilting her chin as she did so. A dozen women in shiny frocks faced her, standing in a row, books on heads, their right knees raised as if to dance the cancan. All were chanting: 'In this way I attain perfect poise.' Another young woman, evidently their teacher, who was crouched before one of their number, adjusting her recalcitrant footwork, stood up when she saw Rose. 'Thank you, ladies.' She turned back to her class. 'That will be all for today.' Books were rescued, shoulders dropped; her unlikely troupe dispersed in giggles.

'Miss Burnham?' Their teacher walked towards Rose, right hand extended, a vision of perfect poise made flesh. She was dressed in black, nipped in below the waist, her feet slightly turned out like a ballerina's. South-east London's very own Pavlova, Rose thought. 'Good evening. I'm Miss Porter. I'm very pleased to meet you. Thank you so much for coming to my little school.' Her tone suggested she was the one to thank. Rose wondered if she should drop into a curtsey to acknowledge the favour bestowed. It was interesting to note how Miss Porter's confident movements commanded the room, a room beginning to fill with a fresh batch of students, and chairs, as the outgoing group gathered their bags and left.

'I'm so glad you could give us your time, Miss Burnham. When Miss Townsend spoke of you so warmly, I felt sure you would be the perfect person to advise my young ladies. I want to impress upon them the need to dress for success.'

'Thank you for inviting me. It's a topic I couldn't resist. But when you say success, what do *you* have in mind? Success so often means different things to different people.'

'Why, in life, of course,' Miss Porter said, smiling broadly, 'whatever their chosen path. Some of my young ladies are clerical workers, some help Mother at home; most hope to marry and establish homes of their own, but there are fewer opportunities for marriage these days and whatever her field of life, the young lady who is confident and courteous, and who knows how to project her best qualities, will carry off the prizes.'

'Indeed,' Rose said. In her mind's eye an imaginary stream of well-dressed young women, eyes forward, books on heads, dashed towards a finishing line. She blinked the image aside. 'And who are your young ladies? What sort of young lady comes to learn elocution, etiquette and deportment?' The ones attending the previous class had looked to be in their early twenties; the women now entering the room and taking their seats looked a few years older, closer in age to Grace. The fact that they all wore similar styles made it harder to identify their backgrounds.

'Why, the daughters of professional men: businessmen, bankers, solicitors; trade, even – its higher echelons, at least. Well, of course, you know Miss Townsend.'

'Yes, her family are clients of mine. I'm making the gowns and going-away outfit for her sister's wedding.'

'Ah, lucky girl.' It was unclear whether the luck lay in Rose's skills or in Mary Townsend securing a husband, although Miss Porter's emphasis made Rose suspect the latter was uppermost in her thoughts. She and Rose were about the same age; Rose wanted to ask how Miss Porter had come to start her own business, but there was no time for that question now. The background noise was rising – a discreet murmur, but a distracting sound, nonetheless. There was no getting round it: Miss Porter's young ladies were gathering to hear all about dressing for success. Rose took her place at the front of the class.

'. . . and some women have the vote,' she was saying, ten minutes in. 'I hope it won't be long before we all do. Whatever the newspapers might like to think, those of us who want the vote are not flappers; we are all modern young women.' Some of her audience looked down at their laps. She must not lose them. 'So,' Rose raised her voice, 'how are we going to dress for this brand-new world we are making?' She had their attention again. 'Shorter skirts mean greater freedom and make it easier for us to live our lives. And those lives are changing. We want clothes we can walk in, clothes we can run in, if need be – we have places to be, and buses, trams and trains to catch. We want to be alert to fashion without being in thrall to it. Of course, I could tell you not to combine red with purple, and that a mixture of stripes and florals will be so startling as to overpower you. But you know that already, don't you? You want to know how to look stylish on a small budget. You want an outfit that can take you from the morning through to the evening and still look distinguished at night . . .' On she went. 'And, finally,' Rose concluded, 'above all, be confident. It is 1925. You are the new women of the 1920s. Dress for success in whatever you do.'

Rose took her eyes from the vague middle distance and allowed herself to focus on the faces before her. There was a sea of smiles and – thank goodness – enthusiastic applause. Miss Porter walked towards her, beaming, and then turned to her charges. 'How very kind of Miss Burnham to share her expert-ise with us and pass on some valuable tips. Some of you may well be bachelor girls; others will want to be Miss Femininity.' Rose painted the appropriate smile on to her face. Where had she heard that phrase before? 'But whatever your role in life, I'm sure you will agree that Miss Burnham has given us plenty to think about. I, for one, am going straight home to overhaul my wardrobe. So, please join me in thanking Miss Burnham with a further round of applause.'

And there was Grace, making her way towards her from the very back of the room. When had she snuck in? 'That was won-derful, Miss Burnham. I knew you'd impress them. And I've found two prospective mannequins for the charity fête. Shall I introduce you now or would you rather wait until we meet to rehearse?'

'That's marvellous, Grace; thank you – but can we wait? I need to get back this evening and it would be difficult to assess your friends in front of their classmates. But thank you, all the same. I'm sure you will have picked the right two.' And if not, she would think about it later. It had been a long day, but Miss Porter seemed pleased and several of her young ladies came to shake Rose by the hand and ask for her card. All being well, she would soon have a smattering of solicitors' and businessmen's wives and daughters heading in her direction – a steady stream of reliable clients to keep things ticking over nicely and support more exciting one-off commissions.

What else do these businessmen's daughters learn here, Rose

wondered, apart from saying, 'How now, brown cow?' and balancing books on their heads? On her way out, she stopped to read a noticeboard crammed with timetables and lists of classes in etiquette, deportment, calisthenics and homemaking: 'Next week: How to Make a Lady Cake.' And there, pinned in the top right-hand corner, was a fan of business cards printed with the words 'Cupid's Arrow'.

20

Was that a coincidence, or was the deportment class linked to Cupid's Arrow – and, if so, how? Cupid's Arrow . . . Miss Holmes's money . . . the Townsend wedding . . . the dresses for the charity fête . . . Rose felt tugged every which way. She needed to clear her head.

Sometimes, when in need of inspiration, Rose headed to Dulwich Picture Gallery. She had made her earliest trips there as a girl, accompanying her father, who had stepped into the gallery one afternoon to shelter from the rain and discovered a liking for paintings. Thereafter, she was her father's frequent companion. Alice was too young when these trips began and Ginny had stayed at home with their mother, where she'd learned to crimp pie crusts and how to get as many discs as possible from a single sheet of pastry, a skill that would stand her in good stead years later when cutting into expensive cloth. Rose had baulked at these domestic accomplishments, however; if she learned to cook well, she might find herself confined to a kitchen one day. A gallery was a much better bet.

At first Rose was lifted to look at the details in the paintings. Soon, she was able to stand on her own two feet and note them for herself: to see the delicate lace, the snaking braid as unfathomable as a maze, and the way light lent translucency to a painted fabric, deceiving the eye into seeing depth where there was none. 'Look at her razzle-dazzle,' her father would say, pointing out the rings on a sitter's fingers ('and the bells on her toes') and encouraging his daughter to stand closer and take a hard look. If some well-heeled gallery visitor looked askance at his worn overcoat – and they often did – he would wink at Rose and whisper: 'A cat can look at a Queen.'

And so, on mornings like this one, Rose took herself to the gallery and stood in front of a painting, these days taking note of fabric, cut and line with a practised eye. This morning, she reassured herself that the hour was not misspent, she was here in the line of research. Would elaborate braiding suit Mary Townsend's going-away dress? The drama should be in the detail, not in overt display. Still immersed in the painting, Rose stepped back and collided with someone. 'Oh, I'm sorry,' she said.

'My error,' a male voice replied, and as she turned, the man smiled.

'I do apologize,' Rose said. 'I was intent on the painting.'

'So was I. And that's nothing to apologize for. You like paintings,' he said. It was a statement, not a question, and a statement of the obvious, she thought. Unlike Rose, he seemed entirely comfortable with this exchange. He had mid-brown hair, a strand of which he now brushed from his forehead, looking at her as he did so. 'What drew you to this one? You looked as if you would step inside it, if you could.'

'I was looking at the clothes,' Rose said. He glanced back at the painting and then returned his glance to Rose and her clothing, trying to get the measure of her, she thought, as she was trying to get the measure of him, a slim man in a grey suit, standing in a gallery at eleven o'clock on a Tuesday morning, and so, evidently not at work. But then, apparently, nor was she. She saw him glance at her hands, but they gave no clues; she was, of course, wearing gloves. Everyday gloves, though, not best leather.

He seemed to be deciding on his next question. 'Are you particularly interested in clothes?'

'Aren't all women?' This fellow had a cheek, starting a conversation with her and in a public gallery. 'At least, we're expected to be . . . I like the complicated pattern of the braiding,' Rose said, conceding that she was not quite ready to bring their conversation to an end.

'The braid on the cuff, you mean?' He stepped closer to the canvas and extended his right hand, revealing his own shirt cuff, a band of white that, although not new, looked freshly laundered. Rose noticed the tracery of hairs on his slim wrist and the glint of a mother-of-pearl cufflink: discreet, not overstated. Her insides gave an unaccustomed lurch. Whatever was she doing, trying to read this man's clothes?

Rose took a step backwards. 'You'll excuse me,' she said. 'I must go.'

'Of course.' He touched the brim of his hat; there was a flash of silver and another hint of mother-of-pearl. 'Good day.' His eyes did not leave her face.

Rose had planned to look at other paintings but was now too self-conscious to do so. Tightening her grip on her drawstring bag, she headed instead for the exit. She felt aware of herself in a way that was new, and disconcerting. Her footsteps sounded loud on the parquet floor; it took an unusually long time to reach the doorway.

21

Really, the cheek of that man the other morning. He might think himself charming, but she knew better. Drat. Now she had puckered her stitches: a simple beginner's error. Rose sighed and went back to the start of the seam. Feeling ruffled in a way she did not care to explore, she began to unpick her work. Ginny was the only one of them getting anywhere this evening. Alice was listening out for the door so that she could rush down to greet – and inspect – the young women Grace had selected for their mannequin parade. The workroom fizzed with anxiety.

At last Alice was rewarded. 'I'll be with you in a minute,' Rose said. 'Do you want to join us, Ginny?'

'No, thank you. I think the two of you will be quite enough.' And, Ginny might have added, one of us needs to focus on the Townsend commission.

Rose heard voices as soon as she stepped out on to the landing. Bursts of laughter and animated talk rose from the fitting-room; it sounded as if there was quite a party going on downstairs. She paused to listen.

'Read another,' an unknown voice commanded.

Grace started speaking: '"*A man who loves a girl really and truly is very seldom selfish. He would think of you, and your future, and your reputation before anything else. Show some pride and strength of will – he will admire you all the more for it.*" That was to a "Fanny Fairyfast".'

'Fanny Fairyfast?' Explosive laughter.

'I wonder what she wrote in to ask,' a different voice enquired.

'Can't you guess?' Alice asked.

Grace piped up again. Your turn now, Miss Carstairs. 'Read another.'

There was some rustling of pages and then the voice recited, ' "*My dear, your friend must not speak to gentlemen in the street if she does not already know them. Whatever is she thinking?*" And what about this advertisement?' The speaker dropped her voice an octave. ' "Ladies, must you go veiled for fear of superfluous hair?" ' More gales of laughter followed.

If they were going to get anywhere this evening, Rose needed to calm things down. She took a deep breath and opened the door. 'Can anyone join in?'

The fitting-room was unusually full. Both cane chairs were occupied, as was the spindly chair near the fireplace. Alice was holding forth in front of the mirror. Grace leapt up from her chair, pushing the magazine into her bag as she did so. 'Miss Burnham, let me introduce you to the two girls from my class. This is Miss Daphne Carstairs' – she indicated a willowy young woman with tightly crimped auburn hair – 'and this is Miss Monica Sedgeway.' The second candidate was slightly shorter, with brown curls softening an angular face. Both had the right figures and, fingers crossed, could be licked into shape without too much difficulty.

Grace opened her mouth to say something further (and perhaps provide Rose with some helpful conversational gambits), but Rose was in no need of introductory pointers. 'Thank you, Miss Townsend,' she said. 'And thank you all for coming this evening. I'm pleased to meet you, Miss Carstairs and Miss Sedgeway. I appreciate you giving up your time. As I'm sure

Miss Townsend has explained, this is all in a very good cause. This evening I will show you how to best project yourself when presenting clothes, and take your measurements. We've quite a lot to get through, so why don't Miss Burnham and I start measuring straight away? Miss Carstairs: if you would like to change behind the screen, we'll get started.'

Two hours later, when all measurements had been noted and Daphne, Monica and Grace transformed into passable manne-quins, the evening came to an end. There would be a final fitting-cum-dress-rehearsal in one week's time, and then the charity fête would be upon them.

The day of the fête dawned warm and clear, the sky the bright, solid blue normally associated with a child's paintbox. It was exactly the kind of weather one would order for the end of June. The driver had a struggle to fit the long dress-boxes into the small van Mrs Lingard had sent to collect them, but at last everything was strapped up and Rose, Ginny and Alice were able to clamber inside. The fête was to be held in a small park near the Crystal Palace. Although only a few miles from where the sisters lived, Rose had never been there before. They reached the park by midday, in plenty of time for the two o'clock start.

A smiling attendant, one of Mrs Lingard's willing helpers, stood at the nearest gate, distributing programmes. Rose took one and scoured the list of that afternoon's entertainments: stalls selling jam and other preserves, a coconut shy, a dog show, a children's fancy-dress and a 'Lovely Ankles' competition, then the final event – and the one she was looking for – 'Summer Sunshine: A Mannequin Parade, with Clothes by Designer Rose Burnham.'

' "Lovely Ankles",' Alice said, reading the details over her sister's shoulder. 'If there's time and there are no last-minute hitches, I'd like to enter that.' Rose guessed that, secretly, she hoped to win.

The mannequins were due to change in a striped tent of the type used to serve teas at Edwardian garden parties. Mrs Lingard had thought of everything: there were trestle tables, a rail for the clothes, a folding screen for changing, half a dozen canvas chairs, a jug of lemonade and some tumblers. She had even thought to provide a set of small steps to help the mannequins mount the bales that supported the makeshift stage on to which they would step out to exhibit Rose Burnham's work to the world. Well, not the world exactly, but supporters of the local orphanage and its environs, the great and good of the neighbourhood, and the not so great or good who planned to enjoy a grand afternoon and were already coming in through the gates.

While Rose and Ginny unpacked the clothes and parasols, Alice provided a running commentary. The park was filling up nicely. It was an exercise in then and now, the older generation dressed in sombre clothing, the younger generation keen to introduce elements of modernity. Some wore hats at precarious, jaunty angles. 'Don't they realize cloche hats should be worn straight, crammed on to the head just above the eyebrows?' Alice said. Every now and then colour made its own bold statement, although no visitor could hope to compete with Alice's leaf-green stockings.

Eventually, the clothes were ready, all hems, buttons and buckles checked. 'That's that,' Rose said. 'We can't do anything more until the others get here. Shall we take a look at the dog show?' The sisters linked arms and strode back across the grass, Alice in the middle, Ginny and Rose on either side. 'Just like the old days,' Ginny said. They didn't even have to adjust their steps to keep pace with one another.

There was much brushing and fluffing-up of fur, and tweaking of bows around canine necks, in the area cordoned off for the dog show. There was much flaunting of pedigrees, too, plus the odd motley-looking pooch which hadn't a hope against the serious entrants. And there *were* some serious entrants. Mrs Lingard knew someone who knew someone from the Ladies' Kennel Association and had invited her to judge the event. First up was a rascally looking terrier led into the ring by a young woman who, with her Eton crop, drop-waist blouse and tie, looked surprisingly up-to-the-minute. By contrast, the judge, a veteran of such occasions, might easily have stepped out of the ark. Dressed in black, black and yet more black, and multiple layers at that, she must already have been sweltering on what was rapidly becoming a warm afternoon.

A gaunt, leggy young woman paraded with a greyhound in a jewelled collar, lending support to the theory that people look like their dogs or else choose dogs to complement their own personalities. A stream of large, small, bouncy and rapscallion characters followed, as the dog show progressed through much trotting and barking (and the occasional embarrassing mishap). At last, the prizes for the best this and that were awarded. One winning owner became tearful; the dogs were rewarded with extra fuss, a young man with a camera snapped the winners and the dog show came to an end.

Rose checked her watch. 'Go on, Alice, you should just have enough time to dazzle the judge with those stockings.'

Much giggling and joshing preceded the 'Lovely Ankles' competition, which took place behind a sheet suspended at calf height between two poles, with contestants invited to sit on a long wooden bench behind it. 'Best feet forward, ladies,' the organizer said, jollying things along as the candidates got into place and shuffled up each time a new entrant joined them. Finally, everyone was seated – and how comic they looked, with their legs cut off in this way. Sixteen legs in all: some thick, some thin, some bony, some curvaceous. A whole row of pale stockings, with two exceptions: Alice's leaf-green legs. And so, the loveliest ankles were judged. First prize went to the young woman sitting beside Alice. Alice came second, and was awarded a pair of pottery budgerigars almost as garish as her stockings.

'They're cheerful,' said Ginny, ever the diplomat, when Alice reappeared in the tent.

'Aren't they just? However, I think they're destined to hang in the scullery.'

The dressing tent was now a scene of concentration and anxiety. The Misses Carstairs and Sedgeway were practising how to walk on a less than ideal surface while listening to Maddie broadcast instructions on where they should place themselves on 'stage'; Ginny was scrutinizing all the hems once more, to be absolutely certain there were no loose threads on those not-quite-so-simple frocks. Grace Townsend had yet to arrive. There's still time, Rose told herself, and, if need be, we will simply have to show one less dress.

'Why don't you sit down, Rose,' Ginny said.

'Yes, come and sit over here with me.' Maddie patted the bale beside her. 'If you're careful you can look at the audience without them seeing you.' She unrolled the tent flap a few inches. 'There's already quite a crowd. Women, mostly, although there are men, too – reluctant husbands, I expect. They know they'll be footing the bill if their wives fall for one of your frocks. And there's quite a mix of ages, but I suppose that's what you'd expect. There's everyone from Old Mother Hubbard and her children sitting on the back row, to the well-heeled who are beginning to take their seats at the front. I wonder if—Oh!' Maddie shot back as if stung.

'Are you all right?' Rose asked. 'What is it?'

'It's nothing. I'm fine,' Maddie said, although the colour had drained from her face. 'It's just that *he's* here,' she whispered, and then, more quietly still, 'the man I told you about: my dancing partner from the Amalfi.' There really was no need for caution; no one else was paying any attention. Daphne and Monica were busy getting changed under Alice's watchful eye, while Grace, who, cutting it fine, had just that moment arrived, was filling the tent with her apologies.

'Quick, look,' Maddie said. 'Over there, by the coconut shy. If you sit where I am, you'll see him, the man who dropped me like a stone after whisking me round the dance floor.' They exchanged places. 'See, the tall man in the blue-striped blazer. There, just taking aim.' Rose could only see the back of his head but, as she aligned herself, she heard the crack of a coconut knocked clean off its shy.

'A grand aim as well as a good dancer.' Rose hoped she sounded less panicked than she felt. She had to get a good look at this man, but her show was about to begin. 'I can't see him properly from here.' But she had seen enough to know that Maddie's dancer was not her own suitor. So, Mr Edward Martin really was a true romancer. Oh dear. 'Are you sure that's him?'

'Of course I'm sure, and anyway, you saw him that night, remember?'

'Actually, it was Ginny who saw him. I only caught a glimpse of you as the two of you were leaving.'

'It's definitely him. Handsome, isn't he?'

'Handsome is as handsome does,' Rose said decisively. 'At least that's what Mum always told us.' How ridiculous: even though she couldn't see the fellow properly and was not on the lookout for a genuine suitor, she actually felt miffed that Cupid's Arrow had supplied her with someone less debonair. 'Come on.' Rose tugged Maddie's elbow. 'You can't think about him now.' And nor can I, she admonished herself; too many thoughts were hurtling towards her. She must get a good look at Maddie's dancer the minute the mannequin parade was over.

Alice was the first on stage, wearing her elaborate cream-and-green coat over a dress kept simple in order to let the coat do the work. She walked to the end of the platform with her coat buttoned, and then spun and twirled to show off its heavily embroidered cuffs and handsome large buttons, before turning again and walking with the coat open and swinging freely, to reveal the simple shift dress underneath. An auspicious start and, by seeing Alice first, wearing a garment finished to such a high standard, the audience was immediately hooked.

Next up were the Misses Carstairs and Sedgeway. By the time they reached the front of the stage and paused with hands on hips, Alice had changed into a different dress and was out on the catwalk again, with Grace not far behind her. With four mannequins parading, the audience focussed, as Rose had intended, on the spectacle as a whole and on movement, colour and line. Miss Holmes's special dress, a garment on which Rose had lavished hours of attention, was saved until the very end. Grace showed this one, twirling slowly, lingering and striking a pose. Grace was in her element. For the first time in her life, she had actually been instructed to show off. She walked the dress to the very edge of the stage, stopped and pouted, relishing every moment.

In no time at all it was time for the final tableau. Maddie stayed backstage, handing out parasols as if her life depended on it, and reminding each mannequin where to position herself to create the right effect. And then the parade was over. The audience began to applaud. 'Your turn now, Rose,' Ginny nudged her. 'This is your moment. You should go out and take a bow.'

'No, I don't think so.' Rose backed away. 'I think we should leave them with the tableau. That will be much more effective.' She *had* to see Maddie's dancer, but she didn't want to risk him seeing her – or disappearing. She must find the man in the blue-striped blazer.

The crowd was just as Maddie had described: a hotchpotch of ages and social classes. Mrs Lingard had clearly worked hard to dragoon the 'right' people, as well as the local neighbour-hood. Rose's audience was starting to leave and, in the distance, people were already heading for the park gates. And then she saw him: Maddie's dance partner, the man in the blazer. He was not far away, and he was not by himself. He was with Miss Lane, the manager of Cupid's Arrow.

He was with Miss Lane! His right arm was linked through hers and she was leaning into his shoulder as they strolled towards the nearest gate. They walked as if nothing could trouble them, looking like a perfectly ordinary couple enjoying a sunny afternoon. Rose watched them both, transfixed.

A few yards further on, the dancer and Miss Lane stopped. Rose saw Miss Lane adjust her jacket collar and then brush something from his lapel. Such a small, fluid gesture and yet so revealing – their every movement confirmed the relationship between them. Rose watched Miss Lane laugh and whisper something in her companion's ear. She could not look away; it was as though she had never seen a man and a woman walking together before.

Rose kept on staring as the pair continued their stroll. So, there was no lone rogue, luring unsuspecting women with counterfeit promises; they must both be involved in the deceit. Poor Miss Holmes: all that quiet longing written on a card and packed into a box for these two fakers to mock. As if sensing Rose's distaste, Miss Lane chose that moment to turn and look in her direction. Rose stepped back smartly. Her face was burning, her hands shook. The brass band oomphed out another rowdy chorus of 'He Makes Me All Fussed Up'.

It was too soon to think further about what she'd just seen, and she had to get back to the tent. They were due to leave within the hour and the dress-boxes needed packing. For now, though, Rose needed to pause. So much had happened in one afternoon, and especially in the last ten minutes. She sat on one of the trestle tables, thankful for an excuse to be quiet. Ginny leaned against her, exhausted. Alice, the only one with any energy left, had gone to explore what remained of the stalls. The parade had gone off well, Rose and Ginny agreed, with applause and smiles in all the right places and, according to Alice, who had been out to check, nearly all the 'Rose Burnham' business cards had been taken – a good outcome that augured well. Grace, Daphne and Monica were warmly thanked, while Maddie, in a rush, as so often these days, disappeared as soon as she could. She said her sister was expecting her, but Rose knew she was still smarting at the thought of her dancer. Rose was smarting, too, but for a different reason. She was wondering what on earth she had got herself into.

She and Ginny were beginning to stir themselves when two women dressed in matching outfits strode into the tent. The shorter of the two made a beeline for Rose. 'Good afternoon. Apologies for the informality, but we couldn't resist coming to say how much we like your work. That blue dress was divine. Apologies – again; we should introduce ourselves.' The speaker proffered a kid-gloved hand. 'I'm Barbara Bressingham and this is my sister Dorothy – Babs and Dolly to our friends. And these are our stalwart companions: Cocoa and Biscuit.' She pointed at the two long-haired chocolate-coloured dogs slavering beside them. 'You've done well today, haven't you, sweeties? Cocoa won Best Bitch in Show and Biscuit was runner-up.' She leaned towards Rose: 'Although we whisper that, so as not to hurt her feelings.' Babs returned to her normal voice. 'A splendid after-noon for us all. Now, we'd love you to make us some clothes. Perhaps a version of the blue dress in peach for me and one in almond green for Dolly? And, we were wondering, would you consider making coats for the dogs?'

'Gosh,' Rose said. 'There's a thought. I'm flattered,' she said, stalling. 'Why don't I give you one of my cards? If you call me, we can make an appointment and talk properly when things are a little less . . .' She waved a hand towards the half-packed boxes and the yards of tissue paper that Ginny was now studiously folding in an effort not to catch her eye.

'Of course,' Babs beamed. 'We'd love to. We'll call next week. Come on, girls.' Babs and Dolly and their canine companions departed. As soon as they disappeared, Ginny raised her eye-brows and mouthed: '*Dogs' coats*'.

'Don't worry,' Rose said, laughing. 'We probably won't hear from them again. People often say they'll call at events like these, but that doesn't necessarily mean they will.'

Mrs Lingard chose this moment to appear. 'Rose, dear, that was marvellous. Thank you so much. This afternoon really has gone swimmingly; such generous contributions towards the babies' cots. I think we have almost reached our target. And did I just see the Bressingham girls? Lady Barbara and Lady Dorothy? You've done well there, my dear. They are definitely worth cultivating.'

'I'm flattered they like my work,' Rose said, hoping to convey that she knew all about 'the Bressingham girls'. She called up a distant memory of a photograph in *Country Life*, or was it the *Tatler*? 'We've agreed to talk next week. I look forward to meeting them properly.'

'Good. Well done.' Mrs Lingard turned and left the tent as briskly as she'd entered it.

Rose turned to Ginny: 'Dogs' coats it is, then.'

22

Despite their professed admiration for her work, the Bressinghams did not call Rose the following week. Fortunately, she and
her sisters were so preoccupied with the Townsend commission
(and especially with Mrs Townsend's ability to change her mind
at each fitting) that this fact did not fully register until the
Friday evening, when they were closing the workroom for the
night – 'shutting up shop', as they called it. Alice was meeting
her friend Maud and had already slipped away, leaving Rose
and Ginny to put everything straight.

'No telephone call,' Rose said, as she made a neat row of her
shears and different-sized scissors, 'which at least means no
awkward moments pacifying large dogs. Imagine' – Rose pulled
a face – 'having to measure and snip four armholes – foot holes?
Paw holes? You see, I don't even know the right words. It's
just as well that Lady Dorothy and Lady Barbara haven't
materialized.'

Ginny gave her a questioning look. She'd been folding strips
of lining material, but now stood with them in her arms.

'I don't mind,' Rose insisted, taking out her feelings on a
stray bobbin that wouldn't slot into an already crowded tin. 'All
right.' She stopped dissembling. 'The Bressingham sisters would
have been quite a coup, I admit. All the same, we *have* had a
letter from Mrs Lingard, thanking us with great warmth and
sincerity, and saying that a Mrs Crowther will be in touch for

an outfit for her daughter's coming-of-age, and that Mrs Lingard herself has something in mind for the autumn. And we have good reason to know that what Mrs Lingard promises actually happens. That's two new commissions to look forward to, and Miss Jennings the civil servant wrote with a new request the other day – so, there will be life after the Townsend wedding. Hallelujah.' And, with that, Rose managed to fit the bobbin into the available space.

'Are you all right, Rose? You've been in an odd mood all week.'

'No, I haven't.'

Ginny's look contradicted her.

'Well, perhaps. I'm fine, really. I'm just . . . I did hope the Bressinghams would call, of course I did, but it's not just that. It's . . .'

'It's Cupid's Arrow, isn't it?' Ginny said with some consternation. 'Honestly, Rose, you mustn't let that dreadful business eat into you.'

'I can't help it, not after what I saw at the fête. You should have seen them together, Ginny. Now that we know Miss Lane is connected to Maddie's dancer, it changes the whole picture. The idea that the agency itself is a falsehood . . .' Rose shivered. 'That's so much more complicated – and disturbing – than if Miss Holmes's swindler were a lone man. Just think, Miss Lane and the dancer must have sat and schemed and planned and picked over prospective candidates. I doubt Miss Holmes was the only one.' She bristled at the thought of those fakers sitting side by side, making fun of their next victim. 'They shouldn't get away with it,' Rose said, pushing her chair under the table with unnecessary force.

'I've been thinking, Rose . . .' Ginny was careful not to catch her eye. 'It will be hard to get Miss Holmes her money back, won't it? Even given what you know.'

The question hung in the air. 'Is that the reader of detective novels speaking, or my sister?'

'Both. You know it will be difficult, Rose. The money may have already gone, and if Miss Holmes won't go to the police . . .' Ginny's voice trailed off. 'I know how much you want to help her – and us – but I do wonder . . . I am just wondering . . . what point there is in you continuing to pursue this, if there's little chance of catching these villains red-handed and getting any money back. And,' Ginny hurried on, 'the Bressingham sisters may still get in touch – it has only been one week, after all – and, even without their custom, our own circumstances have improved – or will do, once the bills are paid. Things are not quite as shaky as they once seemed.'

'But I can't stop now.' Rose fixed Ginny with a righteous look. 'What about poor Miss Holmes?' But there was something else behind her indignation.

'Oh,' Ginny said, 'I know that look. I know that glint in your eye.'

'What look?' Rose asked, affecting innocence.

'I've seen it before. You can't fool me, Rose. You're going to carry on with this, whatever happens, aren't you?'

'Only because someone must,' Rose said, busying herself with nothing in particular. She felt caught out; Ginny knew her too well. She couldn't stop now, not now there was an even larger deceit to uncover.

Part 3

The Cloche Hat: The Female Detective's Best Friend

23

'It's lovely, Rose,' Maddie said, 'especially this room.' It was the first Sunday in July. They had looked all over the house and now occupied the fitting-room's comfortable chairs. They had reminisced over their apprenticeships and remembered who sat where back then, but Maddie lacked her usual exuberance. She was wearing a jazzily patterned blouse, but couldn't live up to its promise. Rose talked of the ongoing preparations for the Townsend wedding and joked about Alice commandeering the dressing table for her hatter's block, but even when she complimented Maddie on the inventive windows she was creating at Webb & Maskrey, Maddie needed prodding into conversation. We're as bad as each other, Rose thought. Finally, she asked, 'Is everything all right? You don't seem to be yourself.'

'I wanted to see your house, Rose, but I had another reason for coming today. There's something I want to talk to you about; I couldn't think who else I could trust. Something happened the other week and I can't stop thinking about it.' Maddie reached into her bag and pulled out a sheet of paper. Rose took it from her and read: 'I KNOW YOUR GAME. YOU'RE NO BETTER THAN YOU SHOULD BE AND YOU WILL BE CAUGHT OUT.'

This missile was written in thick, red capital letters on white paper. The handwriting was large and uneven – childlike, almost – but though its message was the equivalent of a playground taunt, there was nothing remotely playful about it. 'Who on earth would do this?' Rose asked. 'What do you think it means?'

Maddie reddened and tossed her head, a gesture which looked haughty, but Rose knew was wounded pride. 'I don't know. It's jealousy, I expect.' She took a deep breath and drew herself up as if to intimidate the letter writer. 'It must be written by someone who doesn't like the fact I'm making a go of things – or trying to, at least. I visit a lot of departments to gather props for the windows; that gives me a certain amount of freedom. Perhaps someone doesn't like me moving so freely through the store. You know what it can be like.'

Rose picked up the vile note and scrutinized the lettering, as if that would reveal the reasoning behind it. 'The thickness of the block capitals makes it all the more unpleasant, somehow.'

'Doesn't it,' Maddie agreed, taking it from her. 'It's as if her venom is there on the page. She has pressed so hard the words have practically come through on the other side of the paper.'

'*She?*' Rose studied Maddie's face. 'Do you have an idea who wrote this? Do you think you know who it's from?'

'No,' Maddie insisted, indignant now, as if that knowledge would be beneath her dignity, 'but I assume it's a "she". It reminds me of other judgements passed down from one woman to another. I've been thinking of my mother's sister, my Auntie Vi. She always has an ear to everyone else's business and will stand at her garden gate, hand on hip, commenting on someone passing by. "No better than she should be" is the kind of thing she'd say.'

She and a hundred other willing critics, Rose thought.

'I couldn't believe my luck in going back to Webb & Maskrey. I don't want it spoiled by anything.'

'No, of course not. So, you do think it's someone there?' Rose quizzed. 'What about the people you work with?'

Maddie shook her head. 'It can't be them. Miss Denby is friendly and Miss Barnes, too – I can't think it's either of them. That's the trouble: I can't easily think who it *could* be. It was posted to the hostel, but of course the hostel and the store are one and the same. A few girls from other shops room there, but most work at Webb & Maskrey.'

'What about the people you knew when you were there before?' Rose began to construct an inventory of the workroom. 'Queenie Blake is still there. She could be catty sometimes. Or what about Josephine Wilton? She was pointedly silent when I announced I was leaving. Most people said something nice, even if I knew they didn't mean it, but Josephine carried on sewing as if I hadn't spoken. And do you remember when Miss Feldman chose you instead of Josephine to pick out the jet beads for that bodice we did for Mrs Young? She wasn't at all pleased about that. But that was years ago, and all of those are silly, petty things . . .'

'Yes, they're hardly . . .' Maddie's words disappeared. She started her own list: 'The people I worked with on the windows before have left, apart from Miss Carter, that is. And it can't possibly be her.' Rose agreed. Miss Carter was no mere mortal. 'I have visited the workroom,' Maddie said, 'but I wasn't there long – I only called in to say hello for old times' sake. It's hard to recall the details because I've been in and out of so many departments. And anyway, being catty is one thing; this is something else altogether.' She looked down at the letter again.

What odd conversations take place in the fitting-room these days, Rose thought, looking in the mirror at the two of them, sitting side by side, scouring an anonymous letter. 'It must be horribly disconcerting,' she said. 'Peculiar, too. I thought poison-pen letters were only sent to people with something to hide.'

Maddie shuddered. 'Well, whoever it is, it's a wicked thing to have done.' She folded the piece of paper and put it back in her bag. 'It would have been an odd day even without that. I misplaced something Miss Carter wanted for a display. I'd picked up the two hats she'd asked for and could have sworn I'd put them ready, near the window, but then I couldn't find them. Miss Barnes and I looked high and low, but they'd vanished. It was Miss Denby who found them in the end – in the store-room, of all places – and just in the nick of time. I was so grateful she took the trouble to go and look. But I still can't fathom why I left the darn things there in the first place. I don't even remember going there that morning, although evidently I did, which just goes to show how much that letter riled me. And it's not just me; Daisy Johnson's had one.'

'Daisy Johnson – isn't she the young woman at the hostel whose notepaper you borrowed to write to Cupid's Arrow?'

'Yes. She works on kitchen appliances and shows them in the store.' The young demonstrator, Rose thought. 'And a man shouted at her the other day,' Maddie continued, 'told her she should get back into the kitchen herself. Anyway, Daisy burned her letter and said good riddance. She's right: the whole thing is hateful and embarrassing. I want to forget all about it.'

'Do you think it could be someone with a vendetta against working women?'

'Possibly, but if it is, I've no way of finding out who they are. I really would like to forget the whole thing.' Maddie gave another dramatic shudder.

'I expect you're right,' Rose said. However unpleasant, the letter itself was harmless and surely the writer would tire of their theme. But if it was someone with a grievance against working women, she had better keep an eye out herself. Or could the letter have something to do with Cupid's Arrow? No, that was unlikely, and she would have received a letter too. Cupid's Arrow had far more reason to target her than Maddie. 'There was something I meant to ask you. The man you danced with at the Amalfi that night, Maddie, the one at the charity fête: what did the two of you talk about? Do you remember?'

Maddie frowned. 'Not really. Nothing in particular – which dances we preferred and which tunes. We danced almost the whole evening, so there wasn't that much time for chat. It was only when we were walking to the ladies' hostel that there was really time to talk. That's when he asked me about work and I told him where I lived – and you know what happened then.'

'Whose idea was it to go to the Amalfi?'

'Mine, I think. I suggested it because I hadn't been there for ages and thought it might be fun.'

So that was that. The Amalfi was not the dancer's usual haunt. No wonder he was nowhere to be seen when she and Ginny went back there. 'And he didn't say anything to you about Cupid's Arrow?'

'No, why would he? Just how fortunate it was that he'd met someone who likes dancing as much as he does. You know how these things go,' Maddie said, although Rose didn't. 'Why do you ask?'

'No reason. It just seemed odd – him being interested in you having money.'

'There are some odd people about these days.'

'Come on,' Rose said, standing up. 'I'll walk you to your tram.' It suddenly seemed important that she accompany Maddie.

The two of them linked arms and set off for the high street. Rose repeated how much livelier the Webb & Maskrey windows looked these days and Maddie joshed Rose about her empire, but Rose sensed that Maddie was putting on a brave front. On the way back home, her own confidence dwindled. True, there were some odd people about, but the idea that someone could write such filth was appalling. Maddie could be imperious at times; perhaps she had made enemies at the store. Surely, someone at Webb & Maskrey was the logical explanation? The fact that Daisy Johnson had also received a letter seemed to confirm that. If only Miss Johnson had kept hers instead of burning it. Maddie's letter was brutal, but perhaps the letter writer was warming to her theme. Her theme: that made Rose pause. If indeed the letter writer was a woman . . . What if the letters were written by a man?

Surely, a man had even more reason to resent female progress – hence that man challenging Miss Johnson – but why target women in a department store? Department stores were full of women. It was no use; as Maddie said, the letter writer could be anyone. Rose studied the young woman walking beside her and the man in the trilby who had raised his hat in greeting as he stepped down from the tram and stood back to let Maddie get on, and who was now walking a few steps behind Rose. This was ridiculous; she was letting her imagination run away with her. She couldn't possibly suspect every single person she saw. Rose stopped at the junction and waited for a delivery van to pass.

And why on earth would Maddie be caught out? Then again, why ever not, Rose thought. In the last ten months, she had often expected someone to tell her *she* was an imposter; that she was just playing at being a dress designer and that the labels she'd had printed at great expense were every bit as fake as she was. By now, Rose was walking at quite a clip. For once she did not check the hats in Cecile's window or the china on display in Clare's Cabinet. Fraudsters, letter writers . . . all of them preying on women and preventing them from living their own lives. Would she be the next in line? Would she come downstairs and find a poison-pen note on the mat? This was a matter of pride, Rose told herself, turning left into Chatsworth Road. We women must stick together.

Starting up in business felt perilous enough – insecure prospects, ludicrously long hours, little sleep, precarious finances, the need to be constantly on her toes, not to mention the responsibility of employing her sisters and asking them to trust to her luck. Surely that list was long enough, without having to worry about someone else's hostility. But it wasn't just Maddie's letter that had prompted these thoughts. Rose recalled a morning several years ago, eons before she'd thought of branching out alone. She was still living at home and had emerged from the house one morning in a brand-new coat – how she'd loved that coat, her very first piece of tailoring: damson-coloured wool with intricate black frogging, her showpiece garment on completing the evening course – to find that two neighbours had paused to chat a yard or so further up the road. They looked Rose up and down, took in her coat and, although their greetings were amiable enough, she had barely passed the gate before she heard one say to the other, '*She'll* never marry. She thinks too much of herself.'

Sticks and stones, Rose had told herself then, seeking comfort in the childhood rhyme with which her mother had mopped up sisterly squabbles. Sticks and stones, she told herself now. This righteous indignation brought Rose back to her front door. It was far easier to think about a poison-pen campaign than to consider the hornet's nest she might be stirring up at Cupid's Arrow.

Alice was standing in the hallway, removing her hat and gloves. 'Did you see her?'

'Maddie? Yes, I've just walked her to her tram.'

'No, the woman who called not ten minutes ago. I thought your paths might have crossed. I was just coming in, and was standing on the doorstep, when she approached the house. She wanted to know if this was Miss Rose Burnham's address. She didn't leave her name – *wouldn't* leave it – although I did press her. I assumed she was shy, but I don't really think it was that. I thought she must have seen our work at the fête, but she seemed a little bit cagey. It was difficult to know what she wanted. Perhaps she was trying to make her mind up about us and didn't want to be put on the spot.'

'What did she look like?'

Alice screwed up her face. 'Hard to say. She was wearing the most awful muddy colours and a hat you wouldn't believe.'

'Yes, but what did she actually *look* like? Was she tall, short? Did she have blonde hair, brown . . . black?'

Alice equivocated. 'Tallish . . . medium,' she decided. 'Brown hair, I think, but I couldn't really see her hair. To tell you the truth, I was distracted by what she was wearing and by her dreadful, frumpish hat. I'm sorry. Gosh,' Alice brightened, 'do you think she was from Cupid's Arrow? Could it have been Miss Lane? That would cast an entirely different light on things, wouldn't it? But Miss Lane would dress better than that, surely?'

24

'Alice says someone came to the house asking about me, yester-day, just as she was letting herself in,' Rose told Ginny. They were standing side by side in the scullery; Ginny was washing up, Rose drying. Both were wearing cotton gloves, a necessary and daily palaver – a scullery maid's hands and fine silks not being the best of companions.

'That's good,' Ginny said, passing a plate to Rose. 'We hoped that the fête would bring new clients.'

'But this woman must have waited until Alice appeared. Why didn't she just knock on the door?'

'I expect she wanted to get a sense of us before making a formal enquiry – like strolling past a shop window before deciding to go in. Perhaps it's someone going up in the world who hasn't quite plucked up the courage to consult a designer.' Ginny paused in the washing up. 'Why, Rose? What's the matter?'

'Nothing,' Rose bluffed. 'It's just not what we're used to, that's all. You know how formal things were at Webb & Maskrey. It's just a different way of doing things, I expect. You're prob-ably right: it was someone testing the water. That's more or less what Alice thought. Really, the sight of Maddie's dancer with Miss Lane was so unexpected and unnerving that I'm suspecting everyone I encounter. If I'm not careful, I'll be thinking that the Bressingham sisters are part of the plot to lure young women, and their dogs the perfect decoys.'

'Logic and deduction: that's the way forward.' Ginny handed Rose the last plate. 'At least that's what my detective stories tell me.' She peeled off her wet gloves and dried her hands. 'Let's think about what we know.'

Rose put down the plate and the tea-cloth. Now she was ready to speak. 'Miss Holmes has been deceived by a man who pretended to woo her. That much is indisputable. And we've learned something new. Cupid's Arrow appeared to be a genuine agency with a scoundrel on its books, but it now seems that the manager, Miss Lane, is behind – or at least in on – the deceit. She is romantically linked with the man who calls himself Reginald Wilson and, as far as we know, selects likely candidates for him to charm and defraud. What a perfect scheme. Not one lone wolf but a pair of swindlers. There are two crooks at work, not just one.

'The fact that Miss Lane is involved makes the whole thing even more cruel. It's not simply a case of "I think we have found your heart's desire; he looks like Ramón Navarro and lives in Dorking." She has an in-depth knowledge of her clients' every awkward pause and blush, and she passes each detail on.

'If the swindlers are careful and not too greedy, they can fleece any number of women while maintaining a respectable front. And the poor innocents who fall foul of this pair will be too distraught and embarrassed to report the deception, and too ashamed to admit that they've stooped to using a matrimonial agency for fear of ending up "on the shelf". Who would want to confess that to a policeman?'

'On the shelf,' Ginny repeated, grimacing and looking at Rose. 'What a disgraceful phrase that is.'

'Yes, but we know that it's what people say and, worse still, think – and it's one of the reasons these fraudsters may get away scot-free, unless we can catch them at it.'

Calculating, cunning, conniving . . . Rose picked up her shears and cut into the yards of printed chiffon which, when combined with a clinging sheath of eau-de-nil silk, would emerge as an evening gown for Mary Townsend, a new and late addition to the bridal trousseau, and one that felt intensely personal. Indeed, this gown had been commissioned by Mary herself, not her mother.

Something so delicate and alluring should not be sullied by distasteful thoughts, but the more Rose contemplated Cupid's Arrow, the more audacious that enterprise seemed, especially if they had a smattering of genuine male clients to provide the perfect cover. Hence the unsuspecting Edward Martin, the lonely heart who, poor sap, had now been saddled with her. She would see Mr Martin once more, and then gently send him on his way. A further meeting may be awkward for them both, but it was only fair to let him down kindly and, who knows, he may even reveal something about the agency that would help her to assist Miss Holmes.

Dear Miss Holmes – and the other women like her who may have taken equally desperate steps to avoid being left 'on the shelf'. That revolting phrase intruded again – not picked, not chosen, not wanted. An age-old story, if louder now, given a new gloss since the war. The very idea that women had no value unless picked by someone else . . . Rose had never considered the term in relation to herself and was not about to do so now. (And if there *was* any picking to be done, she'd be the one doing it.) Rose wielded the shears again and stood back to assess the result.

The business shielded how she was seen, to a great extent, although frankly she didn't much care. They could say what they liked about her from now on, Rose told herself, as long as she could get on and work. But how did Ginny see herself, she wondered. She had wanted to ask last night, but didn't. That was not mere convention, but sisterly feeling. She looked across now at Ginny, who, oblivious of Rose, was chasing some impossibly small beads with a needle and thread.

It must be strange being almost a widow, and yet not one. Only those close to Ginny knew that about her. Did she regret not marrying Tom on his last leave? Rose knew they'd intended to fix a date. However young they were and however brief their marriage, Ginny would have been a widow now, with status. And there must be many women like her: single, but spoken for – once upon a time, that is. Rose drew herself up. 'Spoken for': that was quite a phrase itself. And what of the young 'widows' who had never got married in the first place and were now bringing up a child? The war disguised so many stories.

Rose exchanged her shears for her smallest scissors and returned to her earlier thought. How did Ginny see herself? Had Tom come home, Ginny would no longer be a seamstress – or, rather, not a seamstress in the same way. She would probably have done some work for the business but, if she'd had a family, she'd have been at home looking after them (instead of now looking after her sisters). Indeed, if she'd married while at Webb & Maskrey, she would have been expected to leave. Most women there saw work as something they did before marriage but, for those who did not, the choice was stark: marriage or a career; one or the other, not both. Rose had made her decision a long time ago.

Rose put the small scissors aside. That was quite enough

cutting and snipping for one morning. And none of these thoughts were helping to advance her current dilemma: how to expose an agency that dangled marriage before its hopeful applicants? Although it now seemed certain that Cupid's Arrow itself was fraudulent, she was no closer to obtaining proof. What she wanted was a photograph of the dancer, to confirm his identity once and for all. Better still, if she could find one of him with another innocent or, even better, cosying up to Miss Lane, she would have the evidence she needed.

Miss Holmes didn't have a photograph, but that did not mean no photograph existed. There was a photographer at the fête; perhaps he had snapped Miss Lane and the dancer and . . . But of course: she had stared at a whole wall of photographs only a few months earlier. Why had she not thought of this before?

Mr Jones was photographing two small boys when Rose returned to Alfredo's Snaps. The boys, dressed in bathers, were lounging with beach balls on an immense shallow tray of sand, set before a blue-washed backdrop. Their mother clearly had no faith in the actual weather (nor perhaps sufficient funds for a day trip). She may have found the ideal solution, however; it was warmer indoors than out that day, and the boys' knitted bathers wouldn't have fared well in the waves, but Rose was Miss Lipton again and Miss Lipton did not make light quips.

Miss Lipton was perfectly happy to take a seat in the corner and wait half an hour, or longer if need be. But Mr Jones was ready to receive her tentative enquiry before then. She was embarrassed to ask, but – Rose lowered her eyes – she wondered if, by any chance, she and her sweetheart had been photographed together in the park. They'd had some lovely walks there on more than one occasion and there was often a photographer about. 'The thing is,' Rose confided, leaning towards Mr Jones, 'it's my young man's birthday soon and I would so love to present him with a signed photograph if, by any chance, we were captured together on film on one of those afternoons. I want it to be a surprise, you see. That's why I've come by myself rather than asking you to take our photograph here. You mentioned that your son takes photographs out and about. I'm sure he must be the young gentleman I've seen.'

'Well, my dear . . .' Mr Jones looked kindly at Rose. 'It is a little unorthodox, but why not? I'm always keen to help romance blossom. Have a look at the wall and, if there's nothing there, we've got some more recent snaps in the book.' He gestured towards an album on the counter. 'Sometimes, for one reason or another, prints are not collected by their sitters, and occasionally we ask a customer if we can make an extra copy to display. Good portraits bring in new custom, you see, and show the range of settings we offer. We never ask solo young ladies for copies of their photograph – that wouldn't do; otherwise, I would of course have asked you.' Such practised gallantry.

'Of course.' Rose stood before the wall of photographs, as she had some months earlier. Now that she was no longer idling before them, passing time, the mass of faces pinned there was almost overwhelming. She must forgo the floor-length gowns and effusive hats, and concentrate on the more recent photographs, especially those of young couples and individual men.

The picture-wall offered whole histories. Some couples looked decidedly awkward together and there were some excruciating wedding snaps – brides and grooms with blanched faces, who seemed to be wondering what on earth they had let themselves in for. Rose told herself to ignore the wedding photos; it was hardly likely that Miss Lane – or whoever she was – and the dancer, if they were married, had allowed the photographer to parade their nuptials here.

Men in trilbies, flat caps; men in overcoats, summer jackets. But no dancer. And it had seemed such a good idea. Mr Jones joined her. 'No luck?'

'No,' Rose said. 'And I did so hope . . .' She did not have to feign disappointment.

'Have you looked at the album?'

'No, not yet.' Rose opened the album and turned page after page of yet more courting couples, more family outings, picnics, weddings, even ducks skimming the water, preparing to land on a pond. She was about to turn the page again when she saw there was a man in profile watching those hovering ducks. And that lone observer was the dancer. He looked somewhat startled, but it was undeniably him. 'Oh,' Rose said, 'would you believe it, here he is. It's not the best of shots and he is by himself, but it's most decidedly my gentleman friend.'

'The ducks must have startled him.'

'Yes,' although Rose thought it more likely the dancer was surprised at being snapped. 'Nonetheless,' she told Mr Jones, 'it clearly is him.'

'We do our best,' the photographer replied, summoning a tone of professional pique. 'Mind you, it was the ducks my lad was after, not your sweetheart.'

'Well, I think it's an interesting composition,' Rose soothed him. 'I tease him about being camera-shy, but here he is captured on film.' She beamed; she was allowed to beam. Mr Jones would interpret it as a ray of romantic sunlight. 'May I order a copy?'

'I don't think you need do that, miss. You can have this one. The ducks didn't come out all that well.'

'Thank you,' Rose said. 'There is just one thing,' she added a few moments later. 'I don't suppose my young man will call here for any reason, but would you mind if this was our secret?'

'Not at all,' Mr Jones replied. 'I expect you'd like to surprise him.'

Wouldn't I just, Rose thought. But first, she needed to show the photograph to Miss Holmes.

25

'How kind of you to call to tell me you've finished tweaking that neckline, Miss Burnham,' Miss Holmes said, employing a double-speak Rose realized must be for Mother's benefit. She and Miss Holmes both knew there was no neckline to tweak. 'It's Miss Burnham, Mother,' Rose heard her mumble, Miss Holmes evidently having placed her hand over the mouthpiece. 'Thank you so much for ringing,' she said, back with Rose again. 'And you've just caught us. We are about to go away for a week, to visit my aunt. May I call you when we get back?'

Drat. She had wanted to see Miss Holmes as soon as possible. 'The thing is, Miss Holmes,' Rose said carefully, 'I have a photograph I'd like to show you. I think you may recognize the gentleman.'

'Oh.' For a few long moments, the line was silent. 'How silly of me to have forgotten that,' Miss Holmes said eventually. 'Yes, of course I'll come and collect it. I have to return some library books this afternoon – I'll pop in on my way home.' Rose stared at the telephone. She had to admire Miss Holmes's extemporizations. For all that she had fallen prey to a deceiver, she was none too bad at deception herself.

'It's not him, I'm afraid. It's not Reginald.' It was later that afternoon and Miss Holmes and Rose were huddled over the photograph. Miss Holmes's voice flagged; she sounded utterly deflated. She had lost all the eagerness with which she'd entered the fitting-room. She held the photograph up to the light and turned it left and right, as if by doing so she might create a different image altogether. But, alas, this altered nothing. 'That isn't Mr Wilson. That doesn't look anything like him,' Miss Holmes added with an undertow of disdain, her unmistakable tone confirming that one woman's handsome beau is another's undesirable. She might almost have been affronted by the suggested link.

For the avoidance of all doubt, Miss Holmes repeated her denial. 'I'm sorry, Miss Burnham, but that really isn't him. Reginald is shorter and stockier, and he has a moustache.'

'A moustache?'

'Yes, didn't I say?' As if a moustache was the first thing one would mention when describing an elaborate fraud. But it would have helped Rose to know this pertinent detail before she had gone looking for photographs. Never mind. 'But,' Miss Holmes continued, 'how – where – did you find this and why did you think there was a connection?'

'I'll be honest with you, Miss Holmes,' Rose said. 'A friend of mine went dancing with this gentleman. They, too, met through Cupid's Arrow, and from some of the things she told me' – Rose paused, intimating that discretion of course prevented her from saying too much – 'I wondered if he and your gentleman were one and the same. I'm sorry they aren't; I did so hope we were about to confirm his identity.'

'I hoped so, too.' Miss Holmes sighed. 'I don't think I will ever find Reginald now.' Some three months had passed since her original revelation, but she looked no less defeated this afternoon.

In that long moment, looking at Miss Holmes's broken,

weary face, Rose realized something she should have known. She wanted to identify the swindler and so did Miss Holmes, but from, oh, such different motives. As desperate as she felt about her lost capital and the way she'd been deceived, Miss Holmes was still smitten. What she wanted more than anything was to see Reginald Wilson again. A single photograph would be something to hold on to, at least. Rose had dangled that possibility before her – and withdrawn it.

'I'm so sorry, Miss Holmes.' How to make up for the fact that she had unwittingly wielded a further blow? 'I won't give up just yet. Perhaps something will come to light while you're visiting your aunt.'

'Perhaps,' but it was evident that Miss Holmes thought it unlikely.

26

So, it wasn't the dancer after all, although he was decidedly no innocent. But what a blow; Rose could still see the defeated expression on poor Miss Holmes's face when she'd held out a photograph of the wrong man.

There must be more she could do – and do while Miss Holmes was away. Perhaps Cupid's Arrow itself would yield new clues, and even the solution to this dreadful business, if she was willing to employ different tactics. She had read a fascinating newspaper article about sleuthing: the patience required, the need to watch for hours on end, if need be, to be sure of catching a criminal at work. All the best detectives were skilled at shadowing suspects. And now that Rose thought about it, this was the obvious next step. She would go to Cupid's Arrow again but, this time, she would stand across the street and watch. Who knows, she might see 'Mr Wilson' and his bewitching moustache, or, come to that, Miss Porter; she had yet to work out the significance behind the fan of Cupid's Arrow business cards pinned to Miss Porter's noticeboard.

That afternoon, Rose tucked herself into a doorway and fixed her eyes on the black door opposite. She was well concealed and, thanks to a hat pulled down over her forehead, unidentifiable. For the first ten minutes she entertained herself by dreaming up advertisements: 'For that element of mystery, choose a cloche' or 'The cloche hat: the female detective's best friend.'

The novelty waned all too quickly. Her shoulders stiffened and the doorway was unfeasibly stuffy, with an unmistakable whiff of tomcat. For the next hour or so, no one went into or out of Cupid's Arrow. She had obviously picked the wrong morning. Business was clearly not brisk, but then romantic encounters rarely run like clockwork, so why should romantic enquiries?

Shortly before one o'clock she was rewarded. The black door opened and there was Miss Lane, coming out of the building and turning left on to Bolton Street and the main thoroughfare of shops. Rose checked her watch, although she need not have done so; her stomach could have told her it was almost lunchtime.

Miss Lane looked different again this morning: neither the cajoling interviewer, nor the Saturday-afternoon romancer. This morning she looked like a purposeful young woman going about her business in a rather handsome suit – surprisingly handsome, in fact. She came to a halt in front of a shady window a few doors further down. Rose paused, too, and, aiming for unobtrusiveness, turned slightly to gaze at the corn plasters and cod liver oil displayed in a nearby chemist's window. Miss Lane seemed to hesitate, but then opened the door beside the shady window and stepped inside.

Rose crossed the road and peered into the dark interior of Madame Estelle's. It was hard to see properly without advertising her presence. Standing at an angle to the window, she watched Miss Lane greet the proprietor and, nodding and gesticulating, and oblivious of the fact that she was being observed, indicate with both hands how she would like her hair styled. Rose sighed. All that waiting, only for Miss Lane to leave the office to get her hair waved.

Madame Estelle – it must be Estelle (if that was her actual name); she looked to be the most senior person at the salon – helped Miss Lane into a gown and showed her to a vacant seat. There was no point in waiting; indeed, there was every reason why Rose should leave. At any moment Miss Lane might look round and see her standing there, nose practically pressed against the glass, or else catch sight of her via the large mirror on the wall in front of the hairdressing chair. She would come back in twenty minutes and see how Miss Lane and Madame Estelle were getting on.

By the time Rose retraced her steps, Miss Lane's head was covered with evil-looking crimpers. It was obviously going to be a long wait. Rose turned away and once more affected an interest in the nearby shops. There were more corn plasters to examine and assorted piles of fruit to count in the greengrocer's window before she judged it safe to return. Miss Lane was still inside but was now submitting to the hairdresser's final ministrations. Madame Estelle fussed round her, adjusting her hair and brushing her collar, calling to mind that far more intimate moment at the fête, when Miss Lane had brushed the dancer's lapel.

Miss Lane smiled at Madame Estelle and nodded in affirmation of her new look. She then took Madame Estelle by both hands and squeezed them; this was evidently not the first time they'd met. Perfect, Rose thought. Women talk to their hairdressers, just as they confide in their dressmakers. Might she learn something here?

Miss Lane turned and walked towards the doorway. Once again Rose moved out of sight and feigned an interest in the chemist's window. The chemist would doubtless conclude there was something she needed but felt embarrassed about.

Some moments after hearing Miss Lane's cheery goodbye, Rose returned to the salon and pushed open the door.

Madame Estelle approached. She was a woman in her forties with a cross-over gown – part dress, part overall – and exceptionally small, tight curls. 'Good afternoon. Can I help you?'

'I hope so. I was walking by and couldn't help but notice that a young lady has just left your salon with a divine hairstyle; so *very* up-to-the-minute.' Madame Estelle looked suitably flattered. Rose amplified her theme. 'It's the kind of style I've been longing for, but couldn't pluck up the courage to choose. Seeing that young woman has decided me. "Why not?" I thought. "Just open the door and go in." Were you responsible for it?' Even if Rose had not witnessed Madame Estelle's titivations, this was an obvious guess; the only other staff in evidence looked like trainees, whereas this woman exuded confidence and – the biggest giveaway of all – had exactly the same crimped look.

Rose offered her *piece de resistance*: 'Quite the West End touch.'

'Thank you.' Madame Estelle patted her own curls.

'Could you please do the same for me? I know I'm a trifle dishevelled, but I wasn't expecting to come to a salon today. It's just that, as I say, having seen that young woman, I don't feel I can resist. And I do need to grab my courage with both hands. She was altogether more modern than I am.'

The hairdresser looked appraisingly at Rose, who, to aid her concealment, was once again dressed in an undistinguished manner. 'Oh, that's the confidence that comes with having a good hairstyle. I'll lick you into shape in no time. I'll just tidy your hair and then I'll crimp you. Come this way and I'll find you a seat.'

Primped and preened and gowned, Rose returned to her

mission. 'You mentioned confidence. Some women just have it, don't they, while the rest of us – I merely speak for myself – are much less sure of ourselves.' Madame Estelle's murmured reply was non-committal. She snipped at a lock of hair. 'I expect the young lady I saw has a glamorous job to go with her coiffure and clothing,' Rose continued, but the use of a sophisticated term cut no ice. Madame Estelle mumbled and carried on scissoring. Rose tried not to look down. She already had a bob; was she now being bingled? More hair fell to the floor. Crikey: was she about to be shingled?

Thankfully, Estelle put her scissors aside. 'That's you tidier, miss. Now for some curls.'

'I expect you do a lot of young women's hair – bachelor girls and so forth,' Rose said, as Estelle advanced with the evil-looking crimpers. Ouch. Their teeth were exceedingly sharp, but one must suffer for one's work. This thought gave Rose a lead: 'I expect a lot of young women talk to you about their work these days,' she tried again.

'Oh, you wouldn't believe the things they tell me,' Madame Estelle said, sounding more relaxed now that she had progressed to crimping. 'I had a young lady in here only the other day telling me how she and her young man long to marry but can't afford for her to give up her job. I thought she was going to weep on me, I did. A teacher she was. And office workers, too – struggling. Some of them look like they don't know what's hit them. I've never fancied an office job myself or wanted to be a teacher. Mind you, we all have to earn a living, even some of those young women who didn't expect to.'

'I imagine the young lady I saw has an interesting job,' Rose persisted. 'It's funny, isn't it, how you sometimes weave whole stories around people you see in the street? That young lady, for instance: she really did have something. I can imagine her living in a smart flat with all the latest gadgets: a cocktail shaker, jazzy pottery and whatnot. Does she work in interior design, by any chance?' Steady, Rose, she told herself.

'No, miss, nothing like that. In fact,' Madame Estelle leaned towards the mirror and spoke across the top of Rose's head, 'she manages a matrimonial agency.'

Bingo. 'Gosh, how very modern.'

'Isn't it just? I don't know that I'd have the nerve – to use one, that is.'

'Me neither, but how intriguing. And that does make sense. It would take a modern young woman to run one. She must meet all sorts. Did she pass on any romantic tips?'

'Well, she did say that many of the women who apply would like a man like the ones on the films. You know, someone with smouldering looks. Mind you,' Estelle chuckled, 'there's not many men as silent as that in real life.'

Rose laughed at the joke. She must think what to ask next. 'And what about the gentlemen – where does she find them?'

'She hasn't said, although she does say she's always busy.'

'A matrimonial agency . . .' Rose pretended to ponder the concept. 'I wonder where she learned how to run something like that. I wouldn't have the first idea . . .' She opened her eyes wide and raised her eyebrows encouragingly, but Madame Estelle did not respond. Instead, she lifted another clump of hair and gripped it with another vicious metal clip. 'And she looked so smart,' Rose prodded. 'Perhaps she was about to matchmake for someone important . . .' But the hairdresser carried on crimping.

Finally, when she reached the end of another serried row, Madame Estelle spoke. 'The young women of today,' she said, 'from the way they dress, it's hard to distinguish between them. When they walk through that door' – she gestured towards the street – 'they might be the daughter of a duke or a washer-woman. Until they open their mouths, of course.'

Rose begged to differ, although not out loud. She could spot differences in dress at twenty paces; quality spoke for itself, and she doubted there were many dukes in the vicinity. Nonetheless, Madame Estelle was right about the different voices – until the Miss Porters of the world succeeded in changing all that with their elocution classes. But this won't do, Rose told herself; a tip-top investigator would not allow herself to be side-tracked in this way. She must get back down to business. 'But Miss—' Rose began, then corrected herself. 'The young lady who was here before me, the one who so impressed me with her stylish hair' – Madame Estelle gave another self-satisfied smile; thank goodness you could never praise anyone too much – 'she strikes me as being really sophisticated; she does look the part, that is. I suppose she must be single to run a matrimonial agency.'

Madame Estelle paused in her crimping. At last. Those metal teeth were brutal. 'I don't think she has a wedding ring,' she considered, 'though I could be misremembering. That's something I always check. When you've been cutting ladies' hair as long as I have, you keep an eye out for these things. It's a good way to start up a conversation, put a new customer at ease and make sure I don't put my foot in it. It can be a touchy subject. Mind you,' she looked pointedly at Rose. 'I can nearly always tell.'

'I'm not married,' Rose said. 'I'm too busy earning a crust.'

'Well, we all have to earn our keep,' she said again; her role must require a ready fund of platitudes. 'There, that's you done.' The crimpers were finally in place. Rose thought her head might explode. 'I'll just apply the lotion. It does whiff a bit. You might have to take shallow breaths.'

Rose was anointed with the pungent lotion. Her eyes watered; any kind of breathing became difficult. Estelle gave a final, determined squirt and asked, 'Would you like a magazine? I've *Home Chat* or *Good Housekeeping*.'

Rose took a magazine from the top of the pile and opened it at a short story. 'The Questing Thirties: Love comes to youth, but middle age must hunt for it. And then, if you are a woman, it flees from you. After thirty, is your place on life's sidelines?' She turned the page and found an article on corsets. 'Know Yourself – Make the Best of your Good Lines, But Do Not Fail to Correct Your Defects' – and an advertisement for 'Rodiod, a remarkable fat reducer: it quickly gives thick, ungainly ankles, double chins, unbecoming wrists, arms and shoulders a normal fashionable contour. Call or send for a jar at once.' And to think that Madame Estelle provided these magazines to cheer her clients while they awaited their own transformations. The fashion page offered an inventive solution to 'Girls for whom Economy is a Must.' Apparently, one dress with a detachable collar and separate sleeves was able to fulfil many functions. With the addition of the collar and sleeves, it became an afternoon frock; minus sleeves, the economizing young woman was immediately dressed for dinner; and with no sleeves or collar, and a pretty flower pinned at her waist, the evening (and, no doubt, Prince Charming) awaited. Rose closed the magazine and put it to the bottom of the pile – that was quite enough guidance for one afternoon.

Forty minutes later, she emerged with an identikit hairstyle. Madame Estelle hovered. 'I hope this is what you expected?'

Rose was able to reply without dissembling. 'Thank you.

This style is quite unlike anything I've had before.' What else could she say? She reeked of perming lotion, was one and nine-pence down, and no wiser than when she'd set out. She didn't even know if Madame Estelle thought Miss Lane was married. But, Rose reminded herself, there was one consolation: at least she was not yet thirty.

'It'll soften,' Rose told Ginny.

'Yes, but what possessed you?'

'Miss Holmes. While I was on the trail of Cupid's Arrow, I saw the manager go into a hairdressing salon. I thought I might learn something if I went in afterwards.' Rose studied her hair in the bedroom mirror and attempted to settle its stiff peaks. 'Sadly, Miss Lane had not chosen the Mayfair salon Tallulah Bankhead favours, but Madame Estelle's in East Dulwich.'

But Ginny wasn't willing to be appeased. 'You need to give this up, Rose. You can't keep trailing after Cupid's Arrow and then have to sit up half the night sewing. Even without the Townsend wedding and all its razzamatazz, there's now Miss Jennings's two-piece. You're trying to do far too much.'

'But Miss Holmes still won't go to the police.'

'I know you feel sorry for her, and so do I – the whole thing is appalling – and I know how angry you are at Cupid's Arrow and what they've done to us all, but I suspect that it appeals to your vanity to think you will be the one to expose them.'

Rose bridled. 'That's unkind.'

'But true.'

'Perhaps,' Rose said, although they both knew Ginny was right. 'But we now know that not only is Miss Lane involved, as well as the dancer; there is also someone else out there preying on vulnerable women. "Reginald Wilson" could be deceiving some other hopeful as we speak.'

Ginny looked at Rose; Rose returned her long, hard look. Eventually, Ginny said, 'What's the use . . . We both know that, regardless of what I say, you're not going to drop this, so why not approach it like a tricky design you can't quite resolve, and then see how best to align the different elements.' Rose had a vision of complicated drapes and folds and then, oh, the joy of the end result! Ginny groaned at the delighted look on her face. 'Why am I saying this to you when, frankly, all your – and our – efforts should be directed towards lace and chiffon and silk. But, as you *are* going to continue with this – and you patently are,' she said before Rose could offer even the feeblest denial, 'you'll need more information. You need to go and see Miss Holmes again as soon as she gets back from her aunt's.'

'And, in the meantime,' Rose said appeasingly, glancing again at the bedroom mirror, 'I have no plans to go anywhere. For the rest of the week, I will be here sewing. I'll catch up on sleep and, gradually, my hair will begin to look a little less corrugated and more like my own. You'll see. Everything will come together.' Rose crossed her fingers behind her back.

27

It was a Wednesday afternoon just over a week later, and Rose was sitting, once more, in the Stygian gloom of The Laurels, looking out at a hypericum and the bank of spotted laurels for which the house was named. The sitting room was a trifle less gloomy today; even its north-facing windows could not entirely eradicate the July sunlight. Cups of tea had been served and, as soon as the usual pleasantries had been exchanged and she'd enquired about Miss Holmes's trip, Rose got down to brass tacks.

'Your letters, Miss Holmes – the letters Mr Wilson wrote to you. Did you keep them?'

'Of course.' Miss Holmes blushed. 'I should perhaps destroy them, but I can't quite bring myself to do that.' Even these words pained her.

'I understand. In fact, I'm sure you are wise not to. After all, Miss Holmes, the letters are proof of Mr Wilson's expressed intentions and your own mistreatment.' Rose paused to let her words sink in, but Miss Holmes was unable to hear them. Rose started again. 'I think you said that Mr Wilson wrote to you on hotel notepaper. I've been wondering if the different addresses might yield some information – help to give a picture of his movements and perhaps to identify him.' She was not prepared to add that she wanted to discover how much, if any, of his cover story was actually true. She couldn't ask Miss

Holmes to face that possibility just yet. 'Would you be willing to tell me the names and addresses of the places Mr Wilson wrote from?'

'If you think it will help.' Miss Holmes offered Rose a seat at the table near the window and left the room. She returned with an inlaid workbox. 'I keep the letters here.' She opened the lid to reveal its pink satin lining. How many keepsakes nestled at the bottom of sewing boxes like this one, Rose wondered. Miss Holmes lifted out the inner tray of needles, cottons and other sewing paraphernalia, and retrieved a slim package of letters from the hidden compartment beneath. The letters were tied with a band of blue velvet ribbon. Miss Holmes put the package on the table in front of her.

From where Rose was sitting, opposite Miss Holmes, and with an expanse of rosewood tabletop between them, it was impossible to read the handwriting on the envelopes. It was agonizing to have Mr Wilson's letters so close and yet untouchable. Miss Holmes fingered the letters as if they might scorch her; she seemed to be willing herself to untie the velvet knot. A knock on the sitting-room door interrupted them.

'I'm sorry to disturb you, Miss Holmes' – it was Sarah, the maid – 'but there's been a mix-up with the laundry and I've got Mr Bradshaw here.'

'Just a minute, Sarah. Will you excuse me, Miss Burnham?' Miss Holmes rose from the table, looking uncomfortably at the letters waiting there. 'I'll just have a word with Sarah.'

The two women stood talking in the hall. Miss Holmes had her back to Rose, but the door remained open; Rose could hear stray words from their conversation, and they could just as easily hear her, or indeed see her, if they were to look. What was she to do? She longed to reach for the first letter and examine the handwriting. There wasn't time for her to read the letter itself – Rose hardly liked to grasp that glancing thought; she would not betray Miss Holmes, or herself, in that way – but the handwritten envelopes weren't private and were waiting there in plain sight. It wouldn't hurt to look at the first one. Rose stood up and walked towards the window, a perfectly natural gesture, something anyone might do to pass the time when their hostess was called away. En route, she peered at the top-most envelope.

The handwriting meant nothing to her. The lettering was rounded with extravagant loops on the 'P' and 'L' and a downward slash on the 'T'. That at least put Mr Martin in the clear. Rose wasn't sure if she felt relieved or not; she had already decided he was a genuine romancer, if not a very accomplished one. But all of that was for another day. Rose studied Miss Holmes's address, determined that she would recognize the handwriting if she saw it again but, to be on the safe side, she had better jot something down. She made a scribbled copy of the key letters in the back of her notebook and looked up just in time: Miss Holmes had re-entered the room.

'Now, where were we?' Miss Holmes asked, resuming her seat and taking possession of the letters once more. Her words were not just a mere turn of phrase; she was patently stalling.

'Your letters, Miss Holmes,' Rose said. 'You were going to check the names and addresses of the different hotels.'

'Indeed.' But she still seemed reluctant to untie the ribbon and release them. Too painful, Rose supposed. As of course it would be. 'I've fastened the knot too tightly, Miss Burnham. I have some little scissors in the bureau that will help me to prise it open.' She began to rise again from her chair.

'Let me get them for you.' Rose couldn't face another delay.

'Would you mind, Miss Burnham? Thank you. They're silver scissors in the shape of a crane. You'll know the type – the beak makes for nice sharp points.' Rose found the small scissors straight away and handed them to Miss Holmes. 'Thank you, Miss Burnham.' Rose sat back down and tried not to look as greedy for information as she felt.

There was no further reason to prevaricate and yet Miss Holmes picked at the ribbon with a delicacy Rose found excruciating. 'The first letter was from Herne Bay, I recall,' Miss Holmes said, pausing again before she'd managed to untie the knot, 'but we'll check the address on each one.' She started opening envelopes, naming a location, date and hotel, before putting each letter aside and moving on to the next: Herne Bay, Eastbourne, Worthing, Broadstairs, Margate and towns adjacent. They were nearly all seaside resorts.

Miss Holmes paused in her search. 'I hadn't really taken that in,' she said, when Rose mentioned this. 'I suppose I was far more interested in the letters themselves, and the promise of our next meeting, than in where they were written from. And, of course, Reginald didn't live in any of these places; he was just passing through for a night.'

'Yes, of course,' Rose said. How easy it was to miss what you weren't looking for.

28

Dear Miss Lipton

*Allegra – How proud I feel to be able to write your first
name, and such a delightful name as yours. How wonderful
that we two are sympatico. If you would care to join me,
same time, same place, on Saturday, I will have a surprise
for you . . .*

Yours
Edward

Rose cringed. She couldn't help it. She had always been
told to listen kindly and do as she would be done by, but 'sympatico'? Really? Mr Martin must have swallowed *The Ardent
Lover's Guide to Courtship* or some other such manual. But a
surprise: what might that be? What had he got up his sleeve?

Mr Martin – Edward – waved two tickets at Rose: two tickets
for a mystery bus tour. How enterprising, how unexpected. No
revelations, then, no declarations or whisking her off her feet,
just two lonely people side by side in an open-topped charabanc.
Where might their journey lead? Never mind the mysterious
route the tickets promised; what about their two bodies pressed
against one another, confined by a tiny seat?
The morning was clouding over. Romance rarely blooms

when drenched. Did Mr Martin have a Plan B? Rose, who had brought a parasol, now noticed that her companion carried a brolly. Oh dear, they looked set for all eventualities. 'This way,' he said. 'Follow me. The chara leaves in twenty minutes.' Mr Martin sounded positively sprightly. How ever was she going to let him know that this would be their last meeting?

All aboard through Sydenham and down into West Dulwich, sweeping on towards what Rose mistakenly assumed would eventually be central London, but then, somehow, the charabanc doubled back. They were now heading into Kent, via Bickley and Petts Wood, destined for who knew what hidden places. The journey would have been uncomfortable enough – too intimate by far in this cramped space – but all too soon Rose was conscious of Edward Martin's burning gaze. He seemed to be taking in her every feature; oh dear, was he about to declare his undying devotion? But, no: Miss Lipton's hat was askew; he was squinting at her corrugated hair. Had his mother not taught him it was rude to stare? Rose straightened her hat and stared back. Mr Martin recovered himself, and so their odyssey continued.

Rose saw large houses dotted among small ones, large gardens too, hinting at distinguished pasts, and then hedgerows, fields and intermittent villages, and still they trundled on, with Mr Martin pointing out things of interest and Rose trapped beside him. At last, they reached the countryside proper, with fields defining farmland and oast houses standing proud. And all the while Edward Martin kept up his commentary: types of farm building, barns and houses; styles of rooftop – pediment, gable, thatch. Against this list, the countryside barely counted. If this was a magical history tour, the magic was wearing thin. At last, Mr Martin changed tack.

'Allegra,' Mr Martin said. 'Such an unusual name, so invent-ive.' He paused. 'A rose by any other name . . .'

This phrase was hardly new to Rose; it had been quoted too many times within her hearing, but on this occasion she blanched. Why now? Had Edward Martin plucked something out of the air, something vaguely romantic he thought she would like, or – grim thought – did he want her to know he had found out her real name?

'Do you read much Shakespeare?' Rose jumped in before he could say anything further. If Edward Martin was part of the Cupid's Arrow plot after all, she didn't want him to realize that she now suspected as much. But Mr Martin merely looked puzzled. 'The quote . . .' she explained.

'Oh. Really? No. It was written on the lid of a box of fancy soaps my mother had. I've never forgotten it.'

Rose nodded her acknowledgement. His reply seemed nat-ural enough.

'When the soaps were finished, my mother used the box for her beads. She only had the one string of beads, but they smelled of scented soap ever after. Such a strong smell, it was – and how it lingered . . .'

'How nice.' But was it? Rose's thoughts still snagged on that quote, although surely her admirer couldn't have invented all that about the soaps, and so swiftly – unless he was remarkably quick on his feet.

'My mother liked nice soaps,' Rose said, and immediately wished she had not. Her mother was too precious to be squan-dered on Edward Martin.

'Women do.' Perhaps scented soaps were not to his liking.

What to say next? Rose wondered. Romance must be such

hard work. But then, other people were not continually second-guessing if their companion was a fraudster or not.

'I once saw a competition in the paper in which women were asked to describe their ideal man.'

'Oh, yes? And were they all after a Valentino-type?' Mr Martin affected disdain, but sounded sulky, like a boy not picked for the team.

Poor man: he was obviously carrying the wounds of past slights. 'No, not all. I think they just wanted someone honest and straightforward, someone who wouldn't let them down.' Although, Rose recalled, some of the replies had been couched in excessively sentimental terms.

'Well, that's fair enough. And yet it's hard to know what women today *do* want.'

Oh dear. Mr Martin's mood was cooling along with the temperature; it looked like their umbrellas could be required at any moment. The whole afternoon had become a decidedly damp squib. Perhaps she should have shown more appreciation of Mr Martin's choice of mystery tour and his interminable explanations. 'I expect we all have our dreams,' Rose said. A non-committal reply seemed best.

But non-committal would not do. Mr Martin was not to be dissuaded. 'Oh, I've had my dreams, but it's a woman's world these days. The mere man barely gets a look-in.' The sneer behind his words was unmistakable.

'Really?' Allegra Lipton disappeared; this was Rose Burnham speaking. 'Is that what you really think?' There was no mistaking her feelings, either.

Mr Martin recovered himself. 'And good luck to them, I say.'

For the next few miles, they travelled in silence, as dull as the day itself. It was drizzling now, which at least gave Rose the excuse to open her parasol and erect a useful barrier. Now she became even more conscious of Mr Martin's damp sleeve pressing against her left elbow.

The drizzle stopped and Mr Martin rallied. 'Look over there,' he said, twisting in his seat. 'This is the bit I like.' This tour was obviously no mystery to him. He pointed to a manor house in the distance, its frontage concealed by trees, its numerous turreted chimneys claiming its right to stand in the landscape. Rose was struck by his newly animated features. His delight was unmistakable and, when the house emerged from behind the trees, she agreed it was a handsome building. Surely Edward Martin's delight couldn't be anything other than genuine? He was quite a poetic soul, really, albeit one with deeply conservative views. Though he was not alone in those.

Someone, somewhere, might find him charming, if his was the kind of charm they liked, and if they were happy to endure all his many facts and lists. But enough was enough. He might be a dull man, but he was definitely not Miss Holmes's deceiver. This would be their last meeting. Even so, Rose did not have the courage to tell him face to face. She would have to write him a 'regretful' letter care of Cupid's Arrow. The words began to take shape: 'Dear Edward, much as I have valued your company, I do not feel we are . . .' Fated? Destined? '. . . to tread life's path together.' Would something like that soften the blow? Yes. She would write the letter tonight and post it first thing in the morning.

29

Roses 'by any other name', letters, seaside towns: what was their significance, and was Reginald Wilson lurking on a seafront right now? These thoughts ambushed Rose at odd moments – like this one, for instance, when she needed all her attention for Miss Jennings's summer two-piece, and especially its edge-to-edge jacket, which Miss Jennings was now assessing. How gratifying – and how reassuring – that the restyling she'd requested last year had resulted in this commission.

Rose stepped back and appraised the result of her latest dawn-chorus achievement. She'd been up until midnight and begun sewing again at five, staring at her work until spots danced before her eyes. The line of an edge-to-edge jacket must be perfect, and the look of this particular jacket was accentuated by the floral trim that picked up the pattern of the dress underneath, Miss Jennings having been dissuaded from choosing all-over florals for both.

Now it was Miss Jennings's turn. She moved towards the fitting-room mirror and, smoothing the foulard silk at her hips and turning to check the effect, looked hard and appraised herself. Turning again, she yawned and patted her mouth with her left hand. The small stones on the gold band she wore on her little finger caught the sunlight. 'Forgive me, Miss Burnham. The week's catching up with me.'

The two-piece, Miss Jennings explained, was her summer

indulgence. Rose wanted to do it justice, all the more so because Miss Jennings spent most days in office drab. Rose might be in awe of her Civil-Service status, but she despaired of her weekday clothes: stolid tweed suits with reinforced elbows and (Rose happened to know) reinforced backsides. Miss Jennings's suits were every bit as hard-working as she was. It was quite a shock to reconfigure her in off-duty florals, but she deserved every wallflower and peony.

'This will have its first airing next weekend,' Miss Jennings was saying. 'My friend and I are lunching out and then spending the afternoon at Kew Gardens – a rare lazy day for us both. Our weekends are usually more mundane.'

'I hope you have a lovely time,' Rose said, 'and that the weather holds. I'm sure you both deserve an indulgence.'

'Yes, weeks spent vetting documents or marking essays may be good for the soul, but they don't offer much in the way of entertainment.'

'Your friend is a teacher?'

'Yes, Miss Compton and I met some fifteen years ago and have roomed together ever since.'

'How fortunate, and what a nice arrangement. How lucky that the two of you have been able to room together all this time.'

Miss Jennings looked down at her dress. 'Yes, isn't it. And Isobel – Miss Compton – loves gardening and is so looking forward to Kew. She's the green-fingered one, so it's lovely to be able to treat her for her birthday.' Miss Jennings blushed. It was warm in the fitting-room this afternoon. 'Oh, this is just the thing, Miss Burnham. Thank you for all your hard work.' Miss Jennings did look lovely, and quite different. The pastel pinks suited her fair hair and soft features. At this moment, she looked rather like a peony herself.

'Miss Jennings,' Rose said later, while her client was changing back into her usual drab. 'You're a woman in a man's
world . . .'

'I think the same could be said for all of us, Miss Burnham,
don't you?'

'Yes – but professionally, I mean. You've risen through the
ranks where few women have managed to do so. Has that ever
given rise to any . . . unpleasantness?'

'Unpleasantness?' Miss Jennings emerged from behind the
screen. 'Within the Civil Service or outside?'

'Either, really. Someone being devious or behaving badly
towards you; someone who resented your position or progress?'

'Oh, Miss Burnham!' Miss Jennings laughed. 'Where to start?
I could mention the wag who put a frog inside my desk on my
very first morning, or the prankster who filled my inkwell with
sand. There were various incidents along those lines. I laugh
about them now and had to pretend I found them amusing
then. This was a long time ago, of course, when women were
still decided oddities in clerical roles. Things like that would be
described as high jinks and I knew better than to complain or
break ranks. I also learned to work twice as hard as the men I
worked alongside and to never, ever put a foot wrong . . . But
one takes these things in one's stride. Everyone I work with has
worked hard to attain their level in the Service and made sacrifices in order to do so. I was told early on to forget you are a
woman but, latterly, especially now that I'm a Principal and
manage female staff, I find that being a woman helps. Why do
you ask? Has something happened to you, Miss Burnham?'

'Oh no, not to me – to a friend of mine. She's received an
anonymous letter. I expect it was someone being spiteful, or
else feeling wounded and lashing out.'

'I'm sorry to hear that. How distasteful. One keeps hoping things will change. There's a new entrance scheme for young women who see the Civil Service as a career. I hope that means things will be different, although one can never be sure, and of course they will have to give up so much.' She continued looking at Rose. 'I don't suppose you've had it easy, either.' Miss Jennings stepped towards her and touched Rose's hand. 'A word of advice, Miss Burnham. There will always be petty-minded people who don't want you to live your own life. Believe me, I do know. But what matters is being true to yourself and what you achieve.

'Now,' she said, in a lighter tone, 'I've been thinking: could you make me a cravat? Something with embroidery, like the ones the older Miss Burnham wears. They look rather splendid on her, and I'd like something I could wear with a white blouse and dark skirt. It's time I spruced up my clothes. Nothing too elaborate, mind. I leave the colour and pattern up to you.'

'It will be a pleasure, Miss Jennings,' Rose said, and it would be, too. She added the cravat to her mental list of 'must do's'.

Before Rose had a chance to consider quite when that additional task would be accomplished, there was a distraction in the offing: the Saturday-afternoon post had brought another note from Miss Porter. Rose saw the envelope on the hall table as she showed Miss Jennings to the door. Perhaps Miss Porter would now like a companion lecture: 'How to Dress Badly: Pitfalls and How to Avoid Them'. But no: the envelope contained an invitation to a party, no less: *Miss Porter At Home, Thursday 23 July, Canapés, 7 o'clock, RSVP 24 Prospect Street.* And how delightful: an engraved card with lettering in copperplate script and her own name added to the top left-hand corner, just as it should be. Would she have to sing for her supper with more conversational entrées on dress, Rose wondered, or might this be her opportunity to establish the link, if any, between Miss Porter and Cupid's Arrow?

30

The front door to 24 Prospect Street was ajar when Rose arrived. She braced herself, walked up the short flight of steps and followed an unknown person into the entrance hall. Miss Porter's soirée was taking place in a ground-floor flat with a large bay window overlooking the street. The double room stretched the full length of the building; folding doors, which were currently open, divided it and its functions in two. An upright piano, topped with a mint-green and pale-pink runner, displayed a row of photographs and small trophies, including an inscribed statuette of a dancer, which had evidently been presented to Miss Porter at some point. A series of framed certificates announced other past successes, as did a hand-tinted photograph in which a junior Miss Porter in a Bo-Peep gown danced with a girl in pantaloons. This section of the room was a statement of accomplishments, while a slightly shabby day bed, a circular table and other prosaic furnishings told of Miss Porter's day-to-day life. Rose had envisaged something more modern, but then few people – herself included – could afford to be as up-to-the-minute as they would like.

Nonetheless, Miss Porter had pulled out all the stops. Another table, in the back half of the room, held the promised canapés and a selection of sandwiches. White bread cut into dainty triangles alternated with small rolls streaked with anchovy paste. Little paper flags posted atop each plate indicated anchovy, cream cheese and celery, tongue. And there were jugs of fruit cup afloat with orange wheels, and quantities of tiny cheese savouries. Some half-dozen young women from the deportment class (although, no one Rose recognized) were nimbly circulating with fruit cup, savouries and small talk – another of their lessons in 'How to'. Miss Porter also circulated, looking animated, holding court.

Rose had decided on a smoky-blue tea-gown and draped her dress with a long, narrow, amber scarf. She thought she'd made the right choice, although, despite the hour, the few people who'd arrived ahead of her were wearing afternoon frocks. Rose accepted a glass of fruit cup and looked about her. The party had yet to acquire its own momentum. Introductory conversations were punctured by the rhythmical thud of the door knocker announcing each new guest. Stray words pierced the air and hung there; a gramophone would have helped. Then several guests arrived in swift succession and suddenly the room came to life.

Miss Porter appeared at Rose's elbow. 'Can I introduce you to Mrs Eagleton, Miss Burnham? Mr Eagleton is a local businessman; their daughter attends my classes and is also here this evening.' She gestured at a sylph-like figure distributing fruit cup. 'Miss Burnham is a designer,' Miss Porter explained, 'and recently came to advise my young ladies how to dress.' Miss Porter's own etiquette was, of course, impeccable.

'How nice to meet you,' Mrs Eagleton said, and proceeded to speak of the weather and her daughter's attainments since joining Miss Porter's class, before asking Rose, did she think waistbands would drop even further? They were practically around one's calves as it was.

The party was swelling nicely. A small group of women, standing shoulder to shoulder, were leaning into one another, deep in a conversation it was impossible to overhear. Three men, in their own larger circle, feet spread firmly apart like a Gilbert and Sullivan chorus, were broadcasting their views to the room. Single, emphatic words – coal – taxes – prices – punctuated their talk. Except for a side-parting, a watch-chain and a Ramsay MacDonald moustache, there was little to distinguish one man from the next. At least the women's clothing allowed them to make a stab at individuality.

'Good evening.' A voice Rose couldn't quite place spoke over her left shoulder.

She turned and immediately felt herself blush. It was the charming man from the Dulwich Picture Gallery. Her insides somersaulted. 'What a surprise,' she managed to say.

'A pleasant surprise, I hope.'

'What brings you here?' Rose dodged.

'Oh, a friend of a friend,' he said, surveying the room. 'Do you think an artist would find something here worth painting?'

'A still life, you mean, or a street scene? Not that it's a particularly distinguished view.'

'Oh, I'm not sure about that. I think Camille Pissarro thought differently. Didn't he paint some scenes here or round about? Although his London was rather different to ours.' The charming man looked at Rose as if he might like to paint her. 'Is there a scene *you'd* like to see on canvas?'

Rose thought for a moment or two. 'Coming back into London on the train,' she said, surprising herself, 'on the few occasions I've been away, there's a particular point where the city starts to take hold and you can feel its energy rising through even the smallest details: the lines of washing in back yards, the yards themselves, row upon row of busy lives lived in tight spaces, people glimpsed through windows; and the train itself, slowing down as if to capture the sight. It's not an especially attractive view, so perhaps a painter would reject it, but whenever the train reaches this point, I know I'm almost home. That scene says something to me about belonging. I can't say exactly what.' Rose stopped, embarrassed, and looked down at her glass. 'Goodness,' she said. 'Whatever has Miss Porter put in the fruit cup?'

He smiled. 'Go on. I'm interested to hear more.'

But Rose had regained her usual self. 'And what about you? Do you have a favourite view?'

'Around here, do you mean? I've been away, so I'm getting used to the place again. It's the same, but different, as places so often are. That's why I like to visit galleries. There's always something there to intrigue me.' He looked directly at Rose. The hairs on the back of her neck prickled, her fingers slipped on her glass . . . But here was Miss Porter at her elbow.

'I'm sorry to interrupt you, Miss Burnham, but can I lure Mr Spender away? I'd offered to introduce him to someone who has just this minute arrived and can't stay long.'

'Yes, of course.' How else could she have replied? How insistent Miss Porter was, always mixing and mingling, and her guests must do the same. This must be another talent her young charges would acquire.

'Will you excuse me?' The charming man put his tumbler down on a bureau and followed Miss Porter. Rose watched his retreating back. Mr Spender: not the name she'd have guessed for him, but then, what had she envisaged? She put her own glass down beside his.

Miss Porter was back again. Evidently, Rose was not to be let off, either. 'Miss Burnham, may I introduce you . . .' and so the next hour passed. From time to time, Rose caught sight of the charming man – Mr Spender – but there was no chance to reconnect with him, the one guest who, as far as she was concerned, was the only other guest here. Their glasses marked the spot where the two of them had stood. During their brief exchange, something indefinable in the atmosphere had changed. The still life on the bureau recorded that.

A voice jolted Rose from her thoughts. She heard her before she saw her; heard the slippery accent that identified Miss Lane. Rose shivered and felt cold, completely different sensations from those she'd experienced an hour earlier. Miss Lane was standing at the far end of the room and, thankfully, looking elsewhere. Rose didn't like to doubt her own powers of disguise, but this was not the moment for Miss Lipton to be unmasked. She needed to make her escape.

'Will you excuse me,' Rose said, interrupting a conversation about sweet peas in which she had no foothold. Thank goodness she was not still talking to the charming man. She turned away and, keeping her head down and making herself as inconspicuous as possible, concentrated on moving towards the edge of the room and the doorway. She heard Miss Porter say, 'Help yourself to food and then let me introduce you.' It would only take a minute for Miss Lane to put one or two of those dainty sandwiches on to a plate. Rose couldn't risk another of Miss Porter's impeccable introductions.

Rose dared not pause in her manoeuvrings or try to catch Mr Spender's eye. She would have to leave without saying goodbye or, indeed, thanking her host. 'Leaving already?' someone asked. 'I must, I'm afraid,' Rose mumbled. 'I suddenly feel unwell.'

There was no one in the hall to delay her, thank goodness. Rose grabbed her jacket and hat, and dashed down the front steps and out on to the street without stopping to put them on. Some yards further down, she leaned against a wall and began to catch her breath.

31

'I was at Miss Porter's house last night, Grace.' Rose was check-ing the position at which the sleeves met the shoulder seams on Grace Townsend's bridesmaid's dress.

'Oh, yes?' Grace said, looking at herself and not at Rose.

'Yes. Miss Porter had a small party and some of her young ladies were there, circulating with canapés and fruit cup. I thought I might see you, too.' Although thank heavens she had not. It would have been impossible to get away if Grace had been present and all too keen to polish her technique for intro-ducing guests to one another.

'Oh, Miss Porter did mention something,' Grace said in an offhand manner, 'but I was busy last night.'

'Where are you up to in your classes?'

'Pardon?' Grace looked taken aback.

'Your deportment classes. Can you drop your shoulders please? Thank you; it's hard to check the sleeves if you tense your shoulders. What was it today?'

'I'm sorry? Oh . . . deportment. More deportment: be sure not to slouch, and that kind of thing.'

Grace Townsend was distracted. Come to think of it, she had been distracted for some weeks, arriving late for the charity fête and for today's appointment: 'I'm sorry, Miss Burnham, I had some letters to post' – even her apology demonstrated an uncharacteristic reserve. There was a subtle difference in her clothing, too; her dress was somewhat more sober and fewer bangles jangled when she moved. Yes, there was something different about Grace.

'Are you happy with the sleeves?'

'Absolutely.' But Grace wasn't concentrating. This was the first time Rose had had to nudge her for a response. What was going on with her?

'You will look a dream in this,' Rose said, expecting the usual exclamatory reply, but none was forthcoming. 'Are you heading home afterwards?' Rose asked, for something to say.

'Yes, I've got some letters to write.'

'More letters?' Rose asked, thinking to make light of her new predilection for letter-writing.

'Yes, Miss Burnham,' Grace said, and left it at that.

That was odd, Rose thought later, while putting the fitting-room to rights. But then why should Grace always be vivacious? Perhaps she was unlucky in love . . . Oh, not another one – Rose banished that possibility. Grace Townsend was entitled to be distracted, just like anyone else. And, anyway, why should everything come back to romance? That was not the focus of her own life. A vision of Mr Spender appeared before her. Rose blinked it away and adjusted the magazines.

'Look what I found on the doorstep,' Alice said, coming into the sitting room that evening and dumping her hat, summer string gloves and assorted bags on to the nearest chair.

'Oh good, you're just in time,' Ginny called from the scullery. 'I'm about to dish up. How was Maud?' she asked, distributing potatoes across three plates, her back turned to Alice and to Rose, who was busy setting the table.

'Very well. She's got an interview at Sapphiro's next week.' Alice named a successful West End milliner.

Rose looked up. 'You're sure you're not tempted to try there yourself?'

'Not a bit. I like the idea of offering bespoke hats as well as gowns. It will give us a certain cachet.'

'As long as you are sure.' Thank goodness, Rose thought. She would hate to lose Alice now. She smiled at her, but then changed her tone. 'What's that you're holding, Alice?'

'That's what I was trying to tell you. I found it on the doorstep. I would have left it, only . . . it's a rose.'

'How lovely,' Ginny said, without turning round. 'It must have blown in from someone's garden.'

'I don't think so.' Rose stared at the rose as if this was the first time she had seen one. 'It's shrivelled.'

'And it can't have blown from anywhere,' Alice explained. 'It was right in the middle of the doorstep. Someone must have put it there.'

'And it has withered leaves,' Rose added. 'And a bow tied around its stem.'

Ginny gasped and, saucepan still in hand, turned to face her sisters. 'I think it really is time you stopped this, Rose. Something very odd is going on here.'

'It's someone's idea of a prank,' Rose bluffed, although her heart had leapt into her throat. 'You've read too many stories in which bad things happen down dark alleyways.' She hardly liked to admit, even to herself, how much this rose unnerved her.

That night, before she went to bed, Rose stepped into the workroom, looked out the largest darning needle they possessed and slipped it into her jacket pocket.

*

Rose was disturbed by a gale of laughter; a harsh, brittle sound that appeared to come from outside. She went downstairs and opened the front door. Miss Lane stood on the doorstep. She was wearing her crocheted dress and a tangle of long scarves, the kind of scarves Rose designed and often wore, but there was something incongruous about these. They were knotted in the wrong places and she was wearing several at once. As soon as she saw Rose, Miss Lane stepped back on to the path and stood, arms open, as if announcing her presence to all and sundry. Miss Lane continued laughing, braying almost. She was notifying the whole street, never mind the whole household.

Finally, Miss Lane spoke. 'Did you like the rose I left you, Miss Burnham?'

Rose woke with a start. Her nightdress was twisted around her legs, and she had hauled most of the sheets on to her side of the bed. It was three in the morning. Ginny was sleeping soundly, and all was quiet – except for Rose's pounding heart. Fear drenched her, wrapping itself around her as tightly as her sodden nightclothes. Three o'clock became three thirty, three thirty ticked towards four. Rose lay in the dark and silence, waiting for her panic to subside.

PART 4

A Grand Adventure

32

'I wasn't sure if you would come,' the charming man, Jack Spender, said in greeting. Rose hadn't been sure, either. She was stunned when his invitation dropped on to the mat at the start of the week. And now, was she really here? 'Although I suppose it's a quick getaway I should prepare for,' he continued. 'You seem to make a habit of disappearing.'

How to answer that? 'Ah, Miss Porter's soirée,' Rose said. 'I suddenly felt unwell, light-headed – the heat. As more people arrived, the room became quite stuffy.'

'I see.' He held her gaze.

Did he believe her? She truly did feel light-headed now. She was still trying to absorb the fact that he'd written, and so soon; she was still picturing the confident swoop of the 'J' in the 'Jack Spender' with which he'd signed his note. He must have written the very day after the party. This was all so new and so fast; there was no etiquette manual for it.

Rose needed to reclaim surer ground. 'I was surprised to receive your note,' she said, and was surprised now to hear how matter-of-fact her voice sounded. 'How did you find me? Did Miss Porter give you my address?'

In reply, Jack Spender took Rose by the elbow and steered her towards the gate that led into the recreation ground where that afternoon's entertainment would take place: an aerial performance promising 'joy flips' and one-guinea rides. His fingers held her securely; she could feel each one through her thin knitted jacket. The sensation blew her question away. What did it matter where he got her address? They were here this afternoon. They passed a stall selling sugary confections and a 'hit the jackpot' machine. The smell of hot spun sugar was overpowering; the thwack of the mallet hitting its target jolted her. Her senses had never felt more alive.

A penny-in-the-slot machine promised to tell their fortunes. Her companion rummaged in his pocket and pulled out two pennies. 'Come on': he handed one to Rose then blew on the other – 'for luck' – before posting it through the slot. The machine disgorged a pink slip of paper. 'You will find your heart's desire,' he read aloud. He looked at Rose. 'Your turn now.'

'May all your life be a grand adventure.' Rose laughed and pulled a face. 'That doesn't tell me anything.'

'Do you mean to say you expected pearls of wisdom?'

'Not for a penny. For tuppence, maybe, although I have to say, I like the sound of a grand adventure.'

'You should be careful what you wish for.' Rose wasn't sure whether he was speaking to himself or to her.

The stall-holders were attracting custom and the field itself was filling up. 'I haven't been to an air display before,' Rose said, to change the subject. 'In fact, I've never seen an aeroplane close up.'

'And you not all that many miles from Croydon? Though I don't expect you've that much time for plane-spotting.' Jack Spender smiled.

'I suppose you come to displays like this quite often.'

'Not really. But I like to renew my acquaintance every now and again, see how the old war horses are holding up.'

'You sound fond of them.' From this distance, the aeroplane they were walking towards looked as fragile as something made of balsa wood.

'It's not all that surprising, when your plane was the one thing between you and the sky. If you didn't put your faith in it, you'd be lost before you even started. And I'm glad to see that some of my fellow pilots have managed to put their skills to good use, though I don't imagine they ever saw themselves criss-crossing recreation grounds or entertaining the crowds with loop-the-loop or one-guinea rides.'

'Loop-the-loop?' Rose repeated. Her insides were performing their own acrobatics at that moment.

'I don't know if we'll get that kind of tricksiness today.'

'My knowledge of planes is limited to something I read about a schoolgirl who hopes to be a pilot one day.'

'She wouldn't have liked to fly where I flew.'

'No, I expect not.' Rose had been about to add that she'd read this in a girls' annual a client's daughter had left behind. She was glad now that she'd not spoken. She pushed her hands into the pockets of her jacket; the feel of its bulky stitches steadied her. They walked in silence towards the fencing that marked off the display area, separating the stalls from the field. Rose told herself that this walk across uneven ground required all her concentration. There was quite a crowd this afternoon, and yet they were the only two people there.

'I like to watch sign-writing planes,' Rose said, relieved to have thought of something that could legitimately lighten the mood. 'You know: the ones with an advertisement streaming behind – except that, on the few occasions I've seen them, it's difficult to read what's actually written there.'

It worked: 'Brasso,' he said, smiling.

'Or Sylko,' Rose suggested.

'Perhaps both: two for the price of one.'

They found a spot with a good view for take-off and leaned against the railings side by side. In no time at all, the pilot appeared and strode towards the plane, his casual entrance as much of a performance as any theatrical bow. Rose saw Jack Spender's jaw clench; he seemed to be taking every step with him. When the pilot climbed into the cockpit and strapped himself in, Rose sensed her companion's coiled agitation. He seemed poised for flight himself.

All heads turned and followed the aeroplane's progress, watched it write its way across the blue. Rose heard Jack Spender's intake of breath. He's up there with him, she thought. I wonder if he ever comes down. The plane rose, swooped and turned; rose again, circled, dived and landed. The relieved smile on Spender's face when the plane touched down was out of all proportion to the graceful performance they'd witnessed. Was watching this display some kind of personal test – an ordeal he had to put himself through? His knuckles stood out white against the railings. For some unaccountable reason, Phyllis Holmes came to mind: Miss Holmes and her own white knuckles gripping her bag as she told her desperate story. Rose blinked hard to dislodge the apparition. Miss Holmes had no place here. Everything seemed out of kilter; her thoughts were all over the place this afternoon. Rose looked again at the man standing beside her. What was she doing here? She had no idea who she was with.

Jack Spender patted his pockets and produced a scrap of paper and the nub end of a pencil. For all that he seemed to have gathered himself, Rose saw that his left hand was shaking.

'I must write down the details of the company the man flies with – you never know, I might return to the skies. There may be some work in it for me.'

Is that wise? Rose wanted to ask. She couldn't imagine this man getting into a cockpit again.

He licked the end of the pencil. 'I have a pen,' Rose said, opening her bag and fishing for her fountain pen. Ordinarily, she wouldn't risk the nib by offering it to anyone else.

'Thank you.' She watched him scrawl a series of letters and the name, while struggling to balance the scrap of paper on the railing. He put the note away and returned the pen to Rose, but continued watching the pilot, who, now safely disembarked, was walking back towards the spectators with a practised jaunty air.

'You seemed to be flying with him,' Rose said carefully. 'I expect that even an occasion like this brings back all kinds of memories.'

'Yes,' Spender said, 'it does.' Some moments passed before he spoke again. 'And even on a day like this, something can go wrong. That's the thing with flying, and with so much else besides.' He looked steadily at Rose. 'You think you're having a grand adventure and that you're in control, but that's so rarely the case. Life can surprise you at any moment and that adventure turn sour. It's something we should all remember.' He held her gaze; Rose felt a new emotion grip her. The shiver of excitement had become something else altogether. And then Jack Spender laughed, and his laughter dismantled her fear. 'And that's why we pilots have parachutes,' he said, restored to his earlier, charming self. His arm brushed hers. 'You've got quite chilled in the shade. We should have picked a sunnier spot. Come on, let's go and find a cup of tea.'

It was nothing, Rose told herself; she was chilly and over-tired. She had spent too long chasing too many phantoms. It was a momentary misreading, that was all, with a companion still haunted by the war. But if that was the only reason, why did she feel she had strayed too close to a flame?

33

Alice had commandeered the table and was fashioning yards of ribbon into a series of impossible rosettes. Ginny was sitting near the fireplace, chewing over a crossword puzzle. Every now and again, she looked up and said to no one in particular, 'Hmm, six letters . . .'

Rose was curled into the chair opposite Ginny's. She had opened her notebook to a fresh, clean page, but there was still nothing written there. She was trying to solve her own puzzle: the shrivelled rose on the doorstep, Miss Holmes, Cupid's Arrow, 'a rose by any other name' . . . By day, she sewed; by night, these things tormented her.

Ginny interrupted her thoughts. 'Here's one for you, Rose. Four down: "A bad 'un who can run", seven letters.' Rose looked blank. 'Bounder,' Ginny answered, when Rose failed to respond.

'Of course,' although that word took Rose straight back to where she did not want to be.

'That's the second time you've sighed this evening. You're not still puzzling over that sinister rose, are you?'

So, Ginny still thought it sinister. Rose had been hoping Ginny would produce a tidy explanation to reassure them both. Obviously not.

'It won't stop nagging me,' she said. She saw again the shrivelled rose and the ribbon tied around its stem. The ribbon made it even worse. 'It has to have come from Cupid's Arrow – a polite but pointed threat, put there by either Miss Lane or the dancer.' Or even Edward Martin, Rose thought, given his odd words about roses. 'More likely Miss Lane, I should think,' she said. 'And it's such a confident gesture, too, taunting as well as chilling.'

'There may be an entirely innocent explanation,' Ginny said, too late to sound convincing. She looked just as puzzled as Rose. 'If we were private detectives, this would be another good moment to consider what we know.'

Rose put down her notebook and pen. 'We know that Miss Holmes's deceiver is not Maddie's dance partner – Miss Holmes was almost affronted when I showed her his photograph – but he is involved somehow, as is Miss Lane. Indeed, the fact that the two of them are romantically linked, and Miss Lane manages Cupid's Arrow, suggests that those two are at the very heart of whatever is going on.

'We also know that the swindler is not Edward Martin – his handwriting is wrong – and yet I feel increasingly uneasy about him, though I can hardly condemn the fellow because he happens to know a quote about roses; after all, he seems to have read up on practically everything else. Of course, he may just be a man who feels hard done by, some poor lonesome who seems a trifle odd to me because I find him dull and have become suspicious of every man I encounter.' Jack Spender included, Rose thought, and then immediately disowned the idea. 'I said when all this started that it would make sense for Cupid's Arrow to have one or two innocents on their books, and I suppose that's just what Edward Martin is. He doesn't strike me as the ideal romantic partner, but his failures on that score may be exactly what took him to Cupid's Arrow in the first place.' Rose shrugged.

'Putting Edward Martin aside for now,' she continued, standing up to rehearse her argument, 'the key problem is that I'm no closer to identifying the bounder who deceived Miss Holmes. So far, all I've done is cross suspects off the list.' Rose paced back and forth. 'The dancer and Miss Lane are clearly not acting alone, and yet the little I know about the two of them is nowhere near enough to convince anyone else of their wrong-doing. Maddie wrote to Cupid's Arrow requesting a dance partner and the dancer obliged. He and Miss Lane could say he was simply offering a service; he also loves to dance, and as a young lady wrote wanting a dance partner – which, after all, is not the usual business of a matrimonial agency – what gentleman could not oblige? He merely stepped in to help.

'There is nothing I can pin on either of them,' Rose said. 'Although they're connected, and may even be husband and wife, if pressed about "Miss" Lane, they'd say it's more appropriate for her to be described as "Miss" – that her single status convinces clients of her fellow feeling. Which brings me back to square one. It's maddening.' Rose stood still and waited for Ginny to comment, but Ginny said nothing.

'Without confirmation of the deceiver's handwriting or his photograph, I am nowhere,' Rose admitted. 'And after all this time, and all I've done. I need someone else to apply to Cupid's Arrow in the hope that their letter reels in Miss Holmes's Reginald Wilson – or whatever his current name is. I can't pose as yet another hopeful applicant.' Rose looked across at Alice, who had been surprisingly quiet up to now. 'Alice, what do you think about submitting your photograph?'

'No,' Ginny insisted, laying aside her crossword puzzle, the better to tackle Rose. 'You can't bring Alice into this. It's too risky.'

'And yet,' Alice grinned, 'I've been waiting for you to ask.' She put down the rosette she'd been working on and sat up straight, all ears.

'Alice only needs to be involved to the extent of sending her picture. She wouldn't have to do anything else – except write an introductory letter.'

'Rose . . .' Ginny said warningly.

'I *am* here,' Alice said.

'Just think: if Alice sends in her photograph and a letter – you needn't go to the agency in person, Alice; Maddie didn't – it will all be perfectly safe.'

'*Safe?* So, you do think there's some danger in this?'

'No, it was just a manner of speaking.' Rose hurried on: 'If Alice writes a letter and submits her photograph, and asks her suitor to contact her via the post office . . .'

'You're becoming inventive.'

'That's what Maddie did and – don't you remember? – that's where Edith Thompson collected the letters Freddy Bywaters wrote; that was how they kept in touch. I think I read that in the *Daily Sketch*. She gave herself a false name and he wrote care of the post office. Though I don't suppose she ever thought the letters she wrote back would see her hanged for her husband's murder.'

Ginny shivered. 'Poor Mrs Thompson. That makes the association even more disturbing.'

'Edith Thompson can't be the only woman to have used the post office to receive letters from someone other than her husband. And anyway, Alice doesn't have to actually meet the man.'

'Spoilsport,' Alice said.

'The key thing is that if she registers with Cupid's Arrow, she'll receive a letter and I'll be able to check the handwriting.

Although I do think it would be helpful if you fetched the reply yourself Alice, rather than me, just to be on the safe side.'

'On the *safe* side,' Ginny stressed. 'So, there *is* some danger in this.'

The shrivelled rose, thorns and all, bloomed afresh. Rose blotted out the image. 'It's just for continuity,' she said.

'Well, I'm game.' Alice brushed off Ginny's resistance. 'I don't think these scoundrels should win. Help me look out a photograph, Rose, and work out what I should say. I'll go and make a start.' She adopted a saccharine tone: ' "Dear Cupid's Arrow, I am twenty-two and so long to be in love. I do hope there is a knight in shining armour out there for me." ' She clasped her hands, as if in prayer.

Rose smiled at her younger sister's doe-eyed look. 'I think you may be overplaying the simpering starlet.'

34

No sooner was Alice's letter written and posted than a letter arrived at Chatsworth Road for Rose. And not from Edward Martin, either – this one made her heart swerve. She seized the envelope and tore it open.

A second invitation from Jack Spender, hot on the heels of the first, and, Oh my goodness, this one contained the precipitate suggestion of dinner. Things were moving at a remarkable speed. My smoky-blue dress, Rose thought straight away. No, he saw that at Miss Porter's flat. Already she was leaping ahead to what she would wear, her thoughts racing towards that simpler calculation rather than admit that her world tilted the minute she saw Jack Spender's handwriting. He wanted to see her again and she him. But was that a good idea? His coiled anxiety, his impenetrable nature; was anything about this wise? And yet how would she know how she felt, if she did not see him again?

The date suggested was less than a week away, and a few days before the final Townsend fitting. Could she really see him then? Yes, she must. And she would make something new to wear. If she got up early every morning and sewed at night, she would just about manage it. She had more time now that the Townsend garments were practically finished. Her dress would be simple but striking – something sleeveless with all the engineering in the skirt, a skirt cut on the cross with a rippling, slanting hemline. A dress that took your breath away.

It was impossible to make a dress in secret. It was impossible to do anything without Ginny and Alice knowing. That was unfair, Rose conceded – and untrue. She had still not told either of them about the aerial display (each had assumed she was seeing Maddie), but the business of making a dress was not something she could so easily hide. All her sisters knew for certain was that she had met someone and would shortly see him again, but the idea of Rose walking out with anyone at all was such a new thing – and the timing so poor, given the Townsend deadline – and now a dress was being made especially, there must be something in it. Even Ginny had taken to humming 'Who were you with last night? Out in the pale moonlight . . .' And the wretched thing about that Edwardian ditty, Rose thought, as she put the final stitches into the last seam, was that now she kept humming it herself. It was maddening how these things took root. And Alice, of course, was enjoying every excuse to prod and tease – like now, for example, insisting on reading them a magazine story she claimed they'd all enjoy but which was obviously directed at Rose.

Alice cleared her throat. ' "Don't be a cad, Cyril's inner voice warned him. If you kiss her, she'll expect you to marry her." ' She emphasized the word 'kiss' and then paused, pointedly looking at Rose. Rose laughed, as Alice had intended, but refused to take the bait. 'What would your Mr Martin say,' Alice persisted, 'if he knew you were meeting a *different* gentleman tomorrow evening?'

'Ah,' Rose replied, matching her playful tone. 'That, we will never know.' She looked up in time to see Ginny glance at Alice and shake her head. It was the slightest gesture, but Rose was grateful, all the same. She didn't really mind the teasing, but she was still trying to decide what this invitation meant. Her thoughts were blurred, her feelings skittish, susceptible to change from one moment to the next. She saw again that shock of white cuff and Jack Spender's fine, slim wrist, and felt again that new sensation undo her. 'Jack', Rose ventured silently, testing that possibility. She couldn't think of him as 'Mr Spender' now.

The dress was ready. Rose held it aloft, turning it left and right to get a sense of the weight and play of the silk. (She'd made a virtue of necessity by combining two differently patterned silks, leftovers from clients' frocks, and was pleased to note she'd still achieved the effect she wanted.) 'What do you think?'

'It's going to look stunning, Rose,' Ginny said, gauging the dress from the way it twirled in her sister's fingers. 'I don't know how you've managed to do it in between finalizing the Townsend clothes.' Although Ginny did know, because, for the past five days, when Rose had got out of bed early each morning to work on her dress, Ginny had stirred before turning over and going back to sleep.

Where did dinner fall in the spectrum of things, Rose wondered. Dinner at The White Gardenia: she hadn't heard of that restaurant, but then, why would she have? She didn't dine out and barely knew the area; had only been in the vicinity to visit Cupid's Arrow and that dreadful hairdressing salon. Going by the address, the restaurant looked to be about a mile further on down the road. How nice to travel in that direction for pleasure. Perhaps she would entertain her companion – Jack – with the story of that salon over dinner, dressing up the awfulness of it all, although she would have to invent a reason why she'd gone to Madame Estelle's in the first place.

Rose felt self-conscious waiting at the bus stop in all her glory. It was as though everyone could read her thoughts and knew what she was embarking on. But what *was* that? This was simply dinner and need mean nothing more. And to think you've always prided yourself on honesty, Rose admonished herself.

When the bus came, Rose decided to sit upstairs. Riding upstairs had been a childhood treat; she must have been eight or nine, their mother unwilling to shepherd three girls upstairs on a moving bus when all three of them were small. But what an adventure: seeing the world at a new height and from a new perspective, sitting in the open air. And playing the bus game, too, her sisters leaning over the rail to pick out someone glimpsed in the street, and then saying 'feathered hat' or some such, and Rose inventing a story about the woman wearing that hat, or dress, or whatever it was they'd chosen. It was a harder game to play in winter, when there was little to distinguish between one dark coat and the next, but the gathering winter darkness and the cold made upstairs forays less appealing in any case and their mother more reluctant to permit them.

The bus game: it was years since Rose had thought of that. It was funny how things came to mind. She might ask Jack about his own childhood. Or perhaps next time. Next time? She was already writing the future, as hopeless as any young girl. Yet twenty-six is not that old, Rose reassured herself; it was just that she was a late starter. Miss Holmes came to mind again and, once more, was dismissed.

The bus kept up its steady progress. Rose took deep breaths to calm herself. Butterflies they called it, but it was more like a menagerie in flight. How strange, the contrast between the start-stop motion of the bus and her own nervous excitement. Rose looked at her fellow passengers; perhaps every one of them had somewhere they were longing to be.

They were approaching Cupid's Arrow. What was going on there this evening, Rose wondered. It was five past seven: Miss Lane had probably left for the day; even fraudsters go home. But she should take a look, just in case. She glanced down at the doorway and recoiled.

Rose leapt back from the rail as if scorched, and then gripped it again with both hands and looked hard at the scene being enacted on the pavement: at Jack Spender talking with *her*, that woman, Miss Lane, on the doorstep of Cupid's Arrow – she in a simple floral dress, he dressed (of course) for dinner. It was all Rose could do not to shout out 'No!' This could not be. It made no sense. Or did it? Rose resisted the very idea. She burned with rage, dismay and humiliation, a scalding mix of all three. How could she have been so foolish? She wanted to put out her hand and call a halt to their words, but the doorstep conversation continued, oblivious of Rose. The bus trundled on, maintaining its steady, dementing progress, and she with it, a useless spectator.

Such rage, such fury. How dare he? Rose bent her head and tried hard to focus on the printed patterns on her dress. She felt exposed; everything that had happened must be written all over her face. Take deep breaths, Rose instructed herself, and open your eyes wide. You cannot cry here; you must not. 'Damn him,' she said under her breath.

How could she have been so naive? All that time she'd thought his interest was real, he'd been playing with her on behalf of Cupid's Arrow. Their urgent attraction was nothing of the sort.

And if he was like the other fakers, then she was like Miss Holmes: entirely deceived, taken in. Taken in by . . . what? A charming man. And what was charm, after all, Rose asked herself, if not a light dusting of bonhomie. Not depth; a surface quality, nothing more. A means to oil the wheels of conversation – or deceit. She put up her hands to cover her face.

That was why Jack Spender was at Miss Porter's. He'd arranged to see Miss Lane – Miss Lane must have been the friend he mentioned. The word 'friend' acquired a serrated edge. Miss Lane must also be the person who had given him her address. And did they also discuss what he should say? How humiliating, how outrageous. To think of Spender and Miss Lane picking over her life, turning her into another of their prey. An angry tear dropped on to Rose's dress. Her new dress, a dress that was now going nowhere. I'm no different from Miss Holmes, Rose thought. This relationship is a sham – and Jack Spender an out-and-out liar.

Ginny and Alice did not ask why Rose came home so early that evening; they knew better than to ask her anything. The next days passed. Rose worked, tweaking and finalizing the Townsend garments, double-checking hems and fastenings already checked, planning for the future of the business. She flung herself into work, sketching dresses, coats and evening gowns whose inventive finishing touches would be tricky to pull off. Rose sketched like someone possessed. Work would be the thing. Work was *always* the thing and would restore her. And if sometimes she was conscious of Ginny and Alice exchanging glances, she knew they would not comment.

35

Rose was finessing the collar of Mrs Townsend's coat, while Ginny embroidered a delicate but elaborate panel for Mary Townsend's going-away dress. They were working in companionable silence when the front door slammed, footsteps pounded on the stairs and Alice burst into the workroom. 'You won't believe this,' she panted, looking from Ginny to Rose. 'The word at Webb & Maskrey is that Maddie's in big trouble. Sarah on Haberdashery just told me. Apparently, Maddie put a load of stockings and cammies in the window. And they are – *were*; they've been taken down now – hung over a folding screen so it looked like a woman was undressing behind it.'

'What?'

'And there was dancing.'

'Dancing? That can't be right, Alice. You must be mistaken.'

'No. Pandemonium it was, apparently.' She might have been naming the latest dance step. 'There was a kerfuffle outside the store. People have written to the manager and all sorts. And it's going to be in the paper.'

'But what about Maddie? Is she all right? Has she been dismissed?' This is utter madness, Rose thought, looking incredulously from Alice to Ginny. When will Maddie learn to keep her head down? And why court disaster when she's already received an anonymous letter? A thought flashed across her mind: had Maddie written that letter, to draw attention to herself? Surely not.

'I expect we'll hear more soon enough,' Ginny said, 'but whatever possessed her? Honestly, Rose, the two of you don't know when to stop.' Rose opened her mouth to protest, but saw Ginny's lips twitching; she couldn't keep her own face straight for long, either. Soon they were both smiling. 'And to think that when we were there, you couldn't even display underwear in the window,' Ginny said, 'let alone stage some kind of lingerie show . . .'

'Here she is,' Alice said, opening the door to Maddie a few days later, 'the talk of Webb & Maskrey and the West End stores: the disgraced window dresser.'

'Oh, don't joke, Alice. It's been dreadful.'

'What happened exactly?' Rose asked, ushering Maddie into the fitting-room so that the two of them could talk in private.

'Oh, it's been ghastly, Rose, truly ghastly,' Maddie said dramatically, halting in the middle of the room, as if claiming centre stage. Rose took one of the cane chairs and waited for her explanation. 'And it was all going so well,' Maddie continued. 'Miss Carter was so pleased with my progress that she told me I'd be in charge for the week that the First Dresser was away. She particularly complimented me on my inventiveness, so I thought, "Right, I'll show you what I can *really* do."

'We have some exquisite lingerie right now, so I decided to create a boudoir scene with a folding screen and clothes flung over the top – lace flimsies, you know – and several pairs of silk stockings, with a dress model poised as if emerging from behind the screen.' Maddie gesticulated, recreating the scene for Rose. 'And then I thought, why not go further and have a real person, someone wearing brightly coloured stockings and dancing? Something eye-catching and absolutely *now*. I asked Daisy Johnson, and she said, why not; she's leaving London any day to open a tearoom and so, in for a penny . . . and she knows all the latest steps. The speed at which she whirls and swirls and kicks up her legs – the perfect way to show off those lovely new stockings and put Webb & Maskrey on the map.' Webb & Maskrey had been on the map for over fifty years, but this was not the moment for Rose to say so.

'I might just about have got away with the stockings and the lingerie,' Maddie said, turning to face the mirror and addressing Rose through it, 'although some customers were affronted by the pretence of a lady undressing, so I'm not entirely sure about that, but to have someone in the window dancing in a skimpy frock was a sin twice over. That's what really did for me. I'd wanted something bold and striking, but Daisy drew quite a crowd and unfortunately someone was bruised in the crush – it was almost lunchtime, you see, and so the street was especially busy – and drat it all, a journalist was passing.

'Anyway . . .' Maddie sat down at last. 'The long and short of it is that Miss Carter came steaming through the store, breathing fire and brimstone. Daisy had finished dancing by then, thank goodness, and left the window. She couldn't sack Daisy because Daisy had already handed in her notice and, bless her, insisted that the dancing was entirely her idea, but I was summoned to see Miss Carter, and "dressed down" isn't the word. I expected to be sacked on the spot; I would have been, in the old days – I know that. It was all touch and go, but, amazingly, Miss Harper, the new head of Lingerie, spoke up for me. The thing is, there was a rush to her department straight afterwards and the sales of lingerie have gone through the roof. Which means that, although I'm in disgrace, it appears I have shaken things up in the way I'd intended.'

Maddie's smile reminded Rose why Ginny described her as looking like a purring cat. 'I've had to be very humble – and, boy, did I feel humble; I really did think I was for it – and I'm now on probation and eating humble pie like mad. Miss Carter sticks her nose in the air whenever she sweeps past, and Miss Harper attempts to look stern, but she curls her lip with pleasure as she's shot to the top of the list for the number of midweek sales. There was a newspaper report – only the *Gazette*, thank goodness, and page fifteen at that – so it could all have been a great deal worse.'

'Well!' Rose sat back and stared. 'You always wanted to make your mark, Maddie. You used to talk about getting your name in the paper.'

'Oh, they didn't print my name, thank goodness. The article was one of those paragraphs tucked away amongst other items.' Maddie intoned: ' "Visitors to a well-known West End store, which shall remain nameless, were aghast – and agog – to discover last week . . ." I think Mr Maskrey knows the proprietor and so managed to keep the piece small and relatively hidden. They had wanted a photograph but, thankfully, there was no photographer available and by the time there was, I'd dismantled the window. I felt such a chump but, honestly, Rose, you would think no one had ever seen a woman's legs before. So, now I'm making up for my misdemeanour by constructing genteel windows – frothy blossoms, children's frocks and so on – and all under the eagle- and ever-vigilant eye of Miss Carter. No more cami-knickers for me, I can tell you.'

'Dressed down by Miss Carter: I don't envy you that.' Rose pulled a face in sympathy. 'Well, I'm glad it's no worse, but seriously, Maddie, what were you thinking? You'd be finished if you were sacked and had to leave without a reference. And I don't understand: the last time we met, you showed me that horrible anonymous letter. I thought you'd not want to draw attention to yourself. This puts you right in the spotlight.'

'I know, I know. Madness: complete and utter madness. But everything has been quiet and perfectly ordinary for nearly six weeks. Nothing's happened since I got that letter. I wondered if it had been written by Miss Harkness, who's since left. She was at the hostel, too, and could be quite snippy – mind you, I'd always thought she liked me. Truly, I really did think the whole thing was over and done with. And Miss Denby and Miss Barnes thought the lingerie a good idea. Miss Barnes didn't say much, but then, she rarely does, but Miss Denby was encouraging. In fact, she was the one who suggested hanging the camisole over the screen so that it looked like someone was undressing. However, I intend to be careful from now on and expect to be doing penance for a good while yet.' Maddie made a show of putting her head in her hands.

Rose reached across and patted her back. 'Let's hope your penance ends sooner than think,' she said, then laughed. 'Though I *am* sorry I missed your window, Maddie. You could have sold tickets for that.'

36

'Romeo, Romeo, where is my Romeo?' Alice said, coming through the front door the next morning and depositing her hat on the hall table. 'There was still nothing for me at the post office.'

Rose beckoned her into the sitting room. 'Give it time, Alice,' she said. 'Even if Cupid's Arrow send you a faker' – And which one? she thought – 'they still need to make him *look* genuine. They need time to apparently consult their files and for your prospective swain to mull over his letter to you. The fact that you haven't yet heard is all to the good, I think. A fake romancer won't want to appear too eager.

'And we need you here,' Rose whispered. 'The Townsends have already arrived and are in the fitting-room with Ginny.' They had indeed arrived en masse – the female Townsends, that is. Mrs Townsend and Grace together in the fitting-room for the first time was quite something. And there was of course Mary, the bride to be, and her young cousin Emily.

They were having their own private mannequin parade, a dress rehearsal of sorts. Rose and Alice now joined them. Mrs Townsend was walking towards the mirror, examining her dress from every angle, turning and walking back again, and then doing the same with her coat: walking with arms extended, then sitting down on a chair and raising and extending her arms yet again to show that she could wield an imaginary knife and fork, and cope with the wedding breakfast.

Thankfully, Mrs Townsend had been dissuaded from her latest idea – for a single ribbon that would dangle from each bridesmaid's wrist; a pointless, if nice and, for some reason, newly fashionable touch, which was all very well if you planned to stand perfectly still and let the ribbon draw attention to the straight line of your dress, but the bridesmaids would be following the bride down the aisle. Rose did not want them to look as if they were doubling as Morris dancers who would shortly waft their ribbons and perform a merry hop. No, that was not the effect she and her sisters had striven to create these past few months. 'That wouldn't do, Mrs Townsend,' Rose told her in such quelling tones that Mrs Townsend immediately disowned the suggestion. 'You look splendid, Mrs Townsend,' she said five minutes later, remembering her Ps and Qs. 'That coat really suits you.' Mrs Townsend turned and smiled gratefully at Rose.

And now to the parade's triumphal moment: Mary in full bridal regalia, walking slowly down the hallway – Rose could almost hear the church organ – and into the fitting-room, and checking that she, too, could stand, sit, eat, turn and do all the things a bride would be required to do in church and at the wedding breakfast. Everyone was on hand, providing not just an audience, but extra pairs of eyes, Ginny assessing the neckline and sleeves, while Alice observed the movement of the dress, with Rose in charge overall.

Much praise was given to the beading on the silk-and-lace tunic, and to Ginny's hard work stitching the tiny cream beads, which were almost too small to grasp. There'd been talk of pearl beading, but Mrs Townsend thought not: 'Pearls are for tears,' she'd said. And then, seemingly unaware of any inference that would be drawn, added, 'I had pearls on my wedding veil.'

Ginny's praise was well deserved. 'I don't know how you have the patience,' Rose had said, watching Ginny flex her fingers yet again and stretch her eyes wide, attempting to fend off tiredness before tackling the next run of beads. But this was an old conversation of theirs; delicate work had always been Ginny's forte.

Soon it was Mary's turn to show her going-away outfit: a silk crepe dress with a scalloped hem, embroidered panels and matching coatee. This was a slicker parade, with Mary no longer the quintessential bride-to-be but a young woman stepping towards her new life, a restyled Miss Townsend (and not a 'Miss' or a 'Townsend' for much longer). Mary's outfit was completed by a petalled hat, elfin-style, one of Alice's creations. Her mother, who had sought safety in a dusky-pink toque supplied by Webb & Maskrey, looked a trifle enviously at a design too young for her. 'Once upon a time, Miss Burnham,' she said wistfully. 'It's Mary's turn now.'

In that moment, Rose saw Eleanor Townsend as she must have been years ago, a beautiful woman who thought that beauty alone would carry her through. She had invested her life in her daughters, but was now wondering, What is there left for me?

37

Now that the Townsend preparations were almost complete, Rose could turn detective again. Her desire to catch the fraudsters was now greater than ever; she would show them all she was not vanquished. She still had not told her sisters what had happened with Jack Spender – the experience was too raw. But she must not let her fury (and dismay) prevent her from seeing the larger picture.

As luck would have it, a trip to the seaside was called for; the sea air would help to clear her head. Even Ginny agreed they had earned a day off and volunteered to play Watson to Rose's Sherlock Holmes, if need be. Alice offered to stay behind and hold the fort, although, in truth, she wanted to finish a chic little hat she was remodelling and planned to wear that evening. Rose wondered when to break it to her that, all things considered, she should concentrate on making hats for clients first. But there was time enough for that lesson to be learned.

It was an overcast day and surprisingly chilly for mid-August, but the glowering skies above Herne Bay did little to deter the crowds. Every other frock was striped or floral; everyone was tricked out in their summer finery, making a valiant effort to look the part. Thank goodness, Rose thought, for the current passion for home knitting, and for the parasols, which were now being put to good use fending off sea breezes. The band was playing, and despite the chill, there was quite a long queue for ice creams. A man on stilts, handing out flyers for the Punch and Judy show that would take place that afternoon, thrust a programme at Rose.

'We'll start with the seafront,' she said, as she and Ginny began to walk along the promenade. 'We're looking for Sea View, which, I suspect, won't be all that far from the railway station.' They found it some three hundred yards further down. One of the many small private hotels along this stretch, Sea View boasted a newly white-washed frontage, white gate posts and a trim front lawn with cockleshell edging. Rose glimpsed equally snowy tablecloths and cruets on the dining tables she could see through the large bay window. Ginny waited outside while Rose went in.

The reception area was empty and its silence so pressing it was almost loud, but a bell on the counter summoned a middle-aged woman dressed in black, who, from the look she gave Rose, announced herself to be the kind of proprietor who could spot a misdemeanour before it even took place and knew how to police her guest house.

'Good morning, can I help you? Would you like to book a room?'

'No, thank you,' Rose said. 'I'm here to meet my cousin, who is staying with you and has invited me here for the day. At least, I *think* he is staying with you,' she said, switching into character. Rose patted the pockets of her dress. 'I was so sure I'd remember the name of Reginald's hotel that I neglected to write it down. Or, at least, I *thought* I'd written it down but, if I did, I failed to pick up the piece of paper. Oh dear. I know the hotel is on the seafront and I *think* it was Sea View, but I've now walked past Sea Mist, Sea Breeze and Seascape, and so I'm beginning to wonder. And didn't Reginald also say something about Beach Combe?' Rose shook her head. 'I'm afraid I'm rather confused. I know he mentioned seashells; I do remember that.' She knew she was safe with this assertion. Almost every building on the seafront had shells decorating their walls, lawns or gate posts.

The proprietor painted on a 'we-get-all-sorts' smile. 'What is the gentleman's name?'

'Mr Wilson, Mr Reginald Wilson, but he's only checking in today and so he may have yet to arrive. He has stayed with you before, though, and speaks very highly of your . . . establishment: so clean, so . . . such excellent service. I know he was here on the sixteenth of October last year, because the sixteenth is my birthday,' Rose invented, 'and he told me where he was staying that day.'

The proprietor gave an audible sigh; patience clearly had its limits. Rose looked pointedly at a printed notice that insisted 'We are here to help'. The proprietor sighed again and pulled the heavy black register towards her. 'Give me a moment.' She found the appropriate page and ran her finger down the first column.

'But I don't expect you saw that much of him while he was here,' Rose intervened, 'even if he was staying with you. My cousin is a commercial traveller, and so is mostly out and about on business.'

The proprietor wrinkled her nose. The bad smell beneath it would have been discernible to even the most unobservant enquirer. 'We are a family hotel, miss. We do not admit commercial gentlemen.' Her index finger, poised on the page, now became an accusation.

'Oh, dear, and I did so hope I'd found the correct guest house. It all looks so lovely, so neat and tidy, and I know how hard Reginald works. I was so pleased to think of him being comfortable here of an evening. He is more like a brother than a cousin, you see. Are you absolutely certain he wasn't here?'

'Absolutely.' The proprietor had obviously heard quite enough family history for one morning. Rose stood her ground. She had no intention of leaving until the relevant page had been properly checked. The proprietor conceded defeat. Her eyes followed her finger down to the bottom of the page. 'There is no Mr Wilson that month,' she confirmed. She slammed the ledger shut.

'Thank you,' Rose said sweetly. 'I'm so sorry to have troubled you, but I did think it was Sea View.' She fanned herself with the flyer for that afternoon's Punch and Judy and strained to get a better look at the brochures and assorted papers on the open shelves behind the now glowering proprietor. 'Oh dear . . .' Rose swayed and gripped the edge of the counter. 'I seem to be having one of my turns. I do apologize for troubling you further, especially when you're so busy . . .' It was eleven o'clock; the hallway and reception area were deserted and the building exuded a deathly calm, all guests having been ushered out for the day. 'I am sorry to impose upon you, but would you mind if I sat down? I've come over a trifle faint. Might I have a glass of water?'

'Of course,' the proprietor said, although she looked like she'd swallowed a wasp. 'Do take a seat . . .' She indicated a nearby chair. The proprietor disappeared and silence resumed, a hot, dense silence that penetrated the airless room. As soon as she could no longer hear retreating footsteps, Rose made for the open shelves. The brochures were lined up in several neat piles – advertisements for assorted attractions and seaside jaunts: the end-of-the-pier show, the Roman fort, a walled garden. And there, towards the end of the row, and filed just as neatly as all the rest, was a tier of envelopes and printed letterhead for the Sea View Hotel.

That's it, she thought. That's how he did it. 'Thank you,' Rose called out to the silence. 'The glass of water won't be necessary. I suddenly feel much better.' She picked up a sheet of writing paper and an envelope and tucked them into her bag. It was clear to her now: Reginald Wilson's hotel story was yet another piece of fakery.

'I've got it,' Rose said, stepping out on to the seafront and waving at Ginny, who was waiting by the railings further down. 'I've got the evidence I wanted. What now?'

'An ice-cream sundae or a cornet, don't you think? We can't leave without having an ice cream. Let's go to that kiosk near the band-stand we passed earlier.'

'Lead on.'

Despite the cool breeze and overcast sky, they did all the things one should do at the seaside: bought ha'penny cornets and walked some distance along the pier and seafront, then back along the beach; waved at the children riding the prancing horses on the merry-go-round and even poked their heads through cardboard cutouts to be photographed as a Pierrot and Pierrette.

'Right,' Ginny said when they were restored to their own selves, 'tell me how you think he went about it.'

'He was quite nifty, really,' Rose said, linking her arm through Ginny's. 'Thorough, too. Essentially, Mr Wilson targeted a number of towns accessible to London, mostly seaside resorts, and then visited the small private hotels there that have their own letterhead. Not all small hotels do, of course, but he needed printed notepaper as proof of his temporary residence. If he ran out of steam, he could always add one or two large hotels to his list. They'd be beyond a commercial traveller's reach, but if his victims didn't know that particular resort, they'd be none the wiser. And if caught out, he could always maintain he'd stepped in to The Grand, or The Metropole or wherever, to rest his aching feet. He could invent all sorts of stories, if need be.'

Ginny smiled at two small boys in shirtsleeves who were racing one another to the pier. For a moment or two, Rose was lost in her own thoughts. She stopped mid-stride, though not to admire the seaview.

'Do you know,' she said, 'I never thought to ask what he did.' Ginny looked puzzled.

'What he sold, or pretended to sell – and Miss Holmes never said. Perhaps she never asked. I can't see the two of them debating the finer points of trade.'

'Well, it's hardly the most romantic of topics,' Ginny said, 'especially if it's Mansion Polish or beef suet. Though I don't suppose a commercial traveller could carry beef suet. Imagine the smell by the end of each week.' She continued to ponder the subject. 'Perhaps it was stockings or a reviving health tonic . . .'

'Oh,' Rose wailed, 'I hope it wasn't Kruschen Salts. ' "Who is the happy wife?" ' she mocked. ' "She who keeps her youth, her good looks and her husband's adoration . . . The happy wife takes Kruschen Salts." That would be the final humiliation.'

'And yet I see you know all the words.' Ginny jabbed Rose playfully in the ribs.

'Yes, because they're so outrageous. But Reginald Wilson must do *some* kind of work. He can't sit idle until their latest scheme comes off – unless they are all living on the proceeds of the last one. Oh.' Rose grimaced. 'And now they have Miss Holmes's money.' This conversation was becoming more unpalatable by the minute. 'What a nasty business this is.' She looked at the pastel-fronted hotels with their seashell decorations. Who would have thought they'd be the means to establish a devious fraud?

Rose gripped Ginny's arm more tightly. They were nearing the end of her explanation and the end of the pier. 'The seaside towns struck me as odd when they came up in the list of places from which Reginald Wilson wrote to Miss Holmes. Theirs had been a winter courtship; how likely was it that he visited seaside towns then? That's what made me wonder if the addresses themselves were fake. But, of course, seaside hotels are especially easy to locate as there are any number of them along every seafront. He may even have picked up the notepaper on an earlier occasion and held on to it for later, and then along came his – next? – victim, Miss Holmes. Perhaps he'd played the same nasty trick on someone else last summer, and that prior conquest gave him the idea, so he pocketed more than one sheet.

'All that was needed was a willingness to travel to and from London, and to construct a suitable story to support his deception. Well worth it, of course, if you can lay a false trail via reassuring, romantic notes posted from those self-same resorts and have every hope of amassing a fortune. It was all very neat, and proof – apparently – that the deceiver was visiting a particular town, just as the postmark said. The fraudster was there, of course; it's just that he wasn't there as a commercial traveller. It was a perfect plan: perfect – and perfectly cruel.' Rose pictured Miss Holmes twirling before the mirror in her cream-and-pink wool crepe suit, allowing herself a secret smile as she contemplated her latest letter and her next assignation.

38

The nefarious deeds of Reginald Wilson, Jack Spender and Cupid's Arrow continued to taunt her, but Rose had not forgotten the need to help Maddie. Daisy Johnson may have some information that could cast light on the poison-pen letter and, now that she was on the verge of leaving London, Rose could not risk further delay. She decided to squeeze in a visit to the ladies' hostel the very next afternoon and ask Miss Johnson about the letter she'd received.

Their introductions were brief. Miss Johnson already knew why Rose was there and, thankfully, was happy to talk. 'If you follow me in,' she said when Rose arrived, 'and walk upstairs as if you live here, I don't think anyone will challenge you; they aren't as beady-eyed these days during the daytime. I'm sorry we can't go somewhere more salubrious, but I need to be out of here first thing and this is my one chance to pack.'

The bedroom – or rather, dormitory – had not changed since Rose had crept upstairs with Maddie years earlier. There were the same cubicles and – surely not the exact-same? – curtains pulled around each bed. The room resembled a hospital more than anything, albeit less hygienic. The hostel had some single rooms on the top floor – twenty-five bob a month, instead of fifteen shillings – but these were mostly occupied by older, longer-stay residents: the Miss Carters of the world, who had attained a certain status but insufficient funds, and so clung on to hostel life for as long as the hostel would have them.

'Maddie told me about her letter,' Miss Johnson said without prompting. Rose appreciated her direct manner. It was becoming quite a strain to have to pussyfoot around each enquiry. 'How awful. I wish I could help, but I can't. Maddie is right; I burned my letter. I knew who it was from, you see. The silly girl didn't even attempt to deny it.'

So, this was a wild goose chase. All the same, Rose thought, now that she was here, she would like the full story. She was warming to Miss Johnson, and anyone who'd had to master that unwieldy kitchen monster and show it off to the public deserved sympathy as well as applause.

'The business with the letter was ghastly, Miss Burnham. Silly, but ghastly. To think that someone would write such a thing – but I knew straight away who had done it. I don't know if you've ever lived in a hostel, but it's extremely claustrophobic. Petty squabbles can easily get out of hand.' Rose looked at the two long rows of narrow beds with their coat hooks, little bedside cabinets and the meagre curtained space between each one.

'This particular roommate had been making snide remarks for a while. She didn't like the attention I got when I was demonstrating kitchen appliances. As if you could be jealous of that! Anyway, she "borrowed" my best stockings. She said she'd only borrowed them, but I knew she would have kept them had I not said they were mine. I'd stitched my initials on the tops, you see, so there was absolutely no doubt. I knew they were mine even when she denied it, and told her so in front of other people. That was my mistake. She was humiliated as well as exposed, so she wrote a horrid letter and left it under my pillow. When I asked her about the note, she decided attack was the best form of defence and so she made sure everyone in the vicinity heard her denials. It was all very unpleasant. Silly, too, as I say. But she's left now. That's all in the past.'

'Might she also have written to Maddie?'

Miss Johnson shook her head. 'I doubt it. She was rather in awe of Maddie, so I don't think she would want to upset her. And anyway, it wasn't a campaign as such; she was just being spiteful to me. It was obvious that her letter related to the business with the stockings. She felt cornered and so she overreacted.'

'Horrible all the same,' Rose said. It was decent of Miss Johnson to refrain from naming the young woman, despite their differences, but she did need to know who it was. 'Was this Miss Harkness?' Rose asked. 'Maddie mentioned her to me.'

Miss Johnson nodded. 'Yes, but, as I say, she's left now and had no reason to target Maddie.' She knelt beside her bed and pulled a dusty suitcase from beneath it.

'Are you leaving London altogether?'

'Yes, tomorrow lunchtime,' Miss Johnson said, redistributing the dust with her hankie. 'My parents are coming up to meet me. I've had enough of hostel life and will be glad to be out of here. I'm going to stay with them for a couple of weeks and then it's a brand-new start. I'll visit London, of course, but I won't be living here again.'

'Maddie tells me you're opening a tearoom.'

'Yes, in Eastbourne, in a pretty little café with a flat upstairs. Well, it will be pretty when I've done with it. A friend of mine lives in Eastbourne and I'll be rooming with her. I'll have to find a tenant for the flat, but I'll need someone to help at the tearoom so that shouldn't be too difficult. I take possession in a fortnight.' Miss Johnson looked triumphant. 'I'll be exchanging one set of kitchen appliances for another, but the difference is that this will be my own business. I'm not afraid of hard work, but store life was getting me down. You'll know all about that, I expect.'

'I do. The hours I work now are much longer and weekends barely exist, but I'm working for myself and come to everything willingly instead of feeling shunted into what I do. It's scary, though, especially as I'm employing my two sisters. I don't know if the business will survive, let alone prosper, but I mean to do my darndest to make a success of it.'

'Me too. I've a small loan from the bank and my parents have also helped. So, fingers crossed. Right now I've a head full of paint colours, tablecloths and curtain material, so there's still a long way to go. You must come and visit on one of your rare weekends and see how I'm getting on. We business girls should support one another.'

'Indeed, we should.'

'Still, I'm sorry this brings Maddie no closer to knowing who wrote her horrible letter.'

'No, it doesn't, but I must let you get on. Thank you for your time, Miss Johnson, and good luck.'

'Thank you. And I meant what I said about visiting.' She scribbled something on a piece of paper. 'Here's my address.'

39

Dear Miss Dare

Cupid's Arrow have passed me your details. I hope you won't think me presumptuous for writing without further ado. I practically swooned when I read your letter: you sound like just the young lady for me. I don't have a photograph to hand –

'What a swizz,' Alice said.

– but I am a gentleman of twenty-six with good prospects and am tall with dark brown hair. Like you, I love dancing and, though I say so myself, I am quite light on my feet.

'Get *him*.'

If you will give me the pleasure of your company, I would be honoured to invite you to a thé dansant.

A '*thé dansant*' . . . Rose came to read the letter over her sister's shoulder. She could now stop holding her breath: the handwriting was not Jack Spender's. She felt quite sick with relief. Whatever his connection with Miss Lane, he was not about to sweet-talk Alice. This must be Maddie's dancer – or even someone else altogether? Although the letter had taken a while to arrive, it had been worth waiting for. 'He sounds like the perfect amour.' Rose curled her lip in disbelief.

'Doesn't he just? I wonder if he's anything like as dashing as he seems to think. I could go, Rose, and just see?'

'It is tempting, I admit. But, of course, if it is the dancer, he may have seen you when we were at the Amalfi or, indeed, when you were on stage at the fête. I hadn't thought of that until now. How does he sign himself?'

'Arthur Pearson, Esq.'

'Not Terpsichorean Terrence then?'

'We shouldn't mock. He could be a genuine romancer.'

'Or another fake Lothario. We've no idea how many fakers are involved. But whoever he is, he is not Miss Holmes's Mr Wilson, nor my Mr Martin – the handwriting is wrong. All the same, I don't think we should waste this opportunity. A further candidate is too tempting to resist. We do need to know who "Arthur Pearson" is. Why don't you reply saying you'd love to go dancing, but would he mind awfully if the two of you met for tea in the first instance? We'll have to think what you'd give as an excuse.'

'My new dance shoes *draw* so – and I'd like to bed them in first?'

'Hmm. Lukewarm. We'll have to come up with something better, but whatever you say, you do need to meet him for tea. That way, I can sit nearby and listen.'

Rose and Alice arrived well ahead of time so that they could secure their tables at the Lyons Corner House on the Strand. The venue was a good choice – large and roomy, but sufficiently busy for Rose to be able to merge into the background in a demure brown cotton dress and trusty cloche hat.

Upstairs at the Corner House was bustling, as usual, its tables a mixture of young couples, groups of friends, bachelor girls and shoppers; the solo bachelor girls toying with poached eggs on single pieces of toast that looked as lonely on their otherwise empty plates as the young women themselves, the shoppers resting their feet, the friends talking avidly above the sound of the ladies' orchestra. Even so, Alice's unknown Romeo would be in no doubt which young woman he was meeting. Her come-hither smile was, if anything, too strong, especially when coupled with her bright lilac ensemble. Was there time to approach Alice and advise her to tone things down? No; Rose decided not to risk that. And it was just as well that she stayed where she was, for no sooner had she removed her cotton gloves and put them down than she heard a man announce his presence at the next table. 'Excuse me, miss, are you Romance? May I join you?' Golly, he knew how to elicit a romantic shiver. Rose glanced in his direction: the dancer was standing a few feet away.

So, Maddie's dancer went by the name of Arthur Pearson. Rose very much doubted that, but, whatever his name, he was the wrong man. How incredibly frustrating. It had been a slim chance, Rose knew, but she had so hoped that this afternoon would be the ultimate unveiling, the moment when Miss Holmes's bounder finally revealed himself. But what an opportunity this would be to see 'Arthur Pearson' at work, and at close quarters, too, provided he didn't recognize Alice. Rose looked down and saw that her hands were trembling; it was a shock to hear his voice and to have him so close by. If she stretched out her left hand, she would be able to touch his jacket. Rose dared not look at her sister, but she could hear her loud and clear. It would be worth the cost of tea and a teacake just for that.

'Ealing, you say. Gosh, that's quite a journey. I'm in Knights-bridge myself. Have you met many young ladies this way? It is nerve-wracking, isn't it? Forgive me, but I do feel most fright-fully nervous.' Her companion barely had time to respond before Alice confessed, 'I must admit, I did contact another agency before approaching Cupid's Arrow, but when the gentle-man who replied described himself as "practically single", I thought I'd best give him a miss. Shocking, isn't it, how some people behave?'

Pearson looked down at his teacup.

'*Have* you met many young ladies this way?' Alice quizzed. 'Do tell. I shan't be the least bit offended.'

'One or two,' he said reluctantly, 'although gentlemanly dis-cretion prevents me from saying anything more.'

'What a swizz, although I am pleased to hear you are a gentleman of discretion.' Alice giggled. Her eyebrows rose to her hairline.

'Forgive me, Miss Dare, but haven't I seen you somewhere before?'

Oh no, Rose thought, but Alice held her own. She barely missed a beat before replying, 'Me? Do you think so? People sometimes say that. I must have that sort of face. Or else they say I look like Clara Bow. What do you think?' Alice turned sharply to the left and right to show off her profile, vamping it up for all she was worth.

'Clara Bow. That must be it.'

Alice came straight back at him. 'Oh, you flatter me, Mr Pearson, but you're charming with it.'

Rose struggled to remain silent. She was almost taken in her-self. Alice was at her most beguiling – or most deadly, depending on your point of view. Arthur Pearson stared. Good heavens,

Rose thought. *He looks genuinely smitten and they've only been talking for ten minutes.*

The Lyons' nippies were at their nippiest, sidestepping tables while holding full trays, dispensing countless one-and-sixpenny late lunches, scalding cups of tea and buttered toast. Rose watched their deft movements as she listened to the *pas de deux* taking place at the next table. *Pas de deux?* It was more like a solo performance. Alice's talk was so surefire it was hard for Rose to keep up. Even Pearson seemed dazed and almost out of his depth. Alice was not so much eliciting information as bombarding him with it. If she wanted to demonstrate her credentials as a ditzy brunette, she was succeeding. She described her dog ('the sweetest little terrier'), her favourite colour ('Prussian blue'), her longing for a car – and her parents' objections ('They think I'm too young. So unfair!').

Rose kept her eyes on the book she was supposedly reading. She had borrowed Ginny's library copy of *Blackmail Isn't Kind*, but there were no tips to be found within it. She must remember to keep turning the pages; it was just as well she wasn't trying to follow the plot. The story unfolding beside her was far more scintillating. Rose read the same words several times while straining every sinew to keep up with the conversation taking place nearby.

'. . . Pa made his money—well, we will gloss over how Pa made his money, but suffice to say, he did. And so, of course, he must lavish attention on his only and beloved daughter. Sorry, am I talking too much? Ma says I do run on. Anyway, the thing is that Ma and Pa are away at the moment – for six whole months; can you believe it? And while they are living the high life, poor little me has been left all on my lonesome. Pa and Ma left me a sheaf of instructions – several whole pages, in fact.

Honestly, you would think I can't fend for myself. Well, I have got into one or two scrapes—Oh, I say,' Alice said, her tone changing to a strangled and apparently shocked giggle. Rose knew she shouldn't glance in her direction, but couldn't resist. Arthur Pearson had leaned towards Alice and was eyeing her like the proverbial spider with the fly: Come into my parlour, Rose thought, but if that's what you're thinking, you have got things the wrong way round.

Alice was clearly having a wonderful time reeling in her catch. Rose was now even more certain that Arthur Pearson – or whoever he was – was up to his handsome neck in all the shady goings-on. He had backed away from Maddie when he'd realized she had no money, was romantically linked with Miss Lane and, at this very moment, was calculating how best to deceive 'Miss Dare'. But they were still no closer to identifying the man who had lured Miss Holmes. And what had they got to hold Arthur Pearson himself to account, or, indeed, to identify him? The name he'd given Alice, and was using this afternoon, was more than likely false, and the photograph of him with ducks mid-flight was not exactly the best likeness. Unless you knew the man concerned, you wouldn't easily pick him out. The police could hardly post an alert for lone men standing at the edge of park lakes. But the photograph was at least something to go on. A photograph, Rose thought: *that's it.* No male applicant supplied a photograph.

'Oh, my goodness,' she said out loud. 'That's it.'

Several heads turned towards her; Alice looked daggers at her sister.

'My napkin,' Rose said and dropped to her knees. She scrabbled under the table. This was no time to be caught out. She started mumbling; eccentricity was probably her best bet.

'Oh dear,' Alice spoke in a stage whisper. 'That poor woman. Talking to herself. That *is* a bad sign. You do get all sorts in here.' The note of irritation was not entirely feigned.

'Yes, that's it . . . that's it,' Rose repeated for the sake of authenticity. If she was to pretend eccentricity, she had better sharpen her act; though now safely ensconced beneath the table, she continued talking to herself. Poor Alice, Rose thought. Her blunder had very nearly exposed them both. She hoped her mutterings sounded slightly unhinged. But she did not feel at all unhinged, distrait or in any way unbalanced. She wanted to tell the whole cafe she had uncovered a vital clue (a clue so self-evident she should hang her head in shame for not having noticed it earlier). But shame was for another day. For now, she must sit quietly and let Alice set their trap. A few moments later, deciding that the imminent danger had passed, Rose retrieved her napkin and sat back down in her chair.

'Now, what was I saying . . .?' Alice turned the full beam of her attention on to Arthur Pearson. 'Oh yes . . . Just before I came here, I saw the sweetest Lagonda in a Bond Street show-room. What a darling motor car and such a heavenly blue. Practically the same shade as my favourite crepe de chine dress. I almost wrote a cheque on the spot. But then I thought, Pa would be furious if he got to hear. Such willpower it took, to resist.

'However, that set me thinking. What I need is a little invest-ment, something that will convince Pa I'm not the silly billy he thinks I am, but a young woman with her head screwed on the right way. I need a little venture I can support, something that will come good in a few months – just in time for Ma and Pa's return. Then, hey presto, I'll be able to show them how well I can look after myself.' At this point, as tutored by Rose, Alice allowed a thoughtful pause. 'The difficulty, of course,' she said, appearing to choose her words carefully, 'is finding the right project and someone I can trust. I know next to nothing about investments. Even when I do my sums to show Pa how much I've overdrawn, I nearly always put the pounds in the same column as the shillings.'

'Well, Miss Dare,' her companion's eyes were now as big as saucers, 'how very fortunate that we have met.' The man purred, he positively drooled. 'I might be able to help you there,' he said, leaning forward. 'It just so happens that I have a pal who is looking for someone to invest in a brand-new business. I could introduce you.'

Bingo, Rose thought. Yes.

'Golly,' Alice crooned. 'How very fortunate. You and I must have been fated to meet.' Now it was her turn to lean forward and turn up her torchlight smile. Rose couldn't help but sneak another peep at these fake spooners. Oh, Alice, she thought, you really are revelling in this.

Arthur Pearson whispered something. 'Oh,' Alice sighed. Rose dared not glance at her again. 'Next Thursday . . . Thursday would be tip-top. I'm off to the cottage in the meantime. Well, we call it the cottage, but it's really our weekend home . . . And do you really think your pal will allow me to invest in his scheme?'

'I'm certain.'

'That would be thrilling. Lucky me.'

'Would you care for another coconut ice, Miss Dare?'

'Thank you, but no, Mr Pearson. I've just noticed the time and must dash. I'm meeting a friend for cocktails later. I've been having such a lovely afternoon I'd almost forgotten that. Until next Thursday, then . . .' Alice stood up and, as a parting shot, blew Arthur Pearson a kiss.

Rose watched Alice weave her way between the tables, with Pearson observing her every step. As soon as Alice disappeared from view he smiled – a smile so big the room could barely contain it. Rose watched him fix his hat at a jaunty angle and set off downstairs with equally jaunty steps. Oh, you trickster, she thought, you are about to trip up.

40

Rose caught up with Alice in a nearby side street. Alice grabbed her by both hands. She could scarcely control her excitement. 'How did I do?'

'I think you've mistaken your calling.'

'Was it too much? I did get rather carried away.'

'It was a mite theatrical, but he seemed to lap it up.'

'Do you think so? You said we'd no time to waste, so I thought I'd better give him the full treatment. I thought that if I was required to behave like an absolute ninny, I might as well have some fun. I must say, I did enjoy myself.'

'I noticed. And where did you learn that accent?'

'Well, we've knelt at the feet of enough young ladies' – Alice extended her vowels – '*to know how young ladies speak.* Though I did wonder,' she said, back in her own voice, 'if I was trying too hard. But what made you cry out like that? If it wasn't for my quick thinking . . .'

'Yes, well done. The fact is it suddenly dawned on me – it's so obvious I can't think how I missed it . . .' Rose explained.

When the sisters arrived back at Chatsworth Road, Rose was startled to see that Miss Holmes had booked an appointment for the following afternoon, though the timing couldn't be better. Now she could test her hypothesis.

'I'm a fraud, Miss Burnham,' Miss Holmes said, as soon as

Rose showed her into the fitting-room. 'I'm afraid I don't want a new dress or a restyling – that was simply something I said so as not to arouse Mother's suspicions. The truth is: I wanted to get out of the house. I've been helping Mother organize material for the church bazaar, sorting through items and inventing enticing labels – "A clever puzzle: three shillings", "Smart pochettes and handkerchief cases: two and six". I've been up to my eyes for days, but I have finally completed the task. You're smiling in sympathy, Miss Burnham – I know you understand. But there's another reason I am here: I was wondering if you'd found out anything new.'

Where to start? Rose offered Miss Holmes a chair and sat down beside her. 'It's more complicated than I first thought, Miss Holmes, and I had wanted to find out more before the two of us spoke again. But I have now realized,' Rose said enthusiastically – then stopped. She'd been about to explain about the photographs, but something about Miss Holmes's expression called to mind the day Miss Holmes entered the fitting-room expecting to be handed a picture of Reginald Wilson, but had instead been shown the wrong man. The look on her face that afternoon, as her hopes drained away . . . And there was her earlier disappointment, too, with the studio photograph that was promised but not taken, because of some trumped-up tale about Reginald being in his work suit.

To highlight the significance of the non-photographs now would torment Miss Holmes all over again. Rose picked up her sentence and amended her tone. '. . . I now have realized that, although the operation is evidently on a larger scale than I'd first thought, without the identity of Mr Wilson we don't have the full story – or a strong case to put to the police. If you do decide to talk to the police, that is. I do hope you will reconsider. I realize this is a delicate matter, Miss Holmes, but I keep think-ing about all you've been through and that there may be other women like you. I'm not sure how these things work, but it may be possible for you to talk to the police without them using your name, if the case were to go to court.'

'Perhaps,' Miss Holmes said. 'And I've been thinking, too. I do realize I am not alone in this. The thought of another woman going through the same thing appals me. I will talk to the police – if you're able to discover something that means the fraudsters are likely to be apprehended.' It was a small conces-sion, but a concession nonetheless.

'With that in mind, Miss Holmes, we should put our heads together again.' Rose smiled encouragingly. 'You are booked in for a fitting, so we can use that time to go over what we know. So, think, Miss Holmes: is there anything you haven't told me? Even the slightest detail, even something that may not seem relevant, might help. And what about your mother? Have you managed to say anything to your mother yet?'

Miss Holmes's face spoke for her.

'But was your mother never suspicious of the letters you began to receive, and their frequency?'

'No. I was generally there to collect the post and Mother thought the letters were from an old school friend. I told her I'd revived a friendship with Marjorie Harper, who now lives near Petersfield. And that much was true; it's just that Marjorie didn't write anywhere near as often as Mother thought. She did ask recently why I hadn't had as many letters lately, but of course we've been away, visiting my aunt, and I told her that Marjorie has been away, too.'

'And she didn't wonder why you were having so many new clothes or going out more often than before?'

'She did ask, yes, but she has become more preoccupied of late. She has her bridge afternoons, and her church and committee work. To be honest, I think she was glad to have me out of her hair.'

Rose nodded. 'But what about the letters you showed me? You had some half a dozen letters or more tied up with velvet ribbon. Did your mother never ask about those? One wouldn't normally tie velvet ribbon around letters from an old school friend.'

Miss Holmes looked askance at Rose. 'Mother would never pry into my correspondence.' She was affronted by the very idea. 'She would never stoop to anything underhand. Mother knows I have private keepsakes – and where I keep them. She does sometimes laugh about me squirrelling away my things. My "girlish trifles", she calls them. But she would never stoop to reading personal letters. And nor would Sarah, if she came across them – Sarah never looks at my things. And even if she did see something unintentionally, Sarah would be on my side. All the same, this was all very private – and I have been deceiving Mother – so, as a precaution, I've always kept a couple of letters from Marjorie on top. Mother has seen Marjorie's handwriting and might of course read the postmark, so if she saw a letter from Marjorie on top of Reginald's letters, she would naturally think they were all from her – especially when I sometimes told Mother it was Marjorie I was seeing when I was actually meeting Reginald . . . Mr Wilson.'

'You obviously gave this a lot of thought.' Rose tried not to sound as surprised as she felt. It really was rather extraordinary how skilled Miss Holmes had become in the minutiae of deceit, but needs must, she supposed. A new thought struck her: 'But the letters from your school friend – that is, the letters on the top of the pile, were they there when you looked at your letters when I was with you that afternoon?'

'Yes, of course.'

'So, the handwriting I saw – glimpsed – on top of the pile that day was *not* Mr Wilson's?'

'No,' Miss Holmes insisted, somewhat fractious now, given Rose's inability to grasp what she had just been told. 'That was a letter from Marjorie, as I've said.' She gathered herself and gave a surprisingly arch smile. 'Although I say so myself, I thought that was rather clever of me.'

'Indeed.' But this news was dizzying. Rose's head spun at the enormity of her mistake. 'And are all the letters at home? You don't ever carry any of them with you? Forgive me for asking such an intrusive question, but it could be important, Miss Holmes.'

Rose expected a barked negative in reply, but Miss Holmes said quietly, 'Actually, yes, I do.'

Miss Holmes reached into her flat leather bag, extracted something from its inner pocket and handed it to Rose. It was a postcard with a lace trim: a hand-tinted drawing of a woman sniffing a red rose, its petals also embellished with lace. On the reverse was a handwritten valentine message: 'from your loving?'

Three short words and a question mark, but those three words told Rose what she needed to know. Finally, the identity of Miss Holmes's deceiver was crystal-clear. Now to unmask Alice's mystery speculator.

41

'Another disguise?' Ginny asked when Rose came downstairs the next morning in her latest manifestation. 'And yet more shadowing?'

'Yes, and hopefully this will clinch it.'

'And isn't that my blouse again?'

'Yes, I didn't think you'd mind. I needed the right collar for this.' Rose indicated the long, dark ribbon tied into a bow at her throat. 'Speaking of which, how do I look?'

'A picture of sobriety. You might be about to shake a tin for the Girls' Reform League'.

'Perfect. I thought that if I took the collecting tin that Mrs Lingard pressed on us, I could do some good while looking out for Alice's mystery man. And, thinking of the conversation that's looming about the state of the accounts, it would be no bad thing to curry a little favour with Mrs Lingard.' Rose gave the tin a preparatory shake.

'Good idea, but how can you be sure he'll turn up?'

'He's bound to. Alice played her part so well he'd be crazy not to appear. Alice won't be there to meet him, of course, but he won't know that until it's too late.'

At a quarter past three, Rose was standing opposite the Underground station at Bond Street, rattling her tin and accosting passers-by: 'Thank you. It's for a grand cause.' She felt somewhat less genial when someone posted a button through the slot, but managed to stay in character. She was getting better at this, she decided: better at keeping a beady eye out without seeming to look at anything in particular. She was glad she had opted for the collecting tin; shaking it was a way of deflecting her own anxiety: what if the mystery speculator turned out to be Jack Spender? That possibility was too dreadful to contemplate, but she would have her answer soon enough. Rose knew she was in good time because, half an hour earlier, she'd checked the cafe where the mystery man, Pearson, and Alice were scheduled to meet. Apart from two sets of women taking afternoon tea, the cafe was deserted.

Rose was now in place and ready to identify the 'Mr John Smith' who was due to discuss a little investment opportunity with 'Miss Gwendolyn Dare'. Miss Dare (who had refused to be left out of the excitement) was doing a spot of window-shopping nearby but was primed to join Rose the minute she received the signal. Like Rose, Alice was dressed differently today. No sultry lilac skull-cap, no flimsy voile dress and expensive-looking lilac gloves. She had gone from an intim-ation of extravagance (and an excess of scent) to a down-at-heel office girl in a sprigged muslin frock who was pressing her nose against a shop window, gazing at how the other half lived. The bustle of Oxford Street would hide them both. A man on the lookout for an absolute popsy, who had never set eyes on Miss Dare, wouldn't give Alice a second glance.

And five minutes later, there he was: the mystery man him-self. Ten minutes before the allotted time, he emerged from the Underground station accompanied by Arthur Pearson. There he was at last, and not merely a mystery businessman, but the man she'd been pursuing for the past few months. A man sporting a moustache – ha, the famous moustache Miss Holmes had initially failed to mention – and, yes, undeniably, indisputably, the very man she sought. Rose watched Mr Reginald Wilson – alias businessman John Smith, aka her own Edward Martin – head west down Oxford Street.

42

She knew him, could identify him in three of his different guises, but Rose still wanted more. What she wanted now was to place him – and anyone else she might see there – at Cupid's Arrow itself. Cupid's Arrow was at the heart of it all. Behind that innocuous doorway lay a swindlers' nest. That was where she needed to go.

Ideally, Rose wanted a cloak of invisibility but, in the absence of one of these, she contemplated a more realistic prospect. A man would draw less attention to himself, so that's who she would be, with the aid of her father's old suit. The following afternoon, Rose scraped back her hair, captured it in a net and pulled on her dad's old trilby. Should she also look out his old pipe, or was that a prop too far? Should she compete by adding her own fake moustache? Perhaps not. Best of all were the suit trousers – what a delightful discovery. This particular pair was too large and had to be secured with braces, but she could see why one or two bold women had taken to pyjama pants. There was no need for ladylike steps; the pleasure of being able to stride was even greater in trousers than when wearing today's shorter skirts.

The final element was the heavy jacket that completed the outfit. Though hardly the thing for late August, and scratchy with it, her father's old jacket was essential for her new look. A number of men wore winter suits all year round, poor devils, so

Rose hoped not to be too conspicuous; she also hoped not to melt. But who knew what might unfold that afternoon? Rose slipped her trusty darning needle into her left pocket and gripped it for good measure.

How could she have ever thought Edward Martin a lonesome innocent, when he was the worst of the bunch? A month had passed since their mystery tour – what new mystery would he have had up his sleeve had she not sent him that 'regretful' letter?

Now that she was on to the fakers and they may be on to her, Rose thought it wise not to stand directly opposite Cupid's Arrow. Disguise or no, anyone looking out of the window might wonder at the strange man loitering there. One of the buildings across the street, but some yards further down, had a deep porch in which she could almost conceal herself; this was far better than the shallow doorway she'd selected last time. The porch led to a suite of offices; people were coming and going all day – no one would look twice at someone waiting there.

Rose pulled the brim of her trilby down on to her forehead and leaned against the wall, its brickwork cool against her shoulders. She knew she could be in for a long wait. The first hour was relatively straightforward. Rose counted delivery vans, then women wearing green. She recited (or, at least, made a start on) her times tables and then turned to the poems she'd learned by rote at school. After wandering 'lonely as a cloud', she heard a newspaper boy call out that evening's headline; straggling shoppers gave way to departing workers; then, bit by bit, the office workers faded away. No one left or entered Cupid's Arrow, but she'd glimpsed some movement near the window; there was definitely someone inside.

The traffic quietened, the street grew quieter with it. Finally, the door opened and there he was – the bounder, the faker, the arch deceiver himself – Reginald Wilson, Edward Martin, or whoever he was masquerading as tonight. He paused on the threshold and, irrespective of the warm evening, pulled up his jacket collar. He might almost have been auditioning for the role of pantomime villain. Oh, you chancer, Rose thought, if you were sporting your fake moustache, this is the moment you would twirl it. Where was he off to now? Had Miss Lane just lined him up with his next victim? Was he already considering which fancy footwork he'd adopt – tearoom, boating lake or mystery tour? Reginald Wilson had swindled Miss Holmes, but Rose knew this man as Edward Martin, and she now had him in her sights.

Martin set off down Bolton Street. Without giving it a moment's thought, Rose fell into step behind him. He paused at the next street corner to let a motor car go by, then crossed the road and continued on his way, down Longton Street, turning right into Highfield Avenue. At first, Rose stayed close to the buildings, the offices and shops quickly giving way to a residential district with tidy privet hedges and tiled paths. Soon, she was walking with no thoughts beyond the rhythm of the chase and her quarry's purposeful strides. She had no idea where this journey would lead her, but was certain she'd discover something, perhaps even the fraudsters' lair. But she must not get carried away. She must concentrate on keeping Edward Martin in view. By now, she'd lost track of the street names; the key thing was to keep up. At some point, Martin stopped abruptly and stooped, presumably to adjust a shoelace; Rose stopped too and then, following his cue, picked up the rhythm again.

Up and across a main road, down side streets and tributary

lanes, the journey was becoming a blur. How would she find her way back? If only she had thought to memorize the route or to trail Ariadne's piece of string. Martin turned left into a leafy avenue. Surely they had walked this way before? Yes: she remembered the house with the geraniums in the window. Any house might have geraniums at this time of year, but not in the very same pot. They were definitely retracing their steps. Perhaps he was meeting someone new and had made a mistake and taken a wrong turning.

Edward Martin was still up ahead. He turned a corner and some ten strides later Rose turned the same corner herself. The street was empty – she had missed him. How had she managed to do that? There was a turn-off a few yards further down. Rose quickened her pace to check; he was not there, either. She crossed a junction and, now frantic, continued down the road. Where had Martin gone? Drat and blast it. After all that effort, she had lost him. He must have gone into one of the houses. Or – dread thought – was he standing in one of the doorways at this very moment, watching *her*?

Too late, Rose realized she was almost the only person on this street and had been for some time. Her footsteps rang out from the pavement and reverberated in her head. Now another set of footsteps sounded behind her. They could belong to anyone going about their business, she told herself. Or was the chaser now the quarry? She dared not turn round and look. Rose slowed right down, and the footsteps slowed down with her. The minute she sped up again, so did the footsteps behind her.

At first, she was not sure, and then, even once she was certain, Rose told herself she was wrong. She was conscious of how quiet it was and of the cold beads of sweat slowly trickling down her back. How could she have been so foolish? She had no idea where she was. She must keep walking while she worked out what she should do. She had reached a row of handsome houses – could she knock on one of their doors? There was a park up ahead – surely there would still be people in the park on a warm evening like this one? Rose turned in through the nearest gate, and chose what looked to be the main path. Two or three steps behind her, someone followed suit.

By now, Rose's heartbeat was as loud as her footsteps. Some desperate paces further in, she realized she recognized this place; it was the little park of the charity fête. Without its tents and stalls, it looked completely different. She had come in through another entrance this evening but, thank goodness, she now knew where she was. Her relief was fleeting, however; she was a long walk from home and, although some distance behind her, the footsteps were still there, marking out her own.

Rose hurried past a romancing couple and a man out walking his dog. Surely, she was safe to continue through the park with other people here? Perhaps she should speak to the young couple or try to attach herself to the man? But would it be safe to trust an unknown man, and how would she explain her clothing? Her clothes would make it more likely that they'd believe whatever Edward Martin said, if – when – he caught up.

Were all the park gates still open? What if she took a blind path? The man with the dog had changed direction and was walking across the grass. Suddenly a familiar voice behind her called out, enraged: 'Nellie, stop this nonsense now and come straight home!' Rose felt her stomach twist. What a nasty trick: no one would interfere in a quarrel between a husband and wife. She hurried on down the path, past flowering shrubs, past bedding plants making bright statements in strict municipal lines. The orderly park mocked her: this was a place meant for gentle strolls, not anxious pursuit.

Rose was striding now, half running. The greenery thickened, formal beds giving way to shady trees. Why had she chosen this path? A new thought struck her. Miss Jennings, the civil servant, lived nearby – but where? When Alice delivered her Kew Gardens suit, she'd remarked on the address but, for the life of her, Rose couldn't now think what it was. Suddenly, it came to her: Bobbin Lane. Alice had said that Bobbin Lane was a little street abutting the park. Rose had no idea which of the several paths she should take. Edward Martin was still shadowing her but, for some reason, made no attempt to catch up. He's enjoying this, Rose thought, my fear and his knowledge of it. Her footsteps struck the path; secondary footsteps echoed after. When she neared the bottom entrance of the park, the echoing footsteps picked up speed.

Released by the gate, Rose ran. She was encumbered by her jacket, however, its bulk as well as its weight. She started undoing its buttons – if need be, she would shrug it off; if Martin made a grab for the jacket, she would swerve and leave it behind. She was out of the park now, turning a corner – and there was a sign for Bobbin Lane, a steep street with a row of pretty little houses. Rose charged up the hill with her pursuer still behind her. Twenty-nine . . . thirty-one . . . thirty-three . . . She sprinted the last ten yards. Thank goodness she remembered the number. Heaving, panting, gasping, Rose hammered on the door of number 39. 'Please, Miss Jennings, please!' she cried out. When, at last, the front door opened, Rose fell into her arms.

PART 5

Miss Derring-Do

43

'Thank you, Miss Jennings,' Rose gasped. 'Thank you.' Her words emerged in staccato gulps.

'Whatever has happened, my dear Miss Burnham? No, on second thoughts, don't try to tell me. You can do that later. For now, just try and catch your breath.'

'There's a man . . . a man,' Rose repeated, still clinging to her saviour.

'Izzie . . .' Miss Jennings turned and spoke to a slim woman Rose had dimly observed standing in a doorway – Miss Compton, she presumed, the teacher with whom Miss Jennings shared her home. Isobel Compton came into the hallway, reached into the umbrella stand and, brandishing the walking stick she extracted, went out through the front door. Miss Jennings shut it behind her. Rose tried to stay upright, but her knees were shaking too much.

'Come into the sitting room,' Miss Jennings said, leading Rose through the first door off the hallway. 'You have obviously had a dreadful shock, but don't try to explain just yet. Whatever has happened, Miss Burnham, you are safe now. Sit down and I'll get you a glass of water. Will you be all right if I leave you?'

'Yes. Yes, thank you.' Even though Rose had sat down, she couldn't stop trembling.

Miss Jennings came back into the room carrying a tray. 'I've brought you a brandy as well. This seems like a situation in which brandy is called for. I think I'll have one, too.'

'I'm so sorry to put you out like this . . .' Rose paused. 'I really must explain.'

'Only when you are ready. Brandy first.' At that moment Miss Compton reappeared.

Miss Jennings turned to her. 'Any sign?'

'No. He must have melted away into the trees.'

'Here. I've poured us all a brandy.' Miss Jennings handed Miss Compton a glass.

The three women sat in silence. Bit by bit, Rose felt the brandy's reviving kick and allowed herself to take in the room: the comfortable sofa and the cretonne covers into which she'd sunk, the matching chairs upholstered in a floral pattern not unlike the one Miss Jennings had chosen for her summer suit. The room was calm and understated. There were a couple of lamps on small tables piled with books, Staffordshire figures on the mantelpiece and a pair of watercolours above the bookcases on either side of the chimney breast.

The brandy steadied Rose and brought the colour back to her cheeks. She looked at the two women sitting comfortably in their respective chairs, politely awaiting the explanation they must be longing to hear, although you wouldn't guess this from their patient demeanour. Rose took a final sip and put down her glass. 'Thank you,' she said, signalling that she was ready to talk.

'This is Miss Compton – Isobel – my very good friend and housemate,' Miss Jennings said, squeezing Isobel's hand.

'Rose Burnham,' Rose said to Miss Compton. 'I'm very pleased to meet you.' She laughed at the formality of her words in these peculiar circumstances; this was not the moment for polite introductions. 'Would you have actually wielded that stick?'

'I may well have done.' Miss Compton smiled. 'I was captain of junior lacrosse.' They laughed again, giddy with the brandy and the situation. And, for Rose, the tremendous relief.

'I should start at the beginning,' she said, 'and I will get back to that, but I think it only right that I tell you straight away why I have landed on your doorstep.' She took a deep breath. 'For reasons I'll explain, I was following a man' – Miss Jennings frowned and leaned forward, intrigued – 'who has done great harm to one of my clients; but, at some point, I realized that he knew he was being followed and had somehow doubled back, and was now following me. I'd been up and down, and round and round, a maze of unrecognizable streets, and then I saw the park and, thankfully, remembered you live here. Thank goodness you were in, Miss Jennings.'

Her hostess smiled. 'We are here most Friday evenings, Miss Burnham: the pattern of the working woman.'

'Of course, and here I am disturbing you both, and in this dramatic fashion. I'm so sorry.'

Rose looked down and, for the first time since her arrival, became aware of her clothes. 'Oh, and I should also explain – that's why I'm wearing men's clothes. I thought I should be in disguise.'

'I did wonder,' Miss Jennings said, 'but did not like to enquire.' She and Miss Compton exchanged wry smiles.

'To start at the beginning . . .' Rose went back to the day she'd first heard about Cupid's Arrow. Without naming Miss Holmes, she explained her shock at hearing her client's story, her concerns for her own business, and the strange paths down which her desire to help had led her. Rose felt her rescuers deserved as full an account as she could give – almost a full account: they did not need to hear about Jack Spender.

'How dreadful – you poor woman – and now that the swindlers know you are on to them, you could be in danger. We must call the police, but it's nine thirty on a Friday evening and the man you were following will have disappeared long ago. I'm not sure there is anything to be gained by contacting the constabulary now. The police will have a great many questions and you look exhausted – and you must be hungry, too. You can stay here with us tonight and talk to the police in the morning.' Rose started to object, but her objections were feeble and insincere. The thought of retracing her steps in the dark was beyond her – and, quite frankly, terrifying. Edward Martin might still be out there somewhere, waiting for her to emerge.

'We can't possibly let you go home in this state,' Miss Jennings insisted, 'and if you speak to the police here tomorrow, we will be able to verify your story of this evening's ordeal. First, though, you must call your sisters, who I'm sure are worried about you. There's a telephone in the hall. Isobel will boil up some water so you can have a hot wash, and I'll whisk some eggs while you telephone. You'll feel much better in the morning and will be able to give a better account of yourself. Although, perhaps don't mention the gentleman's clothing . . .' She chuckled. 'We'll find you some suitable clothes. You're about Isobel's size; I'm sure we can find you something, although it might not be up to your usual standard.'

'Not at all,' Rose said. She could see how Miss Jennings was used to taking charge. 'This is extremely good of you both. Thank you, Miss Jennings – and Miss Compton. This really is immensely kind. If you can find me a blanket, I can curl up here on your sofa.'

'Nonsense,' Miss Jennings said. 'You can have the sp— Isobel's room.'

'I don't want to be any trouble.'

'It's no trouble,' they said in unison.

44

When Rose called home that night, Ginny, faithful and reliable Ginny, remembered where Sergeant Metcalfe was stationed. (That was the last time she'd mock Ginny, Rose told herself, for rescuing someone on the dance floor.) Ginny made a telephone call of her own first thing the next morning, and, thanks to her role as intermediary, Sergeant Metcalfe and his inspector appeared on Miss Jennings's doorstep. Rose wasn't sure which of them was the more disconcerted – she, at being interviewed by the police, or Sergeant Metcalfe, at hearing what she had to say.

Rose was grateful for the comfort of Miss Jennings's plump sofa and its reassuring floral cushions. She was glad, too, that this interview was taking place at Miss Jennings's home and that Miss Jennings herself had offered to sit in. The days of chaperones may have passed, but her presence that morning helped Rose to recover her nerve. Before the police arrived, she made one further call and explained to Miss Holmes, in as few words as possible, what had happened the night before and that the police were now involved.

And involved they most certainly were. Rose was questioned and quizzed and made to feel a decided amateur. She described her appointment with Cupid's Arrow, touched on her false courtship with 'Edward Martin', explained what she knew of 'Arthur Pearson' and Miss Lane, and her pursuit of Edward Martin the night before. It would have been a long and scarcely credible tale had not Sergeant Metcalfe's acquaintance with Ginny lent credence to it. Rose convinced herself there was no reason to further muddy the waters by mentioning Jack Spender; she had given the police quite enough.

'I was slow to realize something I should have seen at the start,' she admitted. 'I supplied a photograph, but my "suitor" did not. Miss Holmes didn't have a photograph of hers, either. I should have realized the significance of this sooner, but I was so caught up with my client's distress and my own concerns that I failed to spot this vital clue: no faker provided a photograph of himself, whereas a genuine suitor would have done so.' Rose spared herself – and, more importantly, Miss Holmes – the desperate account of the studio photograph that was planned but never taken. That was for Miss Holmes to explain, should she wish.

Sergeant Metcalfe sympathized. He um'd and ah'd in all the right places and raised his eyebrows on several occasions, while making detailed notes. Inspector Davey was less easily impressed. What was she thinking, following a man – a criminal? This was not a detective story. Best leave it to the professionals. They would need to talk to her again.

There was no time for Rose to take stock and consider the enormity of the past few days. Maddie appeared at Chatsworth Road unexpectedly that Sunday afternoon and barely allowed Rose to usher her into the fitting-room before she started speaking. 'I've had another letter, Rose. I felt sick this time – still do. Now I know that someone's really got it in for me.'

'Oh, Maddie, that's dreadful. Has anyone else had a letter?'

'Not as far as I know.'

'Did you keep it?'

'Yes, like you told me.'

285

'And what does this one say?'

Maddie produced the letter. 'It's every bit as vile as the first one,' she said, handing it to Rose.

'YOU THINK YOU'RE SMART BUT YOU'RE NOT HALF AS SMART AS YOU LOOK,' Rose read. 'DON'T THINK I DON'T KNOW.'

'And there's something even worse,' Maddie said. 'Something happened at the store, in the main window. I was arranging a new window with Miss Barnes. It's a travel scene, a railway station – something to show off our late-summer coats and the new luggage that's come in. The display's still there, if you're passing. Anyway, there are two models sitting on a bench with their suitcases and hat boxes, as if waiting for a train, and there are posters on the wall behind them – real travel posters: "Scotland Straight as the Crow Flies", "The Cornish Riviera", "Buxton, the Mountain Spa" ... I'd just pasted up Buxton and pulled out Cornwall, but it wasn't a poster at all. Someone had scrawled "I KNOW YOUR DIRTY SECRET" across a sheet of white paper as big as the posters themselves. I dropped it as if it had bitten me. Can you imagine, in enormous red capitals, there, in the window? Who would do a thing like that? There was nothing for you to notice when the paper was rolled up, but what if Miss Barnes had pulled out that sheet instead of me? I'd already got the thing on the wall and was opening it out before I saw what it said. Miss Barnes wasn't looking, thank goodness; she was struggling to get a coat sleeve over one of the model's arms. But what if she'd seen the writing, or if she'd been the one to unroll it?

'I screwed the paper up straight away and hid it behind one of the empty boxes. Then I had to sit down on the bench. "Are you off on your travels as well, Miss Greene?" Miss Barnes joked, but then she saw the look on my face. I'm surprised she couldn't hear my heartbeat. I must have looked queer because she said, "Are you all right? You do look peaky." And she spoke with real feeling. I said I'd come over a bit dizzy but would be all right in a minute or two. Miss Barnes is young and she's a sweetie, so I knew she wouldn't ask me anything else. Then, after a few minutes, I had to get up and carry on.'

'Did you keep the poster?'

'Yes, although it's badly creased where I scrunched it.' Maddie unrolled the paper, squirming as she presented it to Rose.

'I'm so sorry, Maddie,' Rose said. She felt quite sick herself. Someone's campaign was seriously hotting up. 'I don't know what else to say, but . . .' Rose had to ask: '*Do* you have a secret? Is there something you haven't told me?'

'No, of course not.' Maddie tossed her head, her usual defiant gesture. 'But I'm starting to wonder if I did mislay those hats the other month, or if that was part of the same business, with someone trying to catch me out. They'd have caught me out good and proper this time – there would have been a major rumpus.'

'This is getting nasty. You really do need to find out what's going on.'

'Yes, and I've been thinking, it's my birthday in a fortnight. If I arrange a birthday tea at the hostel, will you come?'

'At the hostel?'

'Yes. I know it's hardly the most cheerful of places, but it's the simplest to arrange. I've still no idea who's behind all this, and will have to think who best to invite. If you come too, you'll be able to keep an eye out for anything suspicious. I'll also ask Daisy Johnson – as a friendly face. Will you come, Rose? I really do need your help.'

45

Grace Townsend's bridesmaid's dress had required some adjustments, but was now ready and waiting, as were the court shoes that had been dyed the exact shade of apricot to match. If Rose had anticipated a gasp of pleasure and effusive thanks the moment Grace saw them, however, she was mistaken. Grace was bursting to speak, but about something else altogether.

Grace stepped into the fitting-room brandishing a large brown envelope. 'Look, Miss Burnham,' she announced, taking from the envelope a sheet of cartridge paper stamped with a bold red crest. 'Can you believe it? "This is to certify that Miss Grace Townsend has satisfied the examiners and has attained the level of—" In short, I have passed my typing exams and am now a skilled member of the workforce – or will be, as soon as I can find myself a job.' Her eyes were shining; her smile could swallow the room. 'Isn't it marvellous?' she said, twirling with the certificate and waving it at Rose, the purpose of her actual appointment entirely overlooked for the moment. 'You must have thought me strange in recent weeks, but it was a secret, you see, and I'm not all that good at keeping those. I was bursting to tell you, especially as I know how hard you've had to work to achieve all this.' Her free arm swept the room in a dramatic gesture. 'But I daren't let on. I knew you wouldn't tell Mother, but I needed to be sure I could do this before I uttered a single word.

'You see,' Grace continued, 'I've not been attending my deportment classes. Oh, I did go at first, but then I enrolled myself on a typing course instead. The timing didn't quite fit – which is why I've sometimes been late for appointments – but the deportment class provided cover for my typing lessons. I've you to thank, really – no, truly: you made me realize how important it is to work for something you want. I knew I would have to learn secretly and so present Mother with a fait accompli. I'm now writing all sorts of letters, looking for work.'

You've broken free, Rose thought, looking at Grace's capable hands. 'Congratulations, Grace – Miss Townsend; I think you'll have to get used to being Miss Townsend from now on if you're going to be a professional member of the workforce. You should be proud of yourself – well done. One of my clients is a senior civil servant. Would you like me to ask her about openings for new recruits?'

'Oh, thank you, Miss Burnham, that's extremely kind – but I have my sights set on something quite different.' Grace gave a secret smile.

What has Grace got up her sleeve, Rose wondered as she made her way back upstairs. She had little time to marvel at Grace Townsend's subterfuge, however, or indeed her newly trained, nimble fingers. No sooner had Miss Townsend left than a knock on the door announced Inspector Davey and Sergeant Metcalfe. Rose was needed downstairs once more. Two sets of visitors in swift succession – and yet how very different. She readied herself for the inspector's bluff tones.

Inspector Davey was flicking through *Fashions for All* when Rose entered the fitting-room, although she doubted he'd find anything there to suit him. The sergeant, who was hovering nearby, gave her a reassuring nod. Inspector Davey looked about to offer Rose a seat, but then recollected himself. It was her fitting-room, after all. Rose preferred to stand, and took up her usual position in front of the mirror, the better to see her visitors.

'We've made some headway, Miss Burnham,' the inspector said, facing her. 'As it happens, quite a lot.' Sergeant Metcalfe nodded. 'We know the names of their victims,' the inspector continued, 'and are making contact with them now, your client' – he consulted his notebook – 'Miss Holmes among them. Fortunately, and for reasons I'll explain, it's become clear which people they've conned, so we think there will be no need to pursue their full client list.' Thank goodness, Rose thought: Miss Allegra Lipton and Miss Gwendolyn Dare would be spared a thorough cross-examination.

'We've got their aliases, too – quite a string of them, in fact: Reginald Wilson, Edward Martin, Arthur Pearson . . .' Rose held her breath as the inspector worked his way through his list. There was no Jack Spender on it. She glanced down to hide her relief – and yet, could she be certain the inspector knew every name?

Inspector Davey misread her silence. 'It's distasteful, I know, Miss Burnham, how this kind of caper works. I'm afraid imposters are none too choosy when it comes to borrowing people's identities.'

'So I gather.' And to think that Reginald Wilson and Edward Martin were actually one and the same. All the time she was pursuing Miss Holmes's fraudster, she was being wooed by that very man. But she'd nailed him in the end. What a fluke that the name 'Allegra' happened to contain two of the same letters as the word 'loving', and how perfect that it was a valentine's card that enabled her to identify him.

The inspector coughed and continued. 'The man you know as Edward Martin must have realized the game was up when you sought sanctuary in Bobbin Lane. I expect he legged it back to the office straight away and they dismantled everything then – the office was empty when we got there on Saturday, apart from some odds and ends. Though I don't expect there was that much there to begin with.'

No, Rose thought – just a few sticks of furniture, the magazines and the incriminating card-index Miss Lane kept on her desk. I bet she escaped with *that.*

'I tell a lie,' said the inspector, correcting himself. 'There was also a fake telephone.'

'A fake telephone?'

'The telephone was real enough, but it wasn't connected to any exchange. It must have been there for show – to look convincing.'

'Well,' Rose said. 'It convinced me. Miss Lane was taking a call on the day I went to Cupid's Arrow. It never occurred to me that was a pretence.'

'There you go.'

'There was a card-index box on the desk.'

The inspector shook his head. 'Disappeared. However . . .' He paused for dramatic effect. 'They'd overlooked something crucial: a scrappy piece of paper with "Dance Partners" scrawled across the top. It was half hidden under a big desk blotter. Someone had knocked a glass over, presumably in their haste, and disturbed some papers in the process. This slip of paper must have got caught under the blotter then – and overlooked. Though it seems a scrappy thing, it's actually an incriminating document. Mind you, they were none too bright about that. The paper lists a handful of names, your Miss Holmes among them – although she doesn't strike me as the type of lady you'd invite to a tango tea.' The inspector scoffed, then collected himself and coughed to hide his embarrassment.

But the fakers did go dancing, Rose was thinking. Alice was invited to dance straight off, probably as a result of her overly effusive introductory letter. Perhaps, with the other, genuine women, dancing marked a particular stage in their 'courtship', a stage reached shortly before they were relieved of their savings. The intimacy of the dance floor, cheek to cheek and breath to breath – what better way to instil confidence and a sense of security in an unwitting victim?

Was Maddie's name listed, Rose wondered. But, then, her case was different again. She'd asked for a dance partner in the first place, and then revealed she had no money. Maddie had ruled herself out before she could barely be ruled in. There was a thought: would Miss Lipton have been invited to a dance at some point, had her 'romance' continued? 'My dear Miss Lipton, would you care to partake in a Hesitation Waltz?' Hesitation indeed.

Inspector Davey was still awaiting her response. 'Dance partners,' Rose repeated, adopting a suitably surprised tone. 'Yes,' the inspector confirmed, 'but the paper was, in fact, a handy list of their handiwork: a ready reckoner of their misdeeds and the people they've conned. Those villains led these women a merry old dance indeed.' Rose bent her head to conceal her smile at the inspector's way with words.

The inspector was not done yet. 'We know something of how they went about it,' he concluded, 'but there is more we need to find out – and I'm very sorry to have to tell you this' – Sergeant Metcalfe looked down at his shoes – 'but the fraudsters themselves have vanished. Scarpered. As I say, the office they used is empty – they've done a moonlight flit. They could be miles away by now. But don't worry, Miss Burnham. We'll find them.'

46

Don't worry? How could he say that when she was the one who'd identified them and they knew how to reach her? And what of Jack Spender – was he holed up with the other three? What's more, 'miles away' would be like looking for a needle in a haystack. They could be setting up somewhere else at this very minute, preparing to mislead some other unfortunate woman.

'Well, that's rotten,' Alice said when Rose relayed the inspector's words. 'There must be *something* we can do.'

A gleam entered Rose's eye. 'We could go and take a look at Cupid's Arrow and see if there's anything there the police missed.'

'How likely is that?' Ginny asked.

'I don't know, but, in any case, Sergeant Metcalfe needn't know.'

'That wasn't what I was thinking,' Ginny blustered. 'Surely, if they have disappeared, they'll have taken what they need and the police will have the rest.'

'Well, it can't hurt for you and me to go and look.'

'I'm not sure I like this, Rose,' Ginny whispered as the two of them felt their way down the dark hallway that evening. Although closed, the front door hadn't been locked; the police had evidently not thought it worthwhile to secure it.

'What's the worst that can happen?' Rose whispered back.

'There's no one here. The police are certain they've gone. Can you keep that candle steady? It was dark on these stairs even in daylight.'

'I'm still not sure,' Ginny said, as they continued to grope their way down the hall.

'No one will be any the wiser. We really needn't mention this to your Sergeant Metcalfe. Not unless we find something new.'

'He's hardly *my* Sergeant Metcalfe.'

'Well, I don't think he's anyone else's. Sorry, that was unkind. He has been immensely helpful and is obviously a good sort – as long as you keep him off the dance floor.' Rose led the way upstairs.

The catch on the door to Cupid's Arrow gave easily when she tried it. Even as she reassured herself there was no one there, she pushed at the door with some trepidation. The door swung back onto an empty space. Rose let out her breath: the room didn't just look empty, it looked deserted. 'Isn't it funny how a room you know has been abandoned feels completely different from one awaiting someone's return?' Rose said, glancing about her to get her bearings. 'It smells fusty, too. These windows can't have been opened for a while.' She tried the nearest one and it opened readily. 'Can I have the candle? We should have thought to bring two. The street light isn't quite bright enough.'

Ginny passed the candle, shielding its flame as she did so. 'Keep it down, Rose. Don't swing it. Anyone outside will wonder what on earth's going on – and the flame is guttering.' Rose held the candle towards each corner of the room. 'Right,' Ginny said, standing up straighter now that she was satisfied that the room really was empty. 'I'm ready to summon up my sleuthing spirit. Is there anything you notice here that's different from before?'

Rose looked around. 'The magazines are still here – and are now even more out of date. There's no plant – there was a little plant on the table last time – but, other than that . . .' She moved into the office area, followed by Ginny. 'No filing cards on the desk – unfortunately. The inspector was right about that.' Rose pulled open one desk drawer after another: there was a rubber and a couple of pencils in the first one; a pencil, some blank paper and the blank cards for applicants' details in the other.

'Are you Miss Femininity?' Rose asked.

'Pardon?'

'That was one of Miss Lane's questions when I signed up. I'm beginning to think I'd now qualify as a Miss Derring-Do.'

All that was on the desk were some long-dead narcissi, their soil shrinking within their pot. Rose picked up the pot and immediately put it down. 'Beyond redemption,' she concluded. 'I suppose we might as well try the coat.' She was referring to the man's overcoat hung near the door. It was a heavy coat, too warm for summer weather, which was presumably why it was still there.

'You wouldn't think you'd leave your coat, though, all the same,' said Ginny, as she started checking the pockets.

'You might if you had to bolt . . .' And whose coat was it, Rose wondered. 'Anything?'

'No.'

'Can I try?' Rose handed the candle back to Ginny, then thrust her fingers into each coat pocket: empty, but there was a small hole in the lining of the right one. Working her index finger down into it, she widened the gap between the loosened stitches. 'There's something here,' she said, straining to retrieve it. 'Oh, how disappointing: no map of buried treasure, "X marks the spot"; it's just part of a train ticket, not even half a ticket, just the stub.'

Ginny held the candle closer so that Rose could read what she'd found. 'The destination's missing,' Rose said. 'I can't make out where it's for. "F-A- . . .", it says – and that's the point at which it's been ripped. That won't get us far. Oh well, at least we've tried.' She pocketed the stub, all the same.

47

'F-A- . . . F-A-N- . . . F-A-R- . . .'

'Don't tell me, you're getting hooked,' said Ginny.

'What?'

'On crossword puzzles.'

'No fear,' Rose said. 'Not me. I'm still trying to fathom that ticket we found last night: Fareham, Farringdon . . . We really are stumped if it was Farringdon; you could catch a train to several places from there. I thought it could be a seaside town Reginald Wilson – or whatever we should now call him – tried out on someone else, but I can't think of any that are accessible; Frinton doesn't work. And if the coat belonged to Arthur Pearson – or whoever he really is – I wouldn't know where to start. I've no idea what ground *he* covered.' But, Rose reassured herself, at least that coat didn't look right for Jack Spender. 'And it definitely was a man's coat,' she said out loud. 'Not that women can't wear male clothing' – she smiled, recalling her own moment – 'but I can't see Miss Lane in that coat, somehow. And, for all we know, the coat may have had its own story; it could have been bought second-hand.

'F-A- - . . . F-A . . . Argh!' Rose groaned. 'Frazzling . . . Frustrating . . . And, yes, I know those words don't have 'A' as their second letter. Places . . . places . . . ' She went back to crossing letters off her list. Ginny returned to her reading. 'But there was something else,' Rose said excitedly some moments later. 'The plant on the desk: the plant may have been dead, but it's still identifiable. There was a label on its pot.'

Ginny put down *The Dog Barked Twice*. 'I hope this isn't about to become a horticultural mystery.'

Rose swept on. 'I didn't notice a label the first time I was there, but I did when we went back. "Cobnut Nurseries", it said. I didn't think anything of it, but cobnuts grow in Kent. Miss Lane said she'd picked up the plant that morning . . . and Reginald Wilson said something to Miss Holmes about a cottage in Kent. I thought that was yet another of his make-believes, but what if it wasn't bluff? Don't they say that the most convincing lies contain an element of truth? And, if you then add the ticket stub . . . I know it's a bit of a stretch, but I think they could be in Faversham.'

Ginny put down her book. 'Bravo, Rose. Move over Sherlock Holmes. We must telephone Sergeant Metcalfe straight away.'

'But it's gone nine o'clock.'

'That's all right. I've got the number for the station house.'

'Oh,' Rose said, but decided against commenting further.

And now Rose was speeding towards Faversham, driven there by a detective sergeant, no less. Sergeant Metcalfe was the man behind the wheel for her latest mystery tour. And this particular mystery was about to be solved. Inspector Davey couldn't be spared this evening (what a shame, Rose had told him, when summoned to the police station three days earlier), but although it had surely dented his pride, the inspector understood the necessity of Rose being present, and had even agreed to her modification of his plan. She remembered the conversation well.

First, she'd had to endure half an hour (and it very much felt like half an hour) in which Inspector Davey lectured her on inadvisable behaviour and the danger of amateurs attempting to pursue police work. Fortunately, Sergeant Metcalfe was on hand to mollify his superior by reminding him of Miss Burnham's personal involvement in this case and her sterling work in leading the police to the offenders. Her methods may have been unorthodox – and the ladies' return to Cupid's Arrow exceedingly unwise – but, given the general public's growing interest in detective stories and puzzles of all kinds, it was perhaps understandable that the Miss Burnhams got carried away. Even as it gets better, it gets worse, Rose thought, biting her lip as her defender strove to pacify his boss. Nonetheless, she was grateful for Sergeant Metcalfe's intervention.

His superior fixed the sergeant with a quelling look and took centre stage once more. 'It turns out you were right, Miss Burnham. Faversham *is* the place. Two men who fit the descriptions you gave have been heard bragging and throwing their money around in one of the local pubs.'

'Just two men – are you certain there was no one else?'

'Absolutely. We've now made contact with all the ladies on that "dance" list I mentioned, and the fraudsters tally with your descriptions. A variety of names, of course, but their features fit all right; their methods, too – tearooms, dancing and so forth.'

So, Jack Spender was not part of the Cupid's Arrow team. Then why on earth was he arguing with Miss Lane, Rose wondered, and how on earth did he know her? Had he found out about their game somehow and decided to confront Miss Lane? And yet that made no sense. The possibilities made her head spin.

Sergeant Metcalfe stepped forward. 'Are you all right, Miss

Burnham? This must all have come as quite a shock. This must be a very different world from the one you move in. I don't expect you normally come across tricksters like these in your line of work.'

'No, I don't,' Rose said, 'but, thank you, Sergeant, I'm fine.'

Inspector Davey silenced his sergeant with another commanding look and continued his recitation. 'As I was saying, these two men have been enjoying themselves rather freely in one of the Faversham pubs – always a giveaway and, fortunately for us, locals don't necessarily take kindly to that sort of thing. Too careless by half: people flashing their money about in hostelries stick out like sore thumbs.

'Following your information,' the inspector continued, 'we asked the relevant constabulary to make some enquiries, which is why we know this now. They report that the two men have been seen in a particular pub every night this week. However, we do need to be certain we've got the right pair. We can hardly arrest two men just because they've been overheard bragging.'

'No indeed,' Rose interrupted. 'If you were to arrest all men fitting that description, the cells would soon be overflowing.'

The inspector did not appreciate this dig at his sex. If he'd spoken grudgingly before, he now visibly gritted his teeth. Not a good move, Rose, she rebuked herself. Her relief about Jack Spender must have gone to her head. 'I'm so sorry, Inspector, do forgive me. I know how hard you must have had to work on this case.'

Inspector Davey pursed his lips and continued. 'These things are never as straightforward as people seem to think, especially those who read too many detective stories.' Having aimed his own blow, the inspector took a breath and got himself back on track. 'Ideally, we'd catch the men at their lodgings – where we'd hope to find the woman, too – but we can't go knocking on all the doors in Faversham and we must move fast, before these villains flit again and set up somewhere else. Which leaves us with the public house.

'Now, the thing is, Miss Burnham . . .' The inspector's tone changed completely – it now bordered on emollient. 'You are the only person who has seen both men and, indeed, the woman. This being the case, I'm afraid we need to ask for your help to identify them. I appreciate that a young lady like yourself will never have been inside a public house, but I hope that, for the sake of this investigation and your civic duty, you will be able to put aside your entirely proper reservations and agree to assist. Given your close involvement up to now, I am sure you can see how imperative it is that we act quickly. Your help would also enable me to overlook your' – the inspector glanced at Sergeant Metcalfe – 'unorthodox behaviour up to now.'

'I see.' Rose waited a moment or two before adding quietly, 'Of course I am willing to help.' She tried to sound reticent for decorum's sake, but what she really wanted to say was, 'How soon do we start?'

'Thank you.' Inspector Davey outlined his thinking: 'We'll be in someone else's jurisdiction and so can't plant our size elevens too heavily on their turf. And anyway, we don't have the men. This is how things will go: Sergeant Metcalfe will drive you to Faversham, where he will pair up with the bobby on the beat there. The sergeant and the local lad will then go into the pub and stand at the bar with their pints.' Sergeant Metcalfe perked up. 'You won't be drinking, Sergeant, just *appearing* to drink, so that the two of you are well positioned. You, Miss Burnham, will be primed to identify the men from a safe distance. Have no fear: you will not need to approach them. In fact, it is vital that you do not, in case they realize the game is up. All you need do is give a discreet nod in their direction. Then, Bob's your uncle, Sergeant Metcalfe and the local lad will collar the two fraudsters. The men will lead us to the woman, so we'll have her in no time, too.' The inspector paused – for applause?

'That sounds like a plan, Inspector. I wonder, does the public house have more than one entrance?'

Inspector Davey rifled through his notebook. 'I'm not sure.' He looked quizzically at Sergeant Metcalfe, who looked puzzled and shook his head.

'I ask because if one of the men sees me before I see them, he might somehow manage to escape. I wonder, would it be better if I were to disguise myself in some way?'

'Disguise yourself?'

'Yes, especially as I'm likely to stand out if I go into a public house. As you say, young ladies like me don't usually frequent public houses and so the men may look up when I enter. Men have been known to look up when a young woman enters the room. Of course,' Rose hurried on, 'if we could be sure that I could identify the men by looking through the windows of the public house that would be marvellous, but that may not be the case.'

'No . . .' the inspector conceded.

'However, if I were to go in disguise – as someone selling something, for instance – no one is likely to pay me the slightest attention. The men won't necessarily be sitting near the door, so I may have to walk some way into the pub before I see them. I do think a disguise would help. Few people notice the person selling them something' – Rose knew this from her days at Webb & Maskrey; the shop girls were always complaining how invisible they were. 'And that's even more the case with a casual seller – someone selling flowers for a sweetheart, for example. Unless they want to buy them, few people even bother to look up.'

'She does have a point, sir,' Sergeant Metcalfe said. 'Miss Burnham may not see the men straight away and we don't want to miss our chance.'

Which is why Rose was now speeding towards Faversham. Speeding was not exactly the correct term with Sergeant Metcalfe at the helm, but the car was proceeding in an orderly fashion towards their destination. And what a thrill this was. There had been a moment when Rose wished the ticket stub had been for somewhere more exotic – Paris, for example; she saw herself slinking into a Paris bistro, or perhaps even the lounge at the Ritz. But all the same, what an adventure. Rose would have gladly accepted Clacton, or even Penge, if that was what was required to catch these fraudsters. So, Faversham it was, or would be within the next half hour.

Rose adjusted the individual red roses lying in the wicker basket beside her. Roses – how very apt, and not just because of her name: there was the rose on the doorstep, 'a rose by any other name', the lace-trimmed rose on the valentine's card Miss Holmes still treasured and kept in her handbag. There were so many reasons why roses should be used to seize these dreadful men. 'A flower for your lady?', 'A red rose for your heart's delight?' Rose had yet to perfect what she would say if called upon to speak, but she could hardly contain her excitement.

The pub had mullioned windows and they were none too clean at that: the Admiral's Arms needed a jolly good scrub. It was just as well that she wouldn't be required to look through them.

She'd been right to suggest a disguise so she could more easily enter the pub, even if she did now look like a somewhat funereal Lyons' 'nippy'. Rose had been about to take the shears to some threadbare curtain material emblazoned with flowers when Alice remarked, 'I thought you weren't supposed to draw attention to yourself?' Hence, the funereal look: black overall and pinny, tight black headband and dark stockings. If not a doleful-looking nippy, she might be someone about to embark on some exceedingly dirty work. Which was, after all, entirely appropriate.

Sergeant Metcalfe gave Rose the nod and disappeared inside the pub with the local bobby, Constable Burdock. Five minutes later, Rose followed. And what a murky, fumy atmosphere enveloped her: chairs and tables all higgledy-piggledy, and the room itself wreathed in smoke and reeking of beer. It took Rose a moment or two to adjust to the gloom and the intensely masculine noise: booming, bass-note voices and harsh, intermittent guffaws. The clack of dominoes slapping on to a nearby table provided a sharp counterpoint. The shelves behind the bar were swathed in ancient hops, bygone decorations put there many moons ago and now steeped in equally ancient dust. In this dim, dark room the red roses positively shrieked with colour.

Rose stepped further inside, keeping her eyes on her basket and the uneven wooden floor. The public bar looked to consist of one room leading onto another, with a further room at the far end. The bar itself ran the length of the left-hand wall. Rose looked down at the already wilting blooms. If someone offered one of these to his sweetheart, he'd most likely get short shrift. But where were the fraudsters this evening? Were they hiding in plain sight? It was hard to make out anyone among all the dark, hunched shoulders.

She had to come up with something; she had to locate the two men. Even though she couldn't immediately see them, she might be able to pick out their voices if she listened hard enough. Perhaps she would hear Edward Martin reprise his role as tour guide and relate the history of hop-picking, or the legend behind the initials carved into the beams on the pub's ceiling. And then Arthur Pearson might step up to entertain the clientele with his latest fancy footwork.

Rose peered intently at the room, scanning the different tables without seeming to focus on any particular one. And then she stopped looking and listened. Gradually, almost imperceptibly, a voice Rose recognized made itself heard above the rest.

'. . . women today don't know what's good for them.'

And then someone she didn't know chipped in: 'I agree.'

Oh, no, don't say that, after all this effort, Edward Martin is here with someone else this evening. But as Rose homed in on the voices and inched towards the sound, she saw the two men she was here to trap: Martin sitting with his back to her, talking to the unknown man who'd just spoken, and Arthur Pearson, sitting on Martin's left side, his profile turned to Rose.

Edward Martin spoke again. 'They need teaching a lesson,' he laughed, 'and we know how to go about that.'

Rose lunged: 'How dare you!'

'What the dickens,' he cried out, as Rose leapt forward and pummelled his back with both hands. Sergeant Metcalfe appeared from nowhere. Edward Martin ducked. Arthur Pearson struck out and, by mistake, landed his accomplice a left hook. Martin reeled backwards, stunned to have been hit by his own partner. In the scuffle that followed, the constable took a swing at Pearson, but Sergeant Metcalfe took the brunt. Golly, thought Rose – who had quickly retreated and was now watching from a safe distance – this is pure slapstick: it's better than being at the pictures, watching the Keystone Cops. In the ensuing tussle, a table was overturned, pint pots spilled, and Martin's right arm was wrenched up behind his back. Eventually, Sergeant Metcalfe collared Arthur Pearson and Edward Martin was subdued. Once handcuffed to a chair, he sat opening and closing his mouth like a carp. A black eye was coming on nicely.

Sergeant Metcalfe mopped his brow and rubbed his right knee, at which point Rose remembered his poor wounded leg; the sergeant was evidently used to rather more pedestrian duties. 'You weren't supposed to speak to them, Miss Burnham,' he whispered between gasps when order was restored, 'let alone cause a skirmish. I wouldn't recommend you try that sort of thing again.'

'I know. I'm sorry, Sergeant Metcalfe. I hadn't meant to start any fisticuffs, truly. In fact, I'd no idea I had it in me. I rather surprised myself.' Rose didn't have to pretend embarrassment; she was genuinely shocked by her own behaviour. 'But I was so enraged when I heard what Mr Martin said that my hands itched to give him what-for. I wanted him to know that, though he might think himself clever, it's a woman who has tracked them down. It's a woman who has had the last word.' Rose stood up straighter, all embarrassment forgotten.

'You certainly did that, Miss Burnham.' Sergeant Metcalfe looked hard at the young constable. 'I don't think we need mention all of this to the inspector, Constable Burdock. I don't think every detail need go in your report. We've got the men now; that's the main thing. They won't feel quite so clever after a night in the cells. Ah, perfect timing . . .' Sergeant Metcalfe looked up as two more uniformed men entered the pub. 'Here are your colleagues, Constable, to relieve me and get these villains locked up. I'll be back in the morning, as we agreed, to sort out the final details.' The sergeant drained his glass. 'Purely medicinal,' he said. 'Right. Now I must get Miss Burnham home. It's all been quite an ordeal.'

Constable Burdock winked at Rose. 'Yes,' he said, 'but for whom?'

48

A few days later, Rose opened the door to Inspector Davey. By way of thanking her for 'the Faversham capture', as he termed it (perhaps coining the name with a view to recounting the incident to colleagues), he said he wanted to fill her in on some new details. The inspector may not have thanked Rose quite so warmly had he known the full Faversham story or realized that Sergeant Metcalfe had already filled her in on quite a lot.

'As we thought,' the inspector began, 'and, despite their numerous aliases, there were definitely only two men involved. Quite put out, our fraudsters were, when we persisted in checking if any others might share the limelight. The two men met in the trenches, apparently. That's where they cooked up the scheme, maddened by the thought of women living the life of Riley while they and their fellow combatants were sinking in the mud.

'Once back in Blighty, the younger one married and his wife – your Miss Lane – fell in with their plans.' The inspector referred back to his notebook. 'Arthur Pearson was one of the names he favoured. He's the more suave of the two – seems to have gone for the younger ones, those with a bit more pep.' Rose swallowed this dint to her pride and told herself that it just went to show how successful her disguise as Miss Lipton had been.

'Yes, they were a wily bunch, these schemers, and they knew

how to play a long game; knew that if you want to part someone from their savings, you must build a rapport and get your victim to trust you. The one you – and your Miss Holmes – met courted his victims with small gifts, chocolates and the like, and suggested interesting places the pair of them might visit. He went to quite a bit of trouble, it seems. Swotted up and so forth. We found some books of his at the Faversham house.' On dinosaurs, trees and country houses, Rose thought, but decided against saying so.

'And they were crafty enough to know how far they could go without being had up for breach of promise. The men never actually proposed to anyone, just dropped heavy hints. And they were obviously well organized. One of our lads found a whole box of fake valentine cards. You know the sort: "Will you be mine, signed X." ' Yes, and poor Miss Holmes still carries one in her handbag.

'Oh yes, we've plenty to go on,' the inspector congratulated himself. 'They seem to have worked in tandem, the woman interviewing the female candidates and the two men taking them out to tea or whisking them round the dance floor.'

What a ploy, Rose thought: Miss Lane, the two men and their multiple aliases. Just those three, and assorted props. The fake valentine cards would be an extra twist of the knife for poor Miss Holmes. She hoped the inspector would not mention those when he next spoke to her. Rose wanted to ask if, by any chance, the police had found any other props – dead roses, for example – but she couldn't ask that. They would think her completely batty.

'Miss Lane is a bit of a mystery, though,' Inspector Davey said. 'A cousin of hers has spoken up for her – turned up at the station to vouch for her and said she wasn't a bad sort really, but

had fallen in with a bad crowd. Mind you, I think family loy-
alty may have blinded him somewhat. For someone who's been
led astray, she seems to have taken to the life quite nicely.'

'This cousin,' Rose asked. 'Did he give a name?'

'Spencer,' the inspector said, 'or Spender, something like
that. But we're not interested in him. It's the woman who's
foxing us. You might be able to help us there, Miss Burnham,
being a dressmaker and' – he looked uncomfortable – 'a member
of the female sex.'

But Rose had lost the thread. A cousin? she was thinking.
Jack Spender was Miss Lane's cousin? That was the last explanation she would have come up with. She thought back to the
aerial display and the fear she couldn't quite place. Had he been
trying to warn her, without implicating Miss Lane? But, Rose
thought, he could have had no idea I'd ever met Miss Lane. He
was surely thinking of the war that whole afternoon – of that
grand adventure that was no such thing. But what appalling
luck: that the first man I should step out with is Miss Lane's
cousin. The ghastly memory of Jack Spender arguing with Miss
Lane outside Cupid's Arrow thrust itself before her. Rose felt
every bit as sick as she had that evening, although now for a
different reason. She had got it so very wrong.

'. . . I was saying you might be able to help us there, Miss
Burnham,' Inspector Davey repeated, speaking more loudly.
'There were one or two smart items in her wardrobe – smarter
than you would expect. At first, we thought there might be two
women in on it, but the men say not. And the woman speaks
nicely, or tries to, and yet is not so la-di-dah when cornered. All
in all, she's harder to make out.'

That didn't surprise Rose. The two men may have conducted
the courtships, but Miss Lane was no one's fool. The probing

questions Allegra Lipton had been asked – Are you Miss X or Miss Y? – were all down to her; no man would have dreamed up those. But the inspector was still waiting. 'Most women like nice clothes,' Rose said, 'if they can afford them. And Miss Lane may have had elocution lessons. Some people do these days.'

'So I'm told.'

Yes, that's it, Rose thought. That's how Miss Lane knew Miss Porter. It would be a relief if that were the case; she really had not liked to think of Miss Mabel Porter, she of the junior glissades and inscribed statuette, knowingly directing unsuspecting young women towards Cupid's Arrow. But an elocution class made sense. If Miss Lane was able to adapt her accent, she could move in wider circles and entrap more women. Had she adopted a particular accent for her interview, Rose wondered, and tried a different voice for Miss Holmes? And was that why she'd looked so much smarter the day she left Cupid's Arrow to have her hair styled? She must have changed her wardrobe to match her clients: a smart suit for Miss Holmes, who had made a prior appointment and was evidently well-heeled; a crocheted dress or something equally low-key for those who dropped in off the street. It was so much harder to place people these days; the shake up since the war must allow for all manner of tricks.

Inspector Davey looked quizzically at Rose. 'Has something struck you, Miss Burnham? Don't keep it to yourself if it has.'

'There's a deportment teacher on Markham Street: Miss Porter. She teaches etiquette, elocution and deportment. She had some Cupid's Arrow business cards on her noticeboard. Miss Lane, the manager of Cupid's Arrow, may have had classes there.'

'Thank you, miss, we'll bear that in mind.' The inspector made a note.

'I hope you don't mind my asking, but I am concerned for my client, Miss Holmes: will she see any of her money again?'

'A little, perhaps, although most of it has gone. Gone on fancy dinners, nice outfits, glasses of port and lemon . . .' The inspector seemed to have embarked on his own fantasy spending spree. After a tour around the bright lights, he recalled his duty and coughed to disguise his embarrassment.

'Oh!' Rose gasped. Those swindlers still had her two guineas – the two-guinea fee she'd paid Cupid's Arrow. Now that she had solved the case, this fact seemed even more outrageous. And fancy paying someone a fee to investigate them. That can't be in the detective's handbook.

'Are you with me, Miss Burnham?'

'Yes, Inspector.' A spot of throat-clearing seemed called for.

Now that they had both recovered themselves, Inspector Davey continued. 'The younger man and the woman who called herself Miss Lane had obviously worked out their story, but the two men were surprisingly quick to blame one another – no love lost there, I reckon. I rather think the strains in that partnership were already beginning to show.

'By the by, one of them mentioned something about being followed by a woman dressed as a man. Trying to throw us off the scent, no doubt, or else he has been moving in bohemian circles.' The inspector laughed at his own joke. 'Still' – he brought himself back down to earth – 'we've got them all now; that's what counts. Are you all right, Miss Burnham?'

'I'm fine, thank you, Inspector.' Rose managed to conceal her own smile. 'It's just that it's a lot to take in.'

Having delivered his update, the inspector stood up to leave. As he reached the door, Rose said, 'You mentioned finding a box of valentine's cards. You didn't find any other sample letters while you were searching?'

'Like what, Miss Burnham?'

'Poison-pen letters and that kind of thing.'

'No, nothing of that sort. What makes you ask?' The inspector had a penetrating stare.

'No reason,' Rose said swiftly. 'I just wondered if that was the sort of thing they would stoop to – to intimidate their victims, to encourage them to keep quiet and so forth. You do hear of people writing poison-pen letters, don't you?' It was a question worth asking, Rose thought. The inspector may have some knowledge that could help her solve things for Maddie.

'You've been reading too many stories, miss,' Inspector Davey said. 'Poison-pen letters are an altogether different game.'

And so it proved the following evening.

49

'I think you know Miss Johnson?' Maddie said, turning to Rose.

'Daisy – please.'

'Hello, Daisy' Rose said, smiling. 'It's nice to see you again. I thought you'd be in Eastbourne.'

'I am – more or less – but I'm staying with my parents for a day or two and have just popped up for Maddie's birthday tea. And here's something towards it.' Daisy lifted the lid on the tin she was holding to reveal a handsomely iced sponge cake.

Maddie took it from her. 'Oh, thank you. That's very generous.' Daisy smiled. They were standing beside one of the larger tables in the sitting room at the ladies' hostel. Rose and Daisy had just arrived; the other guests were still hovering, reluctant to select a chair. Daisy, who was looking bright and refreshed in a floral dress, moved towards the nearest one.

'And this is Miss Barnes and Miss Denby, who I work with,' said Maddie, introducing the two young women to her left, both of whom had bobbed hair, Miss Barnes's light-brown bob a lesser version of Miss Denby's sleek black cap. 'The three of us share the Dressers' room.'

'Cubby-hole, more like.' Miss Denby rolled her eyes. 'I don't know how we all squeeze in.'

Miss Barnes smiled tentatively and offered Rose her hand. She looked barely seventeen and was decidedly the team junior.

'Pleased to meet you, Miss Burnham,' she said with excess formality.

'And Miss Purfew you know of old.' Miss Purfew stepped forward. She had obviously made an effort for the occasion, wearing her best lemon blouse and a cameo at her throat.

'Yes, indeed. It's nice to see you again.' Rose hadn't known Miss Purfew well, an exchange of appraising greetings the extent of their former acquaintance. She recalled Miss Purfew flitting between the counters to get a better look at her back in the spring. Miss Purfew wouldn't have that difficulty this evening, as Rose took the chair next to hers. Miss Denby sat down on her other side, next to Miss Barnes. Maddie sat opposite, with Miss Johnson, and fixed Rose with a stare to remind her of her mission.

Miss Denby leaned across the table and, as if bestowing a gift, offered Rose the inside of her left wrist. ' "Shem-el-Nessim: the Scent of Araby". What do you think?'

'Hmm, nice,' Rose said, although a little sharp for her taste.

'Miss Greene?' Miss Denby presented her wrist to Maddie next. She might have been circulating a box of sweets.

Maddie sniffed. 'Ooh, yes. Lovely.' But Rose knew she was also just being polite.

'I thought so, too,' Miss Denby announced. 'Two and nine.'

Miss Purfew rummaged in a tapestry bag and pulled out her knitting. 'You don't mind, do you? I'm desperate to finish this.' She held up several glossy rows for their inspection. 'Artificial silk,' she said, lest anyone was in doubt. ' "Reproduces silk's every charm," ' she added confidentially, quoting an advertisement. 'It's going to be a jersey with a dropped waist and tie belt. 'Chartreuse,' she explained, in case they thought the colour merely green, 'with a sailor collar in champagne, though I've yet to tackle that.'

'Lovely,' Rose said, and this time meant it. 'My younger sister is knitting something similar.'

'Has she reached the armholes yet? They're the very devil to get right.'

'Are they? She hasn't said.'

And so, the tea party proceeded, although not exactly with a swing. The conversation edged forward, was prodded into life, stopped and started again. Once they'd exhausted the usual department-store gossip about long hours, difficult managers and awkward, snippy customers, there were several lulls in their talk. Things eased when, with Rose as oracle, Miss Johnson introduced the topic of summer frocks, but their enthusiasm soon dwindled. Few were in the position to buy a new cotton frock, however cheap, and the hostel sewing machine was temperamental. Maddie chose this moment to go and get the food.

Miss Denby opened her bag and took out her handkerchief. 'Oh, Miss Denby,' Miss Barnes gasped. 'Your lovely bag. It's spoiled. Your pen must have leaked into the lining.' Miss Denby snapped the clasp shut as if the bag itself were at fault.

'Ink. Oh, dear. That can be very stubborn,' Miss Purfew said, looking into the distance to summon a solution. 'Milk: that's what's needed, I think. But you'd have a job to use milk inside your bag, because you would then need to wash it out. What a shame. I like coloured inks myself; I sometimes write in mauve. I gather that coloured ink is rather fashionable these days.'

'Does milk remove red ink, too, then?' Miss Barnes spoke with such concern it might have been her own bag that was soiled, but it wasn't Miss Barnes's considerate tone that caught Rose's attention.

'I'll try it,' Miss Denby said, putting the bag – and the

conversation – behind her. 'Where's Maddie got to with those sandwiches?'

At that moment Maddie reappeared with the plates, and with the food laid out on brightly coloured strips of paper. 'I thought these would jazz things up.' She had somehow contrived to make three plates of sandwiches, biscuits and rings of swiss roll look remarkably attractive.

'They do look good,' Miss Johnson said.

Miss Purfew agreed. 'No wonder your windows are always so clever.'

Everyone helped themselves. Miss Barnes reached for the biscuits, her hand hovering over the chocolate bourbon.

'Oh, I had my eye on that one,' Miss Purfew said, aiming for playfulness.

'Well, have it, Miss Purfew – I don't mind.' Miss Barnes withdrew her hand.

Miss Denby snapped: 'Well, you should mind. You shouldn't let people walk all over you.'

Blimey, it wasn't just Miss Denby's perfume that was sharp this evening. Whatever sparked that had nothing whatsoever to do with chocolate bourbons.

An even more awkward silence settled on the party. 'I was in Marylebone this afternoon,' Miss Johnson said brightly, 'and I walked past the smart hat shop there, Madame Cynthia's – do you know it? There was a little beige monkey sitting on the counter, wearing its very own jacket. So sweet.' The tension eased; everyone was grateful for the change of subject.

Miss Barnes shuddered. 'I don't think I'd like that. Those tiny hands and fingers.'

'I've heard people shop there because of the monkey,' Miss Denby said. 'Apparently, it's become quite a draw.'

'There you are, Rose, you'll have to get one,' Maddie said.

Rose laughed. 'I don't think we're quite ready for that.'

Miss Purfew turned to her. 'And how are things, Miss Burnham? Is everything working out? Or is it proving to be more difficult than you first thought?'

'Oh, it's keeping us on our toes.' How else was she supposed to parry that one? Rose glanced at Maddie. What a complicated evening this was – someone should be keeping score. Daisy Johnson was the only one among them who seemed at all relaxed, but then she was no longer cooped up here. It was all rather hard-going, and not helped by their brown surroundings and these decidedly-hard brown chairs. For all that it was her tea party, Maddie wasn't much help; too worried, no doubt, by the need to establish if her accuser was among them, eating potted-paste sandwiches, swiss roll and assorted biscuits.

The plates were cleared. It was time for Rose to introduce a party game. 'I know,' she said, as if the idea had just occurred to her. 'What about a game? How about a version of "Consequences" I know called, "All for Love"? All the conclusions have to be romantic.'

'If only . . .' Miss Purfew sighed.

'I think I've got some paper in my bag,' Rose said, searching in it, although she knew exactly where the paper was. 'I've even got some pencils – I'm always picking up pencils,' she explained, not wanting to look as if she'd come prepared, 'in case I want to draw something, and then I find I've accumulated half a dozen.' She ripped the paper into small, neat squares. The others huddled round.

Rose handed out the squares. 'Do you all know how to play? We each write down someone's name at the top, fold our piece of paper so that the name is hidden, and pass the paper on, to our left. We then write down a second name, fold it over, and so on. At the end of the game, we will each have written two people's names, where they meet, what they say to one another, and the consequence of their meeting. Everyone invents their own story, but as the papers are folded and passed on, the different stories all get mixed up. No one knows what's gone before, and so you end up with some rather silly and amusing results, which everyone takes a turn to read out loud. 'For example, Charlie Chaplin met Pearl White at the skating rink in Purley. He said: "Would you care for a turn on the ice?" She said: "Oh, Charlie, take it away, your moustache is tickling me." And the consequence was: they eloped.' Miss Barnes looked doubtful. Rose repeated the explanation for her benefit.

They settled to the game. At last, each entry was complete, and each piece of paper unfolded, ready for the stories to be revealed.

'Miss Purfew, do you want to go first? What does the one you're holding say?'

'Harry Houdini met Elinor Glyn in the storeroom at Webb & Maskrey. He said, "How'd you like to spoon with me?" She said, "I don't mind if I do." And the consequence was: They smouldered on the loggia.'

Daisy started reading next: 'Mr Pemberton met Mata Hari at the Motor Show . . .'

'I don't think we should have used real people – people we know, that is,' Miss Purfew said. 'Film idols and so on are all right.'

'Perks it up a bit, though, don't you think?' Miss Denby interrupted. Mr Pemberton, the Under Manager, was obviously her contribution. 'What does yours say, Miss Barnes?'

'Rudolph Valentino met Miss Greene.' Maddie blushed.

There was a general tutting at the inclusion of Maddie's name.

'Well, it is her birthday,' Miss Purfew said.

'And at least you got to meet Valentino,' Rose said, looking from Maddie to everyone else. Goodness, there was so much tension around this table. 'And tell us, Miss Barnes, what did Rudolph Valentino say?'

'How about a game of tiddlywinks?' Miss Barnes paused in her reading. 'That's not romantic.'

'Perhaps it depends on who you're playing with. Shall we have another round?' Rose asked, quickly gathering up the papers, 'now that we've got the hang of it? But can we do this one in block capitals? I could hardly read Maddie's handwriting.' She glanced apologetically at Maddie. And so, another game began.

'Someone's capitals trail down the page,' Miss Purfew complained, when it came to reading out the next round.

'They're mine, I'm afraid.' Miss Barnes frowned. 'I can't seem to keep them straight.'

Miss Purfew sniffed. 'It's a good job you never have to write notices for your department.' All this one-upmanship, Rose thought; she was so glad all this was behind her.

'I think it's time for cake,' Miss Johnson announced. 'Before we all head off.'

'Good idea.' Rose and Daisy exchanged glances. At least no one could say much while munching cake. Daisy fetched the cake she'd baked, and cut and handed round the slices.

'You've all got an earlier start than me,' Rose said, when she'd quickly swallowed her last mouthful. 'I'll stay behind and clear everything up.' And before anyone could disagree, she leaned across the table and scooped up the concertinaed papers.

50

Rose spread the corrugated papers out on the sitting-room table and Maddie put the two anonymous letters and the crumpled poster beside them. What a way to spend a Sunday afternoon. Ginny and Alice were both out and wouldn't be back until later; Rose and Maddie could sift through the evidence undisturbed.

'I know who your tormentor is,' Rose said, smoothing the papers, 'and I think you do, too. I already had an inkling, but these confirm it. I wonder if Miss Denby was already tiring of her game; she didn't seem too worried about revealing herself last night. She was the only one to include people we know – you and Mr Pemberton – and there was the matter of her bag, which turned out to be stained with red ink. She hadn't expected that revelation, of course; that was Miss Barnes's doing.'

Maddie said nothing, but stared somewhat helplessly at the accusatory material.

'Did you never suspect it could be Miss Denby?'

Maddie shook her head. 'No. She's been so friendly and helpful. Yet, now that we do know, I wonder if she was ever as friendly as I thought. I have sometimes wondered about things she's said and done. For instance, she found those hats I'd mislaid – do you remember? But going over it again – and I've thought about it often – I'm certain I wasn't anywhere near the storeroom that day. Miss Denby must have put the hats there

322

herself – and then "found" them. She was obviously biding her time.'

'And I think that's what happened with the letters, Maddie: she got the idea for the first one from the anonymous letter Daisy Johnson received, and when that didn't work, she had to come up with other ideas. Didn't you say she encouraged you to put the lingerie in the window?'

'Yes, she was very keen on that. It was her idea to make it look as if someone was undressing. She really did encourage me – thought it a cracking plan. I knew it was daring, but Miss Denby's encouragement made me think that perhaps it wasn't such a risk after all. And I did think she was my friend.' For once, Maddie looked defeated.

'A false friend, I'm afraid. It's jealousy, Maddie. I'm sure that's what's behind it. She didn't like Miss Purfew complimenting you on your windows, did she? But there's more to this, I'm certain,' Rose said carefully. 'Miss Denby clearly thinks she knows something that will damage you. And I think you know what that is.'

Maddie got up and walked to the window. She stared out of it for some time before returning to the table and sitting down. Rose couldn't work out if she was still debating whether to tell her something or plucking up the courage to say it. What secret could be so dreadful that she'd denied its existence up to now?

'I have a child, Rose,' Maddie said, 'and it looks like Miss Denby has found out.'

'Oh, Maddie, I'd no idea.' Rose tried hard not to stare, but this was nothing like what she'd expected.

'I'm sorry I couldn't tell you, but only a few people know. After all, it's not just my secret. Her name is Esmé and she's nearly three years old, but Esmé thinks I'm her aunt and my sister Bella is her mother.'

'Oh, Maddie,' Rose said again, uselessly. 'I'm so sorry, and all this time. I'm sorry you didn't feel you could tell me.'

'I wanted to, Rose. I've thought about it often these last few months.' Maddie attempted a smile.

'I don't know what to say.' Maddie with a daughter, her whole life changed and yet having to behave as if nothing was different. Rose groped for the appropriate words, but her voice dried in her throat and her thoughts with it. The enormity of this was just too much. 'And . . . Esmé's father?' she asked after a while.

'He died.'

'The war?' But that couldn't be right, Rose thought; the dates were wrong. Not everything came back to the war.

'Yes and no. He jumped down from a bus and his heart gave out. He died there on the pavement. It could have happened at any time, apparently. He was gassed in France and was never the same after that. Esmé's father was Toby Pemberton, Mr Pemberton's son.'

'Oh.' Another wholly inadequate response. Rose didn't know where to look. 'I think I remember hearing something about Mr Pemberton's son,' she said, 'some talk at the store about a tragedy or something. Coming some years after the war, we'd stopped expecting those, although I don't know why that was. I'm so sorry, Maddie. How did the two of you meet? I don't imagine you moved in the same circles.' If she focussed on practical questions like this one, she might have a chance to gather her thoughts.

'We met at the staff entrance,' Maddie explained. 'He was waiting for his father one evening and I happened to come out of the door. Mr Pemberton was delayed and so we struck up a conversation. He was so handsome, Rose, and he had the loveliest smile.' She smiled herself, remembering. 'I pretended I was waiting for someone too, just so I could stay and talk.

'He didn't tell his father we were walking out for ages. Mr Pemberton was not best pleased. He was even less pleased when Toby told him we were going to get married. I can't be sure we would have done otherwise, but Esmé was on the way. I'd like to think we would, though. I did love him. And then, before everything was sorted, Toby died.' Maddie paused and looked into the middle distance.

'After that, Mr Pemberton softened – not immediately, but sometime later – and said he'd help if he could. He'd always been civil with me – it's just that he didn't have me in mind for a daughter-in-law. But then, after Toby died, I think he realized I was his one link with Esmé, and Esmé his one link with his son.

'I held on at the store for as long as possible, but then I had to hand in my notice. I said I was needed at home to nurse my mother. That was the story everyone was told, you included – I am sorry about that – but it was Bella who looked after Mum. I went to stay with my Auntie Vi near Waterloo. She's the one I mentioned who always has an eye to everyone else's business. She got her money's worth with me, I can tell you.' Maddie pulled a face. 'Anyway, Auntie Vi takes in sewing, so I was able to help her out and, being in Waterloo and not venturing far, I managed not to see anyone who knew me. It's funny how easy it is to hide in London, in plain sight, simply by moving to a different district.

'After Esmé was born, I went back home and got a job at Barstock's in north London. What a comedown that store was.

But Bella and Ted had taken on Esmé, and I needed the work. They've no children and said they'd raise her as their own, and gladly. That was always the arrangement. So, as far as Esmé knows, they are her parents and I'm her aunt.' Maddie smiled, but there was little pleasure in it.

'But that must be so difficult,' Rose said. She was still trying to take in the shock of Maddie's story and the dual life her friend was now forced to lead.

Maddie shrugged. 'It was the only way to make things work.' She dropped her guard. 'It is hard, Rose, but I couldn't see another way. I was at Barstock's for over two years – two years, four months and five days precisely. By then, Mr Pemberton had come round, encouraged by Mrs Pemberton, I'm sure. Anyway, he knew I was unhappy at Barstock's and so, when a job came up, he put my name forward. I could have got it on my own account,' Maddie added defensively. 'He wasn't the one to appoint me. Mind you, Miss Carter was hardly likely to ignore the Under Manager. Mr Pemberton explained that I'd had to leave to look after my mother and so I deserved a second chance. Though, as I say, it was Bella who looked after Mum.'

'That was quite a risk for him, in his position.'

'Yes, I realize that now, but I'm not about to give him away. I don't ever mention Esmé at work. I don't even have a photograph of my "niece" on show at the hostel. I only see her at weekends – the perfect aunt, that's me.' Maddie's sigh told the larger story. 'But I don't see how Miss Denby found out. I truly have not said a word. I'll have to leave, of course. I may have to move away altogether. But, first, I need to find out what she knows.'

51

The fairground announced itself to Rose several streets before she reached it. She'd forgotten how raucous and overwhelming that sound was. So had a man nearby – at the crack and retort of a rifle from the shooting gallery, Rose saw him blanch and start, and his wife put a steadying hand on his elbow. How many other men here were back in France, she wondered, and with seething mud, not grass, beneath their feet?

Rose ignored the squeals coming from the helter-skelter, and the stallholders offering candyfloss and coconut brittle, and looked away as Punch knocked seven bells out of Judy to cheers and rowdy applause. She needed to find the Hall of Mirrors, where Maddie and Miss Denby had arranged to meet on their half-day. And there was the Hall of Mirrors up ahead, and a long queue for the swing boats snaking beside and beyond it. Rose joined the back of the queue. That way, she could keep a lookout without being seen. If Miss Denby wasn't to take fright and disappear, Rose had to allow her to enter the Hall of Mirrors first.

'You weren't expecting me, Miss Denby.'

'No.' At least she had the decency to look uncomfortable. Miss Denby held Rose's gaze for a moment and then looked down at her shoes. They were nice shoes too, Rose noticed, with two straps across the instep. But they weren't here to talk about shoes.

'You've been set up,' Rose said, 'just as you've been setting up Miss Greene. She knows you're the person behind all the nasty tricks that have been played on her.' Miss Denby looked back towards the entrance. 'I wouldn't bother, if I were you,' Rose said. 'I know all about it, and the anonymous letters. If you don't talk to me now, you'll have to explain yourself to someone at Webb & Maskrey.'

Miss Denby scoffed. 'You wouldn't dare.'

'Wouldn't I?'

'That would put your friend on the spot.'

'Miss Greene has nothing to hide.' Rose was stunned by her own audacity. She was glad Miss Denby had no idea how much her insides were churning. 'You, on the other hand . . .'

'She thinks no one knows, but I know.' Miss Denby tilted her chin defiantly. 'She thinks she can get away with it, but I've seen them.'

Them? This conversation was taking an unexpected turn.

'The two of them, canoodling. It turns my stomach.'

'Canoodling?' Rose was wholly unprepared for this. She hoped she didn't look anywhere near as surprised as she felt.

'Yes,' Miss Denby said. 'Well, I expect that's what they get up to when they're alone. They think no one's noticed, but I have. I've seen Mr Pemberton and Miss Greene whispering in corners. He's old enough to be her father. I've seen them once or twice these past few months, down by the storeroom and near the offices. Their heads were almost touching.'

'Miss Denby, you have got this wrong.' At last Rose was able to speak with conviction.

'And the way she carries on. She thinks she's the bee's knees. Well, I know better.'

'I thought the two of you were friends. You helped Miss Greene a while ago when she mislaid something . . .'

'I did, but I should have let her sweat, and seen what Miss Carter made of her star assistant then.'

'But, why?' Rose implored her. 'What has Miss Greene done to you? Why befriend Miss Greene and then torment her?'

'That job was mine before she came back.'

'You were Second Window Dresser?' Maddie hadn't thought to mention that.

'No, but I would have been. I was expecting promotion any day, but then Miss Greene swans in. Quite the bobby dazzler, or so she thinks. Says she hopes we'll all be friends. Miss Barnes might be fooled, but I'm not. She wouldn't have got the job if not for Mr Pemberton.' That much was probably true, but not for the reason Maddie's accuser thought. This was like being on a switchback ride.

Rose took a deep breath. She must hold her nerve and keep her eyes on Miss Denby. She couldn't afford to be distracted by the peculiar shapes the two of them were making in the distorted mirrors all around them; this conversation was peculiar enough. 'And that's why you wrote the letters?'

'Yes.'

'And encouraged Miss Greene to put the lingerie in the window?'

'I thought she'd get the sack. I don't know why she didn't.'

'But when she didn't, you realized you needed to ramp things up, hence that horrid poster?'

'How did you know it was me?' Miss Denby challenged Rose.

'You were always close by when something went wrong. Oh, I know the two of you work together, but all the same. You were also quick to offer advice that wasn't always helpful. And then, of course, there were your capital letters in the game, "All for Love" and your ink-stained handbag.'

'I didn't think Maddie had noticed that.'

'She didn't, but I did. What do you think Mr Pemberton will say when she takes your letters, and the poster, to him?'

'She kept them?' Miss Denby looked horrified. 'She wouldn't dare.'

'Oh yes, she will,' Rose bluffed. 'Those letters are cruel as well as unpleasant. Mr Pemberton may decide to pass them on to the police.' Miss Denby's expression switched from horror to disbelief. 'Yes, the police investigate poison-pen letters – didn't you know?' Rose had no idea if that was true, but she needed all the ammunition she could muster. 'And the poster will cause Mr Pemberton particular offence because, had your plan succeeded, that would have embarrassed the store.'

'I didn't mean any harm to Webb & Maskrey – it was Miss Greene I was after,' Miss Denby explained. 'But she won't go to Mr Pemberton, or anyone else for that matter, because then the truth would come out.' Quite likely, but not the truth as Miss Denby saw it. 'She wouldn't do it.'

'You think not?' Rose fenced. 'There is nothing between Miss Greene and Mr Pemberton,' she insisted. 'That's something you've invented because you're jealous. Miss Greene has years of service behind her and is well regarded. She returned to the store after some years away – people are rarely allowed to do that. Why do you think she was?' Miss Denby scowled and studied her feet. 'Webb & Maskrey obviously think highly of her,' Rose continued, 'whereas you are a relative newcomer . . .' She emphasized these last words. Miss Denby stood in awkward silence, a silence punctuated by the squeals and shouts outside and the shrieks and laughter coming from within the Hall of Mirrors itself: 'Look at me, skinny as a stick of liquorice'; 'You want to watch that face you're pulling. If the wind changes, you'll be stuck with it.' The speaker laughed, snorted and then laughed all the harder.

Rose cut through this jollity and Miss Denby's silence. 'I hear that Shipley's are advertising. It's a smaller store, but that can give the right person an advantage. You could be in luck there. But if you're sacked and forced to leave Webb & Maskrey with no reference, you won't find work in another London store. That's something you should consider.'

Rose surprised herself. She was in no position to assert any of this, but her tone was obviously convincing. She could see that Miss Denby was thinking about what she'd said and was weighing up her options. How easy it must be to wield fake authority, if you could adopt the right manner.

'I think you should give what we've discussed some thought, Miss Denby. I should also add that if you do nothing, I will feel obliged to act. Miss Greene is a loyal employee and may decide not to upset the store by explaining what's been happening, but I am not bound by the same considerations. Webb & Maskrey would be appalled to learn that they've been harbouring a poison-pen writer. What is more, as an ex-employee, I know exactly who to speak to about this.' Bluff and more bluff. But it might just work. Rose balled her hands into fists to stop them shaking and watched Miss Denby leave the tent.

'She doesn't know, Maddie,' Rose said, when they met at Chatsworth Road that evening. 'She thinks she knows, but she doesn't. She's seen you talking with Mr Pemberton and thinks you are having an affair.'

Maddie stared at Rose. 'With Mr Pemberton? He's old enough to be my father!' Rose thought it best not to mention that Miss Denby had said the same thing. 'I'm flabbergasted,' Maddie said. 'But that's a relief, to put it mildly. Although I'm still not necessarily safe, am I? I may have to leave Webb & Maskrey anyway, whatever Miss Denby does. It's too close there; someone else could find a way to make mischief.' Maddie sighed. 'I don't know; it's probably too soon to decide. I still can't believe that Miss Denby hadn't guessed, not that there's any reason why she should. I'm so careful when it comes to Esmé. But I've made my bed and I must lie in it. That's what Auntie Vi would tell me – has told me, a great many times. They talk of shame, but I'm not ashamed. Esmé is the best thing that's happened to me.'

Rose enfolded her friend in a large hug.

52

There was one more thing Rose needed to do.

'Sydenham 3491 . . .?'

'It's Miss Burnham, Miss Holmes,' Rose said at the sound of the familiar voice and number. She could tell from the tone of the reply that Miss Holmes was adjusting the position of the telephone receiver. 'The thing is, Miss Holmes, I have a confession to make.'

'Oh dear. That does sound serious.'

'It's nothing to worry about, I promise, but there is something I'd like to tell you, something that I very much hope will help – a couple of things, in fact. I think it would be best if we spoke here. Can you come and see me, whenever it's convenient for you?'

'I came as soon as I could,' Miss Holmes said when, two days later, she settled into one of the fitting-room chairs.

'Thank you, Miss Holmes, but before I tell you more, how are you finding things with Inspector Davey? Are you still happy talking to him by yourself?'

'Oh, yes, perfectly happy, Miss Burnham. The inspector has been as kind and considerate as he can be, given the circumstances. And Sergeant Metcalfe telephoned yesterday to say that some other poor woman who was deceived wants her day in court, so I will be spared that particular humiliation.'

'That's marvellous, Miss Holmes, and must be a tremendous relief. And now,' Rose said, for there was no way to delay it, 'there's something I must tell you.' She plunged in. 'When I said that I wanted to help, I decided to sign up to Cupid's Arrow myself in the hope of meeting Mr Wilson and shaming him into making reparation. I was angry too,' Rose said, in further justification, 'and his exposure seemed only right and proper.'

Miss Holmes's expression was caught somewhere between horror and fascination, and the desire to hear more, much more. 'You registered with Cupid's Arrow?'

Rose nodded.

'And did you . . . did you meet Mr Wilson?'

'I did meet him, Miss Holmes, except that the gentleman I met presented himself to me as Mr Edward Martin, and that's who I thought he was. Incidentally, by the time I met him, he no longer had a moustache.'

The expression on Miss Holmes's face told Rose that, from her point of view, there was nothing incidental about a moustache. 'Where did the two of you meet?' she asked quietly.

'In the Crystal Palace park. We went for a walk around the lake.'

'The boating lake?' Miss Holmes asked even more faintly.

Rose realized she was treading on broken glass. 'Yes, but we did not go boating, Miss Holmes. In fact, we met only three times and had only the most superficial of conversations.'

Miss Holmes sighed. Honour seemed to have been served.

'The reason I'm telling you this is that I want you to know that I, too, was duped,' – Miss Holmes flinched – 'led astray, by the man you knew as Reginald Wilson. I was on the look-out for a fraudster, and yet it took me a long time to identify him.'

'I'm sure you did your best, Miss Burnham.'

'I did, Miss Holmes, but I, too, was taken in. That's my point, really. You have no need to rebuke yourself. Theirs was a clever and elaborate scheme. Anyone would have been deceived. The fact that you *were* is no slight upon your character. This has been a dreadful business, but the fault is entirely theirs, not yours.'

Miss Holmes gave a pained smile. 'Thank you, Miss Burnham. I'm still trying to absorb the thought of you meeting Mr Wilson – or whatever Reginald's real name is – but your words will be reassuring in time. Yes, I think they already are.' Miss Holmes straightened her back as if strengthened by that thought. 'And some people are unlucky in love, aren't they, through no fault of their own? They are unlucky in love and yet still their world keeps turning . . .' She gazed into the distance. She was beginning to fashion a new, more palatable version of her situation, reshaping the experience into something she could live with. Good for her. And 'unlucky in love' did have a certain mystique, like the final tragic act of a weepy at a picture house, when the curtain falls on a sad but staunch and undefeated heroine who survives to live another day.

We all write our own stories, Rose thought, me included.

Miss Holmes interrupted Rose's thoughts. 'Mother has been surprisingly understanding.' It was the first time her mother had entered any of their recent conversations without prompting. 'But the trouble is, she pities me. I see it in her face all the time.'

'I'm sorry, Miss Holmes. However, I think I may be able to help you there.' Rose could see Miss Holmes thinking, What on earth could Miss Burnham have up her sleeve that could possibly relate to Mother?

'That's the second thing I wanted to see you about. I have taken the liberty of contacting someone on your behalf,' Rose explained. '. . . but without mentioning your name or going into any details,' she added quickly. 'I do hope you will forgive my doing so but, when I tell you more, I think you will under-stand why I couldn't mention this before. It's all down to you, of course, Miss Holmes, but I think – hope – you will like what I am about to say.' Rose outlined her plan.

53

Alice pointed to the three hats lined up along the top of the fitting-room cupboard, their hat stands of differing heights positioned in a perfect triangle to show off a mustard cloche hat tickled by a tortoiseshell feather, a jade-green cloche with a complicated rosette at its brim and a skullcap in peacock blue.

Rose and Ginny made admiring noises. 'Your presentation hats,' Rose said. Alice had been to collect her 'highly commended' hats that afternoon. 'Who are they for?'

'The green one's for me. I'm meeting Maud after lunch, and I plan to wear it then. We're going to a tea dance at the Waldorf and that hat's got to earn the entrance fees and pay for our afternoon tea. I intend to flaunt it there and be my own best advertisement.'

'Good idea. And what about the other two?'

'I thought I'd offer the mustard cloche to Maddie. She's in need of cheer after that business with the stockings' – and more besides, Rose thought – 'and who better than Maddie to be a living, breathing model for my millinery? But the peacock-blue has yet to find a home.'

'And I think should be sold, rather than given away.'

'I'm getting to that,' Alice said. 'I've made two or three hand-painted notices. What do you think?' She opened a small folder and showed a series of watercolours of a cloche hat concealing a woman's face, with the words 'Alice Burnham, Milliner' scrolled across the crown. The drawing was the same in each instance, but the colours different in each one.

'Perfect, Alice,' Ginny said.

'Truly,' Rose added. 'Very sophisticated – very *now*. Why don't you ask Grace Townsend's deportment teacher, Miss Porter, if she'll take one for her noticeboard? That way you'll soon have a queue of young women making enquiries.' And this suggestion would go some way towards assuaging her own embarrassment at thinking – though, thankfully, never suggesting to anyone else – that Miss Porter was somehow involved with Cupid's Arrow when, in fact, she was merely a young woman making her way in the world, just as she was. Miss Porter had thought she was helping another young business to find its feet and, according to Sergeant Metcalfe, had been extremely shocked to discover the truth. Rose comforted herself with the knowledge that she had come to the right conclusion, eventually: Miss Lane had attended several of Miss Porter's elocution classes just as the agency was setting up.

Alice was still contemplating her headgear: 'But as for the blue . . . perhaps one of the Bressingham sisters?'

'Perhaps,' Rose said, 'now that they have finally got in touch. But regardless of who buys that hat, and when, I think it would be a good idea to keep one or two on permanent display. That way people will see them the minute they enter the fitting-room.'

'Thank you.' Alice hugged her. 'I was hoping you'd say that.'

'Did the Bressingham sisters say why they hadn't telephoned before now?' Ginny asked. 'I'm afraid I'd given up on them.'

'Yes, they were full of apologies – extremely effusive, in fact – and say that the gap has given them "abundant" ideas for new clothes. A few days after the fête, apparently, they were telephoned by Billy or Joey, or was it Teddy, who insisted they accompany him on a motoring tour and whisked them off to the Peak District and other points north – Hardwick and Haddon Halls, Chatsworth, Eyam and so on, and on to the Lake District, Windermere and beyond. "Such " fun, Lady Dorothy said – and the dogs "adored " it, their basket strapped to the dickey seat. And then – of course – there was Biarritz. They've been there for the past month.'

'How lovely.' Alice's voice expressed the longing they all felt. 'I wonder what the dogs did there . . .'

'Coming back to the real world,' Ginny said, 'have you heard anything more from Miss Holmes?'

'She's better than she was,' Rose said carefully. 'And she coped with the police interviews better than I expected. I offered to be present – Miss Jennings also offered her services – but Miss Holmes said she'd be more comfortable by herself. From what I can gather, the inspector was extremely considerate and so it was easier than she'd feared. It seems she should get some of her money back – at least that's what the inspector thinks. Of course, it all has to go to court, but the police are confident of a conviction. What's less certain is whether she'll be able to repay anything she owes us.' Rose hurried on: 'But I do have a plan for Miss Holmes and, just this morning, received good news on that very front, but I'll save that until I've spoken to her again.'

'Curiouser and curiouser. And what about Maddie, dare I ask?'

'She's still doing penance at Webb & Maskrey, though I think she's on the way to being forgiven. I'll find out more next week.' A great deal more, Rose hoped. 'It's her niece's birthday and she's invited me to her sister's to celebrate. We're promised cake and games.' She paused. 'So, Alice,' she said, smiling. 'When should Ginny and I put orders in for our own new hats?'

'When you can afford to pay for them,' Alice said pertly. Rose laughed.

'She's learning,' Ginny said.

54

Mary Townsend stood before Rose, looking surprisingly serene, and there, hung in readiness on her wardrobe door, was the silk crepe dress and coatee she would wear to depart for her honeymoon. Rose put down her needle and thread. The last button was in place, the last bridal superstition observed – at Webb & Maskrey, and in other establishments, too, so Rose had heard, the final button was always left unstitched until the actual wedding day, and added at the bride's own home – as now – or later, at the church.

Weddings had always created a stir at Webb & Maskrey, even though their preparations did not necessarily go to plan. Rose recalled one young woman who had let herself be dressed but otherwise barely seemed present at her numerous fittings. She was more like a statuette than a living, breathing woman. What had become of her, Rose wondered. Thankfully, the mood was more usually one of mounting excitement, anticipation gaining on the workroom as well as the bride, albeit quietly; it didn't do to speak out in Miss Feldman's workroom. But even Miss Feldman could mellow: Rose recalled a night when she, another fitter and various hands and assistants had all clustered round the same table to complete a bridal gown, and Miss Feldman herself had pitched in. The energy was contagious; seamstresses were generally willing to stay even later than usual to finish a wedding dress.

And now all the fretting and making was behind Rose. The car would be here any moment to take Mary Townsend to church. Her father was pacing in the hallway, having thanked Rose for her skill and hard work, for all her ministrations and 'for managing to keep things in hand', an unaccountable comment which presumably referred to his wife. Although surprised by Mr Townsend's congratulations, Rose felt as gratified as she did in the old days. A good word from both Townsends would undoubtedly help the business.

Equally surprising was Grace Townsend, who, before leaving for the church, had thrust a foolscap envelope at Rose and whispered, 'Read this later. Not here. I hope you will approve.'

The bridesmaids had set off half an hour earlier under the watchful eye of Mrs Townsend, who was enjoying her own moment in the sun. It might be Mary's wedding day, but due homage must also be paid to the bride's mother. 'Of course, it's how one wears these things,' Rose overheard Eleanor Townsend tell a friend, Mary's godmother, when complimented on her own outfit. 'One must have the right figure to carry it off.' And, in this instance, Mrs Townsend was right: the funnel collar and slimline coat did justice to this creed, and so did well by both client and designer.

'Eleanor, my dear, what a triumph,' Mary's godmother exclaimed. 'You must give me the name of your dressmaker.' Rose allowed herself a private smile. Good: the ripple effect had begun.

And now there was just Mary upstairs. 'Thank you, Miss Burnham,' she said, admiring herself in the mirror and turning to gesture at the outfit awaiting the scene-change that would signal her further transformation.

'It's a pleasure, Miss Townsend,' Rose said, but, even

today – perhaps especially today – she couldn't help but think of Phyllis Holmes, who had surely dreamed of a moment like this one and made plans for her future with Reginald Wilson. Unlucky in love, Rose thought. That was at least more appealing than 'on the shelf' and managed to hint at a romantic mystery: 'Oh, there goes Miss Holmes. Unlucky in love, wasn't she?' With those words, Phyllis Holmes would be able to hold her head high. Rose remembered a childhood game she and Ginny had played. Chanting 'He loves me, he loves me not . . .', they'd blown at dandelion clocks and watched their swansdown filaments float away. How early some lessons were learned.

But this would not do. All was well here, and she had somewhere else to be. Rose said her goodbyes and wished Mary Townsend luck.

That somewhere else was the delightful garden tended by Miss Compton and Miss Jennings, which, even on this mid-September afternoon, managed to be awash with colour. Spears of achingly blue delphiniums, and dahlias of every shape and hue, testified to Miss Compton's green fingers. The table was laid for afternoon tea under the shade of a rowan tree. A dish of jam (last year's plum, cropped from the tree at the far end of the garden), a sponge cake, cucumber sandwiches (minus crusts), plus thin slices of bread and butter, stood ready on an embroidered cloth. A canvas-backed chair awaited Rose.

'Come and take a seat, Miss Burnham,' said Miss Jennings. 'I'm just warming the pot. I hope you have recovered from your ordeal?' There had been more than one ordeal since they'd last met, but Rose knew the one to which Miss Jennings referred.

'Have you heard any more?' Miss Compton, who was already seated, leaned forward, eager for news.

Miss Jennings reappeared, carrying the teapot. 'Let the poor woman catch her breath. Do sit down, Miss Burnham, and allow us to tempt you with one of these sandwiches or a piece of Isobel's sponge cake. Her jam's delicious, too. You've come straight from the Townsend wedding, I assume?' She was clearly determined to allow Rose to relax before being quizzed on the subject of interest to them all.

'Yes, though not the wedding itself. I gave Miss Townsend's dress the final once-over and left shortly before the car came to collect her. I've done my part. A wedding is for family and friends.'

Miss Compton barely allowed Rose to finish her last morsel. 'So, Miss Burnham . . .'

Amid tuts and exclamations, Rose told Miss Jennings and Miss Compton what she'd learned about Cupid's Arrow. She didn't reveal all her workings and glossed over some of the more delicate details. The mistake she'd made about Jack Spender didn't figure in her account, for instance, nor indeed the full extent of her role in the skirmish at the Faversham pub. Rose hadn't told Ginny the full story of that incident, either; she still blushed whenever her extraordinary behaviour came to mind.

'Gosh, you have been busy,' Miss Compton said when Rose concluded her explanations. 'How admirable. And will Miss Rose Burnham, Detective, retire now?'

'Another piece of cake, Miss Burnham?' Miss Jennings intervened, sparing her from answering that question. 'Well done, Miss Burnham,' she said, cutting Rose a large slice. 'You kept at it and wouldn't let it drop. The police wouldn't have caught those despicable schemers without you.'

'And are you glad you did it?' Miss Compton asked, adding a generous helping of jam to a slice of bread and butter. 'Was it fun? Most of the time, that is? I realize that evening in the park must have been terrifying.'

'It was quite a lark, for the most part, if only the circumstances hadn't been so desperate – for my client, and for us at the start. I enjoyed my different encounters – my trip to Cupid's Arrow and the photographer's studio, even my conversation with Miss Lane's hairdresser, despite the atrocious perm I came away with. I'll be giving Madame Estelle's a wide berth from now on, I can tell you. But I've no experience – well, very little experience – of romance and so I was hardly the best of investigators for this situation. It turns out that Miss Holmes wasn't the only one deceived. The fakers fooled several women in the same way. The police have already built quite a case against them.' Rose gave silent thanks to Sergeant Metcalfe. Without his involvement, she and Ginny wouldn't have learned half of what they knew.

'And what about your poor Miss Holmes?' That diminutive was evidently catching. 'Do tell.'

'Dear Miss Holmes,' Rose said, wanting to restore her status in absentia. 'There's some good news there. She won't get all her money back – or at least nowhere near the full amount – but I think she will get a little and I've managed to find a solution to another of her difficulties. A young woman I know has opened a tearoom in Eastbourne and needs someone to live in. There's a flat upstairs that the young woman, Miss Johnson, won't occupy herself and so Miss Holmes is going to live there and help to run the tearoom. Miss Holmes had envisaged an entirely different future, of course, but under the circumstances, she's happy enough to accept this one for now. And Miss Johnson is sensible and good-hearted, and will help Miss Holmes to find her feet. It's a good solution for them both and Miss Holmes will at least be independent.' And she'll escape that gloomy house. 'The two of them met last week and, fortunately, took to one another straight away. The timing couldn't have been better. Miss Holmes was thinking of answering an advertisement she'd seen in *The Lady* . . .'

Miss Jennings looked pained. 'I know the sort: "Young woman wanted to help with kennels. Must love Sealyhams." '

'Actually, it would have been something worse. She was about to apply to become a companion, which would have meant picking up someone else's dropped stitches and posting their letters, all the little jobs she has been doing for her mother, only at some demanding employer's beck and call.'

'Do companions still exist in 1925?'

'For the lucky few they do, I'm afraid, and they're every bit as put-upon as they always have been. She'd have had no time to herself, so I'm even more relieved that she and Miss Johnson hit it off. And it turns out that Miss Holmes has an aunt who lives further along the Sussex coast, which has helped to soothe things with her mother.'

'Well done for rescuing her. There you are, you see: that's something else you have achieved. And what about the business: is there news on that front?'

'The Townsends are pleased with their wedding outfits – and have already suggested me to some of their friends. And I've other new clients, too.' Best not mention the Bressingham sisters by name, Rose thought; it was a client's prerogative to name her dressmaker, not the other way round. But at least their reappearance should more than make up for the loss of Miss Holmes's multiple orders. Rose continued her list: 'And Miss Porter, the elocution teacher, has asked if I'll speak to each new intake of young women, so I'll be talking to her students a couple of times a year. Oh, and my younger sister, Alice, has just sold her first hat. Which reminds me: I have something for you both.' Rose reached into her bag and pulled out two parcels wrapped in tissue paper and fastened with ribbon. 'These are to say thank you. I don't know what I'd have done if you hadn't come to my rescue that night.'

'Oh, how exquisite. It's almost like having a birthday,' Miss Compton cried, fingering the tissue paper.

'Isobel does love birthdays.' Miss Jennings opened her parcel efficiently while Miss Compton lingered over both ribbon and paper. 'Oh, the cravat! How wonderful – and such delicate embroidery. The colouring and style are perfect – how did you guess?'

'I'm glad you like it. The design is mine but the stitching – the embroidery – is Ginny's handiwork.' Stitching was too mundane a word for the flowers that flourished there.

'Oh!' Miss Compton exclaimed in delight, lifting a long, narrow scarf from its wrappings and holding aloft a melody of blue, green and mauve silk.

'I thought it would match your summer suit. I saw it hanging on the wardrobe door the night I stayed here.'

'How clever. Oh, thank you, Miss Burnham. More tea?'

'Yes, please. There is one more thing – it's not my news exactly, but it is intriguing. The elder Miss Townsend gave me this envelope earlier today with the strict instruction not to open it until later. It must be good news – the look on her face said as much. I must admit I'm itching to find out. Would you mind if I opened it now?'

'Another surprise,' Miss Compton said enthusiastically. 'Yes, do.'

Miss Jennings and Miss Compton watched Rose open the

envelope with care and pull out a magazine. Rose read the title and strap-line: '*Modern Miss: A New Magazine for the Modern Young Woman*'. A slip of paper clipped to the cover instructed her to 'See page 25' and there on page twenty-five was an article on ' "Independence and the Modern Woman", by our new correspondent, Grace Townsend.'

Epilogue

Kickin' the Clouds Away

It was a late-September afternoon and almost Michaelmas Day, one year on from the date Rose signed the lease on Chatsworth Road. She opened the front door and walked down the hall into the sitting room. Ginny was coaxing the fire and, wonder of wonders, Alice was clearing the dining table of the detritus that regularly gathered there. Rose looked around the room as if for the very first time. Yes, here it was – and so were they.

'It's a bit early, I know,' Ginny said, referring to the fire, 'but it's been cool all day, and I thought it would make a nice welcome.' She sat down in one of the chairs beside it.

Rose was just back from seeing Mrs Lingard – their second meeting that year, a meeting delayed by the Townsend wedding. She would present her final account to the Townsends next week. A speedy settlement had been promised (although she'd heard that one before). 'I should go and get changed,' Rose said, but didn't. She was dressed in her businesslike black. By contrast, the colourful frocks Ginny and Alice were wearing more than made up for her sobriety.

Rose took the fireside chair opposite Ginny's, bent down to unbutton her shoes and stretched both legs in front of her. 'That's better,' she said, as she felt her body relax. 'Mrs Lingard was pleased, I think,' she announced, some moments later. 'At least, she said she was satisfied. She did point out, however, that the Townsend wedding had screeched to our rescue in the nick of time.' Ginny looked up. 'Well, those weren't her exact words – but she did say that the commission had appeared at just the right moment, that we must be vigilant in seeking new clients and establishing our clientele, and that although there is always someone coming through the door in a department store, the same cannot be said for an independent business.'

'She was thorough, then,' Ginny said, peering at Rose to see how she'd survived the encounter.

'Yes, she gave me quite a grilling, in fact. In extremely pleasant tones, of course, followed by a glass of homemade lemonade – the sugar after the pill, as it were. And it's all to the good,' Rose added, reminding herself as much as Ginny and Alice, 'that we have Mrs Lingard's advice,' although she did rather feel she'd been put through her paces that afternoon.

'I brought up the subject of the Bressingham sisters,' Rose continued, 'since Mrs Lingard was impressed when they put in an appearance at the fête, and I mentioned that some of our very first clients are now returning with new commissions. I'd hoped to distract her with talk of the Bressingham dogs, but she was having none of that, and went straight on to ask about other new clients.'

'I do wonder about Lady Barbara and Lady Dorothy,' Ginny said cautiously. 'I don't wish to do us down, but we're not exactly their usual milieu.' She looked at the faded and mis-matched cushions on their chairs, and at the somewhat battered dining table and corner cupboard. They had meant to paint both, but hadn't got round to it yet. There was always some-thing more important to do.

Rose followed Ginny's gaze and silently agreed with her unspoken assessment. The Bressinghams would never step inside this private space, but it was about time the room was spruced up. 'I suspect the Bressingham sisters rather like to convey that they're not hidebound by convention,' Rose said, 'and that if they see someone whose work they like, they can indulge themselves – and give the designer a leg up at the same time.' She saw herself ascending a long ladder with the dogs at its base, barking encouragement. 'I doubt that we're about to replace their usual salons.

'Fortunately, we have learned our lesson – I have learned mine, I should say, and am not assuming their patronage will continue. But I was able to tell Mrs Lingard that, thanks to the Townsend wedding, we've already had approaches from two of their friends. We have also acquired a solicitor's wife and daughter via the talk I gave at Miss Porter's, and Miss Croxley-Smythe, whom Mrs Lingard sent our way last year, now wants a new evening gown, so the next season is starting to shape up. And we have Mrs Crowther's velvet devoré for her daughter's coming-of-age, and Mrs Lingard herself will be coming next week to discuss a two-piece in wool crepe. Quite a rash of commissions, in fact, and of course there is the usual bread-and-butter work.

'Oh,' Alice groaned, 'don't remind me.' She paused, her arms spilling papers, books and stray gloves. 'I still have to tackle Mrs Watson's best dress. I don't know how many more re-stylings that frock will take. Its seams have been unpicked so many times, they're beginning to resemble a colander.'

'I know,' Rose said, 'but needs must. Mrs Watson wants it by the end of the week. But there is more good news' – she leaned forward – 'and it will make a big difference. At the end of our meeting, I suggested that, in a few months' time, we might be able to think about hiring an apprentice. Thankfully, Mrs Lingard agreed.'

'Hallelujah,' Alice said. 'No more doorkeeper for me – or matching silks, although I will miss the Habby gossip.'

'You'll have Haberdashery for some time yet, Alice – and any gossip you can pick up while you are there. I'm rather hoping that, when the apprentice does start, you'll take on the task of teaching her how to match silks to fabrics. And we will have to think about where she will sit.'

'She can share my table at first,' Ginny said. 'That way, I'll be able to keep an eye on her.'

'Thank you.' Rose had known Ginny would say that.

'That's something to look forward to,' Alice said, 'and because I felt sure your meeting would go well, I've treated us all to ice creams.' Rose looked from Alice to the fire and then across to Ginny, who was deciding how to arrange her face.

Alice put everything back down on the table. 'I heard the Wall's man ringing his bell an hour or so ago, and so nipped out and managed to catch him. It may be our last chance this year. Quite a charmer he was, and gave me an extra ice cream.' Rose and Ginny exchanged knowing looks. 'They're keeping cool in the sink but they won't last that much longer. We should eat them before they melt.' Alice headed into the scullery and called out, 'Mine's strawberry, to match my dress.'

Rose looked down at her own coal-black dress, and then at Ginny's leaf-green. 'Yours is vanilla,' Ginny said dryly. 'Like mine.'

'Almost a year . . .' Rose said, looking at Ginny. She was still digesting that fact. 'But, despite some exceedingly wobbly moments, we're still here and still in business, and we didn't have to go to Mrs Lingard cap-in-hand.'

'Thank goodness,' Ginny said. They sat in silence, thinking about what might have happened and how things might have been.

Such an unexpected year, Rose thought and, with that thought, Jack Spender unavoidably came to mind. What might have happened there, if she had not got it so badly wrong? She should have written to explain and yet, what would she have said? 'Dear Mr Spender' – Dear Jack? – 'I thought you were a crook. I'm sorry.' Is that how the letter would start? And, after that, what then? Dare she suggest they step out together to Dulwich Picture Gallery? He would think her far too forward. (And why ever would he believe she'd turn up?) Rose sighed. The thought of Jack Spender still tugged at her.

'Here's to us all,' Alice said, coming back into the room with the ice creams.

'Thank you,' Rose said, taking hers and returning to the present moment. She looked from Alice to Ginny. 'On the way home, I was thinking: now that things are beginning to look more stable, isn't it time we had a gramophone? We could get one and pay by instalments.'

'Instalments?' Ginny frowned.

'Oh, yes,' Alice said enthusiastically. 'That's what people do these days.' She was already looking about the room, wondering where the gramophone could go. 'That's your best idea yet, Rose. And I'll be able to teach you both the latest dance steps – you can show yours off to Sergeant Metcalfe, Ginny.'

'No fear,' Ginny said, laughing and shaking her head. 'I think he and the dance floor are best kept apart, but we have arranged to meet for tea.'

'Have you?' Alice asked eagerly.

'Yes,' Ginny said, her voice a decided full stop.

'We'll need some gramophone records, of course.' Alice began compiling a list: 'Tea for Two', 'Kickin' the Clouds Away', 'Kiss in the Dark' . . .

'Ice creams *and* a gramophone,' Ginny said. 'Things really are looking up. And at least you've done with sleuthing, Rose.' Ginny smiled to reassure her. 'You won't have to go through anything like that again. You'll be glad to have put all that behind you.'

Alice shot Rose a quizzical look. 'Really?'

Rose smiled and took another lick of ice cream.

Acknowledgements

Just as some of the characters in this novel are not who they seem, so I have taken liberties with topography, and other aspects of the book. The south-east London street names are inventions, as are some of the publications mentioned here; the park where the charity fête takes place is a mixture of several in the area. Having spent years writing non-fiction, I've enjoyed making things up.

This novel is nonetheless rooted in research. I've long loved the 1920s and it's been a pleasure to return to that decade. Newspapers, magazines, novels, letters, memoirs and diaries from the period offered a rich fund of material, as did *Costume*, the dress studies journal of the Costume Society, especially its accounts of women who worked in dressmaking – whether in couture or lowlier establishments – during the interwar years. Together, these different sources provided me with an enticing mix of information, texture and detail, all of which I snuffed up in order to create my main character, Rose Burnham, her establishment, and some of the situations in which she finds herself. Those who know Winifred Holby's views on clothes will recognize some of her themes in Rose's talk to Miss Porter's class.

ACKNOWLEDGEMENTS

I am immensely fortunate in having Clare Alexander as my agent. As ever, I am indebted to Clare for her wise, calm counsel, her suggestions and support. My warm thanks to Francesca Best, who bought this book for Transworld, and to my editor Imogen Nelson for her enthusiasm and ideas. Thank you, too, to Katrina Whone, Holly McElroy, Barbara Thompson, Emma Fairey, Ollie Martin and Sophie MacVeigh, and to everyone at Transworld who has worked hard on this novel's behalf. Thanks also to copy-editor Alex Newby.

Royal Literary Fund projects of one kind or another supported me for much of my research and writing: sincere thanks to Steve Cook and David Swinburne. Thanks, too, to the London Library for continuing to support my membership. Its shelves are a joy for every researcher who likes to take books home.

Kate Kellaway and Melanie Silgardo read early parts of the novel. My thanks to them – and to Lynette Challands, Katrina Webster and Euronwen Wood for their friendship and support. Belated thanks, too, to Leticia Costalago, who mended my damaged hands, and without whom much would have been impossible.

Special thanks to GW, who has lived with this novel a long time.

About the Author

Lynn Knight was born in Derbyshire and lives in London. The women of her family passed on many stories along with beaded bags and buttoned gauntlets, and fostered her interest in the texture and narratives of women's lives. She is the author of the biography *Clarice Cliff* (2005), a memoir, *Lemon Sherbet and Dolly Blue: The Story of an Accidental Family* (2011), and *The Button Box: The story of women in the 20th century, told through the clothes they wore* (2016). *Miss Burnham and the Loose Thread* is her first novel.